Rave Reviews

"Deborah magically ta..... heather and mist of another time . . . breathtaking, beautiful, award-caliber writing."—*New York Times* best-selling author Lynsay Sands

"This IS historical romance. If any among us need a poster child for the genre, *A Restless Knight* is IT!"—Dawn Thompson, award-winning author of *The Ravencliff Bride*

"Like a bard of old, MacGillivray spins a tale of knights and ladies, battles of will and trials by combat, myth and magic, and sexual tension . . ." —Kathe Robins, *Romantic Times*

"With lyrical prose and fascinating characterization, Ms. MacGillivray transports the willing reader to a time and place that is filled with magical superstitions, pagan rituals, and a deep love of a land long coveted by the English."—Deborah Kimpton, *Romance Junkies*

"If readers are looking for a beautifully written story full of passion and love, set against the brilliant backdrop of the medieval Scottish highlands, then *A Restless Knight* by Deborah MacGillivray is bound to be a winner."—Kelly Hartsell, *CK2S Kwips and Kritiques*

"With a deft touch that seems blessed by the ancient bards themselves, the author pens a brilliant, breathtaking novel that sweeps you off into the untamed and magical world of the Scots, and moreover a man and a woman who refused to bow to suppression." —Charissa Dionne, *Coffee Time Romance*

AS HE LAY SLEEPING

The man was long of limb, thighs powerful, hard from controlling his mighty destrier. There could be little doubt she stared at a fierce warrior, a knight. When she had sent her brothers forth to find her a stud, she never hoped they would return with one so comely.

"Where did they find you, my braw lad?" Aithinne whispered. 'Twas true, he was a stranger to these parts. She never would have forgotten this man had they met. For Damian was handsome—nay, beautiful.

IN HER BED

Deborah MacGillivray

ZEBRA BOOKS
Kensington Publishing Corp.
www.kensingtonbooks.com

ZEBRA BOOKS are published by

Kensington Publishing Corp.
850 Third Avenue
New York, NY 10022

All Kensington titles, imprints, and distributed lines are avail-
able at special quantity discounts for bulk purchases for sales
promotion, premiums, fund-raising, educational, or institu-
tional use.

Special book excerpts or customized printings can also be created to fit specific needs. For details, write or phone the office
of the Kensington Special Sales Manager: Attn.: Special Sales
Department. Kensington Publishing Corp., 850 Third Avenue,
New York, NY 10022. Phone: 1-800-221-2647.

ISBN-13: 978-0-8217-8037-4
ISBN-10: 0-8217-8037-9

First Printing: August 2007
10 9 8 7 6 5 4 3 2 1

Printed in the United States of America

For
Dawn Thompson
Leanne Burroughs and Monika Wolmarans
and the GEMs (Green-Eyed Men)
and
Sandi!

Her flashing eyes, her flame-red hair!—
How did this Lady of power and delight,
Choose to start her spells that night?

—*B. Badger*

Chapter One

May Day night, 1296, Glen Shane, Scotland

"You leave the Beltane festivities, Damian?" Guillaume Challon asked.

"The smoke from the fire . . . sees my head spin. I feel . . . unwell." Damian St. Giles had not actually uttered a lie to his cousin.

He *was* sick.

Not a typical ailment that might afflict a warrior who had lived with a sword in his hand for too many years. This disease rotted his soul. Devoured his heart. Had he been born a man of lesser character, he could easily ha ve considered murder as a means of "curing" his "sickness." A shame he had scruples. Murder *would* simplify the situation.

Little noticing the joyful May Day celebration about him, Damian turned away from the balefire. With mixed emotions, he paused and glanced over his shoulder at his cousin, Julian Challon. Tall, strong, black-haired, a handsome man, Challon—the feared Black Dragon, once the king's champion—was now the new earl of Glenrogha, lord of this valley and beyond.

At age five, Damian had been sent to serve as a page at Castle Challon in Normandy. Three years younger, Damian worshipped Julian. Later, he stayed to train as squire, then knight, under the hand of Julian's lord father. With his black hair and green eyes so like the Challon sons, everyone assumed Damian was another bastard dragon in earl Michael's litter.

Riches and glory had come to Julian, his birthright as the Challon heir. Damian truly loved his cousin, honored him above all others; not once had he ever begrudged Julian any of the accolades which had fallen to him. Over the decades their bond had only strengthened. It was a privilege to serve Julian, to stand at his side in battle, along with Guillaume and Simon—Julian's bastard half brothers. *The Dragons of Challon,* people whispered. Men feared them. Women wanted them. Too many times to tally, they had saved each other's lives.

All these years, he'd been proud to stand in his cousin's shadow and not see the specter of envy. Never had he envisaged anything could come between them.

Sighing, he closed his eyelids and struggled against the overwhelming despair washing through him. Because he *did* care for Julian, these circumstances were so difficult to bear. Sucking in a ragged breath to fortify himself, he opened his eyes and looked at his cousin. Though he tried not to, he also searched the throng circling the balefire, seeking Tamlyn MacShane, Lady of Glenrogha.

Tamlyn.

The woman who should have been his.

When he failed to locate her, he glanced once more to Julian, words rising up within him. Futile words. Words he'd never speak. Were there a crumb of hope of changing his cousin's mind, Damian would humble himself before all, go down on his knees in a plea to Julian, beg him to release Tamlyn from their betrothal.

He knew it would serve naught. His cousin *wanted* Tamlyn beyond reason.

Aye, their King Edward decreed that his Dragon wed a daughter of Hadrian, the earl of Kinmarch. Julian had chosen Tamlyn. A royal edict had naught to do with why Julian planned to take the Lady Tamlyn to wife. His cousin burned for her, craved to possess her with a driving need that was frightening. And, in a sad way, Damian was happy for Challon. For too long, Julian's soul had suffered in torment. The fey Tamlyn had the power to heal him, make him whole once more. Save him.

Damian knew Julian treasured the brotherly bond they shared. Only no man would come between Challon and his bride-to-be. Without hesitation, he would kill to own Tamlyn. He had already warned Damian of this.

In frustration, he bit back words that would merely turn his cousin's favor from him. Drowning his sorrow in mead was the only course that could see him through this night.

Tilting up the leather horn, he cursed to find it empty. Strange, he did not recall imbibing *that* much. He started to fling it away, when a huge man knocked against him.

Reeling, dizzy from the drink, he first assumed he had walked into a small mountain. His eyes traveled up the wall of unmoving flesh and he gawked, his mind trying to come to grips with what he beheld. Tall, of Viking blood, the stranger stood in a defensive position before three young men.

Damian conceded he had drunk too much, but it was not the first time. Never before had he experienced double vision—triple vision.

The three young men appeared exactly alike, except for clothing. Same light red hair, narrow effeminate countenances, same hazelnut eyes, they were dressed too finely to be anything but highborn. When he peered at their features he could hardly tell one from the other. Triplets? What Devil's work was this?

Mayhap the Scots put something more into mead than just honey. He blinked thrice, hoping to see only one smiling face, yet when he opened his eyelids they remained. Grinning at him, their countenances beamed delight for some unknown reason. Damn unnerving!

Damian's attention was pulled away as the *Culdee*—priest of the Auld Celtic Church—tossed dried herbs into the bonfire. The smoke thickened and spiraled outward, the scent heady, intoxicating. Sweat beaded on his brow.

The one in the middle held out his hand. "Hugh Ogilvie."

Still puzzled, Damian accepted it. "Damian St. Giles, Lord Ravenhawke."

Hugh nudged his look-alike to the left, who nudged back, then Hugh poked the brother on the right. That one sniggered, earning him a thump from the elbow, too, this time sharper, meant to silence him.

The one to the right offered him a cup. "I am Lewis. Try this, kind sir. 'Tis a special brew. Made of heather, ale of the Picts."

A feral war-scream jerked Damian's attention back to the celebration.

A man soared over the flames of the sunken fire,

almost seeming to split the smoke, clad in doeskin breeches that were molded to his legs by the lacing of leather thongs up to his mid-thigh. He wore naught else, though a mask with antlers of a large buck sat upon his head. He executed high leaps, kicking to fly through the air, then with the grace of a cat, landed before Challon.

"Drink," Lewis urged, "and all your wishes shall come true."

"Wishes, bah," Damian scoffed. "Wishes are for fools. I just need to drink 'til I forget what cannot be mine."

Hugh pushed his elbow. "It shall do that, aye. Mayhap more . . . even grant all your deepest desires."

With nothing to lose, Damian shrugged and downed the contents of the tin cup, its fire spreading through his body. "I hope it does. This night I have need of it."

The last triplet refilled his cup, his words sounding as if they ran together. "I am Deward, come, drink your fill, it shall give your thoughts ease. You are not from hereabouts, Lord Damian. You travel far?"

"Nay, I come northward on a mission for Edward Longshanks."

"Then you do not stay at Glenrogha to serve your lord brother?" Lewis inquired.

"Challon is not my brother. I am but a lowly cousin. I merely tarry to see him settled here, then I move on to claim the holding of my grandfather."

The three men looked to each other, then grinned. "Cousin, you say? You look like him enough to be his mirror. Such as we are."

As he felt the effects of the strange brew, his mood suddenly lightened. All the pageantry around the balefire receded to darkness as Damian laughed. "I am taller . . . and prettier."

The three idiots' smiles grew even wider, with Deward—at least Damian thought it was Deward—concurring in his run-on fashion. "Oh aye, muckle prettier, I think, do you not agree, brothers, near perfect, just what is needed, seems the hand of fate, eh?"

The heads of the other two bobbed their agreement. "Oh aye. Perfect, indeed."

The melody lowered, pulling Damian's attention to a lone piper playing a haunting refrain. The notes floated on the warm night air, swirled around him and filled his brain. The music sparked a deep, sexual throb within his blood, consuming his will. Hushed whispers descended over the gathering, followed by the crowd sucking in a collective breath.

Then Damian saw her.

Tamlyn.

As she stepped into the glow of the balefire, her hands took hold of the long veil she wore. Drawing them up, she raised them skyward. Everyone seemed unable to breathe whilst she remained in that position of supplication then, gradually, she allowed the netting to snake down her arms.

Bathed in amber firelight, Tamlyn's kirtle was gold, spun from Highland magic. It clung to her body, with splits up both her thighs. A chaplet of apple blooms crowned her unbound, honey-colored hair, rippling in the soft breeze. A heavy gold torque was about her neck and matching cuffs on her wrists, the only things on her bare arms.

A Pictish princess conjured from timeless Scottish mists.

And Damian wanted her more than he ever wanted anything in life.

A second piper joined the first, playing the haunting tune, as Tamlyn rose up on her bare toes and swayed, rocking to the accent of the drum. The

throbbing beat of the bodhran provided cadence for
the wanton roll of her hips. When the music swelled,
bagpipers joined in. Her body undulated in a dance
so carnal, so profane, that a blinding wave of lust
seized Damian. The wall of desire slamming into
him, through him, proved nearly crippling.

Tamlyn circled the fire. Her lithe, feline movements gained force, matching the power of the
melody as she kicked her legs out and spun. She
flung the net about, trailing it behind her like wings.

Held spellbound, the pounding of his heart
echoed the drum, his blood thickening until he was
lightheaded. He felt sick. This woman was not his.
Would *never* be his. Unable to take his eyes from her,
he watched as she danced on air, lifted by the strange
music. A tune that had a life, a magic, all its own.

She danced for Julian. Just Julian.

Damian reeled from the sense of loss, a pain so
deep his heart almost ceased to beat. For years that
face had haunted his dreams, the woman who
would be his. Instead, she danced for his cousin.
How could his visions—which had never failed him
before—be so wrong in this?

Hugh filled his cup again. "Come, fair stranger,
drink your fill. Forget what pains you."

Damian did as they encouraged, eager to embrace anything that might hold the power to help
him forget. This time the effect seemed even
stronger, burning a path to his stomach, the fever
of the brew coursing through him. Glancing back
to the fire, he saw Julian now danced with Tamlyn.
The dance a prelude to mating. With a blistering
anguish, he knew his cousin would take Tamlyn this
night, make her his. The people of Glenrogha
viewed this as the grand rite, a mating of the Lord

of the Glen and the Queen of May. A good omen
for Clan Shane and Clan Ogilvie.

Closing his eyes, he swayed, sickened to the bottom
of his soul. Everything about him swirled until he
feared he would pass out.

"Kind sir, you appear wan. Come, drink," Hugh
encouraged, once again refilling his cup. "Let it
soothe what ails your troubled soul."

His warrior's mind warned mayhap they offered
a drugged potion, though he knew not why. It little
mattered. He glanced to see Julian kissing Tamlyn
before the balefire. Nothing mattered anymore.
Not giving a bloody damn, Damian eyed the cup,
flecks of herbs floating on the liquid's surface, then
lifted it to his mouth and downed it in one swallow.

"Your brothers have returned, rode hard to get
back to Lyonglen." The old woman pressed, "You
must hurry. The night wanes."

Aithinne Ogilvie nodded, glaring at the goblet in
her hand. Specks of herbs swirled and danced on
the cider's surface. "You are sure?"

The healer smiled. "Now you ask that question.
Thought you were set on this path and naught
could deter you."

Lightheaded, her stomach nervous, Aithinne
watched the pattern of the powder on the liquid
shift in the cup. "Then it was talk. Now—"

Oona cackled, slowly circling her. "Now you have
a braw man, naked as the day he was born, chained
to the bed in the tower. Soon he awakens. Delay not.
Drink the potion. Do the deed. You must lie with
him for the seven nights of the waxing moon, and
more than once a night. As many times as he will
take you. I cast the runes. They speak your path."

"Och, you and those Viking ways. You are a Scot, *Cailleach*."

"Hold the insults, Aithinne Ogilvie. I may be an old woman, but I am not the Crone Goddess. This night is our Beltane. Great magic rises. It touches your cousin Tamlyn at Glenrogha and, like the reflection of a mirror, it affects your life as well. Omens bespeak of a great coming. Tides of change ride on the mounting wind. 'Tis the will of the Auld Ones."

"Still . . ." Now that the time had come to act, she hesitated to take this final step.

Oona smiled, her amber eyes reflecting aspects of a cat's. "Kenning your brothers and their soft ways, they did well fetching this one back for you. Any woman still drawing breath would want him in her bed. Ooo, he's a bonnie man who stands out amongst many."

"I do not want many. What this is all about, remember?" Aithinne grumbled, glaring at the silver goblet.

"You want Phelan Comyn or Dinsmore Campbell coming to Lyonglen to claim you? Then it would be rape, for you would never consent." She rotated about Aithinne, fixing her with bespelling eyes. "Of course, you could have had Robert Bruce. He paid you court. But, no, you turned him down."

"Edward's Lordling?" She huffed. "The new Lord Carrick merely wanted Lyonglen and Coinnleir Wood—the stronghold's a sword to the back of the Comyns, simply to enlarge Clan Bruce's base of power in to the Highlands. I shan't be used for men's games of intrigue. Damn them all. They care naught about me, only want the holdings."

"Then damn them all. This way you keep the power. You wield the magic."

"But to lie with a stranger? Oona, I do not even ken his name." Aithinne's hand shook as she looked at the cup, which contained the power to change the rest of her life.

"Ah, my pretty lass, with a man like that in her bed . . . a woman takes first—then asks riddles. Time and tide are right." Her laugh was lusty. "The man is right. Aye, long of limb, built like a mighty steed. Ride him, take his seed within you, milk him dry. Learn your woman's pleasure. This night and six more. Tarry not. The moon rises late. When its pale light floods the tower room, make him yours. The spell is cast. No turning back—for you or him."

Sucking in a deep breath, Aithinne tried to steady her hand. What a fool she had been to think this would be easy, a solution to the quagmire in which she found herself. First, the lies had been to keep the greedy wolves away from Lyonglen, then to prevent Dinsmore or Phelan from carrying her off, holding her hostage until one sired a bairn upon her, thinking to compel her into a Highland marriage.

One lie begets many. Now she stood here, preparing to surrender her virginity to a stranger. How many lies would this deed breed?

Fear coursed through her. Shaking, she almost dashed the cup against the wall, calling an end to the madness. She could not go through with this harebrained scheme.

Oona had been specific in her instructions, how a man and a woman joined. Of course, living in a fortress it was hard not to have some ideas of the ways of breeding. There were horses breeding, cows breeding, sheep breeding. Her brow crinkled. Seemed the whole bloody world spent a large portion of their life breeding—or talking about it.

Everyone but her, she sighed.

Though Oonanne's tutelage proved enlightening, Aithinne frankly did not understand how some of it was accomplished. She shuddered. No, she could not go through with this foolish, desperate plot.

More lies piled upon the many. It was difficult to keep track of the falsehoods she had told over these past two months. Harder each day to sift mendacity from truth.

Oonanne watched her, clearly scrying her mind. Gifted with the kenning, the old witch read her every thought. Though possessed of the sight herself, Aithinne knew no shield against the woman's powers. Oona's words broke her deliberations.

"You shall regret not following through on the course you already set into motion. Do not turn back, lass. There is but a moment of pinprick pain for a maid, then his flesh is within your body, deeper than you can imagine. Breathe slowly. Take him in, bond to him with fire. Your body has slept for too many years. Let him make you a woman."

She spoke in a singsong pattern, weaving the spell to see her lady prepared. Aithinne knew this. The pull of the words was dark.

"He will suckle your breasts, but not as a babe. Let him. Encourage him. You shall warm to this. He will pinch your nipples—"

"Why? That would hurt." Shocked, Aithinne looked up from the goblet.

"What hurts you in this breath and what hurts when you are with him are two different turns. You shall like it, crave it. Mayhap beg for it. Such caresses prepare your body for his possession."

Fighting dizziness, strange hungers stirred to life in Aithinne. That scared her. Terrified her. Never had she known these things existed within her body, her mind. Despite the slow burn at the base of her belly, she was unsure about opening herself to any man in this manner.

Just as the muscles in her arm tensed to hurl the goblet aside, her brother Deward flung open the door and raced in. "Aithinne! Dinsmore Campbell and his men are at the gates, they demand entry, say 'tis late and they require food and lodging. What shall we do, you cannot let them in."

Eyes wide, Aithinne lifted the goblet and downed the drugged cider in one gulp.

Instead of tasting foul as Oonanne's tansies usually did, this one was sweet. Heat flooded her stomach with the power of *uisge-beatha*—whisky. Tingling, vibrating in her blood, it spread through her, singeing her flesh. It caused a spasm within her womb, a clenching like a fist.

"Sister, fare you well?" Deward looked confused. But then, Deward *always* looked confused.

Steps clattered in the hall and two more young men rushed in, echoes of the first—Hugh and Lewis. When the Creator handed out brains, she figured her three brothers only received one amongst them. She could not even call them half-wits. The triplets were third-wits.

Thundering footfalls brought up the rear. The huge Viking ducked under the door's opening to enter. The instant he saw Aithinne he fell to his knees, fisted his hand and thumped his chest in a salute. "Princess Aithinne, the knave Campbell demands entrance."

She sighed wearily. "Einar, up off your knees and stop calling me Princess."

He arose, bowing. "Aye, Princess."

Aithinne closed her eyes, willing herself far away from this place. Hoping to find she was elsewhere, she lifted an eyelid. She sighed. Her spell had failed. Four shining faces stared at her, eagerly awaiting guidance.

Oh, but for a man who could fight for her instead of lean upon her. Controlling her holding of Coinnleir Wood proved difficult enough. Now she lied and schemed to keep Lyonglen out of either the Comyns's greedy grasp or hands of the ever-voracious Campbells.

"Betwixt a hard place and a rock," she muttered.

It would be so satisfying to have a man to aid her. A helpmate to keep such troubles at bay, a man to share the burdens of both fiefs. Someone to hold her in the dark of night, lend his warmth.

Oonanne lifted her brow. "Careful what you wish, lass. The Auld Ones hear unspoken desires and can grant them."

"I wish that were so."

"Done!"

Aithinne blinked. "Hmm?"

"You wished it so. Remember for what you asked," Oonanne warned, shaking a finger at her.

So tired of these past months, Aithinne rubbed her forehead. She looked up at the Viking and summoned her cloak of lies. "The gates of Lyonglen remain closed. My lord husband feels unwell and wishes no visitors. His pennon does not fly from the rampart. That should tell even a lackwit such as Campbell our gates are closed to all comers, to seek shelter elsewhere."

Hugh let out with a shout and clapped his hands. "Siege! Can we pour boiling oil down upon their white-blond heads?"

She laughed. "Nay, but you may empty the chamber pots on them."

Lewis capered in delight, then scurried off after Hugh and the Viking, thrilled to have Campbells to torment. Only Deward remained, watching her with soulful eyes.

"Sister, how long shall you hide behind an ailing husband when he lies cold in the ground this moon's passing, and he was not your husband anyway, and you do not really have a claim to Lyonglen, and what happens when the dread Edward Longshanks, king of the English, comes and then you shall—"

"Deward, hush your gub. I am aware my predicament and the mounting deceits might see me in White Tower, prisoner before the English king."

"What of the man in our tower, did we not do good, does he not please you? Whilst I look not upon men in fondness as a maid would, he is bonnie. Hugh, Lewis, and Einar agree he is perfect for you, he is bonnie, a strong man, we tried to please you. Do you not like him, he is strong—"

"Deward, shush!" She cupped her brother's pretty face with her hand and smiled into his warm amber eyes.

She had hoped these childish ways of the triplets would lessen as they reached manhood. As they neared seven and ten years, hope faded fast. Still, she loved them. Caring brothers, they would do anything she asked—evidence of that lay in her bed upstairs in the north tower. They were just a little . . . hmm . . . absentminded at times.

Fortunately, Einar protected them. The tall man served as her guard of honor. Every lady of Coinnleir Wood received the gift of a personal Viking warrior-guard as part of an ancient agreement with the Norse King Rolv, some four centuries past. Pushing her to exasperation, Einar dogged her every step. While a braw warrior, he had as much common sense as her three brothers. It was a perfect solution, setting him to guard the lads—that protected her Hugh, Deward, and Lewis, but also kept the Norseman from trailing after her, calling her princess and driving her daft.

"I thank you for your concern and for fetching such a bonnie stranger. You did well, brother. No sister could be so blessed." Or cursed, she chuckled to herself.

"Come, Deward! We tipped the chamber pots over on Dinsmore Campbell! Such glee!" Hugh shouted as he danced into the room, laughing. "Dunny Dinsmore! Dunny Dinsmore!"

"Hie yourself off with him," she encouraged with a smile.

Deward paused at the door, his eyes revealing more understanding than she thought possible from him. "Och, Aithinne, go see our stranger. He is bonnie, we did right by you. Though we love you, sister, you are not getting any younger. Go to the braw man, let him take you this Beltane and, when you cry out in pleasure, we shall jeer at Campbell camped below and tell him your husband swives you again. It shall drive him around the bend."

His rare moment of seriousness past, he dashed out of the room without waiting for her response, his mirth echoing down the hall.

Aithinne stood, exhausted, shaking her head and feeling every one of her four and score years.

Closing her eyes, she imagined the Beltane festival. This year the ceremony was held at her cousin Tamlyn's holding of Glenrogha. The hours of darkness were still warm; the heady scent of apple blossoms would fill the night air. The balefire would burn on the high tor until dawnbreak and Tamlyn had danced as the May Queen. Aithinne could almost inhale the redolent blooms. Hear music floating on the breeze.

What she would not give to have been there, instead

of hiding within the walls of Lyonglen, Dinsmore Campbell lurking about somewhere outside—

"Bolt the postern gate!" she yelled.

Einar popped his head in. "Aye, Princess, it shall be made as you wish."

Oonanne laughed softly as she placed a pot covered with a rag in Aithinne's hands. "Aye, you smell apple blossoms, lass. I set this to warm. My Beltane spelling."

Aithinne breathed deeply, letting the stimulating apple, lavender, mandrake, and heather fill her mind. "What do I do with this?"

"You rub it on his chest—and elsewhere. Have him rub it on you where he takes whim. Nature will do the rest." With a lusty twinkle in the ancient eyes, the healer chuckled.

"Oona, nothing in my life is that simple anymore."

Chapter Two

Armed with only wavering determination and a pot of fragrant unguent, Aithinne pushed open the tower room door. She paused, listening to the eerie stillness, the whole world seeming to hold its breath, as if this instant in time changed the fate of all. A silly notion. One she could not dispel.

A thin shaft of moonlight came through the arrow loop, piercing the velvet darkness. It shrouded the chamber in impenetrable shadows, a cloak for the deed she must do. At her instructions, no fire had been laid, so the hearth remained cold. Clad in just a thin chemise under her light woolen mantle, she shivered, though whether from the chill in the air or misgivings about her plan she couldn't decide.

Aithinne's eyes went to the fat, woad candle on the table by bedside, the flickering flame doing little to light the room. Oonanne said before the wick was one-third gone, the moon's ethereal glow would envelop the huge bed, then the Beltane spell she set would gain force. As a reminder, she had marked the side of the wax with a gash.

It was nearly to that point now.

She turned to the door, her hand pausing on the bolt before guiding it into the slot. Not that she

expected Oona, Einar, or the lads to disturb her.
They backed her, abetted her plan. Oona was likely
off practicing rites to Bel, Lord of Fire, offering ancient May Day invocations. She had done everything to see Aithinne prepared for this choice,
strangely, even encouraged her in the scheme.
Einar might be inclined to stand guard outside the
door and growl at anyone daring to approach, however he was on the curtain wall, too busy ensuring
her brothers did not throw themselves off the bastion along with the chamber pots.

The only person she feared might come to disturb her night's plans was Dinsmore. She had
hoped the obstinate man would decamp after it
grew clear her brothers enjoyed their silly game of
siege. From the arrow loop she spotted his tent on
the hillside, his boar's-head-on-gold pennon flap-
ping in the nighttime breeze.

She sighed. Mayhap she should count her blessings that Phelan Comyn had not taken it into his
cork brain to come play ardent swain just because
Dinsmore had. Once, foolishly, she had thought
Phelan might be the man to steal her heart. He was
a handsome lad, with dark auburn hair and blue
eyes. Only, he could not keep his tarse in his braies.
Disgusted with his lies and wandering eyes, she
wanted no part of a faithless husband. Why marry
if your spouse spent his time swiving anything in a
kirtle? Hardly an advantage for a lass to wed if that
were the case.

Aithinne strode to the bed and set the pot down
on the small table next to the candle. Steeling herself, she finally turned to look upon the stranger
lying on the bed.

In awe, she inhaled sharply. "Oh aye, the man is
bonnie. For once, my lackwit brothers did well by me."

Pulsing heat roared through her as she gazed

upon his comely face and superior form. Never had she seen a more perfect male, one to haunt her dreams. As if conjured from those dark wishes, this man fulfilled every desire hidden in her secret heart.

He rested quietly on his back, the strong chest bare. His torso wasn't boyish like Phelan Comyn's, nor was it hairy as Dinsmore's. Neither appealed to her. This man had only a faint dusting of hair right in the center of his breastbone, then gradually thickened into a line that disappeared under the plaide. The wool tartan was artfully draped across his groin.

"Einar's doing, no doubt. The Viking would have blushed and afforded you the modesty, my bonnie stranger. My mooncalf brothers likely sniggered and would have painted you blue with woad and tied tartan ribbons around your staff. Fortunately for you, my big Norseman was there to keep them in line."

Oona had not stretched the truth. The man was long of limb, his thighs powerful, hard from controlling his mighty destrier. There could be little doubt she stared at a fierce warrior, a knight. When she had sent the lads forth to find her a stud, she never hoped they would return with one so comely.

"Where did they find you, my braw lad?" she whispered as foreboding slithered over her skin.

Where had her brothers *acquired* a man of such quality? 'Twas true, he was a stranger to these parts; she never would have forgotten this man had they met. Handsome—nay, beautiful—he had the fey allure of one born with Selkie blood. Though he was motionless, scorching energy thrummed from this dark warrior.

He was silent, barely breathing. She saw no rise and fall of his chest. Fear lurched within her, worry that her simple-witted brothers had dosed him too deeply.

Had all the arrangements for this night been for naught?

Almost greedily, she reached out and stroked his thigh. His flesh was warm. Her fingers caressed the muscles of steel, dragged up to the plaide, then over the lean plane of his taut belly to his chest. Strong and steady, his heartbeat set hers to rocking, then hers slowed to match the cadence of his as though they shared one pulse. Holding her palm there, she opened her mind to the kenning, trying to see into his inner heart—the soul.

Her mind voice whispered this warrior was rare, special, a breed apart. What was it Oona had said about him—*ooo, he's a bonnie man who stands out amongst many.*

Mayhap such things should matter little. Her brothers had not fetched him so she could walk in his thoughts. What she needed from this man he would hardly miss. Males spread it around to any willing lass with nary a thought. She should feel no guilt in the deed.

Yet, the magnificent stranger tweaked her nosiness. "Who are you? Why come you to the Highlands, my braw knight? Have you a lady wife? Aye, you would be hard on the heart of a poor lass."

Jealousy surged within her, blazing with a dominance that shocked her. She tried to dismiss the reaction, chalking it up to affects of Oona's love philter coursing through her body.

As she stared at the midnight hair, softly curling about his handsome face, images of her cousin Tamlyn formed in her mind. Her spine straightened. Did this man know her kinswoman? She closed her eyes and focused on the thudding of his heart against her palm. The impression remained sharp. Too sharp. He *had* to ken Tamlyn.

From a distance people often mistook her for Tamlyn. Only five seasons older, her cousin was a hand's width shorter, her figure fuller. Their hair was nearly the same shade of deep gold, though Tamlyn's lacked the hint of red that highlighted her own, and one had to be up close to notice the flecks of green in her own eyes, missing in Tamlyn's pure amber ones. The most telling difference in Aithinne's mind was the seven freckles across her nose, whilst her cousin bore nary a speck. Oona assured her they would fade with age, but at times she felt they were warts. Though Aithinne loved her cousin like a sister, she always felt less than perfect around beautiful Tamlyn of Glenrogha.

Twigging the image of her cousin in this stranger's memories oddly twisted a knife in her heart. As if this gorgeous man would look upon her and see someone taller—with seven bloody dots on her nose—and find her lacking compared to the perfect Tamlyn.

Her fingers flexed, almost as though she could reach within him and hold his heart. Own him. Brand him. "Scatty, fanciful thoughts," she murmured in self-taunt.

Despite the self-chastisement, fiery possessiveness arose in her. Aithinne's pulse thudded in her ears as her hand snaked down that shadowy divide of the upper chest and over the hard-corded muscles of his abdomen. His skin burned her fingertips as they traced the path to the brown plaide. She liked touching him. Glancing at his strong hands—hands used to wielding a broadsword—she wanted them to touch her, stroke her.

"Aye, my dark knight, you are the man to awaken

the sleeping woman within me," she confessed, all
defenses down.

Aithinne's eyebrows shot up as the tartan jerked.
Oona had explained how men grew stiff and large
as their hunger to mate rose. This avowal had drawn
a frown from Aithinne. She had seen stallions
before. When she told the crone that, Oona merely
chuckled. "Men are not quite the same, lass."

Her eyes skimmed down his long leg to the
leather shackle about his ankle, the chain binding
him to the base of the heavy bed. Reaching out, she
stroked the hard thigh, then up to the tartan. She
blinked in surprise as the pulsing under the material became quicker, insistent, almost tenting it. Inquisitive, she gingerly lifted the cover. She sighed
relief, thankful Oona had been correct. His male
staff little resembled a horse's. Though she had
never made a study of such things, once she had
seen a stallion ready to mount a mare. The animal's
had been kenspeckled and looked rather leathery.
Aithinne shuddered and uttered a prayer for small
blessings to the Auld Ones.

Over the past seven years her guardian, Gilchrist
Fraser, Lord Lyonglen, had rebuffed a score of
offers for her hand in marriage. Caring little, she
had never raised any objections, simply because no
man before had drawn her interest strongly
enough, saw her willing to bind herself to him. Despite the endless refusals, the suitors came in
droves. Being baroness of Coinnleir Wood and
ward to Lyonglen made her too big of a prize for
greedy men to resist. Most persistent of the neigh-
boring lads were Phelan and Dinsmore.

"I could be a swort hag and they would still
clamor to win me," Aithinne grumbled.

The major headache, and true threat, now came
from Edward Plantagenet. Since appointing himself

Lord Paramount of Scotland after the death of their
King Alexander, the English monarch continually
interfered in all manner of Scottish affairs. One of
those constant meddlings, Longshanks endeavored
to arrange marriages for her, as well as for her
cousins, Tamlyn, Raven, and Rowanne. The English
king was sorely vexed over their persistent refusals

As heiresses of Clan Ogilvie, no man could force
them into marriage. A charter granted by Malcolm
Canmore, two centuries before, reaffirmed and
protected this ancient right of the Picts.

Despite Oona's frequent reminders that 'twas
past time when Aithinne should have been taken to
wife, she was unsure she wanted to wed. Naturally,
she wished for a helpmate, someone to share the
burden of Coinnleir Wood and now Lyonglen. Despite those daydreams, she enjoyed the clout of not
having anyone telling her what she must do—or
what she may not.

That did not mean she lacked all curiosity about
the forces of nature or what happened betwixt men
and women. Until this moment, she had viewed
these matters with a detached questioning. At
times, when she caught one of her maids giggling
and blushing around a soldier, Aithinne wondered
if there was not something missing within her. She
had never yearned to be with a man, not once
pined to give herself in that elemental way.

Mayhap 'twas why she had devised this course of
action so easily. She never stopped to reflect what it
would entail to have a man inside her body, how
she would feel. Such considerations had rarely
seemed important before.

"Now, my pretty stranger, you cause me to wonder about so many things."

Dropping the tartan, she stepped to the pot on the
table. Dipping her fingers into the velvety ointment,

she brought it to her nose and inhaled. The fragrant mix swamped her mind, intoxicating, lulling her, yet in the same breath it caused her heart to thud stronger, amplifying the effects of Oona's potion.

Sitting on the bed, her hand hovered just above this beautiful warrior. If she touched him again, there would be no turning back. The consequences of this night, this act, would have long-reaching effects, forevermore changing the course of her destiny.

"My whole life distills to this instant in time when so much hangs in the balance."

Swallowing hard, she put her fingers to his heart and gently rubbed the silken salve to his skin. A jolt shot to her elbow, then her shoulder. By the time it hit her neck, it split like lightning. Part struck her brain; the second arc slammed into her heart, then ricocheted, reverberating through her being until she shimmered with a scorching force.

The moon shifted from behind the clouds, pouring its ghostly radiance onto the bed. Soon it would bathe the whole surface with its unearthly glow. Anoint the virile warrior with Beltane magic. Oona warned the spell would begin when the moonlight filled the chamber.

"Time to change my mind is running out," she whispered fearfully.

She once more placed her palm over his heart, the rhythm stronger, speeding up. He burned, as if a fever consumed his flesh. Looking at the flat male nipple, she recalled Oona telling her what he would do to her breasts, that she would crave such treatment, even encourage him. Leaning forward, she laid her head against his chest, hearing the coursing of his blood, as her first finger gently traced a circle around his small, brown areola. The skin tightened, flesh pebbling. She smiled in astonishment at the reaction.

Strangely, though she was nervous at what lay before her, it felt so . . . *right* . . . being against him. Shifting to bring her legs up on the bed's plane, she eased them alongside his. His male body was so different from hers. Hard where she was soft, flat while she was curved. She had never touched a male as she now stroked him.

"Never wanted to before," she admitted to the sleeping man.

But as her hand palmed over his warrior-honed body, across the taut muscles to the indentation of his navel, she wanted—nay, needed—to have her hands on this man. The beat of his heart jolted as she rimmed the small dip in his belly. Oddly, she grew aware that the thudding of his heart was in time to the pulsing under the cover.

A slow grin spread over her mouth. "So many mysteries to discover." Inquisitive, she lifted the tartan and pushed it aside.

She had seen men jump into the loch to wash up, caught them dashing out, running for their plaides. Still, she never had a chance for a close inspection. Always ducking her head and scurrying away, she had not wished for one, either.

Each pulse lengthened the flesh. It was dark, swollen. She wondered if this condition proved painful for him.

Aithinne reached out to touch the twitching shaft, surprised how scorching it burned, so soft, yet hard. Now it rode high against his belly and she felt amazement such a change could take place. With impish curiosity, her fingers curled about his throbbing erection, her thumb stroking the distended vein running its length. Astonishing. She felt it altering, thickening within her fist.

The moon's luminosity spread across the bed, revealing his beautiful body in all its warrior's splendor.

His angelic face drew her eyes. The black hair laid in waves, not cut in the Norman style. Nagging questions once more arising, she whispered her worry, "Are you not English?"

Despite logic, or how the Fates had put this warrior in the path of her brothers, she little cared about the riddles his presence conjured. This man would father beautiful bairns. One would be hers. After their time together ended, she would see he returned to his life and would never glimpse this warrior again. However, the image of his naked beauty would forevermore be burned in her mind.

A knight to remember.

In the cold lonely nighttimes ahead, she would think back upon this man and know she had been blessed with his coming. Knew she would never permit another to lie with her.

Aithinne arched up and brushed a light kiss against the full, sensual mouth. Her body lurched, hungry for more, suddenly desperate for more. She leaned into him and fitted her lips to his, intent on taking these secrets from him, kissing him as a woman would a man she desired.

The world spun and she went flying.

Literally.

Chapter Three

Aithinne landed on her back with a thud, the shift occurring so fast she had trouble grasping how it happened. One instant, she was kissing him. Oh, how she kissed him! Then in a blink—she slammed to the bed's surface. The breath had not left her lungs, though the whirling in her brain increased, affects of Oona's concoction. She closed her eyelids to still the dizziness. Slowly, she opened them.

The gorgeous stranger loomed over her—his knees on either side of her thighs, his palms flattened on the bed at her shoulders—pinning her. Her eyes widened as she felt an odd thump against the apex of her legs, heat pooling in her body as she understood what that "thump" was.

Gray-green eyes, the shade of the passes of Glen Shane on a foggy morn, fixed her with an intensity inherent to predators. Mysterious fey eyes that could see more than mere mortals bore into her soul with the power of the kenning. Long, thick lashes ringed them, while heavy ebony brows emphasized their mind-piercing hue. When she stared into them, the world narrowed. Nothing else existed. There was only this man with a warrior's beauty far beyond words.

This rattled her. Never had she met a man with
such power pulsing through him. Never had any
man so affected her senses, her body. Made it hard
for her to think.

Oh, this man was very special indeed.

Formed with sensual curves, his lips could be
given to satyric smiles. Smiles that could coax a
woman to do his bidding with nary a hesitation. His
jaw was strong, bespeaking of a man of great
strength and determination, while high cheek-
bones lent a balancing hint of thinness, softening
the arrogant lines.

Used to the neat beard and mustache Phelan
wore, or the scraggly white-blond chin whiskers of
Dinsmore, it pleased Aithinne her stranger was
clean-shaven. Lack of facial hair permitted the intriguing planes and shadows of his face to show to
their full advantage. Moved by the awe this man
provoked within her heart, her hand reached up to
cup his cheek.

Wavy, black hair glistened in the moonlight with
a dark auburn caste, a shade seen in people with
blood of the Picts. That caused her to again question if he were English or Scot. Three curls fell over
the hairline. Her hand itched to reach out and
brush them off his forehead.

The stranger's face was sinful . . . in ways no mere
man had right to be. The kenning whispered, *Selkie
blood.* The seal people of Scotland were said to possess such allure that mortals could not resist them.
But surely, this made him a Scot?

The pale eyes showed signs the herbs coursed
strong within him. Clearly fighting its influence, the
long lashes batted several times as he focused upon
her face.

"Where . . . how . . . ?" Befuddled, his voice
trailed off.

He reached out with one hand, tracing the outer edge of her lips with his first finger. It shook, but the kenning said it was not from the mandrake her brothers fed him, but some dark emotion within him akin to reverence. The finger edged along the seam, parting her lips, dipping into the moistness of her mouth.

Eyes widening, she cautiously swirled her tongue around it, watching his reaction play out in the pale eyes. The lids lowered halfway as though he reveled in the sensation, held it within his mind. Pulling his hand back, he lifted his finger to his tongue, then closed about it and tasted her, savoring her flavor as one might relish mead.

Oona had instructed her to feed him the Beltane mix—it would sharpen his mind, fight the lethargy of the brew. Aithinne scooted up, stretching to reach the pot by the bedside, only to have him block her with his left arm, indicating he had no intention of letting her off the bed.

"Shhh . . . I but reach for this." She gestured to the nearby pot before dipping her fingers in to scoop out a swirl of the balm.

Black brows lifted, perplexed, yet he made no move to stop her. With shaking fingers, she carried the silken lotion to his sensual lips and spread the salve slowly over their fullness. His tongue swirled out, sampling the herbs—Oona's magic. Then he surprised her by sucking on her first finger, drawing on it rhythmically.

Swallowing hard, her breathing grew shallow, raspy. She tugged it back and touched it to her lips. Tasting him.

His brow creased, obviously in pain. "My head . . ."

Her hand trembled when she reached for the goblet left by Oona, nearly spilling some of the liquid as she lifted it to him. "Here. Drink. It shall ease the pain."

The black brows lifted almost in challenge. "What manner of brew do you ply?"

"Beltane mead."

"Mead?" He rocked back on his haunches, his pale eyes shifting to the ornate cup and then back to her. He finally put his mouth on the rim and drank while she held it for him. With it only half-gone, he paused.

"Drink. 'Tis best if you drink it all," she urged.

The corner of his mouth quirked up in a half-smile. "No half-measures?"

"Half-measures never see the deed done."

"I should not wish to disappoint my lady by leaving anything *half-done*." With a faint nod, he drank the rest of Oona's mixture. As she put the empty cup on the stand, he glanced about the room, confused. "How? I do not understand?"

Aithinne silenced his questions by putting her fingers against his lips. Warlock eyes glowing, he kissed them, sending shivers up her spine.

She advised, "Do not ask, dark knight. Just accept."

"But—"

"No questions this night . . . only Beltane magic."

"Either I am drunk . . . or mad," came his raspy whisper, as if he spoke more to himself than her. "Mayhap both."

The moon's pale rays illuminated the warrior's intriguing countenance. Her reasons for having her brothers steal this man were so mixed she grew dizzy just thinking about them and the possible outcome. Nonetheless, as she stared up at his face cast in half-shadow, she knew the Auld Ones had blessed her with his coming.

"Does it matter?" She placed her trembling

hands on his muscular shoulders, reveled in the contours, a soul-deep ache for this man rising within her.

He smiled crookedly. "Damned if I know . . . damned if I care."

Leaning forward, he closed his lips over hers, moving with the gentleness of butterfly wings. The pressure was too light. Looping her arms about his neck, she arched to him, trying to capture his taste. Shaking in need.

Part of the hunger was the potion. Still, she was wise enough to sense it was *this* man. As if conjured from her deepest wishes, he pleased her. Oh, how he pleased her!

Inside, her body coiled tighter, craving, burning. As she surrendered to his warrior magic, vivid images swirled through her mind. She saw herself carrying his bairn, her body full from nurturing his seed within her, giving his child life and watching it grow. Aye, 'twas the man, not the concoction— a spell more potent than any witch's brew.

The mating need awakened, the scorching fire rolling throughout her body, driving her. Having no experience, she nearly panicked, wanting it all at once and not knowing where to begin.

Running her hand over his flesh, she rasped, "Show me."

He pulled her against his chest, letting her feel his heart thunder its rhythm. Kissing her hair he whispered, the desperation raw, "You are no dream . . . but flesh and blood. Tell me you are real . . . oh, please . . . be real."

"Aye, I am real."

His hands cupped her neck, his thumbs brushing lightly along her jaw. "Then let me worship you . . . as I have yearned to do for so long . . . as I have a hundred times in my deepest dreams."

He chained kisses along her neck as his hands splayed over her shoulders and then down her bare arms. Reaching her hips, he skimmed along her outer thighs, until he found the hem of the chemise. Slowly, agonizingly, he ruched up the fabric, the soft gauzy material rasping over her sensitized flesh to her hips, then waist, over her breasts, tormenting her pebbled nipples to the point of torture. Finally, he whipped it over her head and tossed it aside, leaving her naked.

Maiden modesty flared in her mind, urging her to cover her full breasts with her hands, hide from his devouring eyes. But with Oona's love philter flaming her blood, she throbbed with needs and sensations she never dreamt of. She wanted those pale eyes to look upon her breasts, wanted him to stare at her with unveiled desire. Unsure of the ways of men and women, she trembled, afraid he did not like what he saw before him.

Barely breathing, he just gazed at her.

Fear surged within Aithinne. She crossed her arms over her breasts and allowed one side of her hair to fall over her face to veil her shame, her sadness at failing to please him as much as he delighted her. Pressure built in her heart. It moved up her throat as a tear formed in her eye. Bloody hell, she could not even blame it on those blasted freckles in this dim light!

His right hand lifted her chin, forcing her to meet his stare. His finger caught the tear as it trickled down her cheek. "You cry. Why, my lady?"

Her shoulders lifted in a shrug.

He took hold of her wrists, gently prying her arms away from her breasts. For several heartbeats, he did not move. She couldn't tell from his expression whether he found her lacking in some way.

Finally, he uttered, "Beautiful. Oh so beautiful."

Her breasts tightened, yet felt heavier, fuller. Setting his hands on her shoulders, he eased them up the column of her throat, his thumbs brushing ever so softly. She sucked in a ragged breath, finding it hard to get enough air. He smiled, then leaned to her and brushed his mouth against hers.

His lips were firm, warm and dry, not sloppy and wet as Phelan's were in his rough attempts to steal a kiss. She craved to close her eyes and enjoy the conflagration he spread within her flesh, relish the sweet cider and mead on his lips. Wanted to watch him, see the reaction in his bedeviling eyes. The reason why he was here with her was long gone from her thoughts. She only wanted to touch him, stroke him.

His arms were beautiful, granite hard, clearly shaped from years of wielding a sword and lance; yet, they weren't bulky like Einar's. There was a sleekness to his body, a warrior's elegance, which set him above all men.

Breaking the kiss, he gasped for air, his eyes searching hers as though he spoke to her mind with the kenning. The warmth in the pale gaze spoke adoration, love, a soul-deep wanting—emotions that astonished her.

The mobile lips closed over hers once more. Slanting his angle, he worked her mouth, teaching her the skills of pleasure. Her control shattered as the kisses went on. And on. Aithinne felt a low moan echo in her, yet wasn't sure if the sound came from him or her—didn't care as long as he kept kissing her.

Heat rolled off his flesh, blistering her, branding her as the kiss deepened, became more demanding. His tongue pressed along the seam of her lips. He did naught to compel her to open for him, though when she sighed, the questing tongue seized the advantage, spearing in to stroke over, then around hers. The concept was shocking but she quickly learned the rhythm, the play.

She recalled Dinsmore cornering her once as she came out of the garderobe and trying to force a kiss upon her using his tongue. It was sloppy, made her think of a piece of calf's liver shoved into her mouth. There was no comparison. This man showed her just how pleasurable, how varied kisses could really be.

Leaving her breathless, he trailed his mouth along her jaw, then down the side of her neck, pausing to lave his tongue against the spot where her pulse frantically jumped. Her heart slammed against her ribs, but also felt the force of his in his chest and knew the power of this magic between them reached him with the same measure.

She remained motionless, anxious by the dark craft he wielded so easily. Even so, he drew her, called by instincts older than the dawn of time.

Sliding down the bed, he pulled her under him, the solid weight of his warrior-honed muscles pressing her into the bedding. Her body conformed to his solid planes, her rounded softness met his in perfection. He was heavy, yet she found she relished the sensation. The surrender.

His body moved lower, and in rising hunger, his mouth feasted on her breast. At first, his tongue circled the hard peak of her nipple, flicking it playfully. Then sucking it hard, he drew on it in a rhythm that echoed in her body. Hands clutching his upper arms, she arched to him— wanting it all.

For an instant out of time, he paused to stare at her.

"Is something wrong?" she asked, suddenly scared he would not take her.

He swept the hair away from the side of her face.

"I want to capture your image in my mind's eye. When I am old and gray, I shall conjure this memory and recall the power. Recall you, so beautiful with your golden hair kissed by fire, pooling around you. Recall how I have dreamt of this for so many long, cold years."

His fingers traced through the soft curls at the apex of her thighs, finding them damp from her body's desire, preparing her for his invasion. He moaned as he slid a finger into her, then two. Her hips bucked in reaction as he stretched her body. "You are so tight. I do not want to hurt you." Then he moved the fingers in and out slowly, opening her, stretching her.

"Please . . ." She seemed unable to gasp anything further.

Taking Aithinne's hands, he interlaced his fingers with hers and pushed them up beside her head, his body aligning to hers. His erection nudged against her opening, moistening the mushroom tip with the honey of her need.

"As a virgin, you might feel pain when I breach your maidenhead. I would have pain be no part of this special time. Do not be afraid . . . pleasure is on the other side. Kiss me, brand me, own me. Become one with me," he whispered as he flexed the muscles of his hips and slid into her. He paused when he bumped against the virgin's veil. Withdrawing partially, she felt him readying his muscles to apply the force needed to break through the maidenhead.

Aithinne almost yelped. "Wait . . ."

"Wait?" came his strangled reply.

"Aye . . . you must speak your deepest wish."

He echoed the word as if foreign. "Wish?"

"Aye, for what your heart desires most." She kissed the column of his neck, while silently asking the Auld Ones for a child born from the fire of their passion. The child born of her plans to protect Lyonglen and Coinnleir Wood . . . only she now wanted that child.

Wanted *his* child.

"Look at me," he ordered, his voice rough. "You *are* my wish. I want to see your eyes when I take you . . . when I make you mine."

Aithinne batted her lashes, staring into his shadowy countenance, stunned by the conviction in his words. She heard forever in his declaration. Her heart clenched knowing that could never be, no matter how her soul cried out wanting it.

His male hardness stretched her. She marveled at the hot, pulsing flesh pushing, prodding against her barrier. The fullness was startling, but she recalled Oonanne's instructions to breathe deep and slow, relax until her body conformed to accept his flesh within hers. Surely, this joining was fire magic. Confused by his hesitation, she felt him pull back, but then he plunged forward. A cry escaped her lips, but he caught it, kissing her until the pain receded. Lying still, she reveled in how deep he now was within her, how connected their bodies were.

Lifting slightly, he stroked inside her again, going even deeper, causing her to moan in pleasure, desire, not pain. He whispered against her lips, "My wish—to have you, own you, possess you . . . forevermore."

Her beautiful stranger set a rhythm of plunges that had her clinging to him, her fingernails biting into the flesh of his shoulders. Then clinging was not enough. She picked up the pattern so she could arch to meet his frenzied thrusts. The pace quickened, as wild and furious as a summer storm.

Her body exploded into a thousand white-hot cinders, nearly blinding her vision as he pulled her into a maelstrom of fire. His body tensed as he vibrated, the agony, the beauty, etched on his face as her eyes focused. She clung to him as the scalding heat of his seed poured into her body.

The splendor of their bonding summoned tears to her eyes, so humbling she hid her face against the curve of his neck. To her surprise, he was not done. With a smug grin, he suddenly flipped her over, onto her stomach. Aithinne was puzzled by his intent, but he began by trailing kisses down her spine. He leaned forward, reaching for the unguent, and in strong strokes he kneaded her back, her hips, her legs. Pure ecstasy. When his warrior's hands worked their way back up, his thumbs skimmed the inside of her thighs, then maddeningly traced circles on her soft flesh. His care was both relaxing and provoking in the same breath.

He rolled, pulling her with him, until she was sitting astride his hips. It took her several heartbeats to comprehend that she could ride him, but when she understood what he wanted, she seized the chance to be in control. Or so she thought.

Undaunted, his sensual mouth curved into a devilkin grin as he pushed upward within her. The intensity of it, the fullness, caused Aithinne to shatter inside. Colors, like shooting stars, flooded her mind, overpowering her to the point she nearly slipped into a velvet oblivion.

"Have . . . mercy," she panted out.

"Not a chance." His white teeth flashed, the grin wicked. He reared up and wrapped his arms around her, driving into her again and again, each explosion building into another, his strong body bucking against hers, slamming up into her, harder, deeper, more frantic, until she could only obey his wizard's bidding. Until she lost track of how many times he forced her to find her woman's surrender.

She yielded everything. He demanded and she gave,

then gave more. Not just her physical release . . . but her heart. There was no shielding against him, against the dark words of love he whispered to her, weaving his own Beltane enchantment.

She may have made a captive of him, but this dark knight ensnared her soul.

Aithinne's body echoed with the hot vibrancy of their coupling. Still pulsing, shimmering with his possession, she craved more. Leaning her face into the strong column of his neck, she clung to him, wanting to prolong the sensations. So very right, she felt a part of this special man.

All of Oona's teachings failed to hint at the mysterious power that rose between a man and woman, how quickly she pined for more. How it bonded her to him. Now she understood why women so willingly surrendered the small control they had in their lives, giving over their fate to men.

This time with him was precious, to be treasured. She thrilled knowing there would be more nights like this one.

Six more.

Her heart squeezed. Only six. Then he would be gone, back to his life. A life that did not include her or the child they would make. When she sent him away, he would take a piece of her with him. A piece of her heart.

How could she ever let him go?

In her mad scheme, could there be a possibility he might wish to remain with her? Foolish yearnings. Yet, her heart cried, *make it so.*

All of Scotland knew how Marjorie, Countess Carrick, had made prisoner of Robert Bruce, Lord of Annandale. Annandale had traveled to pay his respects and inform the lady of the circumstances of her husband's death in the Holy Lands. As he rode away at the end of his visit, he was unexpectedly

beset with the countess's guard. They escorted him
back to the castle where she kept him captive until
they wed. The union produced enough Bruce children to say it must have been a happy marriage.

Dare she do the same? Was she audacious enough
to hold him longer than the time Oona said she
must to insure he bred a child upon her? This night
had been founded on a need to control her life,
keep her safe from the men determined to use her
for their material gains. But, could this special man
stay? Be her knight protector? Logic said such a wish
could never be, yet the seed of hope took root in
her heart.

He stroked her hair and then pulled her to him
as he rolled, holding her close. "So long . . . I have
loved you. I had begun to think you were not real."

"I am real."

His words were low, softly spoken against her hair
as he nuzzled the side of her face. "I dreamt of you.
Not every night. When I closed my eyes I wished for
the dream to visit me. Even when I did not dream,
I sensed you, wanted you, craved to be near you. So
long, I nearly gave up hope of finding you. Then I
saw you, saw you were mortal. Only, it nearly
crushed me to know you would never be mine."

Aithinne could not speak, so awed by his heartfelt words. A side effect of the potion he had been
fed—a man could only speak honesty when under
its influence. The words he offered came from his
inner heart, where all truths lived.

"You have seen me in your dreams?" Barely able
to breathe, hope surged within her. Could this be?
Oh, please let it be!

He leaned halfway over her, wrapping his thigh
over hers as if to anchor her, make sure she didn't
slip away from him. Rubbing his cheek along her
jawline, he nuzzled her as a cat would. "Since I

became a knight. Before my dubbing, I spent the night in reflection. Fighting exhaustion, I prayed long into the dark hours of morn for God to guide me to be a knight true, show me the path of my destiny. A face came to me in the darkness, barely more than mist. Details were not strong and I was so startled, I nearly lost the thread of the vision. But I could see the eyes. Your eyes. I had no idea what your coming meant then. Later, you appeared again—when I was wounded in battle, your presence visited me. This time my sight was clearer. I saw your golden hair, shimmering as if kissed by fire. When I thought I might die, you soothed my brow and told me I could not give up. I have loved you, hunted for you. No man could love a woman as I love you."

He kissed her. Not the gentle kiss of worship, this kiss was full of passion, born of the fire of their coming together. His knee shifted her thigh so he could slide over her and into her. He linked his fingers with hers and pushed her arms over her head, arching her body to conform to his, to meet his thrusts eagerly.

The perfection of him being within her, knowing their joining was done with love, moved her so profoundly she could hardly breathe. He had seen her in his dreams! Oh, how beyond belief was this! This man was destined to be hers, willed by the Auld Ones.

His body pounded into hers as he brought them to a shimmering release. Their reaching this pinnacle in the same breath only amplified the sense of their belonging to each other. Oh, this night was indeed miraculous, more than she could have ever wished!

He rained gentle kisses over her face, between gasps for air. "I love you . . . love you . . . love you . . ."

Her heartbeat pounded harder, more erratically, with each declaration, knowing she loved this man.

They were destined to be; together they could forge a magnificent future.

"Forevermore. I will always love you . . . Tamlyn." With his final words, he drifted into an exhausted slumber.

Aithinne could not draw air. The pain was too much. She laid there, frozen, tears sliding down her cheeks. How could she have not recalled seeing Tamlyn's face within his thoughts?

Devastation rolled through her, the hurt burning until she feared she might vomit.

Her beautiful stranger loved her cousin, Tamlyn! He thought she *was* Tamlyn!

She pushed him away from her, curling into herself and choking back silent tears.

Tears of anguish that his heart would forever belong to another.

Chapter Four

Just after dawnbreak Aithinne marched into the Great Hall of Lyonglen. She pulled up, growling under her breath as she espied her brothers lazing around the lord's table, awaiting food to break their fast. Their spirits quite merry. With the foul mood she was in, their inane chuckles set her teeth to gnashing.

"Oooooo . . . nodcocks," she muttered, her eyes narrowing on them. "Let me finish with you, then see if you still have half a mind to laugh."

Last night had been more than a maid could wish for her first time. Her stranger taught her things she never knew about her body, showed her pleasures beyond imagining. Aithinne's lip quivered when she recalled how exquisitely he worshipped her with his hands, his mouth, his heat singeing her flesh. How deep he had been within her. How a part of him she had been. All the sensations he made her feel.

There had been no holding back. Defenseless, she had given her heart to him.

Then the bloody bastard ruined the beauty of their time together by calling her Tamlyn!

It was a knife in her heart. She faced the pain—

and the facts. Obviously, there was no longer any question. Her stranger knew Tamlyn, felt deep emotions for her.

Loved her.

She choked back the rising tears, her hands trembling as she barely controlled the urge to cry. Oh, how much more muddled could her life get? Sucking in a deep breath, she forged the pain into anger.

"From where did you steal him?" Aithinne launched her attack before the idiots realized she was in a horrid temper.

The three of them had a tendency to scurry like rats when she wanted a handful of them, so she kept squarely in the path of their retreat. The silly twits failed to notice her bubbling fury.

Hugh leaned sideways in the lord's chair, his legs dangling over one arm. His hazel eyes looked up at her blankly. Deward and Lewis mirrored his action. All three smiled innocently and inquired in one voice, "Who?"

"Save playing innocent, you lackwits. We have only one stranger you dragged to Lyonglen and dumped into my bed." Putting her hands on her hips, she glared at them. At the edge of her vision, she spotted Einar in the shadows, trying to slip away. "Dare not leave, Einar! You were supposed to see they carried out my instructions to the letter. Sit!" She pointed to a bench.

"Aye, Princess." Contrite, he strived to scrunch himself into about half his size as he walked to the bench and sat.

The Viking was quite comical, but she suppressed the rising chuckle and snapped, "Do not call me Princess, Einar."

Head hanging in shame, he nodded. "As you wish, Princess Aithinne."

She exhaled her frustration. "I did not mean

address me as *Princess* Aithinne, I said do not call me Princess a'tall."

"Aye, Princess," he rumbled, while her three mooncalf brothers giggled and poked each other.

"Och, never mind. I have no time to argue over something that you have failed to learn in ten years. I need to know where they *found* that man. He is a warrior. I examined his clothes—raiments belonging to a noble. So from where did you cork brains steal him?"

Her three brothers looked to each other, eyes rolling, trying not to snigger. Deward kicked Lewis under the table, trying to warn him to silence. Naturally, Lewis kicked back. Harder. Then suddenly they flew at each other, slugging away, while Hugh howled with laughter.

"Oh, sister, it was a glorious night!" Hugh beamed up at her. "We are tired, though likely Dinsmore and his cronies are more bone weary. When all the chamber pots were emptied, we pelted them with stones, not big enough to maim, but enough to royally vex them, since Dinsmore commanded them not to loose arrows in return. The Campbells finally rode back up the hill to Dinsmore's tent. While they jumped into the burn to scrub off the dung, we set their horses free. Took them ages to round them up. Later, while the knaves slept, we slipped back and cut the ropes on the tent. The whole thing collapsed on Dunny Dinsmore. Och, did he curse a blue streak! While his men tried to drag him out from under it, we unhobbled their horses and chased them off again."

Eyes narrowing in fury, Aithinne whipped around on Einar. "You let them do this? They could have been wounded, killed, if Dinsmore's lackeys stood and fought." She threw up her hands when

Einar's head hung lower. "Och, I do not ken why I bother."

"Sorry, Princess."

"Sister, stop slapping Einar's ears with words. The Campbells could not fight. They would do naught to upset you. 'Tis why it is muckle fun to torment them." Hugh smiled and lifted the goblet of ale to his mouth.

When Deward and Lewis fell to the floor, still struggling with each other, she glared at Einar and then pointed to them. Instantly, he grabbed them by their belts, lifted them, and dropped them on the bench. Both young men glared at the Viking and then at her.

"*Enough!*" Aithinne used *the voice* she reserved for listen or else. "I want to ken where you stole that warrior from . . . *now.*" She stomped her foot to focus their attention, but mumbles and shrugs were the only replies she garnered. "You found him—at Glenrogha. After I forbade you to go there, you went to the Beltane festival and stole the man from there. Did you not?"

Their eyes widened at her deductions. Hugh frowned. "'Tis not fair, Aithinne. You promised never to use the kenning to prod our minds. 'Tis knavish to walk in a person's thoughts without his leave."

"I have no need of tricks to twig your feeble-minded actions. The knight called me Tamlyn. That told me all. He is from Glenrogha."

"Aithinne, I need to seek my rest." Lewis rubbed the sleep sand from the corner of his eyes. "Cousin Tamlyn shall not miss him. She already has one just like him."

"Just like him?" she echoed in confusion.

"We made sure we got the right one." Deward looked at her earnestly as if seeking her praise.

Lewis sighed, then straightened his clothing,

mussed in the struggle with Deward. "And mind, 'tis not an easy chore. The place is overrun with dragons."

Fearing they were too far into their cups, her foot tapped out her waning impatience. "Explain *dragon*. Say you dare not speak of the Dragon of Challon—the Norman warrior Edward Longshanks sent to claim Glen Shane. Surely, even you three cannot have done something so reckless as to steal him?"

She reeled, faint from the ramifications of their foolish actions. In her plotting, she had merely sought to simplify her life, give her some small measure of security and control. Now this spiraled into a nightmare, one that would see her in White Tower, prisoner to the English king.

"Sister, do not fash so . . . not *that* Dragon." He grinned over their accomplishment. "We borrowed another."

"What *dragon*?" A dull throb grew behind her eyes from trying to uncurl their lack of sense. Since they turned five and ten and suddenly shot up taller than she, she could no longer take a switch to them. If she tried, they would wrestle her down to the floor and sit on her until she expended her fury in the useless struggle. Thus, she was forced to use her wits to handle them now. Only, using her wit against three ignoramuses left her with a dull throbbing pain.

"Not a real one, Aithinne." Lewis propped his elbow on the table to hold up his head. "The Earl Challon—the Black Dragon—was sent by Edward Longshanks to claim Glen Shane. The English king commanded he marry one of our cousins. Challon chose our Tamlyn and she seems fair happy with the notion. Stares at him with calf eyes, she does. They say his two brothers shall wed with Rowenna and Raven."

She pointed to the ceiling. "Then *who* is that up there?"

"A cousin. He favors Julian Challon, much the same way Tamlyn and you do each other. We thought it a fine jest. Actually our dragon is prettier and taller than Tamlyn's dragon," Hugh said as a yawn popped up.

"You are taller than Tamlyn." Shooting a glare at Lewis, warning their fight was not over, Deward picked up the explanation in his rambling fashion. "Our cousin warms to Lord Challon, danced before the balefire with him, she did. Can you not see Fate, sister? It seemed the weave of magic to us—she lay with Challon last night, you lay with his kinsman. It *has* to be the will of the Auld Ones, dare you deny their purpose, provoke their will?"

Totally flummoxed, she sat down with a thud on a bench. For her idiot brothers that was very deep thinking. "What is his name?"

"St. Giles, Lord Ravenhawke, kinsman to the Dragon," Lewis supplied. "They say Lord Challon sets muckle store in him, treats him as a brother."

"Ohhhhh . . ." Aithinne stomped her feet several times in rage, feeling as if she were sinking in a bog and could not find purchase on solid land. "You blethering lackwits!"

Hugh pursed his face, then sighed. "Now, Aithinne, rein in your freckles. You sent us forth to acquire a man. A stallion . . . a breeder . . ." He sniggered and winked at his two look-alike brothers. "We love you, sister, thus we wanted to give you someone pretty. You must agree we far exceeded that. You would not want to lay with some pitted-faced artisan and have him father a dullard bairn upon you, would you?"

Swallowing to keep back raw emotions, she shook

her head. "Nay, since I have done this foolhardy thing I ken he shall give me a beautiful babe."

Suddenly, images of her holding a black-haired bairn in her lap flooded her mind. The child— a boy—seemed to be about a year old, and was so precious her heart squeezed. In the vision, she hummed a cradlesong to the wee babe and ran her fingers through the thick, wavy hair so like his father's. Despite all the worries and fears rising from the aftereffects of this mess, she *wanted* that child. Ached to hold his small body, suckle him.

Never before had she envisioned the child she'd plotted to conceive. It was just one of those vague pieces to the riddle in her mind, a means to an end to keep Edward Longshanks and the greedy wolves from the gates of the two fiefs.

The only children she'd cared for were her brothers, younger than she by seven years. She was barely nine years old when their parents were lost to a wasting fever. In some ways she'd taken over being mother to the lads when she was but a child herself. She loved the triplets, but they had been tedious to raise, thus she assumed she had used up all desire to have a child of her own. She had seen castle workers' babes when they brought them to show her, but the children never provoked that yearning within her to be a mother.

Now, everything was different. She could see the child she would make with this nobleman, and she wanted it. Would fight for it. The instinct to be a mother reared itself within her and proved nearly overpowering.

"Stop and consider," Lewis pressed. "Can you see yourself lying with someone like Phelan or Dinsmore? Or worse? I think not, Sister."

She exhaled resignation. "Aye, you speak true. I was able to go through with this because I found him so pleasing. Only, if Challon is to marry with Tamlyn, that summons the danger of Ravenhawke being at Glenrogha sometime when I am there. The idea was to fetch a man I would never meet again. There will be no avoiding him with him serving Challon."

Hugh crossed his legs at the ankles and appeared smug. "Nay, Sister. He said he only pays visit to the Earl Challon and will move northward to claim some fief that belongs to his grandfather."

"See, there is naught to furrow your brow over," Lewis concurred.

Not realizing she had been frowning, she relaxed her eyebrows and sighed, confused and worried over this foolish mistake that could prove costly.

"You should keep him," Einar pronounced.

All heads snapped to him in shock. Einar never voiced opinions, merely went along with whatever she ordered. Aithinne's mouth hung half-open. Becoming aware she gaped, she snapped it shut.

Keep St. Giles? She spoke the name in her mind and he was no longer *her stranger*, but St. Giles, Lord Ravenhawke. A man who did not belong to her. Even so, her imagination immediately took the bit between its teeth and ran wild with flashes of visions, showing her images of a possible future with this man. Them laughing, working to protect the people of Lyonglen and Coinnleir Wood. Him making love to her in the dark of night.

Oh, the temptation to keep him was great.

Nevertheless, she could never forget this man was in love with Tamlyn. Her cousin may be betrothed to his kinsman, but St. Giles's heart burned with devotion for her. He coveted her in a way a man did not forget. Oh, men could lie with others, but their hearts were branded. A woman might become St. Giles's lady wife, share his life, but each time she lay with him she would ache inside knowing he loved another.

Much of her life Aithinne felt less pretty than Tamlyn. She heard people comment on the unfortunate red tint to her hair and the freckles on her nose. *So sad, poor Aithinne is not the beauty her cousin is,* they whispered when they thought she did not hear. No matter how she could wish for this man to be a part of her existence, she would never place herself in this soul-destroying lifetime of comparisons. That path held nothing but crushing heartache.

"Einar, keeping him is not a choice. He is not a cat." She tried to make light of it as if he meant it as a joke. Only she couldn't ignore the twist in her heart. Oh aye, she'd like to keep him, but *not* when he loved Tamlyn.

"Vikings took people." Einar puffed up his chest, proud of his heritage.

The lads groaned and repeated like echoes, "Not another sermon on the ways of Norsemen."

"Einar, your people took slaves." Aithinne restlessly tapped her fingernails on the wooden table, trying to cipher what was best to do. "That man would never be anyone's slave."

Einar grunted. "Aye, I cannot see that warrior a slave to another. But you are a princess . . ."

Aithinne groaned, not about to address the same old *a princess can do anything* nonsense. "It shall not matter to this knight."

Einar summoned his stubborn Viking scowl. It worked on her brothers, but he wasted it on her. "You are a witch. Bind him to you. Turn his mind to you, Princess. Take the bond of blood with him."

How tempting. It was true. She could bespell him, turn the man's mind in circles, thus convince him to remain with her. Her heart ached even more. To control his devotion through magic would be as hollow as St. Giles lingering with her because she was an echo of the woman who had stolen his heart, a woman he could never have.

"He must go back to his kinsmen. This night," she said firmly, to convince herself as much as them. Aithinne tried to harden her heart, but she was close to breaking down and bawling like a babe. "Dose him with the potion of blackness and then dump him outside of Glenrogha just before dawn-break."

"No." Einar crossed his arms over his massive chest to emphasize his outright refusal.

Aithinne frowned, shocked. Never had the Viking balked at any of her orders. "You deny my command?"

"Oonanne says he stays the seven nights of the waxing moon. He remains. To do otherwise shall anger the Auld Ones. The Auld Father has woven the skein of this warrior's life. What will be must be."

"He speaks truth." Oona stepped into the light as if she materialized from the shadows. "Lass, you have set the wheel in motion. To alter its path now would call down catastrophe upon all our heads. You made wishes and bargains with Annis, our goddess of the water. If you now refute what she granted, you risk summoning her wrath," the crone warned. "You made your bed, my lass—with a pretty man in it. Now you must lie in it with this braw warrior . . . see the deed done."

"I wish—" Aithinne started.

All five people blurted out, "No more wishes!"

Damian St. Giles ached from every fiber of his being. He wanted to move, tried to move, but found for some reason he could not. His mouth tasted fuzzy, musty, the cursed mead leaving a peculiar aftertaste as if he'd been gnawing on a half-rotten stump. He needed water. Opening his eyes, he struggled to focus.

At first he feared he'd been struck blind. After the shock, he realized his arm was oddly bent so the inside crook of his elbow covered his eyes. He attempted to shift it, but the flesh was numb from being in that position too long.

"Damnation!" With effort he lifted it away, grimacing at the pain. He batted his eyelids several times to rid the haze clouding them, and then pushed up to a sitting position, stretched, and yawned. "Where the bloody hell am I? I presume I still live since I taste such agony."

His words bounced off the stone walls, garnering no reply.

Running his hand through his hair, he struggled to gather his thoughts. Beltane . . . the festival on the tor. He recalled that much, bringing to mind the beautiful night and the sight of the dancers, the smell of the fire. Remembered he had been miserable, and stupidly drank too much in effort to drown his sorrow.

Tamlyn. He summoned her visage to mind, so stunning as she danced around the balefire. She had shimmered, like some faery queen his Scottish mother used to tell him about at night when she put him to bed.

But Tamlyn had danced for Julian. Her eyes saw naught but Julian.

Despair twisted within him. He was gifted—cursed, he sometimes thought—with his mother's Highland sight. The kenning she had called it. For years he'd seen a woman's face in his dreams, and knew with complete certainty she was destined to be his wife. So when he came to Glenrogha and saw that face, he was devastated to learn it belonged to the Lady Tamlyn, Countess Glenrogha.

Only a fool could not see Julian wanted her more than life. Worse, it pained Damian to admit Tamlyn returned Challon's feelings. His cousin needed Tamlyn. She was good for him, soothed his troubled soul. She could save him from the darkness threatening to claim him. Still, no matter how many times Damian told himself they were a match blessed by the gods, he could not stop his heart from crying out that Tamlyn should have been fated to be his.

Tamlyn was in love with Julian, and Damian knew, without doubt, Julian would kill to keep her. It hurt, but he accepted their feelings, would stand silently by when they wed in a few sennights, and offer his heartfelt blessing upon their union.

He acknowledged this finality of Fate. Yet, his dreams had not ended, only strengthened. His heart refused to listen. Why?

How could the kenning be so wrong—so insistent—in this?

Foolishly, he had tried to drown his feelings in drink.

"Drink . . ."

The word conjured a vision of three men who looked alike to flash before his eyes. They had offered him a special heather ale . . . promising it would cure what bedeviled him, make all his dreams come true.

He searched his mind trying to find a recollection beyond that point. Strangely, there was naught, outside an image of a very tall warrior—a Viking. With an exhale of frustration, he looked around to get his bearings.

The room was unfamiliar. The chamber was darkened, the only light source from the arrow loop. He

did not need to call upon his fey sense to ken he
was not in Glen Shane.

"So where the bloody hell am I?"

He glanced at his body half covered by the tartan.
Naked. Nothing odd in that. He slept in the raw.
Yet, as he sought his clothing, he saw none of his
belongings. In fact, the whole room was rather
devoid of personal items. There was a trunk at the
foot of the bed, the huge curtained bed, a table at
the side and a chamber pot in the far corner.

"Thank goodness for small considerations." Deciding to make use of the latter, he scooted to the
bed's edge. The rattle alerted him, along with the
pressure around his ankle. Lifting the woolen
sheet, he stared at his leg, his mind having a hard
time accepting what he saw. "That will teach you
to drown your sorrows in Highland mead, you
nodcock."

He was chained to the bloody bed!

Restless, fighting within herself, Aithinne paced
petulantly in her room. Hearing the door open,
she dashed the stray tear from her cheek with the
back of her hand and pretended that nothing bothered her. All her emotions were off-kilter by this
whole matter. She wanted it over with and St. Giles
far away from here this night. Mayhap then her
heart would be safe. Contrarily, her body had other
ideas. Just the thought of him caused the fire
to flare within her, the need to be with him arising
to twist her insides until she thought she would
go mad.

The door pushed wide and Oona came in carrying a tray. The amber eyes quickly appraised
Aithinne's mood. "Time draws near, Lass. Here is
the tansy for you and the warming pot of the salve."

"I don't want the potion or the unguent."

Oona clucked. "Did I ask if you *wanted* them? Cease this quarrelling within yourself, Aithinne Ogilvie. Worrying over things you cannot change is time wasted. Change what you can in life. Accept aught else."

"I tell myself this. Saying such and believing it are two different beasties."

"You begged wishes and our Lady Annis granted them. Now you find they are not precisely as you hoped. The Auld Ones only give so much, Aithinne. They expect you to work to shape the rest of your destiny. You wanted a child—keep your bargain and you shall have one." Oona eyed her slyly. "Only now you want the man, too. That is the trouble, is it not, lass? You have lain with him, bonded with him—a bond of the flesh, the blood, the soul—and now ken there shall be none other for you. Do not hide from these truths, lass. You merely delude yourself when you do. You want him? Claim him. The solution is there. Reach out and seize it. Any woman with Ravenhawke in her bed would not have to be told what to do."

Aithinne snatched up the goblet and downed the thick liquid. "Sometimes I really mislike your peering into my thoughts."

Oona shrugged as she set to unbraiding Aithinne's long hair. "The Auld Ones saw you created in Tamlyn's mold. But you are *not* Tamlyn. They touched your hair with faery fire, gave you the green flecks in your eyes. Where you two are most different is within. You want him? Use these nights of the waxing moon you have left. Summon the faery fire to burn her from his memory. You can, you know. I looked into his mind when I went in earlier to leave him food."

"He was awake?"

"He slept still. My spell sees he cannot stay awake for long periods. He becomes exhausted, confused, and must rest. The herbs make him not remember."

"What did you see?"

"Ah, not even going to feign disinterest?" she taunted. "I saw images of a woman. He does not understand them. Just *thinks* he does. 'Tis up to you to help him find his way."

Aithinne huffed. "You speak riddles, Oona."

"You think to see your path made so easy? This is the journey you wished for, but are you willing to fight for what you want, pay the cost? Too muckle in your life thus far has been easy."

"Easy? Have you mislaid what sense you were born with? I lost my parents to a fever when I was but nine. I raised the lads when I was a child myself. Thankfully, I became ward to Gilchrist. He was a dear man—"

"A silly man, he indulged your headstrong ways, just as the Shane did Tamlyn, Raven, and Rowanne, and neither man prepared the lot of you to deal with the world outside these glens. The four of you did as you pleased, spoke and every wish was carried out. Times change. Scotland moves into dark days ahead. The strong-willed females of Clan Ogilvie must learn to deal with males and their world. These hungry men no longer ignore our glens. Greedy eyes espy Glen Shane and Glen Eallach. Long has Edward Plantagenet coveted these holdings. He has sent the Dragon of Challon to claim Tamlyn. Think hard lass, you will be next. Mark my words."

Aithinne swallowed hard. "The kenning has shown thus?"

"Several seasons past the Laird Shane sought out Evelynour of the Orchard, our seer. He wanted an augury. He had met a man they called the Dragon and wanted to ken more about him. The Shane felt he would one day come for Tamlyn, that he would make a good match for his youngest daughter."

Aithinne's eyes widened in astonishment. "The Lord Challon? Longshanks sent him, yet The Shane believed he was destined for Tamlyn?"

"Evelynour saw him in visions. Dressed in the color of ravens, even mail and armor plate, he came in fog and riding a black stallion of war. At first, she was confused by the foretellings. There was a reflection—*two that were near as one*. Slowly, she discerned one warrior wrapped in the shade of the ravens. The other wore gray of the fog. One carried the device of a dragon on his shield, on the other a double-faced bird—a raven and a hawk. *Two* men, not one. Lord Challon is the first, the one who dressed in black. The man who came for our Tamlyn."

"By the Lady Annis." Aithinne smacked the palm of her hand against her forehead. "What have the lads brought down on our heads by stealing St. Giles from Glenrogha?"

"Mayhap 'twas our Annis granting you a chance to alter your destiny. Longshanks sent Challon to claim Glen Shane. Whom shall the English send to claim Glen Eallach? In the past, the Comyns held muckle sway with the king. Edward might have given Glen Eallach and you to Phelan, with no by your leave, then there would have been naught you could do to change his mind. Now King John Balliol has raised the Scottish standard, summoning all Scots to fight against the English invasion. The Comyns foolishly answered the call. They have lost favor with Longshanks. So where does Edward cast his eyes to find a lord for Glen Eallach? He twigs Gilchrist was too old to protect Lyonglen and your holding of Coinnleir. He will want a young warrior, a strong one, able to stand against both the Comyns and Campbells."

Aithinne sat as the old woman combed her long hair. "'Tis why all these lies and deceit. If I can produce a child for Edward Longshanks, a heir—Gilchrist's heir, then—"

"Aye, he might. He might also think a wee babe too small, that you and the bairn would need a champion. Mayhap a smart lass would find her own man before the English decides it for you. A man who already holds the king's favor."

The potion was hitting her blood, making it hard to focus on Oonanne's words. She tried to contemplate what needed to be done, looking for an avenue out of this quandary. Only her mind echoed with Einar's words. *Keep him.* It now seemed as if Oona pushed her to do the same. It would be so easy to do. Could she dare?

But at what cost to her heart?

As a woman, she wanted a husband to love her, to share the joy in the life they could build together. As lady of Coinnleir Wood—and now Lyonglen—she had too many others to consider. This was not about her happiness. This was about both fiefs surviving the coming war. About the future of her brothers.

A rider had come with word of the Scots' defeat at Dunbar, just days past. Nearly all of Scotland's nobles were made prisoner to the English king or lay dead. Edward would waste no breath before he moved to refashion the nobility of the land. If the nobility were not humbled before him, swearing fealty, he would see Englishmen set in their places, on that she would wager her life.

Her destiny could not be ruled by her feelings. It must be guided by the good for all of Glen Eallach.

If only St. Giles had not called her Tamlyn.

* * *

Aithinne sucked in a deep breath and entered the tower chamber before she could change her mind. The scent of peat hit her nose, telling her Einar had been there to see to St. Giles's needs. There was a wolf throw on the bed; a fire had been laid to dispel the room's chill. Last night she dared not risk the firelight. This night—pain lanced through her—he would likely think her Tamlyn again.

She swallowed, nearly choking on the hard knot in her throat, wanting to escape.

The subtle scent of herbs mixed in the smoke. Oona's fine hand. The rich aroma of apple petals saturated the air, May Day blossoms providing a strong bespelling of love rites. She little needed Oona's philter to stimulate her body, pushing her toward mating with St. Giles. All through the day, all she had to do was pause and think back on images of the night before and everything came roaring back, the heat flooding through her blood to the point where it was sheer agony to stay away from him. Her body throbbed to his invisible brand.

"When I said I did not require the potion, it was not playing coy. I have no need of it. He is the magic." She whispered the forlorn admission. "He may be chained to my bed, but I am the true prisoner of his powers."

Shame pulsed in her. She would join him this night knowing full well he loved Tamlyn. Oh, she resisted coming to him, not following through on her threat to have Einar take him back to Glenrogha. Her body held sway. Age-old mating instincts had awoken within her and there was no silencing their drive.

It was as though he wove a dark enchantment,

and with their joining he became a part of her. St. Giles was in her blood, in her heart, he consumed her soul. There was naught she could do to shield herself from his charms.

Never had she grasped how desires of the mind could wield such influence over one's physical being. Oh, she had seen her cat when it came into heat. The feline had been quite humorous, howling and crawling around on her belly with her tail crooked to the side. Putting a hand to her stomach, Aithinne had a new sympathy for puss and was glad desire did not affect a woman in the same fashion.

Her eyes moved to the bed, hungrily seeking St. Giles. He rested half in the shadows, the tartan carelessly flung across his hips. With his body heat, he obviously didn't feel the chill of the room. She would have been shivering and huddled under the wool. His left arm was carelessly bent across his brow so it covered his eyes.

For several heartbeats, she stared at his beautiful form. He was so lean, so hard. A sleeping warrior prince awaiting the faery queen's kiss to awaken him. Unable to resist, her hand reached out and touched him, stroking the strong thigh muscle. He was everything she could want in a man, as if Annis conjured St. Giles from her loneliest wishes.

Use these nights of the waxing moon, summon the faery fire to burn her from his memory. Oona's words echoed in her mind along with Einar's advice to cling to him.

"If only it were as simple as saying, aye, I would keep him." Regret threaded her voice.

The logical side of her mind arose, trying to sway her heart by reminding her of the anguish of him whispering Tamlyn's name. How absurd to even consider he might wish to stay, to open herself to the sorrow that would come. Foolish indeed.

Aithinne hung her head, closing her eyelids

against the tears forming. Too late, for one dropped to his leg. Why she was suddenly so sad, overcome with a grief that was nearly devastating she could not say. She should send him away now—this night— before she bound her heart, her soul more deeply to this beautiful warrior.

She stepped back from the bed, her breath caught in her throat. His arm had been removed from his face and those pale green-gray eyes watched her with an intensity that was frightening.

For a heartbeat, she was not sure he was fully awake. Then he stirred, faster than she could blink. Never could she have dreamt anyone could move that quickly. Before she could take another step backward or even inhale in shock, his hands took her upper arms and sent her flying through the air.

She slammed hard to the plane of the bed, all air knocked from her body. He straddled her thighs, pinning her. As she tried to rise, he used the chain across her neck. Stretching it between both hands, he pressed the heavy metal to her throat, causing her to strangle.

Chapter Five

Aithinne stared up into the face of a fierce warrior, a battle-hardened man capable of killing without hesitation. This aspect of St. Giles terrified her. Frantic, her hands pushed at his shoulders, against his chest, but nothing she did moved him or caused the pressure on the chain to let up.

"Who are you? Tell me why I am shackled in this room," he growled the words.

She searched his eyes, at first dreading he had not eaten the food which contained Oona's potion. As his eyes struggled to focus upon her face, she realized the brew still held him under its sway.

He raged in fury and anguish, "Demon witch robbing my mind, why bespell me so . . . use my dreams against me? You destroy me."

Aithinne trembled in true fear. This was something she had not foreseen—the warrior unleashed, his strength used against her. She had presumed the herbs and Oona's spells would see him compliant the whole time he remained captive in her bed. Another error.

Mayhap it was the Selkie blood she sensed coursing within him. With that fey magic, he might hold the power to resist Oona's crafting of the Beltane love philter. If so, then the situation quickened to dangerous. She had no way to gauge how a warrior enraged would act with his judgment clouded. Panic rose as her mind warned that a knight used to surviving in battle would act to protect himself from sheer instinct.

Though the weight of the chain had not increased, it still cut into her throat, making speech impossible. Shoving against his shoulders proved futile. While a sturdy lass, she was helpless against the strength of his powerful arms. She could sooner shove around a bloody horse.

Instinctively, she sussed fighting this warrior was not the key. With a trembling hand, she reached up and traced her finger over the arch of his upper lip, then slowly along the fullness of the lower one. The tension on the chain slackened as his focus drew to her hand on his mouth, then back to her pinned to the bed, choking.

Brows furrowed, he flung the links aside as if he had held a snake. His hand shook as he gently traced her throat with his fingers, following where the chain had bit into her skin. In the moon's shadows she saw the glimmer of tears form in his pale eyes. "Be cursed . . . I . . . regret . . ."

Aithinne coughed, nodded, and then tried to sit up.

"I mislike this lack . . . of control," he whispered hoarsely, fighting to speak the words. "It rubs against the grain of a warrior . . . why enchant me thusly? Why taunt me with a vision I cannot have . . . offer me my most cherished dream . . . torment me in a hell of my own fashioning, because I know it can *never* be?"

Unable to meet his probing stare, Aithinne lowered her eyes, feeling empathy for his confusion, the raw frustration. St. Giles was a dynamic man, one used to command. Shame flooded her, showing just how shortsighted she had been in not thinking this whole scheme through.

Truly, she was not a selfish person, one careless of other people's needs or feelings. Only, she had many responsibilities weighing down upon her shoulders these past two months. No one was there to help ease the burden. So many depended upon her to protect them, looked to her to shield all in Glen Eallach in this time of war with the English. Edward Longshanks terrified her. How was she, a mere Scots lass, to stand in the path of the most ruthless king to ever sit on the English throne?

So desperate was she for a solution to her quandary that in all her plottings not once had she considered how the man might feel. Most males seemed too apt to spread their seed around to any woman willing to lie with them. Thus, she had presumed he would welcome, even enjoy, the couplings, then just sleep the rest of the time.

In her mind everything had been so straightforward, her aims clear. Now the threads of her plans were unraveling about her. Rage and rebellion burned in this proud man. Her actions troubled his spirit and, because of their bond, that anguish echoed within her. Her head dropped forward to hide her dishonor, allowing the tears to silently trickle down her face.

He lifted her chin with two fingers, then rubbed the droplets on her cheek with his thumb. "You cry, Faery Queen? Do tears of the Fae taste different? If I sample one, will the price be my mortal soul?"

Her breath sucked in on a gasp as he leaned forward, kissing the tears from her countenance. His tongue flicked out and lapped their taste. The corner of his mouth lifted faintly upward. "My mother believed tears from a faery can bless one with immortal life. In spite of this, she cautioned there is only one way to make a faery cry—to break her heart. Have I broken your heart, my Fae Queen?"

More than he could ever know, her mind mourned. She put her fingers to his lips to stop the flow of words, unable to bear his concern. "Words wound deeper than any knife, my lord. Often they fester and never heal."

Frustrated, Damian backed off the high bed and tried to stand. The room spun. He caught the bed-post, holding on until the world righted once more. Scores of questions pressed inwardly upon his beleaguered brain, but his head hurt too much to think. Bloody hell, just breathing hurt!

Until he looked at her.

When he stared at this vision of beauty, he forgot the ache, forgot exhaustion. His blood renewed and he wanted her with the frenzied urgency that seized a stallion when he scented a mare in heat. The urge rising within his flesh was primitive, raw, more than a man could contain. The muscles in his jaw flexed, trying to rein in control.

Who was she? Why was he here?

Images assailed his mind. Of him making love to her throughout the night. Had that been real or merely a wish of his feverish, drug-muddled dreams? He tried to focus on her, but ended up slumping to sit on the cold stone floor. The swirling blackness sucked at him, waited to claim him again.

Had the whole bloody day passed in a blur? Night must have come again.

Earlier, when he awoke the first time, he had staggered to the arrow loop to look out, see if he could figure where he was being held. The high hills that he saw from the narrow opening were unfamiliar.

He was held prisoner, likely in a Scottish strong-hold. But why?

Times were troubled, seeing loyalties shift at the flip of a coin. The English had moved northward, and Longshanks's battle-seasoned troops from Flanders led the sweep through the Lowlands. What was left in their wake had not been a pretty sight. The sacking of Berwick turned the stomach of the most grim-bitten warriors. It sickened his soul that men were capable of such blood-churning atrocities. He saw how it nearly destroyed Challon.

A runner had come to Glenrogha with report of the battle at Dunbar. The English routed the disor-ganized Scots in a single charge, their leaders fleeing along with the common soldiers. Word had it only Sir Patrick Graham stood and valiantly fought to the death. Thousands of Scots were killed on the field of Spottsmuir. The resounding defeat saw the biggest measure of the Scots' nobility dead or in irons.

With the times so unstable, he wondered if some Scottish lord, who managed to escape the slaugh-ter, had now taken him hostage in an effort to barter more generous terms when he came unto Edward's Peace. If that were the case, then his life was not on the line—for now. Feasibly, they kept him drugged to save confrontation until they could ransom him back to Julian or Edward.

Only why did the woman come to him? Was she real or a figment of his clouded mind?

He turned his head to watch her, but the shadows from the firelight danced and played trickery on him. If he reached out and touched her would her skin be warm? Would her hair be soft if he buried his face in it? Or was she a demon assuming Tam-lyn's form? His head lolled back; it was too much to unriddle.

Earlier, when the door had opened, he had

expected it to be the woman again—*wanted it to be her*. His body pulsed, nearly tortured with hunger. When he had opened his eyes it was to see the hag lighting the candle. Even though he was awake and watched her, he lacked the will to stir. His warrior's instincts rebelled, rage boiling up in his throat at being helpless, vulnerable. Nonetheless, he could do naught as she stepped to the bed and looked down upon him.

She placed some twig with dried leaves under the bedding and then touched a drop of oil to his head. "Aye, my bonnie lad. You are the one Evelynour of the Orchard saw in her visions, the warrior wrapped in the color of fog. Your coming is the will of the Auld Ones. You are what my lass needs." Closing her eyes, she hummed a strange tune. The sound floated about him to crowd inwardly until blackness claimed his thoughts again.

He wasn't sure how long he drifted. Until *she* came . . . the woman with flame hair, soft about her shoulders, and smelling of apples and heather. His body shuddered with desire, every muscle recoiling in a craving that was awe-inspiring. He had to grit his teeth to remain still when her smooth hand stroked his thigh, branding him, sending his blood to boil.

Oh, he wanted her. In a thousand ways. He could spend a month, a lifetime, taking her and still it would never be enough. Never enough.

She slid off the bed and knelt before him, lifting his chin. "This shall soothe your pains." Her thumb slowly brushed a swirl of fragrant unguent over his lips.

Being stubborn, he refused to open his mouth, fearing what the salve would do to him. The heady scent filled his nostrils, setting his heart to beating in the low cadence of the bodhran he had heard at the May Day festival.

She ran a hand up his arm. "Your skin is chilled. I will feed the fire to warm the room."

Trying to resist her siren's pull, he pondered: if he was held for ransom, why was she here? Logic scattered, he was unable to resist. His tongue swirled out, tasting the warm lotion. Its power instantly wiping out everything from his mind.

Everything but her.

He wanted more of it. Wanted more of her.

His thoughts moving faster than his actions, before he could reach for her, she rose. A woozy fool, he drank in the sight of her curves, the way the thin baize clung to her rounded hips. His eyes traveled up her waist to the high peaks of her full breasts, holding him spellbound with the way they pushed against the gauzy material, each breath forcing the tips into the fabric, tempting him to madness.

She moved to the fireplace to add a couple of peat bricks, prodding at them with the poker to see they caught faster. Then she turned. And Damian couldn't breathe.

With the firelight at her back, the long hair cascading around her shoulders and down past her hips, it appeared as if she were born from the flames. The image burned into his muzzy brain, one that would forevermore remain sharp, and with his dying breath he would recall the power of this instant in time. The thin chemise was rendered transparent, somehow more arousing than if she stood naked before him. Damian drank in her fey beauty, his muscles girding in desire so blinding, he had to fight for air.

She came to him, her hands taking hold of his upper arms. "Come, the floor is cold."

Pure animalistic male, his muscles unfurled as he rose, pressing his strong body against her softness. He felt her tense, heard the small gasp of surprise. Heat rolled off her flesh. He greedily absorbed the warmth to where he no longer was aware of the chill in the room. Leaning into her, his mouth hovered just above hers, catching her breath.

She arched to him, wanting his kiss, her eyes so expressive, so open as they watched him. They widened in shock as he moved so fast she had no time to react. His hand took the back of her neck, holding her rigid as his mouth took hers, savaging her supple lips. He used his teeth, his tongue, working her mouth until she gave him what he wanted.

He spun with her to the wall by the arrow loop, pinning her next to it. The stones were cool against her back, but he was all fire, devouring her with a fathomless hunger. The sensations whipped through his blood. Painful. Agonizing. Unlike anything he had ever experienced. No woman before had ever provoked such an unleashed hunger to claw within him.

Her hands clutched his shoulders, her sharp nails scoring his skin, but he could not focus enough to tell if she hung on or fought him. He refused to break the kiss. Refused to gentle his demand.

His right hand snaked down her waist, then over the rounded hip, pausing to squeeze its firmness. Gathering the thin material of her chemise slowly up her thigh, he touched the smooth flesh. Damian growled predatorily as the fingers of his left hand sifted through the nether curls. She squeaked in the kiss as his middle finger slipped over her mound, along the wet crease and then into her body. Her legs clamped around his hand as if to prevent his full penetration, but he turned the action against her, using the inside of his wrist to rub against that sensitized button, making her ride it.

He jerked his head back, gasping for air, reveling in the sweet fire of her woman's heat. She clung to him, burying her face against his neck, her gasping breathing matching the pace of his. He backed the finger out, stretching her. She was so tight. Aligning his second finger, he slowly inserted them both, giving her body time to reform to allow his blunt intrusion.

"Please . . ." she moaned.

"Sweet mercy." Damian's body tensed to steel. He shook with a yearning so crippling he could hardly force his muscles to act. Dropping his head to lean it against hers, he enjoyed how her every breath pressed her breasts against the plane of his thorax, how her hips flexed against his wrist in unsure movements. "Please what, my lady?"

Reaching up, her hand took hold of his neck and pulled him down until their lips met. He devoured her mouth with a ravenous hunger, trying to direct this unleashed force within him. He sensed he scared her, but he could not pull up. He kissed her, caught her gasp into his mouth, their moans becoming one. This was raw, primitive, a stallion scenting his mare and ready to mount her. Even through all the pounding drive to mate, there was something more that brushed against his mind, something rare, beyond the cravings of the flesh, leaving the sensations all the more intense, excruciating.

A sense of rightness, of coming home.

His hands took her hips and jerked her high against the wall. Her arms clasped behind his neck, hanging on. "Wrap your legs around my waist," he panted.

As she did as he asked, he drove into her, giving her no chance to adjust to him. Though tight, her channel was slick, welcoming, so he plunged to the hilt. Everything felt so perfect, making him a part of her.

So right. Of coming home. Of belonging.

Aithinne awoke to sunlight filtering through the arrow loop. Alarmed that she had slept too late, she jerked, trying to sit up.

St. Giles slept peacefully against her, holding her closely. He rested on his side, with his strong leg over hers, his right arm an anchor about her waist. When she stirred, he flexed his muscles, pulling her back to his chest.

Indulging, she permitted herself to lie there and imagine this was any morning, pretend they were husband and wife and that every day they would awaken to this sense of peace and security in each other's warmth. She had not meant to stay so long with him, her only excuse—she enjoyed being held through the night in Ravenhawke's embrace.

Memories of her night with St. Giles roared back, enflaming her body. He had taken her, time after time, with a relentless drive that left them both spent. Of course, that was Oona's love philter spurring the endless need. Still, she sensed more compelling him to claim her. What that *more* was she did not want to stop to consider.

It was late. She should not have risked lolling in bed with him this long. Now that she knew him to be Lord Challon's cousin, the cloak of darkness was even more important. He needed dosing with Oona's potion again, to keep the spell reinforced. Yet, as she tried to slide out from under his weight, she was possessed of two minds. He required the tansy to strengthen the spell cast, already she feared he was slightly resistant for some odd reason. Nevertheless, she would have to wake him up for that.

For a safety precaution, she was determined he never see her in sunlight. If she gave him the brew, he would have no clear memory of her—at least Oona assured her that was the case. Once again, nagging doubts in her mind arose. She sensed a strong resistance in this warrior.

As she shifted, he tightened his grip on her, clearly intending on not letting her go. "Hmm . . . need to . . . use the chamber pot."

He smiled in his exhaustion, then his hand cupped her breast, the thumb lazily brushing the tip of her tender nipple. Instantly, her body responded to his command, but just as she was getting concerned he might awake fully, he relaxed and she was able to slip away from his hold.

Picking up the gown from the floor, she shimmied it over her head, then reached for her mantle, intending to leave. She glanced back. Like him, she had only seen St. Giles in moonlight. The temptation was too much.

She moved to the bed, chancing so much just to gaze upon this handsome warrior. She flinched as she saw scars upon his perfect body, then recalled the first time he had taken her, he spoke of the vision, of seeing her face—Tamlyn's face—coming to him and telling him he could not give up after being gravely wounded in battle. Foolishly, she traced the scar running along the right hip, fought tears welling up within her throat at the pain he must have suffered, how close he had come to dying.

Choking back a sob, she turned and left the room.

She hurried down the hall. The sun was up and the people of Lyonglen were already stirring, going about their morning chores. She hadn't meant to tarry so long, preferring her comings and goings to the tower room were done under as few eyes as possible.

When she heard steps on the staircase, she pulled up and tugged her woolen mantle around her. Her cheeks burned red as she knew whispers about what was going on in the tower room were surely on everyone's lips.

The servants at Lyonglen were scared of this war with the English. They not only knew of her deceptions, they encouraged them, fearful if her plans did not succeed they could well end up with an English overlord. Even so, she hesitated showing herself in her rumpled condition, coming straight from him, his scent still on her skin.

The hurried steps continued upward.

Deward saw her at the top of the staircase, his eyes quickly running over her. The imp smiled. "Sister, hurry, you must come, there is a rider under the standard of the Black Dragon, he asks for you—"

"Lord Challon is here?" Her hand went to heart as fear spread through her. "Mercy, does he ken . . . about . . ."

"Nay, 'tis not the Dragon, just a messenger from him. He asks for you, hurry, he has been waiting since dawnbreak, we dare not tarry longer." He continued on in his non-stop fashion as he took hold of her upper arm to speed her down the steps.

She tugged against his hold. "Deward, you lackwit. I cannot go below stairs dressed in this manner."

"Beg pardon, Aithinne, I was not thinking, you do look like a well-loved lass, our stranger pleases you, does he not, you and he will make a beautiful bairn together."

"Hush your prattle. Run, call Aggie. Scurry."

Leaving her brother to fetch her maidservant, she hastened into her room and pulled a dark blue woolen kirtle from the wardrobe. By the time she finished a fast wash, Aggie came in tsk-tsking the whole way. "Och, lass. Is it true? The Black Dragon is at the portcullis?"

"Nay, just his messenger. Quickly lace me up, then see the servants are kept away from the Great Hall. I would not want someone to make a misstep."

"Lass, they support you—"

"I ken, but I fash about someone accidentally revealing too much without meaning to. So hustle."

"Let me plait your hair."

"No time. This will have to do." Pulling out a ribbon of blue, she tugged the long mass of her hair around and secured it. She wrapped a sash of tartan across her shoulder and tucked in the braided leather at her waist. "I only hope I shall appear a lady, not a serving wench."

Her brothers and Einar awaited her in the Great Hall, all four sets of eyes going to hers, waiting her lead. Deward nodded at her appearance as she took a seat at the head of the trestle table. Taking a deep breath to compose herself, she tried to think upon her cousin Raven, Lady of Kinloch. She was always so collected in her demeanor, able to look a man in the eye and not flinch. Aye, this day Aithinne would pretend to be her beautiful, dark-haired kinswoman.

"Einar—"

He thumped his chest. "I live to serve you, Princess."

She closed her eyes for an instant to reign in frustration. Cousin Raven did not get frustrated. But then, Raven did not have a mountain of a man calling her Princess all the time. She sighed, sidestepping their usual *do not call me princess* argument. "Stand to my left and slightly behind me, at attention. Sword in your hand, tip resting on the floor. Appear relaxed, yet on guard."

"Aye, Princess, it shall be as you wish—"

"Deward, please sit to my right, and keep your mouth shut. Lewis to my left. Hugh, lean casually against the fireplace. All of you, let me do the speaking to this man." She nodded to the servant to open the huge doors of the Great Hall.

A warrior in mail and plate came forward with a guard of two. The handsome man's eyes went to Einar, instantly targeting the biggest threat in the unfamiliar situation, then her brothers, and finally came to rest on Aithinne sitting in the lord's chair, feigning the air of a princess.

He offered a slight bow. "My lady, my name is Gervase, knight for the great Black Dragon, Lord Julian Challon. He sends his greetings."

"The Dragon's name is kenned to us. I should assume few have not heard of his valor in the service of the English king. May I have food and drink fetched for you and your men? Have a room readied for you?"

Lewis kicked her under the table, his eyes flashing a warning not to invite the soldier to tarry at Lyonglen. She booted back. Then Deward kicked Lewis as well. She forced a winning smile and then kicked them both.

"Thanks, kind lady, victuals would be appreciated. The ride from Glenrogha was long. However, we dare not linger. My Lord Challon eagerly awaits word of his cousin."

Hugh sipped from a tankard of ale, choked on it.

Aithinne wished she could lash out at him as well. Hopefully feigning innocence, she inquired, "Lord Challon's cousin?"

"Aye, he went amissing on May Day and has not been seen since. With these troubled times, his absence grows worrisome to my lord. At first, we figured he was off with a wench, enjoying himself. He is known for having a way with the ladies."

Aithinne's spine stiffened as an angry blush flooded her cheeks. She forced her hands to remain relaxed instead of gripping the chair in reaction to the lance of pain that stabbed her heart. She had never been jealous before. It was not a sensation she liked.

"Interesting, but I fail to see how this has import to us here at Lyonglen."

"We searched throughout Glen Shane, then my lord ordered our paths widened and the quest moved into Glen Eallach. None have seen Lord Ravenhawke. Lord Challon frets that mayhap stragglers from Clan Comyn lingering in the hills since Berwick set upon him and have taken him for ransoming. The Dragon sets great store in his cousin, thinks of him as a brother."

Guilt ate at Aithinne. Another aspect not considered in her scheming, that someone could worry about St. Giles' absence, fear he might have come to harm. Moistening her dry lips, she opened her mouth—to what?— tell the man she held St. Giles upstairs, chained in her bed?

Fortunately, Hugh stepped to the table under guise of setting down his empty tankard. He softly placed a hand on her right shoulder and gave a gentle squeeze.

"It does the Dragon well to place such high value on his kinsman, but we cannot aid you in this mission. We have seen no dragons of any sort about the keep," Hugh said with a slight air of boredom.

Aithinne was impressed. She did not think any of the three could muster such a degree of sophistication. Maybe the lads were finally coming of age.

The knight Gervase's gaze skimmed over her in assessment, question in his eyes. "Are you certain? He is a handsome man, black hair, pale eyes—"

Einar shifted one-step closer to her—only a slight

move—yet it drew Gervase's attention. The man recognized that the tall Viking perceived the continued questioning of Aithinne as an insult.

Gervase inclined his head toward her. "Beg pardon, my lady, my words were ill-considered."

Her will taxed, she remained unmoving under his piercing scrutiny. Too used to having no shield against Oona kenning her every thought, a blush spread up her body. She felt as if Challon's warrior could see telltale evidence of her having been with Ravenhawke. Turning away, she was unable to hold eye contact with this man.

"Einar, see that these men and their horses are fed before they must set off on the trail to Glenrogha." She rose, stepping away from the table. "Now, Sir Gervase, I must take my leave. There are many chores. Lyonglen does not run by itself."

Aithinne tried to slam the door to her room, but the three idiots were on her heels. Lewis, in the lead, had the door hit his nose. He pulled up short to rub it, and Deward and Hugh crashed into his backside, which started their typical shoving matches. Too upset by knowing Lord Challon was seeking high and low for his cousin, and when he didn't find him would be back—mayhap this time himself—she had no patience for the lads' childish antics.

She picked up the unlit candle and threw it at them. Lewis ducked but it hit the side of the door and broke into chunks. The other two put up their arms and tried to deflect the pieces.

"Hold your temper, sister mine. We have done naught—" Lewis started, but dodged as she grabbed the empty chamber pot.

They scurried in three different directions to

make her choosing a target harder. "Of all the brainless . . . halfwit—*third-wit* . . . ah . . . ooh—"

"Lackwit is the word you usually hurl at us, Sister." Deward peeked up from behind a chair. "Nodcock in extreme circumstances.

"Nodcock!" Aithinne stood vibrating with rage, much too practical to waste a perfectly good chamber pot on one of their hard heads. "Life is not cruel enough. I send you out on a simple errand to collect a man no one will miss and what did you come back with? The Dragon of Challon's cousin! Of all the stupid, mooncalf—"

Hugh poked his head around the door's edge where he'd hidden. "Now, Aithinne, save your temper. All will turn out fine. You will see. The man will go back and tell Lord Challon his cousin is not here."

Aithinne looked around for something, anything to bean him with. Finding naught, she tossed her hands up in exasperation. "Of course he will. Then Challon will become even more concerned and will lead his troops on a more thorough search. What happens when he comes back, you dunderhead?"

Deward shrugged. "I suppose he comes and we tell him the man is not within the curtain. Aithinne, it is not like he has eyes that see through stone, so how can he know his cousin is in the tower, and why would he think we have reason to hold his kinsman, he will just go away."

"Deward, hush your never ending prattle! Most people take breaths when they talk." She closed her eyes, rubbing her temples, pain pounding to the point where she wanted to cry. "Och, we are doomed. I have trouble enough between Phelan and Dinsmore driving me to distraction, now you bring down the fire of the great Black Dragon."

"Sister"—Lewis came and put his arm around her shoulder, urging her toward the high bed—"you

are just tired. You need rest. Hugh shall fetch Oona
and she will give you a tansy to speed you to rest.
Einar will keep guard and we can decide what is
best to do this evening."

"He goes back. Tonight. No more arguments,"
she insisted, knowing it was the only option left.

Maybe if they could get him back to Glenrogha
by dawn, no fire-breathing Dragon would descend
upon Lyonglen and make a charred meal out of
her.

Chapter Six

A shrill cry—like a woman screaming—echoed through his fuzzy brain, rousing him from his dreamless sleep. The noise came twice more. Then nothing. Drowsing, Damian wondered if it were merely part of a dream.

He might have drifted back to the black void of slumber, but the coolness of the bed caused him to stir. With a smile, he reached to pull her warm body close, wanting just to hold her, to bury his face in her soft hair. Stretching, he struggled to open his eyes, for once not feeling so drugged. She was not there. As his mind cleared, he ran his hand over the spot where she had lain. The feather mattress still bore the impression of her body, but it lacked any of her remaining heat.

"So, my Lady Midnight is real and not a figment of my dreams." Damian was not in the habit of talking to himself, but it gave him a sense of reality missing since Beltane. "At times, I feared mayhap I had been wounded in battle and could not recall, and now fought for my life as I had when the Welshman's sword found the split in my mail."

His dreams of her back in that dark time had been strong. She had come and soothed his brow, whispering tender words. Her ghostly presence had kept him hanging onto life when his mind was scorched by fever, or chills had racked his body.

Sitting up, he once again took tally of the details of his peculiar situation. The chamber was in a tower, judging by what little he could view through the arrow loop. He was sore. Very sore. That brought a smile to his lips as he considered how he got in that condition. But there was no wound from a fight.

"Things are looking up. I am not injured, nor have a mind-fever. So someone feeds me a potion to see I stay in this muddled condition. The question is who and why?" He held his fingers to his nose, scenting her. "But she is real. Oh, she is real. Tamlyn?"

His mind worried around the edges of that burning question. He tried to concentrate on the woman's face, but admitted the herbs he ingested saw everything slightly out of focus. Also, he had yet to observe her in more than moonlight and shadow. While his heart cried out for it to be Tamlyn, logic bespoke such actions were not within the Lady of Glenrogha's character. Pain lanced through him as he acknowledged she might conceivably keep Julian a sex slave in a tower, but upon his look-alike cousin she did naught more than smile in a sisterly fashion. As badly as he wanted it to have been Tamlyn these past nights, his warrior's sense said it went against the grain of truth. Tamlyn MacShane was a lady of honor. Though Damian would like to deny it, she was falling deeply in love with Julian. She would never do anything to dishonor that love or hurt Challon.

So who was this woman who came to him at night? Was she some Highland Lamia his mother warned him about, seeking to suck his soul dry? Did she pluck images of Tamlyn from his mind and refashion her visage to trick him? Trick him into what? What purpose did she hope to achieve by keeping him prisoner? By laying with him?

At her mere scent his body bucked, saying he craved her yet again. How many times had he taken her during the night? Endlessly, it seemed. The corner of his mouth quirked up at his newfound stamina. "Mayhap, I shall inquire what is in the strange love philter—once I half strangle you for chaining me in your bed. Then, my Lady Midnight, I shall turn the tables and shackle you in mine."

He experienced mixed emotions as he grew more certain that she was not Tamlyn. He wanted this woman with a fever that gripped his body. Even as the potion wore off, he still hungered after this mysterious lady of the night. Nonetheless, his heart felt a grieved disappointment.

"Tamlyn was never mine." The muscles in his throat swallowed back tears as he admitted the cold truth.

Damian pulled the plaide to his face, inhaling her intoxicating scent. Willing her to return to him. To have her again he would gladly give his soul, and anything else she might ask.

The next time he opened his eyes, sunlight streamed through the arrow loop, showing it must be late in the day. His stomach grumbled, reinforcing that assumption. He was hungry and thirsty—and in a very foul mood. They were drugging the water or the victuals, mayhap both. He had to eat, and most especially required water. However, with his head near splitting, his temper out-paced reason, leading him to vow not to break his fast.

"Short of sitting on me and pouring it down my throat, I shall touch naught of what they fetch me," he grumbled to the empty room. Struggling to his feet, he wrapped the plaide around his hips and started toward a screen that concealed the chamber pot. Forgetting the stupid chain shackling his ankle, he tripped. "That bloody rips it."

He snatched up the links and yanked, accomplishing nothing. Frowning, he pulled again, this time with all his warrior's muscle. With the strength of his rising fury, he put his full weight against it, jerking over and over. It cracked and pinged, but the chain and bed held.

The rattle of a key sounded in the lock, interrupting his display of bad humor.

Her image rose in his mind. A deep throb pulsed through his blood and instantly his shaft flexed and thickened. "Down, my fair fellow. My Lady Midnight has never come to me in the daylight before. You likely rear your head when 'tis only that strange crone, come to ply witch's wares and potions and cackle at you." His arousal slowed. "Aye, thought you would feel thusly."

The door finally scraped open and a huge man halted, half through the doorway, as Damian raised the chamber pot. Clearly of Viking blood, the man grinned and then rumbled in a deep voice, "'Tis empty. I changed it out whilst you slumbered."

Furious, Damian flung it anyway. Damian gave the big man his due, he moved fast. Quick as a wink, the massive frame was behind the door, using it as a shield as the metal pail crashed against it.

Still smiling, he poked his head back in. "My princess will not like you denting a good chamber pot." The huge man moved past him to set a plate of meat, cheese, and bread, and a pitcher on the small table by bedside.

"Princess?" Damian questioned, since the man sounded as though he truly meant the title. Surely, he had not been carried off to some north country to a Viking stronghold. Vague images of the three lads with a Scots burr arose within his memory. Consequently, he discounted the likelihood.

The man nodded. "My princess."

Thirsty, Damian glared at the clay jug. "More mead?"

"Just water."

Too dizzy to stand, Damian leaned against the bedside. "Where are my clothes?"

"You have no need of them. Eat. Food you do need."

"Where am I?"

"In the tower of my princess."

"Why?"

The man blushed and grinned, but said naught.

"What is your name?" Damian grew quickly aggravated with the half-truths he dragged out of the affable giant.

"Englishman, eat."

Damian crossed his arms over his chest. "So you can foul my body with more of the witch's potion?"

The long white-blond hair shook as the man looked him up and down. "I adjudge you none the worse for the wear, eh? Most men would kill to be in her bed."

"*Her?*" Damian arched a brow. That simple gesture sent pages scurrying in terror to please him. Evidently it failed to hold the same power over behemoths.

"My princess."

Damian rolled his eyes, back to the princess nonsense again. "Why am I being held by your *princess?*"

"You ask too many questions, my lord."

"And you answer too few. You do not like questions? How about a command instead? Tell me the name of your *princess.*"

"Eat. Rest. You need your strength." He offered another of his smiles.

The man was too trusting. As he turned to go, Damian jerked up the chain, causing the giant to trip. Damian flew at him, landing on his back and wrapping an arm around his neck. Most men would have a hard time rising from that position. Exerting little effort, he pushed up with Damian nearly riding his back like a horse. With his trough of a hand, the Viking reached behind him and grabbed a fistful of Damian's thick hair, then with a small heft, flung him forward over him. Suddenly, Damian found himself flying through the air, heels over head, then crashing hard to the stone floor.

Aithinne leaned her head back and closed her eyes, relaxing in the hot water. With all the pressing duties of running Coinnleir Wood and Lyonglen, she rarely had time enough to loll as this. At the end of a long day, she was too exhausted to wait for water to be boiled, then hauled to her room for her to have a full bath. Oona insisted a soak in the herbs would ease the woman's pain of being with Lord Ravenhawke. She had to admit it was helping.

Damian. She had never spoken his given name, fearful of the dangerous power it would have over her heart. The final thread to forevermore bind her to him.

This night she would send him away, back to Glenrogha. *Back to Tamlyn.* A burning knot formed in her heart. With every fiber of her being, she wanted to follow Einar's advice—*keep him.* Despite, she could not risk his powerful cousin coming to Lyonglen, hunting for him. She needed to live quietly, not draw King Edward's attention until she was heavy with child. By then she would be in a better

position to face what needed doing. Having the
Black Dragon battering down the curtain walls in
quest of St. Giles was a terrifying prospect, a risk she
could not dare.

Thinking of the child she sought to conceive
through this harebrained plan, she slicked her wet
hand over her belly. His child would grow there. She
would carry the bairn for the passing of nine moons,
breed with his seed inside her. An ache rose in her
to hold the wee babe, so strong it was painful. The
sensation awed her, humbled her. Never had she anticipated feeling these things, to want the child so
badly that tears filled her eyes.

"A heartbreak in the making. The wee bairn will
be a constant reminder to me of the father."
Aithinne shut her eyes tightly, unable to bear the
thought she would see Damian taken to Glenrogha
as soon as it grew dark. Despair pressed in on her
mind, knowing she would never see him again.

"Aithinne!"

The scream jolted her. She snatched up the sheet
of woolen baize, pulling it across the tub for modesty as the door flung open and Deward ran in. She
quickly dashed the tears from her eyes with the
back of her hand.

"Sister, you must come . . . Einar has your warrior
down and is sitting on him, and he bit our Einar,
then Hugh tried to help and I think he bit Hugh as
well—or maybe that was Einar trying to bite Ravenhawke and missed and gnawed on Hugh, then
Lewis tried to hit your Ravenhawke with the chamber pot—fortunately, it was empty—"

"Chamber pot? Einar biting St. Giles! By our
Lady Annis!" Aithinne jumped out of the tub, clinging to the material, her mind awhirl with Deward's
nonstop explanation.

"Nay, Sister. Did you not listen? Ravenhawke bit

him and then maybe Hugh—but that might have been Einar biting Hugh, but he meant to bite St. Giles back and—"

"Och, hush!' Her brain felt about to burst from listening to him. "They hit Ravenhawke with the chamber pot? Och, have maggots gotten into their skulls? If anything happens to St. Giles, the Earl Challon will bring this fortress down around our ears."

Snatching her kirtle off the high bed, she made a face at her brother. He stood rocking foot-to-foot in impatience, waiting for her. It took several breaths before he understood what the glare meant.

Eyes flying wide, he said, "Oh!" then spun around so she could slip the gown over her head. As she dressed, he asked in a worried voice, "Sister, you do not think they killed your Ravenhawke, do you?"

She paused. "Killed? You failed to mention anyone getting killed. Surely not! Deward, do not beg trouble. Einar would never permit anyone to get killed . . . I hope."

Hurrying down the hall and up the winding stairs to the tower room, she tied the sides of her kirtle as she trailed after Deward. This was her fault. She had failed to dose him with Oona's potion before she left him this morn. Now he might be injured in the scuffle with her childish brothers and Einar.

Her hand pushing open the door, she pulled up as she eyed the scene before her. She sucked in a shocked breath. St. Giles was on the floor, a plaide about his hips. Hugh sat upon the man's right arm, while Lewis, whose hair stood strangely on end, roosted on the other. Glowering stubbornly, Einar used his knee on St. Giles's thighs, pinning the warrior to the stone floor. The knight was wake, though he remained still, likely viewing resistance a wasted effort at this point. She gasped when she spotted the idiots had stuffed a rag in his mouth.

"Of all the muttonhead . . . dimwitted . . . chicken brain . . . sheep-dip . . ." Aithinne was at a loss for words to express how incensed she was by their rash actions.

Lewis and Hugh scrunched up their faces and looked to each other, echoing the question, "Sheep-dip?" Hugh rolled his eyes. "Sister is in a bother again."

"Get off him, you . . . you . . . worms!" Putting her fists on her hips, she used the do-or-die voice.

They did not move. Not even Einar. Her spine straightened in shock. They never failed to scurry to obey her when she used that tone—or at least get out of her arms' length.

"Sister, if we get off the man," Lewis sighed with an exasperated frown, saying he thought surely she should see his logic without being told, "he will bite me again."

Aithinne glared at him. He hunched his shoulders, trying to make himself smaller, less of a target for her ire. Eliciting the desired response from Lewis restored her sense of control. "Get off him or *I* shall bite you!" When they sat unmoving, she frowned and then knelt down to tug the rag from Ravenhawke's mouth.

The eyes were clear, sharp—and focused on her in blazing fury. Oh, what had her carelessness wrought? She knew this was the first time he had seen her in the daylight, the first time his mind was unmuddled by Oona's spells and concoctions. A blush rose to her cheeks and she realized her hair was a mess and she looked a fright. Thankfully, the only light came from the arrow loop and threw deep shadows into the room. Keeping the sun at her back and allowing her long hair to fall about her shoulders as a veil, she pulled the rag from his mouth.

"You!" he growled.

She jerked back at the force of the hurled word. "Me? Uh . . . huh . . ."

"Aye, you . . . you redheaded Lamia . . . I am going to snatch you bald." The way the muscles around his mouth tightened assured her he meant his threat. "I am going to truss you up like a pheasant, then I am going to turn you over my knee and bea—"

Aithinne shoved the strip of cloth back in his mouth. "Sorry . . . even tempers are needed just now—and since there is a dearth of those around this fortress—you please hold those . . . ah . . . mmm . . . suggestions for the present, my lord."

St. Giles's eyes narrowed on her, silently promising what the cloth stopped him from speaking. She sucked her lower lip into her mouth and then glanced around. Four shining faces waited for her to tell them what to do. She sighed relief as Oona scurried in, carrying her herb box and a pitcher.

"Oona, they hit him on the head—" Aithinne fussed.

"Aye, I heard. Whole bloody castle heard." The old woman leaned over, putting the palm of her hand to his heart. "Strong and steady, my pretty. A fine stallion of a man you are. Did you coldcock him, lads?"

Lewis shook his head. "Only stunned him. He is a scary fighter. It took all of us to get him down."

Hugh's shoulders vibrated with a suppressed chuckle. "The man must have a skull of iron. I think it did more harm to the chamber pot than his head, Sister."

Oona ran her hand over his scalp and nodded.

"Nary a lump. Eyes are clear, focused. Madder than an old wet hen are you, my fine braw warrior?"

Oona's smirk caused the muscles in the knight's square jaw to flex. His gray-green eyes bore into Aithinne's, making her swallow hard. She hated he was being handled in a fashion that would insult and infuriate his warrior's spirit, all because of her negligence. And what she had to do now would not make him any happier. Only, she had no choice. Too much was riding on this turn of events.

She looked to Oona. "You have the forgetting potion ready?"

The elder woman's head snapped up. "Forgetting? I thought you wanted—"

"You thought wrong. The forgetting potion— please. The madness ends this night." She tossed her hands up in despair as she looked down at him, fighting the tears that threatened to flood her eyes. "'Twas never my wish . . . I sorrow . . . I never intended . . . och, by the Auld Ones." She took hold of the cloth to tug it out, hoping he would not fight them on drinking the tansy.

"You redheaded witch . . . I shall make you pay if it's the last thing—"

Aithinne shoved the rag back into his mouth again. "Very well, we must try this another way. Um . . . we could . . . hum—"

"I can hit him on the head again, Sister," Lewis offered, a little too eagerly.

She glared at her brother. "Cosh him once more and I will take the chamber pot to you and it won't be empty. They will call you Dunny Lewis. Let us apply logic. You have him pinned, if Deward holds his head still—"

Deward backed up a step, refusal clear upon his face. "Deward is not holding bloody anything on him, he bites, he bit Einar and Lewis—though mayhap that was Einar trying to bite him and getting Lewis instead—"

Aithinne rolled her eyes in exasperation, not wanting to waste time with another of Deward's rambling explanations. "Och, shut your gub and do as I tell you. Hold his head still while Oona and I pour the potion down his throat."

"But, Sister, he bites—"

His complaint was cut off as Lewis leaned toward him and delivered a punch, admonishment for being a coward. And as her brother's weight shifted to reach their sibling, St. Giles's powerful arm pushed Lewis off. The lad tumbled forward to crash into the stone wall. Hugh sniggered while Deward scurried behind the door, using it as a screen.

Deward called, "Quick, clot him one with the chamber pot, Sister."

Lewis tried to stand, only his knees failed to hold his weight and buckled. Being knavish, Hugh laughed at his brother's misfortune, neither paying heed as St. Giles jerked the cloth out of his mouth and flung it against Aithinne's chest. Faster than she could blink, he reached up and grabbed a hand full of her hair at the base of her neck and yanked her forward.

Nose-to-nose with the angry man, Aithinne fought against getting lost in the pure male scent coming off his skin, so intoxicating it clouded her mind to where she could not gather her thoughts. "Get them off me, *Princess*, or rue the day. Then you and I shall have a nice long talk—in the light where I can see you."

"Let go of my princess," Einar rumbled his offense, grabbing hold of St. Giles.

Not thinking, he yanked back on the man's arm, which caused the hand holding her hair to tug back on her head. Tender-headed, she tried to pry his fingers from her locks. With Einar's weight off his thighs, Damian brought a knee up, slamming it against Hugh. Then Lewis jumped into the mess and it was hard for Aithinne to extricate herself from the four struggling men.

Deward had hold of the empty pot, hovering over them for the opening to thump St. Giles. He finally swung and hit Einar instead. "Och, sorry, Einar, I did not mean to cosh you, but St. Giles moved and—" He swung again, catching Lewis, knocking the poor lad tappy.

In pain, Lewis tried to grab his head, but one arm was tangled with Hugh and the other with Ravenhawke. Aithinne barely ducked all the flailing fists, flying from every direction.

"I am going to be bald!" Aithinne wailed, crushed by the mass of bodies. Sucking in air, she used *the voice.* "Enough!" This time they paid attention, though St. Giles's fingers still had the locks of her hair in his fist.

"Get his arms, you bloody idiots." Oona took control of untangling everyone. "Einar, pin his legs."

"Take care, he has my hair—owww—" Aithinne cried out.

Oona laughed. "Why is naught ever easy around you, Ai—"

"Oona! Hold your tongue, old woman!" Aithinne worried should the crone speak her name before Ravenhawke. Names had such magic, the power to conjure one, that she feared him hearing it. Why she never used his. If she spoke it aloud before letting him go, it would set a spell to conjure him back to her when she whispered it on the wind on a night of a full moon.

Either ignoring her, or hearing too late, Oona finished, "—thinne Ogilvie. Matters not. Once we

get the potion down his gullet, between that and
my spells, his mind shall hold no memory of you or
this place."

Aithinne flinched from the invisible blow those
words brought to her heart.

"Touch me, witch, and I shall stake you through
your heart," Ravenhawke threatened.

"Ah, if only I were two score younger, my pretty
warrior, I would love for you to try." She ran her
hand over his muscular abdomen, then winked as
he glared daggers at her. "Let go of her hair, lad.
The poor wee lassie gets sore-headed."

"If I release her, I lose my leverage. I have been
fed foul potions, stripped naked, chained, tossed in
her bed, and—" His gaze returned to Aithinne, setting her heart to pound as she read his thoughts,
saw the images of them together. How could he
recall these things?

Distracted by his warrior's perfection, Aithinne's
breath stopped. His locks of black, kissed with the
dark fire of the Celts, were not in the Norman style.
Long and curling softly about his ears, they brushed
the back of his neck. The knight was handsome—
nay, beautiful—everything for which a woman
could wish. Eyes the shade of the green hillocks on
a foggy morn were ringed with lashes so thick and
long a woman would cry envy.

As she met and held his stare, the world narrowed. The others in the room may as well have not
been present. There was only this beautiful knight
that she wanted more than her next breath. The
knight who would never be hers. A man that loved
her cousin, not her.

She ran her thumb along his jaw. So strong. So
stubborn. The small mouth, etched with sensual
curves, was seductive, though touched with a trace
of what might be arrogance. A black curl carelessly

fell over the high forehead, prompting her to reach
out and brush it back.

Aithinne nearly blanched at the willful, razor-
sharp intelligence flashing within his angry eyes.
Damian St. Giles was the *last* man she would want
to face as an adversary, but it was too late for that.
Much too late. They were lovers for only this short
span; he would hopefully give her the child she
wanted more than her own life. Only, they could
never be friends. Never share a life. Never was such
a cold word.

Images of this knight possessed her, singed her
with an ancient fire . . . of her hands on the bare
flesh of his chest, of how it felt to be kissed by this
dark warrior, of his flesh being buried so deep
inside her body that he touched her heart, bonding
her to him, making her his. Visions that would
haunt her the rest of her days. She stared into the
soul-stealing eyes and trembled with fear of what
her foolish plans had wrought upon this proud
man. Shame filled her, yet she could not take her
gaze from him.

"Fetch Oona's pot," she nodded toward it, speaking to Deward, yet unable to look away from St.
Giles's piercing stare.

Doing as instructed, Deward edged forward and
gingerly passed the pot to Oona. "Watch him, he
bites, he bit Einar, and then bit—"

"Brother, do hush before I lose my temper."
Aithinne glared.

Oona held out the pot. "Give him a taste, lass."

"More witchery, *Princess*?" His expression said he
dared her to try to use the balm on him.

Cautiously, Aithinne dipped her finger into the
pot and then swirled it over his lips. Stubborn man
set his jaw, clear by the flattened lips that he wasn't
going to taste the unguent. It was imperative they

get the potion into him, or his powerful cousin would likely gag, truss her up, and deliver her to Edward Longshanks as a Midsummer's Eve sacrifice. Her hand quivered as she stared into Damian's beautiful countenance, the features made harsh by his fury and the deep shadows in the room.

Offering him a sad smile, she stroked the curve of his cheek with her trembling thumb, feeling love—regret that love could never be—rising within her. "Forgive me, Damian."

She spoke his given name aloud for the first time. Instead of straining against the hold he had on her hair, she leaned forward and brushed her lips against his. The set of his mouth was not welcoming. Even so, she did not let that deter her. Dragging her tongue against his lower lip, she tasted Oona's Beltane unguent, the sweet with a hint of apple. Its power sped through her and warmed her blood, the magic hitting her heart, opening it to where she had no shield against this warrior.

A wall of emotions slammed into her. The ache of yearning to belong to this man burned through her heart, needing, aching for him to love her and not her more beautiful cousin. Craving that his seed would take root in her body so she could keep that small part of him, a child she could hold and cherish. *His* child.

She trembled, nearly overpowered by her want for him, ashamed that her schemes had used him in this manner. Most painful of all was the regret that they had not met at another place and time, maybe a period before he had fallen in love with Tamlyn. If she thought there was a chance to burn Tamlyn from his mind, she might risk bringing down the wrath of his terrifying cousin, even defy an English king for him. This man was special. There would never be another to compare.

The magic hit him, and instead of resisting, he kissed her back, kissing her with all the fervor the potion sped through him. A small part of her clung desperately to the thought there was something of her in the spell, too, that he did not believe he kissed her look-alike cousin, but her. Only her. For this tiny shard in time, she wanted to taste him, savor the passion burning between them. Believe for that heartbeat he was hers.

Lewis to her left chuckled, then Hugh on her right leaned over her back to deliver a tap to his brother. Fearing another scuffle might break out, she motioned with her right hand for Oona to be ready, then snapped her fingers at Deward and pointed at St. Giles's head.

Putting her left hand to his jaw she broke the kiss, pausing to stroke the days' growth of beard. Unlike most men, he had kept his face scraped of hair, in the Norman way. She liked that he did. Enjoyed looking at the strong line of his face that was too beautiful to be called handsome.

Her mind whispered *remember me* though she knew Oona's spell and the tansy would rob his mind of the memories of this week, of her. She smiled sadly. "Sometimes, my lord, life unfolds in a manner just too unfair."

Damian opened his mouth to reply, but she would never hear the words. She nodded to Deward. Obeying, he snatched handfuls of the black hair on either side of St. Giles' head. The same instant, the others bore down on his limbs with all their weight to keep him pinned.

"Grab hold of his nose, lass," Oona ordered, "then he has no choice but to swallow."

Before he could protest, Aithinne pinched his nostrils together to force him to breathe through his mouth. As he finally gasped for air, Oona quickly poured the liquid through his lips, then Aithinne clamped her hand over his mouth to prevent him from spitting it out.

The fey eyes flashed daggers of hatred, silently speaking the command to let him up, promising retribution when Aithinne refused to obey. Her breath held as she waited until the muscles of the strong throat worked, carrying the potion that would burn her from his mind. Tears welled as she watched those haunting green eyes, saw the fight go out of him as the herbs hit his stomach and instantly started to do their work.

Her hand shook as she released her pinch on his nose. She expected the fury to surface with a stream of threats to follow. Instead he just watched her, and she soon knew the reason. In the struggle, she had failed to keep her back to the light coming in through the arrow loop. He now saw her full-faced and in the beam of filtered light.

He tried to raise his arm, but Lewis was still restraining him. She nodded to her brother to release Ravenhawke, even though she feared he might try to snatch her bald again. His hand, callused by years of wielding a sword, lifted to the side of her face. Unable to stop herself, she leaned into the palm relishing this final touch.

His thumb reached out and brushed the tear that trickled down her cheek. "You cry, Faery Queen? Do tears of the Fae taste different? If I sample one, will the price be my mortal soul?"

Aithinne's eyes batted rapidly. Shocked, her mind screamed that he had uttered those same words before. He should *not* recall them. The potion and Oona's spell should rob him of all memories. Once again, she questioned if he were of Selkie blood, if that could make him more resistant to the elixir. It was imperative that he com-

pletely forget this time here with her. A shiver of
dread rippled up her spine. However, his whispered
words blotted out the apprehension.

"I shall pay it—gladly. I love you. Always have.
Always will."

Her sharp teeth nibbled on her lower lip to keep
the sob from escaping.

Deward let go of Damian's locks. "Sister . . . did
you not hear? A man speaks only the deepest truths
after partaking of the mandrake."

Aithinne watched as Damian's thick lashes fluttered, the potion starting to course through him,
felt the muscle of the arm relax. As his hand started
to fall away from her face, she caught the back of
his hand in her palm and pressed it, once more,
against her cheek while she sat silently weeping.

Barely aware of the others rising, she watched
him slowly slip into sleep, slowly slip away from her,
out of her life.

Einar crossed his arms and puffed up his chest in
stubbornness. "Keep the man, Princess. He is yours,
bonded to you through the grand rite of Beltane. If
Odin wills it, you shall carry his babe. A babe needs
its sire. This man loves you. You heard his words."

The tears only came faster, as she shook her
head. "Nay, he believes me to be Tamlyn. He loves
her. He only thought me to be my cousin."

Unable to stand the pain, she jumped to her feet,
looking to Oona. She stood crying, too. With a
soul-racking moan, she fled the room.

At the edge of the woods before Glenrogha,
Aithinne halted her palfrey and waited for Hugh to
help her down. She barely noticed his actions; her
eyes remained fixed on Einar. The big man lifted
Lord Ravenhawke from the back of his heavy horse

as though Damian weighed naught more than a wee child. Since time was of the essence, they had needed to move swiftly through the night to reach Glenrogha before dawnbreak. Carrying Raven-hawke in a cart was out of the question. Fortunately, Einar was strong enough to hold Damian before him. The gentle giant handled the other man with ease, holding Damian half across his shoulder.

"Where do you want him, Princess?"

Aithinne pulled out the plaide she held under her mantle and unfolded the woolen fabric. She pointed to a spot at the edge of Glenrogha's dead angle, where everything had been cleared so the enemy had nothing to hide behind. "There will do."

She wanted Damian found quickly, yet she had to ensure no one within Glenrogha spotted them. Her golden hair with the flame cast was distinctive; even from a distance she would be recognized. That was a chance she could not take. Her trembling hands pulled up the deep hood of her mantle hiding her locks.

Aithinne's stomach churned with cold trepidation. Her brothers were supposed to ride hard, far away from Glen Eallach and Glen Shane, to seek out a man who was a stranger. Instead, they fetched the cousin of one of the most powerful men in the land, Julian Challon. She could only hope he was merely paying a visit and would move on to claim his grandfather's holding, as Hugh assured her he intended to do.

She spread the plaide beside a small shrub and waited as Einar placed St. Giles down upon it. Kneeling, she carefully pulled half of the tartan over the sleeping man, as a droplet fell on his forehead. At first, she assumed it was her tear, but then another hit her hand, and she saw the morning sky had started to mist.

Lovingly, she ran her thumb over one raven's wing brow, then the other, burning the image of his sleeping face into her mind. The image she would carry away. Leaning over him, she brushed her lips over his cool ones. "*A cushla mo cridhe*—pulse of my heart."

There were so many things she wanted to say to him, how sorry she was he had been caught in her frantic struggle to save Lyonglen and Coinnleir Wood. Explain that since women had so few options to control their life, they had to be bold and seize whatever means they could to protect the people depending upon them. That she honored her guardian in his dying wish by struggling to keep Lyonglen out of the hands of the Comyns or the Campbells, and now away from the dread Edward Longshanks. Most of all, how she wished they had met at another point in their life, before he loved Tamlyn, a time when he would have had room in his heart for her.

Words she didn't speak.

Pressing her forehead against his, she closed her eyes against tears flooding her vision. "Be happy, be safe, Damian St. Giles."

Einar came to help her to her feet. "You err in this, Princess."

She walked away not looking back. "Too late. 'Tis done."

Hugh stood holding the reins to her mare, watching her with soulful eyes. He seemed as if he started to speak, then changed his mind, instead offering his hand to help her mount the black horse.

She shook her head. "Move the animals over to the wood's edge out of site. I stay here and watch. I shan't leave until someone comes and finds . . . him."

She could not say his name. Must never say his name again. Her warrior from this day forward would be nameless. It would be too much of a temptation to whisper it on the wind some moonlight night, and summon him to her.

"Riders approach from the south, Sister." Lewis touched the blue woolen mantle covering her arm. "Come, we must be away from this place before they see you. They ride under the standard of the Black Dragon. Hurry, Sister, that is Julian Challon."

Aithinne watched the man on the fearful black steed. He rode with the mantle of power upon his shoulders, like a warrior king of old. A man all of Scotland feared. The man who would marry Tamlyn.

"Sister, come," Deward pressed.

Pulling the mantle about her face, she watched as they rode on past without spotting the sleeping man. Mayhap she had mistaken in putting him at the edge of the bushes. Her body jerked as she saw him sit up, then throw back the tartan. He looked around, as if getting his bearings. Rain fell heavier now, so he pulled up the plaide, arranging it about his head and shoulders.

The he turned and looked at her.

It was silly, but she took a step back. He couldn't see her hidden in the shadows, though somehow it was as though he could sense her.

Fanciful thoughts, her mind chided. Pulling the hood forward more, she put the knuckle of her hand to her mouth as he remaincd fixed, staring in her direction. Then he finally rose to his feet and started off down the road to Glenrogha.

Aithinne watched until he was out of sight, then turned and mounted her palfrey.

Chapter Seven

Damian looked up at Tamlyn MacShane as she set the plate filled with roast meat, cheese, and bread before him. She offered him a curious smile, her amber eyes observing him with a wary expression, but naught more. Why did he almost expect other emotions to be there? Feel deep disappointment when they were not? He had to clench his jaw to keep from reaching out and taking her hand; he wanted to touch her.

Julian stood by the fireside, paring his fingernails with a *sgian dubh*—the knife he had taken from Tamlyn when they first met. His cousin now favored that knife, kept the sheath tucked into his belt, almost a talisman, a touchstone that assured him as long as he possessed it he kept hold of the Lady Glenrogha. His stance was one of assured negligence, though Damian knew Challon was recoiled, ready to spring at him should he perceive any untoward attention paid to his betrothed.

"Challon has been worried about you, Lord Ravenhawke. Fashed that you had been beset by men from Clan Comyn and held for ransom . . . or worse." Tamlyn's rebuke was clear. "We are glad you are safe and have returned unharmed to us."

It sounded as if she were chiding him for going out drinking and wenching his way across the countryside with nary a care how it would upset Challon. He would like to disabuse her of the notion, but he needed an explanation of where he had been to offer, and that was *not* forthcoming.

From under hooded eyes, he watched the beautiful woman in clothes of a commoner, whilst working to unriddle his mystery. He had been gone for days, they said, and no one knew where. Not even himself, at this point. As he tried to focus on his mind, dig deep into his memories, he found it vexing that while flashes of images were almost summoned to mind, they were jerked away before he could seize them. Bloody frustrating.

As she poured the tankard full of ale, a frisson crawled up his spine. Damian pondered why the action, such a simple act, caused a ripple of unease within him. "Challon and I are pleased you returned this morn. We feared you would not be here in time."

Damian placed his knife down on the table, suddenly not hungry. "Oh, and why is that, Lady Tamlyn?"

"Because—" she started only to have Challon push to his feet and come toward them.

"Because Tamlyn and I wed on the morrow." He placed a hand on Tamlyn's graceful shoulder. Sliding it up to her neck, his thumb brushed Tamlyn's pulse point. Possession was stamped in Challon's every action.

A dirk to Damian's heart. "Wed? On the morrow? The banns cannot be called before then. Why such a rush to get to the church steps?"

"Aye, the banns have not been called, howbeit I spoke with the *Culdee* priest and he agreed, with the turmoil facing Scotland, it is for the best if I move to secure this glen, thus he granted dispensation.

Tamlyn and I have a life to build here at Glenrogha. We think it wise to give the people of Glen Shane a true sense of stability, show they are under the protection of the Black Dragon. Let all know—English and Scot—I rule here now as the new earl. In these troubled times 'tis of import to move ahead with our lives."

Tamlyn smiled up at Challon, love clear in her amber eyes. Damian felt an oily blackness coiling at the pit of his stomach, the foulness pushing him to want to shove his fist through something. Swallowing back the grief, he nodded. "Then accept my blessings upon your union. I wish you both all the happiness you deserve." Pushing back on the bench so he could rise, he said, "If you will excuse me, I should like to seek my rest."

Challon nodded. "You look fair exhausted. You should take caution in your carousing, cousin. You no longer are a young man."

"Younger than you, Challon," he snapped before he could bite back the words.

Challon arched a black brow, unused to the surly tone from the man he considered a brother. Regret rose in Damian, but he was unpleased by Challon's uncalled-for rebuke. Julian had spoken so before Tamlyn to ensure that she viewed him as a knave, out drinking and swiving without thought to Challon's worry.

Conceding the point, Julian gave a slight nod. "True, though I am smart enough to wed on the morrow and settle down to hearthside. Mayhap your disposition would benefit from you doing the same."

Damian could not stop his eyes from wandering over Tamlyn's face. "In a breath, if only I could find the lady of my heart. Consider yourself lucky, Julian. Very lucky, indeed. By your leave, I shall retire."

As Damian started up the staircase, he looked

back, catching sight of Tamlyn standing close to Challon. A flush tinged her cheeks as she brushed a stray curl off Julian's forehead. He stood spellbound by the gentle action, the tenderness a clear sign that his cousin had bonded Tamlyn to him. They were one, in spirit, in soul.

Tamlyn would never be his. In utter despair, he closed his eyes, fighting the black wave of longing for something that could never be.

Forgive me, Damian.

Opening his eyes, his head snapped around to see who had spoken the words. There was no one about. For an instant he thought it had been Tamlyn who uttered the plea, but she still stood before Julian, speaking lowly with him.

He blinked his eyes several times, trying to still the rising noise in his mind, the images that floated just out of reach. Mayhap he was ill with some brain sickness. Closing his lids he tried to conjure the voice again, but failed. It had sounded like Tamlyn . . . yet . . . yet, it seemed deeper, huskier, a voice a man would crave to hear in the deep hush of night.

His groin bucked hard.

Odd. Why should his body react to ghost words, when it had not experienced any reaction to being close to Tamlyn? Yes, his heart cried out to touch her, but it was on a pure level of love, his soul craving his mate, someone who could show him how his life should be. This response of his body to whispered imaginings was strong.

"Damian, you are losing your bloody mind." Sighing, he trod on up the stairs.

Aithinne sat huddled in the big bed in the tower room, her heavy, wolf-lined mantle wrapped about her tightly, blocking the chill. She could not stop shaking, but it had little to do with the dampness of the chamber.

Her mind was torn. She knew she had been right to return Damian to Glenrogha. Even so, she dreaded that by sending him from her too soon; mayhap the Spell of Making was broken and she would never carry his child. Anguish rose up inside her. Oona stated there was no way to tell for sure until she ran her monthly courses—or failed to— so it would be over a fortnight until she would have some idea if her plan had succeeded. Not sure she could stand the suspense, she pressed Oona to use the craft to see knowledge on the path her life would take. Oona said there were too many things pressing inward for her to get a clear image of what would be.

Fearing that answer, she begged for her to fetch Evelynour of the Orchard. The strongest of the Three Wise Ones of the Woods, she was named after the goddess of the orchards. Born with fey ability to call upon the thistle and the ravens, she had vision that saw beyond the mortal world.

"Evelynour will come, tell me what I need to ken." She whispered to the darkness, like a small child trying to keep swort demons at bay.

Without a knock, the door opened and Einar ducked down to enter. In his left hand he carried a plate of food, while the other gripped a heavy trunk, slung over the right shoulder. Dropping it with a thud, he placed the plate on the small table at bedside. "Some meat and cheese, Princess. Cook made you fresh bread. Eat." Not waiting to see if she would do as he advised, he moved the chest to the foot of the bed, and then set to building a fire in the cold hearth.

"What is the trunk for?" She glared at the food, feeling no appetite.

"You are not happy elsewhere, so I ordered your belongings fetched up here. The rest will come shortly. We shall soon have you comfortable in a room fit for a princess." He tossed a peat brick upon the catching fire. "Now eat."

"Thank you, Einar, but I am not hungry." She pulled her knees to her chest and wrapped her arms around her legs, huddling against the cold. Against the despair.

"I do not recall asking if you were hungry, Princess. Eat. Life's riddles never are solved if one sickens due to the lack of nourishment." He stood, dusting his hands off on his thighs. "All of Glen Eallach depends upon you. You must be strong for them."

"Sometimes, Einar, I weary by all depending upon me to see them safe and well-fed through each winter."

Einar came to stand by the bed. Crossing his arms, he lifted his pale brows in an I-told-you-so air. "You should have kept Ravenhawke. I asked Odin for his blessing for the child. The Auld Father will give you what you wish. But you need someone to protect you and the babe, Princess."

Aithinne forced a smile. "I have my very own Viking guard for protection."

"You need more. Troubles prowl this land in the skin of a leopard."

"Leopard? You mean Edward Longshanks?"

"Aye, I do. He wears three golden leopards on his surcoat; 'tis his standard. Methinks the device serves him well. The man will not stop until he possesses all of Scotland. Your having a child might not be enough to keep his schemes at bay. Glen Shane forms the entrance to the heart of the Highlands.

'Tis why he sent the Black Dragon to claim the holdings of the Ogilvies and Shanes. At the Beltane celebrating 'twas spoken that the Dragon's brothers shall marry with Lady Tamlyn's sisters, Rowenna and Raven. The old king has long pushed for marriages of alliance for The Shane's daughters to men loyal to him. Now that he has secured the whole of Glen Shane, his eye will turn to Glen Eallach and you—his chance, Princess, to claim all that has been denied him. He has not sent a warrior to take over Lyonglen—yet. He still thinks the old lord lives. Once he hears tides of his passing, mark my words, the Leopard will send a warrior. Lyonglen and Coinnleir Wood are key positions. With Glen Shane and Glen Eallach in his grasp, he holds a knife to the back of these Highland chiefs."

"You speak things I already have sussed, that is why I sought to have a child. Lyonglen held great favor with the English king. He did not rise to Balliol's standard and rebel. 'Tis my hope, if Edward believes I carry his child, that he will honor that friendship and allow me to hold the fief until the child is old enough to rule. I could with this English king's blessing."

"Aye, you could. Only, the Leopard places little faith in women and their ability to control a fief, I hear. What will you do when he sends a warrior, mayhap demands you accept the man as your lord husband?" Einar clearly was not dropping the topic.

Aithinne trembled against such fears, and whispered, "Do not speak such things. Words hold the power to make them truth."

"You should have kept the warrior. He was a man worthy of you. He would fight for you, protect you. 'Tis not too late. Go see him at Glenrogha, Princess. Humble yourself before him and beg forgiveness. No man could resist you on your knees before him."

"If it were only that simple." She laid her head against her knees.

He shrugged. "Life is simple, Princess. 'Tis people who insist on making it troublesome. You want him, go fetch him."

It might be that simple—if not for the fact he loved Tamlyn. Knowing her cousin was forever out of his reach when she wed Julian Challon, would Damian not accept a look-alike alternative? Forevermore torn, Aithinne would always ken his heart belonged to Tamlyn. Every breath she drew she would live in fear that he would see her as lacking in comparison, taller, with hair that had an ugly red cast, and seven bloody dots on her nose.

"Einar, I think I prefer you when you just grunt your answers."

Damian's heart pounded, slamming against his ribcage, his blood vibrating through his body to the point of pain. She sat astride him, her naked body bathed in the silver glow of the moonlight, her head lolling as she rode him, lost to the sensations of their bodies being joined. He bucked inside her, her slick channel tightening about his erection like a fist, squeezing the length of his burning flesh. It was not enough. He wanted to be even deeper inside her. Grabbing her at the waist, he brought her down hard as he slammed upward. From that angle, he forced her to shudder with the release of her passion. Her moan was nearly enough to drive him over the edge, yet not enough to satisfy the ravenous demon riding his back. Wrapping his arms around her back, he pulled to sit up, arching her to where his mouth could latch on the full breast. He was not gentle, drawing hard in a rhythm that matched the rough flexes of his flesh within her body.

"Father, you must awake."

Someone shook his bare arm, snatching him away from the dream of moonlight and her. The man animal in him was furious at the disruption, however the warrior's instinct took hold and he came fully awake, his hand around the dagger he slept with under his pillow. His grip relaxed when he stared into the face of his son.

Moffet. It was still hard to believe this young man, nearly tall enough to look him in the eye, was his child. He felt proud. He felt old. He knew many thought the lad to be Challon's bastard son, the clear stamp of the black hair and green eyes marking the boy as of Challon blood. Damian had not really considered that factor before asking Challon to accept him as page, then squire; he just wanted Moffet to learn from the best. To be the squire to the Dragon of Challon would set Moffet on the road to a secure future. None would dare cast aspersions on Moffet's origins when he stood next to Julian Challon. Had not Julian forced acceptance throughout the land for his two bastard-born half-brothers?

The issue of Damian's misspent youth, Moffet came to him when just a small babe. His mother had been one of the serving wenches at Castle Challon. Older than Damian by three summers, she had brought him the fevered pleasures of the flesh, coming to him nightly for the passing of several moons. Later, when she whispered tides that she carried his child, he learned she actually loved another. The man would marry her, only he did not want to raise another man's child.

Damian quickly learned the sting of betrayal. Anya had deceived him, deliberately set out to get with babe, an eye on bettering her future. She would turn the child over to Damian in exchange for a settlement so she and her new husband, a woodman on the Challon holding, could start off with life far above their station. The woman cared nothing for the infant she carried, only the gold coin she hoped to get for him. It left a bitter taste in Damian's mouth that he had to buy his own son, that a woman could set out to conceive a child as a tool to getting what she wanted in life. However, when he held the little boy, he knew each coin had been well spent. He would have paid a fortune ten times over for the small black-haired babe.

"I sorrow to break your slumber, Father. My lord Challon requests you join him on the bastion."

"What is the hour?" Damian slid to the edge of the bed, then reached for his hose and tunic and began dressing.

Moffet picked up Damian's mantle and held it while he finished buckling his baldric about his hips. "Should be near matins, though 'tis hard to tell in this Scottish holding. They don't keep to the hours of prayers as we did in Challon Castle. Dawn-break has not yet come."

Taking the mantle, Damian swung it around his shoulder. "Shall we see what your lord wishes at this ungodly hour?"

Aithinne stood on the roof of the tower room, staring off into the night as it lightened from blackness to a deep blue. Dawn would soon come, but she hadn't been able to find her rest. She tried to retire to her room on the third level, the room that had always been hers while she was in residence. Mayhap she should have taken possession of the lord's chamber to further her pretense that she was now the baroness of Lyonglen. Only something prevented her. The castle servants were aware the frail man had slipped into the otherworld over two moons passing. They also knew what was at stake and would keep her secret. Oddly, she had always felt at home in Lyonglen. It was a rambling castle of stone, but it had warmth to it, as if built to please the eye as much as for fortification.

Now she could not summon that ease, that sense of belonging here anymore. Some part of Damian St. Giles had marked this place, marked her soul.

Putting her hand on the crenellation, she stared off in the direction of Glen Shane. Her mind cautioned that this malaise was not good, she needed to put Ravenhawke from her thoughts. Forget him. Mayhap in time she would achieve the noble aim. For now, he haunted her. Visions of their time together, what he taught her about the magic of a man and a woman joining, stayed constantly with her. Sometimes she wondered if the potion had done its job and obliterated her from his mind. In weaker moments, a selfish part of her wanted some fragment of their time to remain with him. She could not stop wondering where he was, what he was doing.

Pulling her mantle closer, she shivered against the damp morning air, watching the *haar* shift like aimless gray ghosts across the valley. Once more, she wondered where Damian was. She could close her eyes and try to summon his image, use the kenning to try to touch his mind, but that would be the road to ruin.

"Mayhap I am the one who should have taken the forgetting potion."

Damian paused halfway up the tower steps when he spotted his cousin. For a heartbeat, he remained motionless, judging Julian's mood. Knowing his cousin well, he had an idea what this secluded meeting at dawnbreak was about. Tamlyn.

Challon would take Tamlyn to lady wife this day, but that merely made legal what clearly happened on Beltane. She now belonged to Challon in a way no blessing of the church could ever give. Damian envied his cousin. Oh, he did not expect everything to be smooth sailing for Julian and Tamlyn. There was the concern of her father, Hadrian, Earl of Kinmarch, now prisoner to Edward. Julian had stormed the man's castle and taken him captive, by Edward's command. Damian had a feeling Tamlyn would not let the matter drop.

Still, their bond brought deep yearning within him. He wanted a home, a family. He, as well, had been a warrior for too long. He wondered if he would find those things waiting at his grandfather's holding, pondered if his grandfather would welcome him or resent that Edward had sent him to assume command of the holding. Well, he would find the answers to these things soon enough. He wanted to be away from Glenrogha as soon as possible.

Challon's head turned at his approach, but he waited for Damian to break the silence. The corner of his mouth quirked up. Julian was a master at wielding silence like a sword. Usually it failed to have an affect on him since he knew his cousin too well, only, with the big voids in his memory gnawing at him, this dawn meeting left him with disquiet.

"Rather odd, to find a man about to marry out here all alone," Damian commented. "I wouldst think there were other . . . more comfortable places you could be."

"I granted Tamlyn the time before our marriage, giving her space to adjust to our wedding. I wanted to honor her before her people, have them see she comes to the union with her full blessings. I want peace here. The people of Glenrogha love their lady. Her happiness is important to them." Challon's eyes looked over him in an air of detached assessment, though Damian sensed that wasn't his mood. "So where were you these past days?"

Damian had hoped his cousin would not ask that question. Stalling for time, he yawned, then shivered. How could he explain the lack of knowing, or worse, the bizarre flashes that skittered through his mind at the odd moment? "Truth?"

"I would not have asked otherwise." Challon's tone had an underlying hint of shortness.

Damian shook his head. "The truth—I lack any idea where I was."

Challon frowned, clearly not expecting this response. "I know you said that before, but figured you just did not wish to speak about it before the others. At first I assumed you were off with some wench. As days passed, I grew concerned you had been set upon by some of the brigands from Clan Comyn, either held for ransom or killed. You worried me."

"And here of late, I might have thought that prospect would please you," Damian teased, hoping to drop this line of questioning. He misliked not having the answers.

Challon turned around and leaned his hips back against the crenellation, crossing his legs at the ankles. "I would never wish you harm. You have always been a brother to me. Nothing changes that. I merely warned you to turn your thoughts of Tamlyn elsewhere. I need her, Damian. If I lose her . . ." He paused, looking to the waning night sky, which was lightening to a deep blue. "If I lose Tamlyn, there will be nothing left of me. She is my salvation."

Damian nodded sadly. "I know. I am happy for you, Julian. Truly. Tamlyn and you have my full blessings."

His cousin reached out and embraced him, hugging him tightly. "Thank you, my friend—my brother. Come, we need to break our fast and prepare for my wedding. We can ponder where you were and why you cannot recall aught of your adventure, over some of cook's fresh baked bread."

Damian patted Challon's shoulder. "Go on without me. I want to stand here and enjoy the solitude a bit longer."

Julian nodded, started to turn away, but paused. "Mayhap the Faery Queen stole you away. 'Tis what these superstitious Scots whisper. When no trace of you could be found, the serfs swore the real Queen of Beltane came and stole you from this mortal world."

Damian wanted to laugh off the silly notion, only he felt suddenly lightheaded. "Ah, you unriddled my secret," making a jest of it. Inside he was *not* laughing.

He watched the man they called the Black Dragon go back into the castle. Once the king's champion, Julian had at one time held great sway with Edward, though less since the nightmare of Berwick. Strange the paths of life. Julian, though deeply troubled, had found his paradise here in this forgotten pocket in the Highlands, whilst life had set Damian—who favored him so much people oft mistook them to be twins—upon another path.

Twins. What was it about the word that sent another peculiar ripple of disquiet along his spine to lodge in his brain? His mind worked to capture the elusive feeling, seize hold of something to unravel this sense of nothingness plaguing his memory.

Half-measures never see the deed done.

The voice was clear within his head, sounding so

like Tamlyn. Yet not. It was deeper, whispered, huskier. Trying to focus his thoughts on the wisp of words, striving to pull an image to match them, he failed.

"But what deed, asked the crazy man?" he spoke to the dawn breeze.

Damian watched as Challon dismounted and went to lift Tamlyn from the black palfrey. The fine-blooded mare, named Goblin, had been a bride's gift from Challon to his lady. Eager to please Julian, Moffet rushed forward to take both horses' leads. Challon's stallion, Pagan, nuzzled the mare's neck, murmuring to her. Challon lightly smacked the nose of the randy horse and pushed him back, so he could help Tamlyn from the sidesaddle.

In a manner befitting a man once the king's champion, Challon had gone to great expense to see the wedding take place in a lavish style, despite the rush. Damian understood. Challon sent a declaration to the people of Glen Shane that while he was conqueror of this glen, he now held it and would fight to possess it; he was a man worthy to be their lord.

Absentmindedly, Challon fingered the gold Pictish torque about his neck. Tamlyn's gift to the man who would soon be her lord husband. Emotions were clear on Julian's countenance; he clearly reverenced the meaning of the present, a token to the new earl of Glenrogha.

Julian had confided he designed Tamlyn's wedding gown. While not the customary color for a ceremony, she was dressed in black trimmed in gold, her gown matching Challon's surcoat. Damian swallowed the lump in his throat as Challon took

Tamlyn's hand and led her to the steps of the ancient kirk.

The throngs of Glen Shane's people, lining both sides of the road, fell in behind them, following. Malcolm Ogilvie, dressed in his robes of the *Culdee* priest, stood on the top step, waiting. A hush fell over the gathering as Tamlyn's uncle began the ceremony.

As the words went on, Tamlyn nervously glanced about her. Damian watched her, unable to take his eyes from the lovely woman. Tamlyn's beauty had little to do with the raiments she wore. Most days found her dressed in a common kirtle and sark. He had to admit, Challon had an eye how to showcase his bride. In the black kirtle trimmed in gold brocade, and her golden hair flowing down her back, she robbed Damian of his breath.

Even so, something niggling bothered him. His mind worried, trying to pinpoint what was wrong about the woman who stood before him. It was bad enough his mind held a blank spot of what happened this past week, now it seemed to be playing tricks on him. Tamlyn's hair seemed washed out in some manner.

Then her eyes collided with his. He saw so many things in those amber depths, all so fleeting it was hard to name each. Damian recognized the time had come to let go of the false dream. Tamlyn was never his. She belonged to Julian, not only by royal decree, but by choice of her heart. His mind whispered its sorrow, *be happy, my love.*

Her eyes widened in surprise for a heartbeat, then the expression shifted to alarm as Challon turned, glaring first at her, then to Damian and finally back to Tamlyn. A deep blush of shame rose to her face and she lowered her gaze, clearly saying she knew it had not been proper for her eyes to tarry so long on another man when words were being spoken to bind her to Challon.

Challon lifted a warning brow at Damian. Knowing Challon was right to be irritated, Damian turned his stare to the priest.

Barely listening to the words droning on, he focused his attention on chasing the will-o'-the-wisps within his mind. He felt like a cat chasing his tail. Acceptance rode hard in him that Tamlyn belonged to Julian, only he could not dismiss that the kenning had lied to him. So wrapped up in the preponderances, he failed to notice the *Culdee* had called for Tamlyn's consent to the union. It was important for her to declare this, as the women of Clan Ogilvie could not be forced into a marriage. Their ancient Pict laws permitted the women the right to choose their own husbands. It was imperative that the people of Glen Shane see Tamlyn gave herself freely to this English lord.

Tamlyn didn't reply. At first there was a stunned silence. When the priest asked for her consent a second time, a buzz fluttered through the thong of people. Come to witness their joining, murmurs asked why Tamlyn did not plight her troth. The *Culdee* looked from Tamlyn to Challon, a flicker of question in his eyes. A flush of irritation colored Julian's neck as the priest prompted Tamlyn for the third time.

She turned toward Julian, wearing, oddly enough, an expression of confusion and pleading in her golden cat-eyes. His patience clearly gone, he drew a breath and opened his mouth to speak, when her voice rang out.

"Aye, I take this man as my lord husband. To honor him above all others, provide him comfort, support him in times of the troubles, and give him daughters and sons."

Challon stared, surprised by the lengthy declaration. It was obvious he'd never expected her to make such a clear assent before all.

Tamlyn radiantly smiled up at Julian as he took her hand and led her into the church.

Damian watched them enter the ancient kirk, feeling a door shut within his heart.

Chapter Eight

"Princess Aithinne!" Einar rushed through the stillroom doorway, then fell to his knees and thudded his fist to his chest. "Riders are at the gate demanding entry."

Aithinne closed her eyes and prayed for strength. After fighting queasiness all morn, the last thing she needed was to face Dinsmore Campbell again. For the past three weeks, the man had done naught but try to gain entrance to Lyonglen. The Campbell knave simply refused to take no as her final answer. She feared her ruse of an ailing husband was near end. Soon, she would have to don mourning raiments, and announce Lyonglen's passing. She had hoped to prolong the period before sending out those tides, waiting to make sure she was with child.

For now, staring at that stringy, white-blond hair and scraggly chin whiskers might set her stomach to heaving once more. Of course, these past two morns it required little to set her lurching for the chamber pot. Putting a hand to her belly, she drew a steadying breath.

"Dinsmore? Again?" She sighed.

"Nay, Princess."

Unhurried, Aithinne finished tying the string of yarn around the bundle of heath, milkwort, marsh marigold, and silverweed, then hung them from the rafter to dry. Stalling. The nervousness in her belly was suddenly something other than sourness. The kenning tingled, shifting through her with a sense of foreboding, pressing inward on her thoughts.

An image of St. Giles flashed before her mind's eye. Instantly, the knot in her stomach tightened into a hard fist and her breasts tightened. Longing lanced through her. It never seemed to lessen. Did the wanting never stop? She bit the corner of her lip, pondering how she could miss someone she did not really know. Their nights together had been a mere handful, but he had claimed a part of her soul. As if she were no longer complete. No sooner had her heart whispered his name than anguish flooded her being. She could not help wondering where he was, what he was doing. Was he happy?

Shortly after returning St. Giles to Glenrogha, tides of Tamlyn's marriage to the Black Dragon had been carried to Lyonglen. Part of Aithinne quietly rejoiced that her beautiful cousin was now bound to the English warlord. The other side of her mind perceived it mattered little. She had looked into St. Giles's thoughts, painfully heard his truths. He loved Tamlyn. She sensed the honor within this warrior; Damian would never wound the trust of a man he looked upon as a brother. While he would never have her, sadly, love for Tamlyn would always live silently in his heart, leaving no room for another . . . *for her.*

Oh, she did not doubt he might accept her, knowing she bore the likeness of her cousin. But that would be a living hell. Each time he looked at her, with every caress of his hand, Aithinne would watch his gray-green eyes, fearful of seeing the disappointment in her not being Tamlyn. She swallowed hard, forcing back the anguish.

Three sennights had passed and Damian still haunted her dreams. In long dark nights since, she had tossed and turned, her body recalling each touch, his taste, the feel of him moving inside her. With near obsession she wanted him, and worried one day she might crave him so badly she would foolishly toss common sense to the wind, risk her heart, and go to him. It was misery not being with him, but a misery she could tolerate. Living with him when he loved Tamlyn would be more than she could bear. Each day would see her love wither, her soul die.

Hugh, Deward, and Lewis pushed through the door, wedging themselves into a jumble of arms and legs. The more one struggled to ram past, the more entangled they became. She smiled at their nonsense, the normality of their antics bringing her a small measure of peace. Fussing, all three finally shoved forward, landing in a heap at her feet. Lewis punched Deward in the shoulder. In turn, Deward took a swing, only to have Lewis duck, so the blow landed squarely on Hugh's chin. Stunned, Hugh flopped onto his back, not moving, whilst the other two fell upon the each other, fists flying.

Knowing such idiocy could go on until they wore themselves out, she eyed Einar and nodded. He leaned over and picked up Lewis and Deward by the back of their belts. Sitting up, Hugh tried to take advantage of being free to swat his brothers, only Einar put a foot to his back and pushed him to the floor. Lewis tried to twist, so he could bite Einar on the thigh, but the Viking just gave him a shake, like a puppy would a rag.

"By Saint Ninian's shinbone, you bite Einar and

you will shovel out the garderobes!" Using *the voice*, Aithinne stomped her foot. The lads stilled, knowing she meant the threat. Shaking her head, she pitied the lasses who one day would wed her brothers.

"Sister is in a bad humor again." Lewis sighed, rolling his eyes.

Deward nodded. "She blawed the past two morns, she feels puny, she—"

"Oona says she is with child and we should treat her gently," Hugh informed them, then reached out and punched both Lewis and Deward on their noses.

Aithinne snorted at their idea of gentle. "All three of you cease acting as buffoons and tell me who is at the gates if not Dinsmore. I certainly hope it is not the English storming the curtain wall, or they would capture this place before the three of you stopped fighting amongst yourselves."

"But, Sister, it *is* the English," Hugh insisted.

"English?" Aithinne had a sinking feeling her day just took a turn for the worse.

Aithinne anxiously peered down through the merlons to the mounted warriors below. "Gor! That is a full complement!"

Knights, squires, even hobelars, were behind the bannerets carrying the pennon of Challon—the green dragon rampant on a field of black. Bile rolled in her stomach as she considered there would be no putting off the Black Dragon, as she had with Dinsmore and Phelan, with lies of Lyonglen being unwell.

A racket broke out behind her, the same ruckus that always preceded her brothers' entrance. The three always walked through a doorway with each wanting to be first. She exhaled disgust as their

arms and legs shoved, tugged, and slugged their
way over the threshold.

"Och, not again! Silence! Do you never cease?"
she snapped, causing them to pull up, then approach quietly.

"Sorry, Sister," Deward whispered, peeking over
her shoulder.

Sparing their immaturity little mind, she turned
back to the stone wall. Dread bubbled in the pit of
her stomach as she stared down at the barded
riders. One knight, all in black and mounted upon
a black charger, drew her eyes. Not wearing a helm
like the others, the spring breeze ruffled the wavy
black hair. For an instant her heart lurched, fearing
it was Lord Ravenhawke.

"Open the gate in the name of the king!" he
called, the tone conveying he expected to be obeyed.

With piercing eyes, the warrior looked straight at
the tower roof, as though he sensed her observing
him. He was so handsome, he took her breath away.
But he was not St. Giles, the kenning whispered.
One like him. What had her brothers said? *His kinsman. A cousin. He favors Julian Challon, much the same
way Tamlyn and you do each other. We thought it a fine
jest.* Only, it was no jest. Oh aye, he favored his
cousin. Only there was a darkness coiled within this
man, something she couldn't quite place, as if the
color of the ravens he wrapped himself in also
cloaked his soul. So this was the mighty Black
Dragon, the man now Tamlyn's lord husband.

"Who demands entrance to Lyonglen?" the Captain of the Guard shouted down in challenge.

"Challon, overlord of Lyonglen. I demand entrance."

Stunned, Aithinne jerked back from the crenellation, reeling. Overlord? Did that mean Edward
Longshanks had given Lyonglen to the Dragon of

Challon as well as all of Glen Shane? Why had no tides of this been dispatched? Of course, mayhap the English king did not send advance word, fearing that under the current political clime they might use the time to supply against a siege.

Aithinne closed her eyes against the wave of dizziness trying to claim her. The kenning said she did not want to let this English earl into Lyonglen, yet understood she had little choice. Near to fainting, she put a hand to her stomach, wondering at the cruel irony of fate.

She had missed her monthly courses. With a sly smile, Oona pronounced Aithinne carried the child she sought to conceive; the nausea of the past two morns confirmed this. Only, had the elaborate plans been for naught?

"All this time, the Earl Challon was the overlord here and merely waited until after his marriage to Tamlyn to come lay claim? Surely, the Auld Ones jest." Aithinne's laughter was not mirth, but one of vapors.

Panic coursed through her to the point she could barely think. What of Coinnleir Wood? Would she be permitted to retain control of her hereditary holding, or would that, too, be stripped from her with no regard to the ancient Pictish laws of her clan?

Evidently she swayed, for Deward gently took hold of her elbow to steady her. "Aithinne, do not beg trouble, as you say, let us meet with this Dragon of Challon, see what he has to say. Mayhap 'tis only a formality, that you shall now look to him for guidance and protection, not a bad thing, do you not think? A dragon as protector at a time like this?"

He was right—she must face Tamlyn's lord husband, find out what the earl wanted. After all, he was kinsman by marriage now; possibly that would work in their favor.

An invisible knife twisted at her insides as she nodded to Einar, who in turn signaled permission for the guard to raise the gate. She watched the riders enter through the portcullis before she lifted her skirts and rushed to the staircase, descending them two at a time.

"Oona!" She called, hurrying into the tower room and going to the wardrobe. "Where are you, Oona! Annoying woman, never about when I need her." Flinging open the doors, her eyes searched her kirtles. "What to wear, what to wear . . ." She needed to gird herself in female armor, summon all the confidence she could muster to face this treacherous situation. Yanking out the dark green velvet kirtle, she paused, selecting instead the black brocade. She tossed it on the bed and began unlacing the ties at her sides.

Aggie rushed in, looking about her. "Why all the fashing, lass? You would think Edward Longshanks himself has come to lay seize to Lyonglen."

"Och, him I could handle. Dragons are another matter. Where is Oonanne?" Lifting her hair over one shoulder, she turned so Aggie could untie the lacings up her back.

"You ken that crone, about only when she wills it. Hold still, Aithinne. You wiggle like a puppy. Why all the trouble?" her maidservant asked.

"The Dragon of Challon has come, claiming to be our new overlord."

"Merciful heaven, does the beastie breathe fire?" Aggie's simple mind accepted the pronouncement as a real dragon had come to batter down the gates of Lyonglen. Maybe she was not far off.

"I must suss this out, amongst other things. Have cook fetch bread, cheese, and any cold meats left from yestereve's supper," she instructed. "And wine. The good French stock, not the dregs from last summer we serve Dinsmore and Phelan."

"Stop twisting about, lass, or you will pop out of this dress. You would look a wanton with your breasts already swelling due to the bairn."

Aithinne's head whipped around. "What bairn?" Only Oona, Einar, and her brothers knew; she was startled to hear Aggie speak of it as common knowledge.

"Lass . . . lass . . . I have been taking care of you since you were a wee one. Oonanne can fuss all she wants, trying to muddy the waters, but I ken you breed with that man's bairn."

"But how? Oona only said this morn she believes I am with child."

Aggie smiled and arranged Aithinne's long hair about her shoulders. "A woman breeding has a special glow. That shimmer is upon you. Never have I seen you more beautiful, lass."

"Well, let's hope that faery shimmer dazzles a dragon," she said under her breath.

"Is that the bairn's da?"

Aithinne shook her head. "Nay, but his kinsman, now mine, too. The Dragon of Challon is Tamlyn's new lord husband. He says he is the new overlord of Lyonglen. That scares me."

Aggie fetched the gold braided girdle and helped Aithinne place it about her hips. "Mayhap 'tis not such a bad thing, especial if he is kinsman now."

"Where is my circlet? I want all my weapons about me." Aithinne affixed the circlet across her brow and took a deep breath.

Hurrying down the winding steps to the Great Hall, she felt ill-prepared to face her fate.

Aithinne drew up short when she entered the wide double doors. It was well after nooning, so the workers had already cleared away the meal. Several now fetched wine, bread, and cheese and set them on the long trestle table. She remained in the shadows for several heartbeats, studying this Dragon of Challon. Tamlyn's lord and husband.

His hand on the mantle of the fireplace, he stood staring into the flames with deep reflection. Word had spread through the Highland of this mighty warrior presence—King Edward's champion, a fearsome knight in battle. He was dressed in black, no adornments, even the heavy mantle that hung about his shoulders was of the same unrelenting pitch.

Aithinne steeled herself to look upon him. Though her brothers had said he was similar to St. Giles, still little prepared her for just how strong the resemblance was.

Putting a hand to her heart, she closed her eyes and opened herself to the kenning, trying to brush his warrior's mind, wanting to suss out what she was dealing with in this English knight. Oddly, he was initially closed off from her. Focusing her mind, she was suddenly sucked into a vivid image of him on his knees, kneeling before another, younger man. His body jerked, choking back tears, as Challon cradled a body in his arms. The lad so very like him, he could have been this man ten years earlier. She fought tears of empathy as his intense sorrow pressed inwardly upon her mind and heart. This lad, so beautiful, was too young to have died.

Aithinne swallowed back the sorrow which threatened to overwhelm her.

She must have drawn a sharp breath, for his head snapped up and his eyes collided with hers. She looked into Julian Challon's face, saw the madness of grief hidden within the green eyes. The force nearly robbed her of air. The redoubtable power of this man was terrifying.

Staring at him full-faced, for a heartbeat it was as if she looked at Damian. The dark green eyes widened for an instant, then narrowed on her. The iron control dropped, but only for a fleeting instant. She should have expected the reaction, after all, in the shadows she must appear so like his bride. While she had been expecting a man who resembled Damian St. Giles, she doubted anyone had warned him how much she favored his lady wife.

Challon was not as tall as St. Giles; still they favored each other, enough to be brothers.

Mustering her most regal stance, Aithinne lifted her chin and strode forward to greet him. "I am the lady of Lyonglen. I bid you *ceud mile failte*, Lord Challon."

"I asked to see Lyonglen," he said quietly, but the words held thunder within them. "He sends you in his stead?"

His level stare set her to quaking, but she forced herself to step fully into the firelight. As she did, movement caught her eye. Another man was in the corner. He shifted, but the veil of the dimness hid him. Something drew her, an odd unease unfurling within her, but Lord Challon slapped his leather gauntlets against his palm, jerking her attention back to him.

She tilted her head and smiled. "Lord Challon, I am taller than your Tamlyn, and when you are near, you will see I have green flecks in my eyes. Aithinne Ogilvie, baroness of Coinnleir Wood, in my own right. Tamlyn is my cousin."

He glanced to the man in the deep shadows, and then back to her. "I do wish my lady wife would have mentioned the resemblance. It is astounding."

"Aye, it is." The man stepped from the darkness and into the light.

Aithinne blinked. St. Giles. She jerked her eyes back to the Dragon, fighting a wall of emotions flooding her. Challon's brow merely lifted at her reaction.

Aithinne tried to compose her wits. She'd been pushed off-kilter by Lord Challon's arrival and his claim to be Lyonglen's overlord. Now she recalled the kenning brushing her mind with an image of St. Giles. She had sensed his presence. She felt cold, as if all the blood drained from her, then she felt flushed. A strange buzzing like bees sounded in her ears.

Aithinne flinched as her eyes met the gray-green ones of Damian St. Giles. A man who had been her lover. The man who fathered the child she now carried.

It took all her will not to faint.

Chapter Nine

"Beg pardon, Lord Challon. Tides that the Black Dragon has a twin brother failed to reach Lyonglen." Aithinne pushed the lie over her teeth, hoping it strong enough to guise her shock at facing the one man in the whole land she never expected to meet again.

Willing her feet to remain plastered to the stone floor, she steeled herself not to flinch as Damian St. Giles slowly strode the length of the room to reach her. He moved with a regal grace, a warrior comfortable with power and command. Likely one used to getting his way in all. That sort of self-value often led to an edge of arrogance in a man, and this air touched Ravenhawke's mien. Her heart pounded, slamming with a bruising force against her ribcage. Even so, she had to stand, a timid rabbit, while this predator moved in for the kill.

Her breath hitched as he drew closer, seeing the haunted, gaunt appearance to his arresting countenance. Shadows tinged the skin under his eyes as if he had not eaten well or slept, consequences of watching Tamlyn marry his cousin, she presumed. Aithinne sensed great honor within this man, as well, his respect and devotion to Lord Challon were

clear to her. Thus, the conflicting emotions surely
must be tearing him apart. Her heart squeezed,
kenning this man was hurting inside, aware she
could do naught to ease his grief.

The pressure increased in her chest as she stared
at Damian St. Giles. Flames of desire flickered
within her, despite the overwhelming panic forged
by his dominating presence. So handsome, he wore
a dark blue surcoat over the mail shirt, a simple
braided leather baldric about his hips, and like
Challon, had leathern hose instead of the ones of
mail. Frozen by fear, she remained still, barely
breathing, as his eyes roamed over her features and
then down to her fist clutching the green garnet
amulet suspended between her breasts.

Veiling his thoughts with a sweep of his long
black lashes, he reached out and gently took her
hand from where it rested next to her heart. Un-
curling her fingers from around the dark green
stone, he raised them to his lips, then paused.
Those pale eyes lashed into her soul, stripped away
all protection against him. Their force sent a dread
slithering through her being, and more concern
arose. Had the spells and potions done their mission? Finally, with a half smile, St. Giles brushed his
lips over her knuckles.

Since the potion and Oona's spelling were
crafted to rob all memories of his time with her, for
him, this was the first chance he studied her in
comparison with Tamlyn. A slight quiver racked her
body as she fought not to burst into tears, his unfor-
gettable eyes almost seeming to count each bloody
freckle on her nose.

Finally, he inclined in a faint bow. "Damian St.
Giles, Lord Ravenhawke, your obedient servant, my
lady. I am not Challon's twin, not even his brother,
but merely a humble cousin."

Perceptive, the Dragon lifted his brow. "You have met before?"

The question was addressed to Damian, but Aithinne afforded him no chance to answer. "Nay, my lord. Had I ever met two such handsome men, alike enough to be brothers, I would surely recall. Men such as you are hard for a woman to forget."

She tried to retract her hand, only the vexing man held firm, refusing to let go. Aithinne bestowed an aloof smile upon Ravenhawke, then tugged against his grip again. His fingers tightened, the incisive eyes alive with challenge. Nervous, wondering what Lord Challon made of his cousin's strange behavior, her eyes shifted to Tamlyn's husband.

"Damian, release the Lady Aithinne's hand," Julian Challon advised softly. "You may continue becoming *acquainted* later, after I settle concerns which brought us to Lyonglen."

St. Giles gave a faint nod. "'Til then, my lady. My breath is held in anticipation." Instead of releasing her hand, he replaced it against her heart, then stepped back.

A frisson crawled up her spine. Part dread. Part her body's traitorous response to him.

"Lady Aithinne, if you would be so kind to send for the baron. We must speak with him upon pressing business. We carry a missive from King Edward."

Challon's tone was calm, but coldness spread through her blood as her worst fears became reality. Here the lies would start. She hoped she was mummer enough to lend believability to her falsehoods. Her throat constricted, but she forced out the words.

"It is with respect, Lord Challon, that I must decline this request. Lyonglen is not well."

Challon nodded, the air of impatience upon him once more. "We heard stories of his being ill—why he failed to rise to Balliol's standard or Edward's. Later, tales tother were carried across the countryside about his marriage. Whilst I regret he ails, we still must meet with him—forthwith—upon matters most urgent."

She clutched the amulet hanging from the chain about her neck, squeezing it so tightly it cut into her palm. The pressure warned, ease the grip, but she could not relax her fingers. If she did, she might start shaking and never stop. A large stone of green garnet—the same gem reputed to adorn the Holy Grail—it focused her powers and gave her strength to face this ordeal. Striving for an air of regal detachment, she forced a composed demeanor.

"'Tis not possible, Lord Challon. I regret your journey from Glenrogha was made for naught." Aithinne found pride her voice managed to convey the right note of finality.

Challon's eyes narrowed; he was obviously unused to anyone failing to obey his command. "Lady Aithinne, I have spent the past two fortnights dealing with women of Clan Ogilvie, so I should not hold surprise at your refusing to follow my charge. Methinks you share more in common with my lady wife than a few physical traits."

The Dragon took several paces toward her, undoubtedly to browbeat her with the force of his redoubtable presence. Those dark green eyes had the power to rip away her mind's defenses, lay bare her every thought. Aithinne gnawed on her lower lip, studying this formidable man for several breaths. A dark fire burned in this warrior, an ancient fire, one that burned brighter than any man she ever encountered. Bloody discomforting. Never had she seen a man surrounded by such a dark, arcane aura.

Aithinne was relieved Julian Challon had wed her cousin, Tamlyn, and Edward had not sent this warrior to Glen Eallach to claim the holdings and her. While sinfully attractive, this man was frightening. Aithinne stood in dread of this mighty Black Dragon, so aptly named. Only fools and blind men would not be frightened. And whilst at times she felt the fool, she was not blind to the power of Tamlyn's mate. Unable to meet his penetrating gaze, she looked away—had to for fear of him scrying all her lies.

Her eyes collided with St. Giles's enthralling stare, and suddenly his daunting cousin vanished from her thoughts. As imposing a figure as Julian Challon cut, it was Damian who drew her. Odd, upon first laying eyes upon both men, she had been struck by their likeness. Now, as she stood so close, that similarity lost the impact; it was their differences that held her spellbound.

Her body, her soul, her heart was ensorcelled by Damian St. Giles, forevermore bound to this dark warrior.

"Lady Aithinne, you fail to understand the situation. I am not *asking* to see Lord Lyonglen—I demand it. Edward made me overlord of Glen Eallach. As such, my orders shall be obeyed in all."

"*All* of Glen Eallach?" She barely could speak the reply.

He inclined his head. "All—including Coinnleir Wood, which is what I believe you ask."

She sucked in a deep breath, her jaw clenching against the rising fury. "Edward has no rights here. He is not king of the Scots. My titles and lands pass to me through ancient charter through Clan Ogilvie. Right of Line guarantees thusly—"

"Aye, my ears are fair numb with listening about your Pictish ways," he dismissed with impatience. "I

married an Ogilvie heiress, eh? Edward is Lord
Paramount of Scotland. His commands become law
by suzerainty. The Scots army is broken. All Scottish
nobles are either dead or made prisoner to the
Plantagenet."

"Or their loyalty is *bought* by English gold and es-
tates," she recklessly sneered. "Despite Edward
Longshanks's thoughts on the matter, Coinnleir
Wood is mine."

Challon offered her a fleeting smile. "Mistake
this not, my lady. I hold both glens through charter
from Edward. There is no changing this. Your
cousin—my lady—has come to terms with this, and
I believe she does not find her lot in life such a
hardship. Enough talk. I will see Lyonglen—now."

Aithinne tried to swallow, but could not. Her
throat was too dry. She struggled to keep her attention on Lord Challon, but her eyes kept straying to
Damian.

She steadied herself for the coming confrontation. "I am sorry, Lord Challon, you may not see Lyonglen. He is ill . . . gravely ill."

Damian's expression narrowed on her. "How ill?"

"Too ill to receive anyone. If you will explain the
situation to me, I will try to convey it so that he un-
derstands. I make no promises, mind." A reasonable offer considering she was unsure just how
much a man over two months in his grave would
listen.

"Lady Aithinne, I shall see Lyonglen. *Now*," Challon insisted.

Aithinne took a step back, glanced to Damian, but
saw his reflection was as implacable. She had hoped
they would accept her excuse and go away without
her having to drag out her arsenal of lies before
them. The more she told them, the less believable
they sounded even to her. Without thought she

backed up a step, then caught her cowardly retreat and straightened her spine. "I am Lady Lyonglen. I deal with all matters concerning the holding."

"Beg pardon?" Challon frowned, then glanced to Damian. "I understood you are lady of Coinnleir Wood—Lyonglen's ward, according to Tamlyn. You state you are now the Baroness Lyonglen as well?"

"Aye. Lyonglen's pennon does not fly from the rampart and our gates remain closed to all comers. I only permitted entrance to you and your men because you are now kinsman through marriage. My lord husband . . . feels unwell and wishes no visitors."

Damian's head jerked back, then he roared a question—an accusation—at her. "Husband?" This time she did back up as he started toward her, looking as if he could strangle her. Would *enjoy* strangling her! "*You* are my *grandmother*?"

Aithinne gaped. Surely, the man was mad. Utterly mad. Odd, she did not note the taint of lunacy before. Of course, with the spells and potions she had not witnessed him in a normal way. "You . . . you . . . think you are Lyonglen's *grandson*?" Shaking her head, she reeled. "Nay, my guard—husband had no children by his f-fi-first wife. Well, actually there was a child, a daughter—"

"My mother," he snapped.

Aithinne knew she must look a dolt, but she could not stop her head from going side-to-side in denial. "But she died years ago . . . nearly two score passing . . . same time as his lady wife, a dreadful fever that took many of Glen Eallach's people."

"My grandmother died of the wasting sickness. My mother recovered and lived. When she married my father—a Norman—Lyonglen disinherited her. He swore her name would be forevermore blotted from his life. Seems he kept that vow well."

"But . . . but . . . ." Heat flooded Aithinne's face

and the hall swirled about her as the enormity of his words hit her mind.

"I am the grandson of Gilchrist Fraser, Baron Lyonglen. Due to his age and infirmity, and in honor of their friendship, Edward Longshanks sends me to assume control of Lyonglen. I was granted charter here and am now the new Baron of Glen Eallach. He felt it would be—"

"Noooo!" Aithinne grabbed the back of the lord's chair and used it as a crutch to stay standing. The whole bloody world was pressing in on her. She had to suck air deeply to keep from tossing up the small amount of food in her stomach.

As if the enormity of Ravenhawke's announcement was not enough to swallow, a noise arose at the doorway leading to the kitchens. A monster comprised of three heads, six legs and six flaying arms tried to shove through the doorway.

"A beastie so terrible that Nessie would flee," Aithinne moaned.

Ravenhawke and Challon swung around to face the threat, their hand-and-a-half swords unsheathed and in their grips. Without word, they had moved to a position of protection before Aithinne, their backs to the other, showing they had fought in this manner many times before.

In mêlée fashion, the three young men tumbled into the room and then at the feet of the two imposing warriors. Finally aware of the situation, they glanced up at the Dragons of Challon, and for the first time comprehended the error in their entrance. Mouths open in shock, their eyes full of awe traveled up the warriors' long bodies to the gleaming swords raised in a position to strike.

On their heels, Einar came running in. Breathless, he fell to his knees before Aithinne and slammed his fist to his chest, then he intoned in his deep voice, "Beg pardon, Princess, they would not listen. You must come. There are men at the gates!"

Aithinne cringed, fearing even the strongest spells and Oona's dark potions would fail to blot out the memories of three lackwits who looked alike, and one equally distinctive moving mountain of a giant who called her Princess. "Can this day get any worse?" she muttered under her breath.

Damian rotated around to glower at Aithinne. One black brow arched. *"Princess?"*

"Och, the poor man is barmy." She tried to smile as she motioned for Einar to rise, whilst she moved to stand before her brothers. When he failed to do so, her foot reached out and surreptitiously kicked the Viking. Aithinne ignored Ravenhawke's challenge and focused her attention on her brothers. "More men? Pray who comes now to disrupt Lyonglen's peace?"

Deward looked at her as he struggled to rise. "Aithinne, Dinsmore—"

"Not again!" She threw up her hands in exasperation. "You know my orders concerning that knave—"

"Nay, Princess." Einar informed her, "This time he *demands* entrance, says he comes on the command of Edward Longshanks. By the English king's leave, we must open the gates and permit him to enter and to see Lyonglen."

Deward worried, "What shall we do?"

At the tides that Dinsmore Campbell came bearing orders from the English king, Challon and Ravenhawke exchanged silent questions. Damian gave a faint shake of his head, clearly telling his cousin he failed to believe Edward had sent Dinsmore Campbell.

A tightness filled Aithinne's chest as she stared at Ravenhawke, regretting so many things. Only it was too late. Way too late. Girding herself for the coming storm, she summoned the image of her cousin, Raven, to her mind and tried to wrap the same mien of regal coolness about her. She did not know what sort of bluff Campbell was putting forth, but there was only one way she could answer it.

"My lord husband is too unwell to receive men plying their pale aims . . ."

Hugh, straightening his clothing, gave Lewis's ribs the point of his elbow. "But, Sister, Dunny Dinsmore—"

For the first time, Lord Challon actually smiled. Lowering his sword, he chuckled. "Campbell's new name is rather fitting." His lack of respect for the man was clear in his words. He turned to Damian. "You rule here now. What say you? Shall the new Lord Lyonglen receive this pretender?"

The muscles in Ravenhawke's jaw flexed as he scowled at Aithinne. "Would your lord husband—"

Lewis blurted out, "Oh, but he's not really her hus—"

Both Deward and Hugh clamped a hand over Lewis' mouth stopping him from revealing that Aithinne had never married Gilchrist Fraser. Dizzy, fighting nausea, Aithinne could hardly concentrate on the new developments, let alone weigh their possible repercussions.

"Not really what, *Princess*?" Damian moved closer, his eyes noting her wan complexion.

She swallowed hard, backing up steps as St. Giles closed the space between them. "Not . . . really . . . really . . . well enough . . ."

Seeking aid to escape the man nearly stalking her around the end of the lord's table, she looked to Lord Challon. His expression reflected concern for her appearance as well. "Lady Aithinne, are you in poor health? You mention Lyonglen ailing. Are you so sorely afflicted, too?"

Aithinne yanked the lady's chair before her, a shield to stop St. Giles. She glanced from the angry man back to the Dragon. "I have been . . . *distressed* by matters of late, my lord."

"My lady!" The Captain of the Guard hurried in. "Beg pardon, but the Campbell is yelling if we do not open the gates and permit entrance, he shall battle his way in. He has a large force with him and swears he carries the might of the English king. I have ordered the curtain wall manned and all are at ready. What shall we do? It's clear he means to attack."

"Attack?" Aithinne gasped. "Why—"

She knew why. Dinsmore was suspicious about Lyonglen. No one had seen him for months. Rumors of his illness had been impossible to contain after the Scots king, John Balliol, raised his standard. A runner had come with word, demanding Gilchrist should rise to John's call and muster the garrison of men at Lyonglen. She had to give a reason why her guardian was unable to join the Scottish forces.

She feared giving no valid reason would make it appear he backed the English. That would leave Glen Eallach vulnerable to the Comyns to seize the holdings they had long coveted, punishment for Lyonglen appearing to support Longshanks. Had they not already done the same to Clan Bruce? Pressed and with few options, she had at first sent forth word that her guardian was too ill to lead his men for the Scottish Army. What a mistake! At the news that the elderly man was not in good health, both Phelan and Dinsmore came sniffing around, wanting to know just how ill the man was.

She knew both men saw Gilchrist's weakness as the opportunity they had waited for. Both had tried to gain entrance to Lyonglen, demanding to meet with the baron on urgent matters. Knaves, the lot of them! They only wanted to get in so they could seize her. Both had bragged, years before, that they would take Aithinne and force her to the marriage bed, their arrogant boasts reaching her ears.

With this fate looming before her, Gilchrist sadly drew his final, ragged breath as the first peacock butterfly came with the spring. His last wish had been for her to keep Lyonglen safe, away from both the Campbells and the Comyns, his final words, "Seek the way of the raven." With no other choice, she had concocted the "marriage."

At four and a score, she despaired she would never find a man she wanted to wed. She liked being lady of her holdings—if arrogant, greedy men would just leave her alone! With the "marriage," she could continue to control Lyonglen. The plans formed and her course set, doubts immediately intruded with word of the English crossing the borders.

Aithinne knew Edward Longshanks, the most ruthless king to ever sit on the English throne, wanted to possess Scotland—and would. Was not his stranglehold on Wales and Ireland a clear sign of the fate that lay before the Scots? Edward would marry her off as a prize to a noble loyal to him. However, if she were to get with child and claim the holdings as his birthright, maybe Edward would grant her leave to remain in Glen Eallach without the monarch forcing her into a loveless marriage.

Ravenhawke caught hold of the chair's arms, lifted it and used it to back her against the table, pinning her there, so she could not continue her retreat from him.

"Now, *Princess*, time for some truths from you— though I am coming to see you are unfamiliar with the notion."

The pale green-gray eyes bore into hers, holding her in thrall so she could not look away. All about her receded to near shadow as she could only see him. Images of their time together, his hands upon her breasts, his mouth, twisted within her. The wanting was a knife to her insides. She wondered what he thought about her, if his body recalled what his mind could not.

The fey eyes watched her, undressed her body in front of him, before moving back to lock gazes once more. Then he stripped her mind. Oddly, he said not a word, just watched her. The anger slowly shifted to a questioning, then surprise.

The long black lashes flew wide and Damian St. Giles uttered, "He is dead."

Panic surged within Aithinne. She had never run into a male with such powers. There was little doubt this man had been touched by the blood of the *Sidhe*. She had pondered this—feared this—before, only it made more sense now Aithinne knew his mother had been Scottish.

Made more sense . . . and was more treacherous.

Chapter Ten

With his powerful cousin at his side, Damian St. Giles stood upon Lyonglen's bastion, observing the two score men below. Campbell's array of troops of foot, archers, and hobelars—lightly armed and protected horse soldiers—was impressive, though typical of the Scots, a ragtag-looking bunch at best. Damian was surprised Dinsmore could raise such a large force after the English had crushed the Scottish army weeks before.

"Methinks not all Scots fought alongside of Red Comyn at the Battle of Dunbar," he commented to Julian. "Campbell assumes Lady Aithinne commands here, and thus with a hail of arrows, she would crumple to his feeble assault."

Julian smiled smugly. "Dunny Dinsmore has not counted on the Lords of Challon being in possession of the keep, eh?"

"Good thing we are." Damian's eyes swept down the row of men-at-arms along the wall, sizing up Lyonglen's guard. Many were past their fighting vim or flabby around the middle. "Overfed and not trained hard enough."

Julian crossed his arms over his chest and nodded at the evaluation. "It appears you have your

work cut out for you. Edward was right to send you
here. The position keeps it coveted by Clan Bruce,
the Comyns, and the Campbells. The fief, especially
when combined with Coinnleir Wood, is too big a
prize to leave under the hand of a weak lord—or a
lady, even though she is one of these warrior
women from Clan Ogilvie. With Glenrogha and
Kinmarch in my possession, Guillaume installed as
the new lord of Lochshane, and Simon taking command of Kinloch, Glen Shane is secure. By your
claiming Glen Eallach, Edward shall hold the heart
of the Highlands in his fist."

Damian glanced back to the men below. "You
mean the Dragons of Challon claim it."

Julian's war-seasoned knights and soldiery were
interspersed amongst Lyonglen's troops, on lend
until Damian could pull men from his smallholding in Parvon, Normandy. Though he knew his face
little showed recognition of the fact, he had taken
note of the wary Scots' eyes going to their lady to
see if she raised objection to the two English lords
assuming command. Witnessing Aithinne's acceptance of the situation, her men seemed to relax.
Once assured their lady gave approval, all looked to
Challon for orders.

Used to standing in the shadow of his powerful,
older cousin, Damian did not resent this. A mantle
of power few men ever achieved rode comfortably
on Julian's shoulders instantly, drawing the respect,
awe, and admiration of those around him. Julian
Challon was born to command. Men understood
and reacted to this instinctively.

"Begin as you shall go," Challon advised lowly.
The words carried only to Damian's ears, urging
him to step into the power as the new lord of Lyonglen before the soldiers fixed it in their minds to
look to the Dragon for direction.

"Aithinne! I know you are watching!" Wearing a supercilious smirk, the blond man at the head of the troops stood up in the stirrups of his saddle and shouted for all to hear. "Open the damn gates, Aithinne Ogilvie, or I command my archers let loose their arrows. I give you to a count of ten. Then . . ."

Aithinne tensed at the threat, but Damian reached out and touched her shoulder, lending backing. She seemed surprised, wary.

Stepping so he was visible between the merlons, Damian smiled. "And here I would have bet my gold spurs you could not count so high, Campbell."

The Scotsman's head snapped back and his eyes narrowed, squinting to see who mocked him. The man tried to keep the smile upon his face, but it was clear he was less than happy to spot Damian St. Giles standing on the boulevard. "I demand to see Aithinne Ogilvie. Assure myself she is safe. I come in the name of King Edward of England."

"The Lady Aithinne is protected—by Edward's command. You and five of your guard may enter the bailey. All tother remain outside. Agree to these terms or my men shall cut you down where you stand." Damian nodded to Challon's men to see his will carried out. Instantly, with unified precision, all the men along the wall stepped to the crenellations and presented their bows, arrows notched and targeted upon the Campbell force.

Dinsmore's affable expression remained plastered upon his face, despite understanding Castle Lyonglen was now under the command of an English lord. The dolt obviously decided to bluff it through. "Very well. Five it shall be, Lord Ravenhawke—though King Edward shall not be happy his messenger is greeted by such a reception."

Damian flashed a wicked grin, calling his challenge. "Aye, Edward shan't be." Lifting his hand, he signaled the portcullis raised and the bridge across the dry ditch lowered.

Aithinne waited until she saw Dinsmore and the five horsemen cross over the wooden bridge, under the murder-holes and into the bailey proper, before rounding on him. "You are letting him in? Why? He is—"

"A buffoon, a liar, and a knave." Damian whipped around to face her.

"Do not underestimate him, Lord Ravenhawke. Oft the lowliest, knavish cretin is the most dangerous man in the land, simply because they ken no honor," she countered hotly.

He glared at her, the woman claiming to be his grandmother by marriage. Why did he lack all belief in her tales? Or more precisely, was it he did not *want* to believe? Swallowing back all the questions bubbling within him, he asked, "And what of highborn ladies, *Princess*? Do they know the way of honor?"

Damian almost laughed when her mouth worked like a fish out of water. He had a feeling the Lady Aithinne was possessed of a glib tongue with a sharply honed edge, a woman used to having her way in all. For too long she had run roughshod over an old man, simple boys, and a silly Viking, he adjudged. Much to her consternation, she was now confronted with a man who would not dance to her tune.

"Cat got your tongue, my lady? Pity that."

Damian permitted his eyes to rove over her enchanting face, then slowly down to her full breasts, showcased in the tight bodice of the black gown. Crippling desire for her rolled through his body like thunder. Though less ornate, the kirtle was similar in style to the one Tamlyn had worn to marry Challon. But, as he stared at this flame-haired harridan, he had a hard time conjuring the image of the lady of Glenrogha to mind for comparison.

For that first breathless instant when Aithinne had stepped from the shadows in the Great Hall, he had assumed her to be Tamlyn. From that point on, his eyes only took stock of the differences. She was a bit taller than her cousin; her breasts, though slightly smaller, were full, firm, and high; her waist, more narrow. In the daylight, her hair shimmered. Though a shade near Tamlyn's, this heavy mass seemed kissed by faery fire.

He smiled inwardly at the faint dusting of freckles upon her nose.

Faced with the existence of Aithinne Ogilvie, Damian comprehended the blunder of his assumptions before. In error, he had seen Tamlyn's face and believed she was the woman who had haunted his visions. As he looked into the amber eyes flecked with the dark green—a shade similar to the stone she wore around her neck—eyes he could get lost in, he nearly forgot all around him. With an odd mix of feelings, he realized he stared into the face from his visions.

Only she was his grandmother!

How cruel were the Fates! He thought God laughed when he found Tamlyn only to discover she belonged to Julian. Now that he had unriddled the crux of his silly confusion, he was more perplexed than ever.

If Aithinne was not lying and had actually wed Gilchrist Fraser, then she would be forever more beyond his reach. The church would never consent to a marriage between them because of the degree of kinship. His grandmother! What a sick jest of destiny. He pushed away bile rolling through his stomach.

First to deal with Dinsmore. Then he would lay

claim to this Pictish *Princess*, even if he had to make
her his leman. She was his and he would own her—
in one manner or another. No man would ever
touch her again. He would kill any who dared try,
starting with this Campbell idiot.

Grabbing her upper arm, he tugged her toward
the tower stairs. "Come, Princess, we must hurry
to greet your ardent swain."

Aithinne rushed into the Great Hall with Ravenhawke right on her heels. She was leery of what
manner of farce the man intended to play with
Dinsmore, fearful he was not giving enough caution in permitting the Campbell threat inside the
curtain wall. She was not happy. Many oft deemed
Dinsmore as no threat, for when people peered
into those beady blue eyes, set too close together,
they assumed they dealt with a man missing the
wherewithal to be a hazard. More than once she
pondered if the stupid man was aware of his lack-
ings, and instead of trying to hide the defect, he
employed it to disarm others. They failed to see
him as a true menace simply due to his appearing
naught more than an overgrown child. Over the
years, Aithinne had seen that mistake cost men
unwise enough to accept Dinsmore on face value.
There was something off about the man. It made
her skin crawl.

"I do not ken who is the bigger fool," she raged,
"the fool or the fool who receives the fool. I have
struggled for several moons' passings to keep that
imbecile outside the pale of Lyonglen. And what do
you do as your first act as the *new* lord? You invite
the adder in. Of all the imbecilic actions! Go ahead
and cuddle the snake. When he bites you in the

.nroat, do not whinge to me about the mistake you make this day, Lord Ravenhawke."

"You, as a woman unable to command proper—"

In umbrage, she sucked air. "Not command proper? I will have you ken—"

St. Giles shrugged, unperturbed at the sharp edge of her tongue, and continued on as if she had not interrupted him, "—did well to keep the wolf outside the gate. I, on the other hand, do not labor under the same limitations as a female. Better to see Campbell and call his bluff. He lies. Edward sent me here to assume command. No one knew that outside of his privy council, especially not some low-ranking Scottish noble, who neither supported his own people nor came unto Edward's Peace. Now, Princess, I need a quick rundown of what has been happening here. By your words, I presume this is not the first appearance of this cretin at the gate. This past month he has been yapping and worrying at the hem of your gown, instead of fighting for either side in the war. Am I right?"

"Aye. He saw his chance to try and worm his way inside. The sun has never risen on the day that I would believe any of the lying words out of that pathetic excuse for a man's mouth."

Unnerved that he kept following her, Aithinne skirted around the table. She barely spared a glance to Lord Challon as he entered behind them and sat in the lady's chair, then leaned back and propped his heels on the edge of the table. Aithinne frowned at Tamlyn's mate. When he ignored her, she walked over and knocked his feet off the table. She saw St. Giles hide a chuckle behind his hand at her daring to chastise the great Black Dragon.

"I doubt Tamlyn permits such behavior at Glenrogha, Lord Dragon."

"You have feelings for this man?" Ravenhawke nearly growled, drawing her attention back to him.

In response, Aithinne could not stop the unlady-like snort from popping out. "Loathing, disgust, re-pugnance, revulsion, nausea, abhorrence—"

"Enough. I gather you hold a low opinion of the man. Something we share. Has he feelings toward you?"

Aithinne moved past his cousin, trying to remain ahead of St. Giles, just out of reach. The bloody man kept on stalking her. "Oh aye, greed for Ly-onglen, greed for Coinnleir Wood. The son of a shoat bragged he would steal me away, beget a bairn upon me, and be lord of these holdings. Before I permit that foul vermin to touch me I would rather slit my own throat."

Damian's powerful gaze narrowed on her. "Mayhap he lacks a comprehending that you have a taste for older men . . . *much older.*"

Aithinne swallowed hard, then shrugged as if she did not understand the meaning of his words. "Well, they do possess a more even temper."

Their discussion was halted as her three brothers rushed into the room in typical fashion. St. Giles observed the young men's antics of pushing and shoving, before turning to glare at her. "Are they always like this?"

She sensed rebuke in his question, her spine stiff-ening in response. She had tried, really she had. Just they seemed to go on as they pleased, her cor-rections on how young men should comport them-selves bouncing off their ears. "Mostly."

He frowned. "They are weaklings. Why are they not in training to be knights?"

"How dare you—"

The arrogant man cut her off again, barking at

the lads still struggling to seat themselves at the trestle table. "Enough! Sit!"

Aithinne was shocked when all three immediately did as commanded. So did Einar.

He turned his attention back to her, the incisive eyes fixing her with an intensity that made her look away, unable to meet the force. "Tell me—*Grannie*—is there aught else I should know about this Campbell? Is he aware my grandfather—*your lord husband*—is dead?" The way he stressed words bespoke he did not accept her lies at face value.

"Nay." She sighed. "The lackwit might cling to suspicions. He has been most persistent in trying to gain entrance. Mayhap he has deduced such and wishes to seize the holding before Edward passes it to some noble loyal to him."

She moved to the other side of Challon, hoping to use his presence as a shield. Only Ravenhawke reached past his cousin, catching her lower arm. She tugged against him, but his grip was firm.

"Come, Princess—"

"Release me, Lord Ravenhawke." She used *the voice,* only to discover it failed to have any reaction on this man. Even her brothers noticed, sniggering and elbowing each other. She glared at them silently chuckling at her predicament.

He spun her around to face him, the intensity of his eyes making her breath catch. "Do not dare the presumption to issue orders to me, *Princess.* You will do as I tell you, precisely as I tell you. I shall handle this greedy Campbell in my own way and pace. Know this, I will brook no interference from you. You follow my lead, do not speak unless I grant permission, and you remain by my side at all times. Is that understood?"

She started to open her mouth to protest, but

words failed. No man dared speak to her in this
manner. Ever.

He jerked her toward him so they were nearly
nose-to-nose. "I . . . am . . . understood?"

Aithinne's jaw muscles flexed as she kept the tor-
rent of words behind her teeth. Dealing with him
was going to be difficult enough without angering
him on smaller issues. "Aye, my lord."

"Why do I feel you say aye, but compliance is the
farthest thing from your mind? I warn you—
Grannie—play me false on this or undermine my
authority in any fashion before Campbell, you will
rue the day," he threatened.

Inside she quaked at the force of his promise, but
she refused to quail before him. "I have done nothing but rue the day since I laid eyes upon you, my
lord."

"Too late, my lady, you have made your bed and
now must . . ." He paused, the eyes searching her
face as if suddenly seeking an answer.

Lightheadedness filled her again, as she feared
once more the potions and spells had not done
their work or that the powers she sensed within left
saw him more resistant.

Einar distracted her by announcing, "They come,
my lord."

Ravenhawke shoved her to the left side of the
lord's chair and placed her right hand on the high
back. Changing his mind, he dropped that hand
and instead arranged her left one around the
amulet. "There. Do not move." He barely shoved
himself into the chair, slumped down and donned
an expression of ennui as Dinsmore was escorted
in. Casually, Damian reached for her wrist.

She steeled herself as Dinsmore's pale blue eyes
ran over Damian in the lord's chair and her standing by him. He pulled up short, as his gaze stopped

on the Dragon of Challon, sitting next to his cousin, his hand on Aithinne.

"Aithinne, what goes here?" Dinsmore queried.

Damian looked at the edge of his fingernails, then up to the Scotsman. "I did not pass leave for you to address my lady direct."

Dinsmore's hooded lids narrowed on St. Giles. "Aithinne and I are *old* friends."

"Do not address the Lady Aithinne by the familiar and only address her when I grant leave—"

"What is this, Aithinne? Is he holding you hostage? I want to see Lyonglen. Assure myself that these English curs are not holding you and him prisoner."

Damian's hand tightened over hers, giving it a small squeeze. "I would err on the side of caution, Campbell, and not hurl insults either at me—or my powerful cousin. I believe you know Julian Challon— the King's Champion."

Campbell had the sense to know he had pushed beyond the pale. "Beg pardon, Lord Challon. These times are trying. I am merely concerned the Lady Aithinne has come to no harm."

Damian motioned with his hand for the servant, entering with a pitcher of ale. "Your men surely would like drink after a thirsty ride?"

"Aye." Dinsmore looked to them and gave a short nod, granting leave to them. "Where is Lyonglen, I seek him on urgent business."

Damian's countenance expressed puzzlement. "Where?" He lifted his hand and turned his palm up. "Why . . . here. Where else would I be? Is this some silly riddle? I just saw Edward a fortnight ago. I thought we had settled all business at that time so I confess at some interest in this . . . *missive* you carry."

Worry flickering in the pale eyes, they shifted to

Aithinne, then to Challon, then back to Damian.
"Jest not with a simple Scots lad, Lord Ravenhawke.
I asked to see Lyonglen— Gilchrist Fraser. I wish to
make sure he fairs well. Rumors fly through the
countryside he ails."

"Flying rumors are about as reliable as flying horses,
I find. Though oft, there is a kernel of truth, too."
Damian's eyes went to the bread, cheese, and wine
being placed on the table. "I have been unwell. I
thank you for inquiring. Come, Aithinne, sit and eat."

Challon arose and offered her the lady's chair,
pulling up another so she sat between the two Englishmen. Aithinne forced herself to take sure, slow
steps since her stomach was jittery, unsure what sort
of slight of hand Damian St. Giles was attempting.
She watched as he sliced a wedge of cheese and
held it up for her.

"Come, my lady. The cheese is soft and tasty."
Lashing out with his foot, he kicked a bench in
Campbell's direction. "Sit. Join us."

Dinsmore hesitated watching both men, then finally sat upon the bench.

Damian pressed, "You should eat, Aithinne."

The thought of eating made her shudder. "I
would rather not, my lord. My stomach likes not
the idea of cheese."

He shrugged. "See . . . poor lass, she still ails after
all these weeks. I hope the bloody wasting illness
has kept away from your holdings, Dinsmore. The
only people around here that were not affected
with this strange malaise were the lads," he motioned to her brothers, "and their keeper. I am only
learning this morning of what sort of mischief they
had been up to while I was abed and am considering a suitable form of punishment for their antics.
Aithinne insists they are just high-spirited and in
need of a mien to vent their enthusiasm. Of course,

as the new lord here, I will be overseeing their training . . ."

The three heads turned toward Damian, but his glare soon had then looking down to the plates before them. Einar frowned, but kept his eyes on Ravenhawke, curious. Campbell wasn't so accepting of the news. He jumped to his feet, knocking over the bench.

"Enough of this prattle and farce. I demand to see Lyonglen. I came on a missive for Edward to assure he is well."

Damian leaned back. "Edward? Not King Edward, surely? He knows I am well and here carrying out his orders."

"Not you! Gilchrist Fraser," Dinsmore thundered as if he spoke to a half-wit.

Damian looked as if he just now understood what Dinsmore was on about. "Ah, you mean my grandfather—"

"Grandfather!" Dinsmore's face turned red from frustration. "Fraser has no grandchildren. Everyone kens this fact!"

He shifted to one side in the chair. "Actually, he did. My mother was Gilchrist's daughter. Of course, he was not pleased when she married a Norman knight and cut her out of his life. Howbeit, Edward was kind enough to see the charter to Lyonglen passed to me, instead of giving it to—"

"You!"

Damian closed his eyes and rubbed his forehead as if it pained him. "Do stop screaming all your responses, Campbell. I still feel unwell after this sickness. My head aches."

"What sort of mummery is this? Grandfather? Charter—"

Damian sniffed. "Not that I owe *you* explanation. After my grandfather died—"

"Died!"

Damian glared. "I will repeat once more—sit and use a civil tone or I shall have my men chuck you outside the pale. I *am* Lyonglen now. Edward granted me charter, as my birthright. I have assumed command. And all have been ailing here. End of my explanation—and my patience."

"Aithinne, what are these lies?" Dinsmore demanded. "What about the rumors of your marriage?"

"No lies, Campbell. Keep your tongue in your mouth or risk losing it." He lifted Aithinne's hand to his mouth. "I am Lyonglen. Aithinne is my lady. And you have worn out your well-come."

Mouth agape, Aithinne stared at the new lord of Lyonglen as though sure he was insane.

Chapter Eleven

Aithinne rushed into the bedroom—her old room, out of habit—and straight for the chamber pot. There wasn't anything on her stomach, thus all she managed to do was wretch. Fortunately the pot was clean! It would have been the last straw. She tried to choke back the nausea, but just as she thought it was controlled, her entire being pitched and rolled. Finally, dragging herself to the urn with water, she cupped a little in the palm of her hand and drank, then poured the rest into the basin and splashed it on her face.

Feeling a bit more stable, she paced. As worries pressed in on her mind, panic arose. To counter, she hit her forehead with the palm of her hand, allowing the pain to offset the growing anxiety. Under normal circumstances the knocks should hurt. "This day, they feel rather well-come. Stupid! Stupid! Stupid! I am cursed! Doomed! The Auld Ones use me for sport! I give them jests with this brainless muddle I have gotten into. OONA! Blasted woman, where are you? Could anything be any more convoluted than this situation? His grandson! The whole time I plotted and planned, trying to keep Lyonglen from the Campbells,

Comyns, and Bruces . . . Gilchrist had a grandson! Och, of all the—OONA!"

Aithinne, I have no heir. You, and you alone, can save Lyonglen, protect our people. Gilchrist had spoken those words over and over to her whilst he faded away, growing weaker each day.

The elder Gilchrist Fraser had been so kind to her and her brothers after they lost their parents to the wasting fever, taking them in and affording them the protection of being their guardian. To learn he had a child, and totally cut his lady daughter from his life, caused her to view the old man she had loved and admired in a different light. It was hard to reconcile he had turned his back on his daughter and the son she bore, to the point he had denied their very existence to all. Never would she have thought the Lyonglen she knew capable of such cold-heartedness. The image was upsetting to Aithinne, and set her to think her life was built upon dark lies.

"OONA!"

The woman finally floated in. Oft, the crone did not seem to walk as other people, but glided from spot to spot. Not in the mood for those witch's tricks, Aithinne wanted answers.

"You kenned there was a grandson?" she accused.

Oonanne ignored her and set about to mix a potion. Pouring water into the cup, she stirred it and then held it out to Aithinne. "Drink this. It holds the power to ease your troubled mind."

"Death shall ease my troubled mind! Then I shan't be plagued by three third-wit brothers, a childlike Viking, and an old woman who hides things from me. Do you have any idea in what a bloody mess my life finds itself? Ravenhawke—the man who was in my bed—is the new lord here now."

Oona sighed and held out the cup. "You overset yourself. 'Tis not good for the bairn. Drink."

"Child?" Aithinne had nearly forgotten about the babe she carried, so distressed by Dinsmore, a Dragon, and his bloody cousin. She clutched her mid-section and moaned.

"Och, stop this fashing and down this, Aithinne Ogilvie." Oona employed the tone a mother would in speaking to a child.

Frowning at the bothersome female, Aithinne snatched up the cup and gulped the foul brew. "Blllckkkkk—that is dreadful." She glared at the dregs in the bottom. "I hope this potion works better than the ones you fed Ravenhawke." She fixed Oona with an accusing glare. "I have this sinking sensation he remembers. Oh, merciful heaven, what if he remembers? Were the tansies not strong enough? Did your crafting of the spell fail? Have your powers weakened, old woman? Och, what am I to do? Answer me!"

Oona shrugged, seemingly unbothered by the whole situation. "Change what you can. Accept what you cannot, lass."

"Oh, like I could not riddle that much out myself." She paused and put her hands on her hips. "You kenned about Gilchrist's daughter."

"Aye. Most of Glen Eallach here about two score years ago likely recall the lass. A lovely eyeful she was, much in the image of the *maither*. The old man was not right in the head after the fever claimed his lady wife. Then when he presented the daughter at English court, she eloped with a Norman knight, after the baron refused permission for them to marry. He seemed to die even more inside. His heart withered. He was good to you and the lads, but he never opened himself to loving and losing again. He forbad her name to be spoken at Lyon-

glen. I think she tried to send word a couple times,
asking to see him. He refused. She had chosen her
path, he said; she was forevermore dead to him.
After a few seasons no word came of her ever again.
I never kenned about the grandson. Mayhap that
was her purpose for trying to reach the old man—
giving him tides of the babe's coming."

Aithinne exhaled, "What of the kenning? Surely
this is something you should have foreseen? Why
did you not suss who he was from the very start?"

"As one touched by the blood of the *Sidhe*, you
ken often images are not clear. Visions are true, but
we mere mortals can oft read their meaning wrong.
His aura was mixed, confused by his life threads
being intertwined by Lord Challon's. This man has
the power. It must have come through his mother."

"Could his Scots fey blood see him more resistant
to your spells?"

"Mayhap. This warrior is potent in ways I have
never seen in a male. Both of these men of Challon
are too much alike to understand the dreams and
visions. Too different in the same breath. I warned
you to be careful for what you wished. You wanted
a child. You have one. In seven moons' passings you
will hold that babe. A son. Much like his father. He
will see that, Aithinne; ken you used his body for
your own gain, even if his mind does not recall it
all. One way or t'other he will understand when he
sees the child."

"Oh, I wish—"

"No more wishes, lass! We have more than
enough of your wishes to deal with!"

Damian stood on the bastion, watching the
Campbell men ride away from Lyonglen. "Fair

speed and never darken our keep again, eh?" he muttered.

The wind had shifted, rising off Loch Eallach, swirling about him with ghostly, playful hands that ruffled the locks of his thick hair. The smell of rain was heavy in the air, the knowledge enforced by the gathering storm clouds looming over the passes. A thunderstorm would soon hit. Likely a strong one. He would welcome its power, the force when it broke, embrace the fury.

"Mayhap Campbell will get a thorough drenching soon," Challon commented with a smile. He turned dark green eyes to study Damian, too perceptive by half. "Wish to talk about it?"

Leaning into the crenellation, Damian allowed the wind to buffet his face. Inside, his emotions were jumbled. He was not sure where to start to unravel them. Being moody and, like most men, not particularly fond of articulating problems, reactions, or perceptions, Damian preferred to brood. He knew Julian had questions. Bloody hell, *he* had questions. Perversely, with no immediate answers before him, it was simpler to give into the need for silence.

"Not particularly."

Challon nodded. "I am sure the Lady Aithinne's resemblance to Tamlyn confuses you and—"

"The two favor one another. Despite, I see their differences more than the similarities. A lot of people look at you and I, and think we are mirror images. Not so."

"We are two men with Challon traits," Julian concurred, "yet dissimilar by whom life has made us."

Nodding, Damian forced a grin. "Aye, I am taller . . . and prettier." At the words, the chuckle died before it escaped his chest. *I am taller . . . and prettier.* One of those odd echoes of déjà vu which haunted him since his return to Glenrogha.

"What troubles you?" Challon noticed his reaction and was curious by the sudden change.

Damian tried to pull in the peculiar instant sticking in his craw, pick it apart until he understood what it meant. The moment of time remained elusive. "I am not sure. I need to think upon it more. Things, words, images hover at the edge of my thoughts."

Challon rubbed his thumb over his chin. "Guillaume mentioned you shared drinks with three young men who looked alike and that they had a huge man at their back, just before you vanished on Beltane."

Near perfect, just what is needed, eh? Once more, words echoed within Damian's head. Damn frustrating. "Did Guillaume say more?"

"Only that you were drinking with the four, then later you were gone. So were they. I doubt finding another set of men fitting that description, eh?" Challon paused and then looked out in the direction toward Glen Shane. "I miss Tamlyn. I should have brought her, but I was not sure what sort of resistance we might run into with the Scots stragglers from Dunbar still hiding in the hills, or what we would find here. I am pleased your stepping into the role as baron of this glen is being done with little disturbance. The sooner everything is settled, the sooner I am back at Glenrogha with Tamlyn."

"I am sorry this matter took you away from your lady," Damian said, for the first time not experiencing the taste of deep regret Tamlyn was not his. "She is good for you, Julian. Never let Edward know how he blessed you with this marriage."

"This I know well." He patted Damian on the shoulder. "I go now to see that Pagan is settled in the stable, then to sup. You come? It has been a long day for us both. More unsettling for you though, eh?"

"I shall catch up with you later. For a spell, I would like to walk the length of the bastion, absorb this holding is now mine." The concept was still too new to him. He wanted to savor his first impressions as lord of the holding.

"Then I leave you to your brooding and thoughts of the Lady Aithinne."

Damian offered him a half-smile. "Why do you assume I shall think upon the lady?"

Challon chuckled and then walked away, shaking his head.

Welcoming the solitude, Damian slowly strode along the boulevard, trying to grasp that this glen and the fortress truly belonged to him now. He was lord of Lyonglen. It was a rich holding, land his by right of birth as well by favor of Edward. Only, it would take time to feel at home here. Usually far-seeing in his aims in life, he suddenly felt oddly adrift. He had served Julian, as Earl of Challon after Lord Michael died. Served too many years, too many battles to count. Challon had given him the smallholding of Parvon as a reward. Too busy, ever the warrior protecting Julian's back, he had rarely stayed there, thus felt no roots to that fief. Could not care less if he ever saw it again.

Here in Glen Eallach there was the chance to build a future. The time had finally come to settle down, marry, raise a family.

Those musings conjured Aithinne's face to mind. Did she tell the truth about wedding his grandfather just before the old man's death? If she had, it wasn't to gain money and position. As baroness of Coinnleir Wood, her title and lands easily were equal to Lyonglen's. Why then would she weave this fable of now being baroness of Lyonglen? More to the point, why had he let Campbell believe she was his lady wife?

"Possession," he hissed under his breath. "Like some dog hiking its leg, I wanted to mark her as my property and did not stop to think. Damned if—"

A scream split the storm-darkened landscape. He turned the corner, hand going to the hilt of his sword. His eyes looked out over the wall, trying to see where the call of distress came from. Only silence greeted him. Just as he began to wonder if he dreamt it, the plaintive squeal suddenly rose again.

Only this time, his mind experienced some sort of slippage. He had heard the same screams before. Only when? Where?

One of the guards on regular patrol came around the opposite corner. He nodded in deference. "Good eve, my lord. 'Tis only the peacocks. Fool birds sound like a woman being strangled."

Damian finally spied the ridiculous peafowl streaking across the pale after the peahen. As he stood watching, the landscape from this angle evoked a familiar chord within him. The soldier moved on, but Damian paid little heed as he pinpointed how the scenery was different, why this should seem so memorable when he had never seen it before. Feeling as if it were part of a dream, he spun around and looked upward behind him. The North Tower dominated the fortress, a giant sentinel of the glen. Anyone approaching Lyonglen could be easily spotted from up there.

He leaned his hips back against the crenellations, then stretched out his legs, crossing them at the ankles. His right hand rubbed the back of his neck as he contemplated the tower. Not sure why he felt compelled to it, he pushed off the wall and started into the fortress as lightning cracked, followed by the deep roll of thunder.

His mood was almost summoning the storm to break overhead.

Rounding the turn of the first floor, he hesitated at the stairs curving upward. Damian was unsure what drew him. Nothing familiar about the winding staircase. Nothing causing that echo in his memory as the view from outside had. Urgency to see the tower drew him forward, propelled him to take the stairs two at a time.

At the pinnacle he came to a stop, facing the long hallway that ended in the huge black-oak door. Closed. His hand on the latch, he could almost envision the room in his mind's eyes. Without bothering to knock, he shoved it open.

Mixed emotions filled him as he stood, his eyes taking in the richly furnished room. A fire burned lowly in the huge fireplace, with bearskin rugs before it and again on the floor by the bed. The large wood-canopied bed had plaid curtains of red, which were tied back, long drapes nearly covering the heavy, ornate bedposts. A wolf-pelt cover was folded cross the foot of the thick mattress. A bed fit for a king. The sense of disquiet rising, he leaned against the post, trying to isolate images crowding in on his mind. This room seemed so familiar, yet different.

Going to the large fireplace, he plucked a long straw from the broom propped there and lit the tip from the flames of the peat fire. He walked back to the table by bedside, and used the straw on the wick of the candles. Once there was more light, he studied the bed more closely. *Her bed.*

On impulse he knelt by the foot post, running his fingers over the base. A shiver crawled up his spine as he felt the gashes in the wood. Marks gouged all around the circular post.

"One thing for certain, I am not dreaming these."

* * *

"Are the rooms readied for the Lord Ravenhawke and the Lord Challon?" Aithinne inquired of the maidservant as the woman carried in fresh linens.

The graying woman nodded. "Aye, my lady. All was prepared as you asked. Rooms for both lords are waiting for them. Fresh water is in the urns, and I am just taking in linens—"

"Aithinne!" Deward came running down the darkened hallway, then jumped as a clap of thunder rattled the fortress's stone walls. "You must come, Sister. The man . . . he goes to the room."

"What man?" Aithinne knew that question was a waste of breath.

There was only one *man* and only one *room*. She merely did not want to believe it. She had hoped by placing both Challon and Ravenhawke in the South Tower that the new lord of Lyonglen would stay far away from the other tower for the time being. It was obvious that since Ravenhawke would be living here, this bridge would be crossed sooner or later. Aithinne just preferred that it be later . . . *much later*.

"Of course, nothing ever goes as I would will it. Why should I expect aught different in this?" She exhaled her frustration, her fears.

With rising dread, she grabbed the sides of her kirtle, lifting it so she could hurry her steps. At the top of the staircase she drew up short upon seeing the half-opened door and the flickering light at the end of the hall instead of expected darkness. She knew he awaited her. Like a coward she could turn and flee, claim being unwell—the truth. Nonetheless, she realized it was merely a matter of putting off the coming confrontation. He wanted answers—about his grandfather—possibly about the memories fighting to surface.

Aithinne dithered before the threshold, taking a deep breath to still her pounding heart. Wasted effort. There was no being at ease around Damian St. Giles. Pushing the door open the rest of the way, she froze. She thought she had prepared herself to face this man alone, but she had not anticipated seeing him in her bed again. It brought back all her feeling for him, all her vulnerability. All the need.

He had lit several candles, lending the room a warm glow, and casting his sinful body in half-light. Arrogant man was sitting up, his back to the headboard, his right leg casually bent and crossed over the other. One black curl fell over his forehead in a mussed, little boy fashion, but there was nothing boyish about this man. Everything about him called to the woman in her.

"The lord's chamber has been readied for your possession, my lord." She tried to keep her voice level as she entered the room.

He shrugged. "I rather like it here. It feels comfortable . . . familiar."

"The tower is currently my quarters, but if you would rather stay here than in the master chamber—" She half turned as if going to make arrangements.

"Come here." He watched her with a curious expression. "Come here, Aithinne. I mislike yelling across the room to have a simple discussion."

"'Tis not proper. You are half unclothed, my lord."

Damian's eyes ran down the length of his bare chest, the long legs encased in the leathern hose and to his bare feet, as if he just noticed his state. "Aye, I am." The lids over the pale eyes lowered to a hooded expression, one that was lethal. "Lady Aithinne, I gave you an order, in a polite fashion, yes, but I still expect it to be carried out. *Come . . . here.*"

Sucking up false courage, she started to step away from the door only to have him add, "Close the door—then come here."

Aithinne held still, her hand on the door almost afraid to release it. Before this day, she could not recall any man ever giving her orders. Her father had been a gentle soul, never commanding his daughter do this or that. Gilchrist never corrected her, never issued edicts for Aithinne to follow. She had always been in control—of her life, of her brothers. This morning began with the Dragon of Challon demanding the gates be opened. Now his too-comely cousin was being deliberately provoking, issuing instructions, merely to remind her she now had to obey him as the new Lord Lyonglen.

"Aithinne, I am in a peculiar mood this night. Do not present me with a reason to let loose the poison boiling inside my mind. You shan't enjoy it." The slow rise and fall of his chest showed he drew measured breaths, clearly an effort to control his violent emotions.

Deciding his caution was worth heeding, she closed the door and crossed the room. He said nothing, just stared at her. Outside, the lightning cracked close, making her jump, though she noticed he did not even bat an eyelash. On edge, she glanced at the arrow loop to the flickering streaks of light from the spring thunderstorm, then back to the dominating male in her bed.

He had been there before, but this was a different side of Damian St. Giles. The potions had soothed the warrior's nature, letting the gentleness in his soul come to the forefront. Now the warrior ruled, and she judged his nature to be as wild and untamed as the tempest outside. She knew so much about him, yet he was truly a stranger. For a fleeting time she had held a shard of this powerful, fascinating man. Only now she realized how little she knew about him.

Odd to have given herself to him, surrendered to his caresses, taken him inside her body. In this breath she comprehended how unfamiliar she was about his tempers, his moods, or the manner in which he handled people and situations. On the surface he appeared calm, relaxed. A fool might accept that. She was no fool. Ravenhawke scared her.

In her life she had dealt with Gilchrist, three brothers that were vexing but little more, a frustratingly obtuse Viking, and greedy men who sought to use her. Not once had she ever feared one as she did this man. And it was not a fear that bespoke a concern he might harm her. She knew gut deep this man would never hurt her, never beat her or raise hand to her. His power was more terrifying. Damian St. Giles held the prerogative to destroy her world, and reform it to his whims, the power to crush her heart.

She had to get away from him before it was too late. "In the morn my brothers and I shall return to Coinnleir Wood—"

"I did not grant leave, Princess. You go nowhere without it," he snapped, steel in his voice.

The flatness of his statement disarmed her. Her stomach tightened, though she felt reasonably certain she controlled her outward reaction. "I did not ask permission, Lord Ravenhawke. I am baroness—"

"My charter from Edward is for Glen Eallach. That includes Coinnleir Wood." He smiled, but it lacked true mirth. "Since I am overlord of your holding, you need to seek my permission for all you do, Princess." The gray-green eyes watched her, almost seeming to glow with triumph as he witnessed her struggling to rein in her temper. "You do not care for the situation. You will earn your place now."

"My place?" Heat flooded her face and her fingers curled in fists at her side. "And pray just what is my *place*, my lord?"

He remained motionless, like a big cat intent on watching its prey. "That remains for me to decide, dependent upon the truths I uncover about you, Aithinne. Mark this. You are mine to do with as I please. And at this moment I would please a lot."

"Mayhap . . . we should continue this discussion another time . . ." The storm was worsening outside, but it was nothing compared to the one she saw in his fey eyes. Breaking away from the stare that ripped into her mind, she turned on her heels and started to leave.

"I did not dismiss you, Princess," he called after her. When she continued walking, he threatened, "Do not make me come get you. I will."

His tone saw her halt. She believed he would do just that, almost feared that he wanted her to force the issue. She tried to steady herself, but her heart kept up the unsteady rocking, made worse by her body's traitorous response to him on an animalistic level. Her breasts were tight, swollen, sensitive. Oona said the child was causing some of this, her body accepting his life within her. But her nights with Damian St. Giles had taught her about the small changes in her due to wanting him.

At this moment, she was close to hating him. No man dared order her about like some common serving wench. She did not trust him, frightened what his presence in her life now meant, terrified of the repercussions if he discovered her deceit. That little stemmed her body's craving for him. It took all her willpower not to go to him, put her hands on that hard belly and slide them up his chest, to take his mouth in a bruising kiss, taste him as she had every night in her dreams since she let him go.

"Aithinne, come here."

Thought barely more than a whisper, she knew better than to defy him. Swallowing to moisten the dryness in her throat, she walked back to the bed to face the arrogant man.

"Your wish is my command." Her tone conveyed it was anything but.

The corner of his sensual mouth quirked up. "Take your clothes off, Aithinne."

She tried to weigh his mood. Was he testing her? Did he mean it? "Go to perdition, Lord Ravenhawke."

The small muscles in his jaw flexed, rising to the challenge. "It is not just my wish, Princess, it is my command. Take . . . off . . . your . . . clothes."

A tremble rippled through her. She fought to keep from slapping that smug expression off his much-too-beautiful face, held tight against the part of her that wanted to do precisely as he demanded. The wanting rose in her, thrummed in her blood to where her body felt on fire. She never knew this drive existed within her before. Was not sure she liked it now. Only the emotions were overpowering to the point she could barely think.

Only want him.

He shifted, swinging his long legs to the floor, rising so his lean, hard body was close, too close. Aithinne's mind screamed for her to run before it was too late. Somewhere inside her she accepted it was already too late. This man held her in thrall. He placed his hand on the flesh just below her neck, fingers splaying as he stroked up her throat. His thumb caressed her jaw, and then his palm agonizingly dragged down the expanse of skin to the edge of her bodice into the cleavage. Her breasts already sensitive, almost strained upward to meet his touch, wanting it to go lower.

The expression in the hooded eyes said he knew her weakness, that he held the supremacy. All she could do was stand and tremble. And want.

"Your flesh is cool, Aithinne . . . so soft . . . so very soft."

He skimmed his hand up to her throat and then down, over and over, each time a little lower. Her breathing hitched as she wanted his hand on her breasts, each inhale pushing the crests up, almost offering them, praying his pass would move to her stiff nipples.

Finally, the rough fingers grazed over the pebbled peak, drawing a ragged breath from her. Arcs of lightning crashed about the tower; the fury of the storm seemed to feed off their rising passion. One finger flicked back and forth, as her body echoed the lighting within her flesh. His caress grew rougher as his finger and thumb tweaked the nipple, increasing the pressure as he saw it spiraled her need for him.

Finally he shoved the bodice off her shoulders, exposing her breasts to the cool air. Damian sucked in a breath and held it as his burning eyes watched both his hands cup her pale flesh. Brushing his thumbs back and forth he whispered in near awe, "Tell me to stop, Aithinne."

"Stop, my lord."

"Tomorrow . . . tomorrow I will stop."

His mouth found hers, kissing her savagely, as the tower shook from the power of the storm surrounding them, as they shook from the power of the storm within.

Chapter Twelve

Damian fell crossways on the plain of the bed, Aithinne half under him. He relished the feel of pinning her with his weight, surrendered to the animalistic mating instincts surging in his blood, controlling his actions. The lightning's white brilliance flooded the room through the arrow loop, bathed Aithinne's enchanting beauty with its eerie glow. Driving him to madness. Damian stared, ensorcelled by this pagan goddess offered up, half-naked before his hungry eyes. Her full breasts were so pale, the nipples tight and jutting. Every aspect of all his dreams conjured to life.

Now this moment was here, that he knew she was real, he was suddenly scared spitless. But Damian St. Giles was never one to back away from a challenge.

Threads of déjà vu wove through this instant in time, echoes of dreams which had haunted his life surfaced in his mind, overlaying each touch, each sensation. Yet, they seemed more than mere visions. These feelings seemed rooted in reality, as if he had actually lain with her before. In a manner of familiarity only lovers possess, his body seemed to know hers, what touch would make her gasp, what would bring a sigh to her lips.

He had not intended to push the situation to this end. His mood perverse, he'd merely set out to provoke her, bring her to heel. The need to possess this woman, to mark her as his, was a demon riding him with spurs, driving him to treat her in a fashion not worthy of a lady highborn. Rules, manners, expected codes of conduct, simply went to blue blazes when balanced with his primeval need to claim her. At this point, all the questions hovering around her, even conventions of God and king mattered little. He would do what he must to own her.

He took her mouth, gently at first, basking in the pounding she set loose in his blood, then savagely, kissing her as though he were a drowning man . . . and only she could offer him salvation. He smiled in the kiss as her fingers bit into the muscles of his arms, hanging on. It was precisely the reaction he wanted from her.

In the morning he would face the damnable riddles of Aithinne's life, decide some immediate course of action. This night, he needed to be close to her, feel his flesh against hers, taste her, hold her, be inside her. Before anything else intruded upon their world, he was determined to bind Aithinne to him, ensure she knew they belonged together no matter what.

Brand her so she'd never let another man touch her.

He chained kisses down her neck, as his hands moved on her, pushing the kirtle down over her hips. She shivered. He felt the small frisson crawl over her skin, under his mouth. He savored it. He desperately wanted to draw this out, revel in every magical moment, only the need to mate thundered through his body, exorcising control and any hope of reason.

Her breath sucked in on a sharp inhale as he

glided his hands up, cupping the weight of her breasts. His thumbs brushed circles around her sandy-colored areolas, then across the stiff peaks of her nipples that protruded more with each stroke. Her body was so quick to react. Aithinne gave herself up to him, open to all he would show her. His groin cramped in a surge of white-hot need when he took one breast into his mouth, drawing hard, laving his tongue against the tiny bud.

Pulling back to gasp for air, he muttered, "Responsive wench," as his thumb circled the ruched areola, wet from where his mouth had been.

Her raspy sigh of delight empowered him. As she closed her eyes, he stopped toying, took the nub between his finger and thumb and gave it a light pinch, then rolled it. Her hips bucked against him, but not in pain. Too lost to the sensual vibrating in her blood, he led her along the razor-edge of desire, pushed her arousal another notch higher.

He raised up slightly to unlace the front of his breeches, then grinned as her shaking hands eagerly helped him slide them and his braies off his tensed hips. Again, the thought intruded that she was too keen, her movements too sure, though not in the practiced art of a wanton, merely in the manner of a woman who holds secret knowledge of how to pleasure her man. More questions, but ones that paled when his hands took hold of her rounded hips

Aithinne drew a ragged breath as he glided over her body, his mouth catching the sensitive lobe of her ear. He sucked on it, his tongue swirled around it, teasing, tormenting, while his knee pushed between her soft thighs, opening her for his blunt invasion. Her body bowed against him, feeding the fire of wanting within him until his insides twisted. His need for this woman was devastating, humbling.

He was claiming her in the most elemental way.

But as he stared into the amber eyes, with their rings of green flecks, he suddenly understood it was she who was claiming his heart, his soul. Their coming together was meant to be, foretold in his visions. The longing he felt for Aithinne went deeper than the flesh, reached to his timeless soul, touching him in a shattering way as no woman had before. The way no woman ever would. Only Aithinne.

The minx was a liar, he was certain of it. The smile crossed his lips and he felt every measure the predator. He would ferret out the truths from her, expose all her darkest secrets, and take his own time in doing it.

He wanted to touch her. His hand snaked up the inside of her silken thigh, brushed over her soft nest of curls, nearly growling as his finger slid into the liquid heat. Her narrow channel was tight, but accepted his finger as he delved deep into that scalding heat, then her inner walls clenched around it, wanting the friction. She made a raspy sound in the back of her throat that sent a shudder through his tensed muscles.

He relished his hard body pressing her into the mattress, wanted her soft hands clutching the arch of his spine as he entered her. Later he planned to set her over him and show her how to control the pace. He wanted inside her now.

First . . . the thud of his heart slammed against her thigh as he glided downward. Then his mouth moved on her—her burning core. At first her hand shoved against his shoulder as if resisting, but soon her sharp nails scored his flesh as she wanted more. Incapable of thought, he drowned in the blinding pleasure, the rough lap of his tongue against her moist flesh.

Gasping to draw air, she splintered into a thousand pieces, coming against his mouth. Barely able to hold back, he pushed up on his knees and then into her with a solid, sure thrust, setting her to keen loudly, until he closed his mouth over hers, catching her pleasure and making it his. His pelvis slammed against hers, over and over, in a near violent force. Some shard of him worried he might terrify her until he felt her hips lift to meet his, their bodies moving apart and coming together in a beautiful dance of passion, of love.

Lightning streaked upward through his flesh, hitting his brain, and then magnifying downward to slam into his groin. His body bucked, his seed pouring into her welcoming heat. His possession was complete. She was his. Would forevermore be his.

Barely able to remain conscious, he tried to keep his weight from crushing her by rolling to the side and pulling her against him.

"Mine," he whispered the brand against her hair, feeling a peace he hadn't known before. A peace of finally finding home.

Before stepping from the fortress, Aithinne paused to pull up the deep hood of her mantle about her face. A shiver crawled over her skin, though it had little to do with the heavy morning fog that blanketed the whole area. The reaction came from the distinct sensation she was being watched. Glancing around the bailey she saw no movement; it was still too early for even the servants to be up and about, as she hoped. She wanted to be halfway to Coinnleir Wood before anyone noticed her absence.

Her stomach pitched again, but she suspected it was from fear, not the morning sickness coming due to the bairn. With a sigh, she hurried her steps toward the stable at the far end of the courtyard.

As she entered, she hesitated to look back across the bailey, expecting to see someone tracking her actions.

"Guilt eating at my soul," she muttered under her breath.

Several horses murmured throaty welcomes as she silently moved down the long row in the deep shadows. They came to hang their heads over their stall doors to get pats, Aithinne touched their cool velvety noses as she passed. The last stall—the biggest one—had one of the outside double-doors open, letting in the gray light.

A tall, young man stood brushing a magnificent black destrier, whilst speaking in low soothing tones to the restless animal. She had to blink, as the beautiful lad bore the clear stamp of Challon in his features. Same black, wavy hair, same near perfection of face. She estimated him to be the age of a squire, still too young for knighthood, but soon another Challon male to steal the hearts of unwise lasses. She smiled.

As if sensing her presence, he glanced up and then nodded in deference. "Good morrow, my lady."

She noted the stallion was the one the Dragon had ridden yesterday. "You are with Lord Challon?"

"Aye, I am his squire, Moffet. Is there aught I may aid you with? Shall I call the stableman?" He looked around, obviously finding it peculiar she was alone at this hour.

She offered a reassuring smile to the angelic lad. "Nay, do not bother to call him. I am merely going for my morning ride. Please do not let me take you from your chores, Squire Moffet." She started to turn, but hesitated, curiosity biting. "How do you like serving the lady of Glenrogha?"

Tamlyn MacShane was a gentle woman in most

matters. Aithinne wondered if the gentleness would extend to her lord husband's squire who was very obviously his bastard son. If the situations were reversed, she was not sure how she would react to her husband having a son by another woman. Still, the lad exuded such a charming openness on his expression that she could not help but warm to him. It was not his fault, the nature of his birth.

"The Lady Tamlyn is patient with me, kind." The full lips parted in a smile, showing his reply came from the heart. "She fusses at my Lord . . . but in a nice way . . . you understand? He fusses back, too, but she just says 'yes, Challon' or 'no, Challon' and then does what she wants. The earl does not know what to do with her ways. He grins a lot though. 'Tis good to see my lord happy again. He has been sad for too long."

Aithinne nodded, taking the bridle for her mount off the hook. "Sounds like our Tamlyn. I would be too fearful to say yes or no to the Dragon and then ignore his wishes. He seems a more fearsome warrior. These men of Challon warm to giving orders."

"My lady," once again the young man looked around, "do you not take a guard with you on your ride? Lord Challon is concerned about the men wandering the hills since the great battle at Dunbar. Troops under the standard of Ravenhawke were attacked. My father would not be pleased that you plan to go out alone—"

"No, he would not."

Aithinne jumped at St. Giles voice. He stood holding his sword in a casual grip, though she did not mistake the negligent mien as a reflection of his mood. Wearing naught but the leathern hose and a simple white sark, which rode loosely on his square shoulders; the wavy hair was rumpled. He looked half asleep—and angry. In a casual movement he leaned the sword, tip down, against the wooden wall.

St. Giles came forward with slow stalking steps, halting a few paces away from her, and just stared at her with those pale unearthly eyes. Eyes that saw too much. Accusing eyes. "Going somewhere, *Princess?*"

Aithinne swallowed hard, wanting to back up, but there was no place to go as the stall's door was at her back. She decided to bluff it through. "I ride each morn. I find it helps me face the day and all its problems."

"I informed you last night I did not grant you leave to return to Coinnleir Wood, Princess. You go nowhere without it," he stated with an implacable force that set Aithinne's temper to spiraling.

Sensing the dark undercurrent of emotions, Moffet glanced nervously to Aithinne and then back to Damian. "I told her you would not want her to go out alone—"

Aithinne gasped, "You said your father—"

"Aye," he nodded, his green eyes shifting to St. Giles, almost wary as if he was not sure he should have spoken up.

She backed up a step, her spine bumping against the stall door. "Father?"

Damian glared at her coldly, almost daring her to react wrongly, then reached over and loosely hugged the boy's shoulder. In an affectionate manner he ruffled the back of Moffet's hair. "Aithinne, this is my handsome son, Maromme—though my mother called him Moffet and it stuck. A Scottish name, I believe. He is fortunate to be in training as a squire to Challon, though I would very much liked to have handled his education myself. Moffet, make your pretty to the Lady Aithinne, Baroness of Coinnleir Wood."

The lad smiled shyly and he gave her a small bow.

"She looks like the Lady Tamlyn, Father, though her eyes are more green."

Aithinne tried to control her reactions. She already warmed to the gentle lad, but knowing he was Damian's son sent a hot poison through her, to the point of being so painful she wanted to double up and cry. It was silly, but she felt betrayed. Ashamed of such thoughts, she misliked the reaction. Though it was beyond her understanding or control, she hurt knowing this child was a product of his passion with another woman. Thoughts flew through her head as she tried to grasp some degree of sophistication at learning this boy was Damian's.

"Yes . . . I wouldst imagine being a squire to the Black Dragon of Challon is an envied position. I . . . I am sure you serve your lord proudly, Squire Moffet."

Damian's grasp tightened about the boy, then hugged him to his side. "Go seek your breakfast ere you begin all these chores. I know Challon does not expect you up at the crack of dawn and without nourishment."

The young man paused. "Merry part, Lady Aithinne."

Aithinne forced a smile for the innocent lad. "Merry part, Moffet."

Picking up the sword, Damian laid the flat of the blade back against his shoulder and watched the lad walking away. Aithinne sensed he was waiting for her to say something, nevertheless, she judged this was a time when it would be best to keep the words behind her teeth. Jealousy, for it could be none tother, burned within her to the point where she could hardly think straight. Was he married? Had he a lady wife somewhere? Or was Moffet a merry-be-got, a child of some castle worker somewhere or a leman? Did he plan to install her here at

Lyonglen? Her cheeks burned, pain too much for her to sort out. All she could think of was finding some place dark and quiet and have a lie down before having to think things through.

"Naught to say, Aithinne?"

She licked her lips and then tried to don a false face. There was little use, she feared; those damnable eyes seemed to rip away the lies she was building for protection. "He . . . he is a . . . handsome lad."

"Aye, hearts will be broken as he comes of age." He nodded, love clear on his face. "He makes me feel very old, Aithinne. He grows too fast. Already his voice is cracking. He is damn near as tall as Challon. A few more moons' passings and he will look me in the eye on the same level. I am not prepared to be a father of a grown man."

"You and . . . your . . . lady wife must be very proud of him."

"I am proud. I have no wife, lady or otherwise, Aithinne, and you know it." His gaze skimmed over the hooded mantle. "You were planning on going to Coinnleir Wood. Why?"

She tried to step past him, unable to handle this confrontation when she was so shaky inside. Taking hold of her arm, he spun her around to face him. His anger stilled as his hand slowly lifted to push back the hood of the mantle, then gentle stroked down her hair as he lifted the loose braid out.

"Sorry, Princess. Your life has changed. You go nowhere without my permission. Same with your brothers. You are under my protection now—"

"Protection? Imprisonment sounds a better name for it, Lord Ravenhawke."

He shrugged. "Not so, yet it little matters. This is what will be."

"You do not own me, my lord. You think because I obeyed your commands last night—"

He grabbed her and pulled her against him, to where his mouth hovered over hers, his stare challenging her, possessing her. "Own you, Aithinne? Aye, I do. Get used to it. We have a lot of things to get settled, a lot of your lies to cut through—"

"Lies!" She tried to jerk back. "How dare—"

"I dare much, Aithinne. For you, I will likely have to defy God and king, so save the high dudgeon. For now you shall take my arm, and with a smile on your face, we shall stroll back into the castle or by damn, I will take you right here, up against the stall door—and I care little who sees." His grin was unrepentantly wicked. "For my choice, I prefer the latter, but I am trying to be nice."

Jerking away from him, Aithinne stomped off without another word. His mocking chuckle sounded softly behind her.

"I thought you might take that option." His long strides quickly had him walking beside her. "Are you not going to ask me about Moffet? I saw the questions racing through your mind. You are a very easy person to know, Aithinne. All your emotions are there on your beautiful face."

Curse his black head! Why did he have to say that? Oh, yes, she was beautiful, but not as beautiful as her cousin Tamlyn. Had she not heard the refrain all her life? Her throat hurt as the tears welled up, but she was damned if she would let him see how affected she was by his words. She sniffed. "Good, then you know what I am thinking now, My Lord Arrogant."

"Hmm . . . I think that sobriquet is a hint." He reached out and caught her arm to slow her pace. "I thought perhaps after we break our fast you would show me around the fortress, introduce me to the villeins and serfs. I should like to get to know them a bit ere I call for them to kneel to me in

fealty. I need to work to secure Glen Eallach. I think
you comprehend the many forces that would seek
to use this valley."

Aithinne nearly stubbed her toe, as her eyes
locked with his. Reality intruded that this situation
was more than just her and her pride; it was the
people here in this glen and in her holding. All
looked to her to see that life continued in a safe
fashion. Being their lady carried a heavy burden,
she knew well, that had driven her to desperate
measures to get with child. Had she not wished for
a strong man to help ease the load she carried?

If only he did not love Tamlyn. How wonderful it
would have been if he came to Glen Eallach
yestereve and they met for the first time. None of
her lies and deceits between them. If only . . .

Aithinne muttered under her breath to herself,
"Nay, I swear off wishes. Hobgoblins to trouble the
mind."

"What is that you say, lass?" he leaned toward her
with a smirk.

She frowned at him. "Just you never mind, Lord
Big Ears."

Damian shrugged, taking no insult. "Aye, I am arrogant and have big ears . . ." he glanced down at
his groin, then added, " . . . and big—"

"Och, you certainly have not learnt any manners—"

"Feet," he finished. "Well, since you think it un-
mannerly to speak of the sum of my body parts,
how about you ask about Moffet instead. You know
you are chafe to do so."

She picked up the sides of her mantle to keep it
from dragging in a puddle. " 'Tis hardly my concern."

"And when did that ever stop a woman from
meddling?"

At the steps to the castle, she turned to face him.
"And you Dragons of Challon ken all about women,

do you not? They fall in your beds at the drop of a kerchief—"

"You did."

She couldn't look away, as they both recalled how in the wee hours of the night she had surrendered all and asked nothing in return. How if she was not very careful she would find him in her bed again and with no more willpower to resist him than before.

Knowing this was not safe banter, she figured discussing Moffet was less risky, despite the reactions within her heart. "Very well, my lord . . ."

"What, no My Lord Arrogant, or My Lord Big Ears, even My Lord Big—"

She interrupted because the expression on his face said he was not going to say feet this time. "Tell me about your son. I see love in your eyes when you watch him."

"Aye, you do. I am very proud of the lad. It hurt like the blazes when I turned him over to Challon—"

Aithinne followed him up the steps leading to the bastion. "Then why did you? I think that is the saddest thing, for a mother or father to send the sons and daughter to be raised in another household."

"Is that why you failed to send your brothers away?" he queried as they reached the boulevard proper and began to slowly stroll along the walkway of the wall that surrounded the inner bailey.

Aithinne's spine tensed as she sensed the coming rebuke from a warrior born and trained, so ingrained in that way of life that he sent his son from him to train with the best, a man who would see no way other. "I lost my parents to a terrible fever. I did not want to lose my brothers. I did not want them trained for war, to ride out and kill or be killed. I did not want them to be made into killers."

"Is that how you see me, Aithinne?" Damian whipped around to see her full-faced for the answer. "A killer."

Under those probing green eyes, she stepped backward. "I know men go to war, sometimes *have* to go to war . . . I just did not want my brothers to be warriors."

"You made them weaklings, Aithinne—"

She exhausted her fury. "They are gentle souls—"

"My son is a gentle soul. He is learning the way of manhood from one of the greatest warriors England or Scotland has ever seen. Challon will show him the way to survive in this world and by being the squire, then knight of the Black Dragon, he will secure a place in these isles where he mayhap will not have to fight and kill. But if the time comes when he needs to protect himself or those he loves, he will be able to do so. It might mean the difference between his life or death. I want him to have those tools in his hands."

Aithinne was unused to people criticizing her choices. She had been chatelaine to both fortresses and people did her bidding. Outside of Gilchrist, there had been none of rank to dare upbraid her in the manner Damian St. Giles just had done. Her pride stung.

"I would prefer we not discuss my brothers," was all she could summon.

His brows lifted in challenge. "Very well. We will not discuss them . . . now."

Ignoring him, she started to walk again. "Moffet's mother . . . you were wed?"

"Nay." He paused by a crenellation to stare out across the glen. "I was very young. Of course, I did not think so then. She was a maidservant at Castle Challon. Being young, arrogant, and foolish—and thinking with my nether regions—I assumed she loved me."

Aithinne was unsure she wanted to hear his love for another. Damian being with this other woman was a knife to her guts. Still, she was not one to shy away from the truths where this man was concerned. It only helped her to ken what a mistake last night had been.

"Did you love her?" She watched this beautiful warrior, the breeze stirring the dark locks, locks kissed with the hint of Celtic fire, blood from his mother. Emotions swamped her: loathing for this faceless woman who had given him such a beautiful son; rage at him for daring to share with another what they had shared last night.

"In the hot bliss of youth I fancied I did. She was so beautiful I hurt just to look at her. You have to be a man full grown before you understand what love really is, how it is so much more than the passion of flesh."

A gust of wind kicked up, stirring the thick *haar* about the grounds like restless, earthbound ghosts of the ancient Picts. The coolness of the fog went to her bone. *More than the passion of the flesh.* More than what they had. She suddenly felt very, very tired.

She heard herself ask, as if the words were spoken by another, "What happened to her? Is she still alive?"

"Aye. I hear she is doing well. She wed the man she loved. They have several children."

She swallowed back the bile rising within her, fighting the tears clogging her throat. "That is well, I suppose. What I asked about . . . was what happened betwixt you and her."

He sighed. "My secret, Aithinne. I shall have your word on this. Challon knows, but none tother. I would prefer Moffet never learns the circumstances of his birth. Aye, he kens he is bastard born, but then several men of Challon have borne the bar sinister upon their shields, so 'tis no shame to my son. Challon and I will see he marries well, he will become a knight, a powerful one some day. No one will dare look down their noses at the most favored knight of the Black Dragon, the grandson of Gilchrist Lyonglen. Your word, Aithinne. I tell you and then we shall never speak of it again."

She nodded. "I give my word, Lord Ravenhawke. I like your son and would wish him no harm."

"Damian." When she looked confused, he smiled. "I ask you to call me Damian. I wouldst have us be friends, Aithinne."

Friends? Oh, aye, he would offer her friendship, and in the depth of night take her body because she was so like Tamlyn. Friends? Why did that make her want to break down and cry?

Instead of railing at him for wasting his love on another, she nodded. "Damian, I give my oath."

"Anya was a couple summers older than I. Already she was in love with her woodsman, but she wanted something better in life. She bartered her body, later my son, to gain that. She deliberately seduced me, fully intended me to get her with child. Once she was heavy with that babe she told me about her loving another. He would wed her, but he did not want to raise a bastard of mine. That much suited me. This child was mine. Bear the taint of bastardy he might, but the blood of Lyonglen, the blood of Challon flowed through him. He was not going to be raised as some baseborn villein. I think she must have sensed this possessiveness within me. She saw the child as a tool. She would sell him to me for gold and silver, enough to give her and the woodsman a much better lot in life than they could have achieved on their own." Lines bracketed his mouth as he frowned, anger, pain, betrayal etched deeply in his expression. "I bought my child, Aithinne. Spent a small fortune in Anya's eyes. The price I paid was damn cheap. He is worth every pence, a hundred times over. I would die to save him. I came out of this Devil's bargain with the real thing of value—my son."

The tears she had been struggling against filled her eyes at the love he spoke of. She sympathized with his feelings of betrayal.

Moreover, she reeled as though she had been slapped as she comprehended how grave was the wrong she had done this man in having her brothers ply him with drink and then dump him in her bed. She, too, had used him to get with child. While her reasons mayhap were less mercenary than gaining coin, she had sought to use his body, his seed to get with child, hoping to use the child as a tool to keep her freedom and to protect Lyonglen.

She knew with a sinking feeling that one day this man would look at her with the same resentment, mayhap worse, as he now displayed in speaking of Anya.

God in merciful heaven! What had she done?

Chapter Thirteen

Damian turned to frown at Aithinne's brothers. They needed frowning at. Gad, six and ten years of age, yet they held the swords as if they were gripping adders. He feared he had a task ahead of him trying to turn these milksops into men. He liked them, despite their annoying eccentricities. Hugh and Lewis had the habit of finishing each other's thoughts, whilst Deward's talk never seemed to stop. Listening to him made Damian want to gasp for a breath somewhere in his long recitations.

He suppressed a smile at their disgruntled expressions. Upon learning they were now to spend the mornings training on the lists, they ran to hide behind Aithinne's skirts, begging for her to intercede. The lady of Coinnleir Wood had not warmed to the reality that she no longer had final say in matters at Lyonglen, especially where her precious brothers were concerned.

"Swords do not bite. Get a firm grip on them or this will happen—" Damian swung his weapon with all his might against Hugh's, the blades clanging together.

Since Hugh's hold on the pommel was too loose and far back on the hilt, all the vibrations of metal-meeting-metal traveled up the sword and straight into his arm and shoulder. The poor lad tried to keep his grip, but the blade clattered from his hand.

Damian extended his arm and leveled his blade tip to the young man's heart, staring down the gleaming steel at him. "That is how easily you can die in battle." He almost laughed when Hugh swallowed hard.

Unfortunately the lesson was lost on Lewis. He immediately held up the sword before his face, examining the blade. "This groove . . . what's it for? I heard tell it was to let the blood of the victim flow freely once you pierce his body. Is that so, Lord Ravenhawke?"

"Ugh." Deward shuddered and turned so pale, Damian feared he might faint.

Damian sighed and lowered his weapon. "The groove is to let the sword be strong, yet lighten its weight. Blood does not need help to flow. So, it's not a blood-gutter."

Deward's Adam's apple bobbed as a green tinge filled his cheeks. "I do not think . . . I want to do this, they can just kill me and have done with it."

Rolling his eyes in disgust, Damian collected the swords. "Swords require strength, which you lads have not developed. Can you even hold a lance?" He handed Lewis one of the practice lances from the rack. Lewis and the lance hit the ground as he went down on his knees. "Forget the lance and tilting for now. Have you had *any* training?"

Hugh brightened and grinned. "We are very good with our staffs."

Damian could not help the chuckle that rumbled in his chest. He had a feeling Aithinne's brothers were not any better at swiving the lasses than they were at the art of warfare. "Ah, I let that pass without comment." He took up the long poles and tossed one to a brother.

"Why does he chuckle at the notion?" Totally perplexed, Hugh turned to his brothers.

Lewis sniggered and poked Hugh in the belly with the end of the wooden staff. "Methinks, Sir Brother Nodcock, he is jesting at our expense, meaning our manroots."

Damian lost it, "Manroots? *Man . . . roots?*"

He was laughing so hard, tears came to his eyes. A mistake. The three faces suddenly turned fox-sly. Exchanging a silent communication, they shrugged, then came at him at once. Damian took a blow from Deward on the right thigh, Lewis caught him on the hip, though Damian did manage to deflect Hugh's swing. But as he had cautioned them with the sword, a warrior needs a firm, well-placed grip or the vibration from the blow to the weapon would travel up his arms, making it hard to hold—which is precisely what happened as he countered the well-aimed strike from Hugh. Since he lacked a good grip, his shoulders absorbed the impact to the point they tingled and grew faintly numb. Raising an eyebrow in reassessment, Damian decided Hugh had some strength after all.

Determined to give them a setdown, he changed the positions of his hands to deal with these rascals better. Even so, he had to admit they were actually rather good when they worked as a single mind. Worse, they labored in conjunction with each other, like some pack of small dogs nipping at your heels. They timed their attacks, keeping him busy countering their thrusts.

Gradually, the vexing Scots shifted, circling to come at him from all directions at once. Deward jabbed the back of Damian's right knee, causing his stance to buckle. Next, Hugh managed an on-target swing so he was forced to counter with his staff raised. That permitted Lewis to deliver a jolt straight to his stomach, too close to the groin for comfort. Had Damien been able to flex his stomach muscles, he could have absorbed the blow well enough, but being as it was lower, male panic kicked in and he flinched. Seizing the opening, Hugh knocked the staff out of Damian's hands, then Lewis and Deward shoved at the back of his knees whilst Hugh used his pole as a lever between his ankles. In one, two, three, the lads had him down—Deward's knee immmobilizing his right arm, Lewis applying his weight to the left, leaving Hugh to triumphantly sit crossways on his thighs.

"Never underestimate the Devil's spawn," Damian cursed under his breath.

His mind spun and suddenly he was lightheaded, though it had nothing to do with losing this skirmish to the lads. Rather, it was one of those odd flashes of déjà vu, as though he had already done this same thing with Aithinne's brothers. The echo was so strong, he closed his eyes and tried to cast his mind into the image, for once grab the shards of the dream. He could almost see it, wrestling with Aithinne, her brothers, and the Viking. The face of the old crone floated before his eyes.

Cosh him once more and I will take the chamber pot to you and it won't be empty.

With the words the whole scene vanished from his mind with a pop, the vision once more gone. He gritted his teeth in frustration.

Opening his eyes, he stared at the three grinning faces. More than willing to take advantage and catch them off guard, he asked, "You wish to explain why Aithinne is lying to me?"

Their smug expressions disappeared. Deward and Lewis both looked to Hugh for silent guidance.

Any hope of gaining answers vanished as Aithinne came rushing into the practice yard.

"What are you doing to my brothers?" Hands on her hips, she glared at Damian, still pinned on the ground. Her frown said she considered him similar to some sort of slimy creature found at the bottom of a cesspit.

Damian turned his head to look at each brother in turn. "I am teaching them a valuable lesson by forcing them to hold me down. I would think that obvious, Princess."

They sniggered, but she huffed exasperation, then tapped her foot in impatience. "Get off him, you dolts. Of all the stupid imbeciles, cork-for-brains, gorked—"

"Gorked? I will have you know, sister, we were wide awake," Lewis complained.

"—asinine, chicken-brained—"

Deward rolled his eyes. "Aithinne tends to rattle on, calling us names all the time, though I am unsure how we can have chicken brains and cork for brains in the same breath."

Damian rose and dusted the mud from this clothing, whilst his eyes skimmed over the frowning woman. He could not resist the taunt. "Aithinne does seem the excitable sort."

"Aye, 'tis true, but Oona says it is worse now because of the ba—" Deward cut his sentence off, turning white then beet red under Aithinne's withering glare.

"—bad temper and freckles," Hugh finished for his brother.

Aithinne's head whipped around. Damian felt sure Hugh was relieved his sister did not have a knife in her hand, for she looked ready to cut out his liver. Damian turned his attention to Deward, observing him. Hugh finished Lewis's thoughts.

Lewis would end sentences for Hugh. Only Deward went on and on. This was the first time either of his brothers had finished for Deward.

"Sorry," Hugh offered, seeming to shrink away from her. Bending over to pick up the staff, he then half-whispered to Damian, "She hates for anyone to notice her freckles."

"You lads may run along and partake the noontide meal. We shall start anew come morning." Replacing the weapons and motioning for his squire to return them to the armory, Damian ignored Aithinne.

Her expression thunderous, she rounded on him once the others were out of eyeshot. "I thought I made it clear, Lord Arrogant, that I do not wish my brothers trained as killers."

He sheathed his sword and adjusted the baldric about his hips. "And I thought it clear you have no say in the matter. I am lord here now and I will not stand by whilst you keep the lads as childish milksops."

She looked about as if seeking one of the staffs to take to him. "OOOooooo, you—"

"The lads are right—you do have freckles and a temper." He reached out and tapped her nose once for each pale freckle.

Oh, did she have a temper! Aithinne drew back and made to slap him—hard. Fortunately, he had good reflexes and caught her wrist before the flat of her palm hit his face. He used the grip to jerk her close.

"Do not ever mistake, Aithinne, to hit me. I shan't ever hit you, so I expect the same respect from you in return. Try it again, you will find yourself turned over my knee and I will use my hand on your bare bottom. Of course, there are some who find that a pleasurable pastime. Care to find out?"

To his shock, she suddenly burst into tears, staring at him with so much hurt in those hazel eyes, his heart squeezed. Her mouth opened, then closed, as though unable to put into words the sentiment she wished to express. Instead, she spun on her heels and fled.

"Bloody hell," Damian growled, watching her retreating back. "Females and tears. Bane of a male's orderly existence."

After the noon meal, rain had begun to fall again, the dark moody day reflecting Damian's melancholia. He stood in the small clearing in the woods, next to the spot where his grandfather had been buried, not really sure what he should be feeling. He never knew the man. To the old baron, Damian's mother and he did not exist. He wanted nothing of them. Anger burned bright within Damian at that slight. He had seen bastards treated with more respect. As he had grown up in the household of Michael Challon, he had been aware that Guillaume and Simon were treated with the same respect as Julian. They were sons of Challon, and though bastardy tainted their birth, they were never deemed as unwanted or unwelcome in the vast Challon holdings. Yet, while his birth was of high nobility, Damian always felt as if he were the true bastard. Simply because an old man denied the marriage of his parents, denied his very right to exist.

He was not sure why that troubled him so. Many times he had reflected on the matter, hoping to set right how he thought about it. He had hoped to meet his grandsire, find some measure of peace with this issue that haunted him. Now the old man was dead. Damian was left with an emptiness, an indefinable sorrow. Surely, he should feel naught toward someone who begrudged his very life. Oddly, as he stared at the mounded earth with the stone stacked on top of it, he was sad, left with questions and thoughts of what might have been had he returned sooner.

He heard her silent steps approach off to his right, though he feigned ignorance of her presence. The subject of Aithinne Ogilvie and her precise status in his grandfather's life was at best touchy. Thus far, he had avoided this issue, convinced she lied about being Baroness Lyonglen. For the present, it mattered little. She would not let go of the pretence easily and there was too much to do to secure the fortress. Fighting with her was not the way to go. He needed Aithinne's support to earn the deference and trust of the villeins and serfs of Glen Eallach.

She remained quiet for several breaths, as if unwilling to break his solitude. Finally she held out a hand-sized rock to him. He glanced at it, touched by the gesture.

"We add a stone to a grave each time we visit. Lets them ken we remember them, keep them safe in our memories," she explained.

He stared at the stone for a moment and then accepted it. Leaning over, he carefully placed the stone at the center of the pile. Frowning, he noted there were bones of one or more small animals there. "Some sort of sacrifice?" he asked, puzzled.

"Och, not a'tall. Oddly, cats seek out the stones to sit upon. I guess they are warm, holding the sun's heat. They drag in rabbits and such, their supper."

Damian closed his eyes and lifted his face to the rain, allowing the mist to fall upon his countenance. Part of him was pleased she had come, cared enough to bring him the rock to add to the cairn. The other part was faintly irritated because her presence brought all those damnable questions he was in no mood to face just now.

"What sort of man was he?" he finally asked, opening his eyes.

She was so beautiful, standing so solemnly, tears in her eyes. Why did he think the tears were for him, not Gilchrist Fraser? Her dark green woolen mantle, trimmed in black wolf fur, framed her haunting face. Flashes of images of her naked above him in the moonlight, riding him as she found her power as a woman, surged in his blood. He would like nothing better than to lay her down on this cool earth and bury himself in the hot magic of her sweet body. Instead, he had asked to know about the man who was his grandsire.

"I once thought him the gentlest soul. He became our guardian after my mother and father had been lost to the dread fever that hit several glens." She pulled her mantle, blocking the chill of the rain, the chill of the memories. "Then I learnt how he cut his only daughter from his life. That makes me wonder how well I really knew him. He spoke of me being like a daughter to him. Had I wanted to marry against his wishes I suppose he could have turned his back on me in similar fashion. I cannot imagine having no worries about those I love—are they well? Are they safe? The act seems too heartless. It makes me fear my whole life was built on a foundation of lies."

She recognized as soon as she spoke the words the trap she has just stepped into. The green streaks in her widening eyes seemed more pronounced, as she regretted using the word *lies*.

The side of his mouth quirked up in a taunt. "They say confession is good for the soul, Aithinne. Want to tell me about your *marriage*?"

She drew herself up and glared at him, every inch a princess. "I save all urges to confess myself for my Uncle Malcolm, the *Culdee* at Kinmarch Kirk."

"Princess Aithinne!" The Viking came running up, fell to his knees before her and thumped his heart with his fist. "Riders come."

"Einar, up off your knees." Aithinne rolled her eyes. "By the bones of saints and sinners, not Dinsmore again?"

"Nay, Princess. The pennon is argent, with a bend azure and three golden garbs—'Tis Phelan Comyn," Einar informed her.

A small kernel of irritation bloomed within Damian's mind. "Another of your suitors, *Princess*?"

She swallowed hard at his tone, the expression in her eyes hurt, wary. "At one time, I considered him such. Now I am smart enough to see I am but a pawn in the game of power he plays with Dinsmore and the Bruces. All men want this glen. The easiest way—they think—is through me. I long ago grew determined not to permit these clans to use me for their means to pale ends. The Bruces desire a stronger foothold in these Highlands. The Comyns and Campbells work to see they don't get it. Both would hold the advantage over the other if they got their greedy hands on Lyonglen. Robbie Bruce finally married Isabella, the daughter of Donald, Earl of Mar last year, so Dinsmore and Phelan think they have a clear field now in reaching me."

He made a dismissive pass of his hand. "Einar, carry word to the guard that I come."

The Viking looked to Aithinne to see if she wished it so and did not move until she gave him a faint nod, granting him leave. As the man rose, he gave a slight bow of deference—to Aithinne—and turned to go.

"Einar," Damian called after him. "From this

point forward, when I give you an order—obey it. You do not look to the Lady Aithinne for commands. Is that understood?"

The big man nodded. "All of Lyonglen is under your command, Lord Ravenhawke. Only I am not part of Lyonglen. I am the personal honor guard to the Princess Aithinne. I serve her. Only her. My homage is to her."

Damian took a step forward, only to have Aithinne catch his arm to restrain him with her gentle touch. "Einar, from now on you accept orders from Lord Ravenhawke. He is lord here now. I am sure he will not give you any instructions that will be counter to my good."

"Aye, Princess." Hesitation was in the pale blue eyes as he looked at Aithinne.

She kept the pressure on Damian's forearm until Einar was gone. "I was not countering you, Damian, but I have spent nearly ten summers trying to change Einar's charge. I cannot even get him to stop calling me Princess in all these years."

Damian placed his hand over hers about his arm. "Very well, Princess. Let us go offer well-come to your suitor."

Julian Challon was seated at the lord's table, once again his legs were crossed at the ankles and propped up on the table. As he saw Athinne approaching with his cousin, he arched a black eyebrow at her and dropped his feet to the floor. She suppressed a smile, recalling Moffet saying how Tamlyn said yes or no to this powerful warrior and then did as she pleased. She wondered if it was that easy for her cousin to handle her Dragon in this fashion, pondered if that should be the tact she took with Damian.

Sadness filled her. Tamlyn might be able to get away with such behavior, but it was because Lord Challon was in love with her. Aithinne did not have such a hold over St. Giles.

"We proceed as before, Aithinne. You do not speak to this man. Allow me to address the issues. You only answer him if I grant leave," Damian instructed.

Aithinne pursed her mouth, resenting the handling. "I am accustomed to speaking for myself, Lord Ravenhawke; I have spoken for all in this glen for nearly half of my life."

"Now I do so and you look to me for leadership, Princess." He almost shoved her in the lady's chair and then took his seat, as the double doors were opened.

Phelan Comyn marched in, three of his men at his back. His scheming blue eyes quickly took stock of both Challon and Ravenhawke. They passed over Aithinne, but she noticed there was no lingering to take in details. As she told Damian, Phelan's real interest was in possessing Glen Eallach, not her.

Phelan was still a handsome man in Aithinne's eyes, nearly as handsome as St. Giles, only his virility paled when compared to that of the men of Challon. A force vital pulsed from these Norman warriors, a presence so dominating few men could stand comparison without coming up short in the eyes of the beholder. Not just their physical beauty, there was the strength from within that shone through their green eyes, an air of being born to rule. All accepted this as a natural order of things.

Aithinne saw Phelan recognized this, too. A flicker of question, of fear of these English Dragons, passed through his eyes before he blinked to guise his unease. "I see it is so . . . Lyonglen is riddled with dragons. I thought Dinsmore had lost

what little wit he was born with when tales reached
my stronghold of a grandson of Gilchrist assuming
title and land here, when the whole area kens the
old man had no family."

Damian's faint lift of his brow said he barely toler-
ated Phelan's ill-chosen comment. "Dinsmore—
never the brightest ray on the horizon." He leaned
back in the chair and slumped down with an expression of boredom. "At least you have the wherewith-
all not to march in here with some cock-and-bull
story of coming on a missive from Edward."

Phelan chuckled, but it sounded tight, forced.
"Not one of his wisest moves."

"So you have heard the tides of my assuming title
here—yet did not fully believe them as you thought
Lyonglen had no heir. Wrong. My mother was Lyonglen's daughter. She married a Norman knight.
I squired for Lord Michael Challon, now serve his
son Julian." He exhaled slight impatience, and then
steeped his fingers. "There is my history . . . not that
I felt the need to give it. I just figured to save all the
questions."

Phelan gave a half-hearted smile. "Possibly some.
Howbeit there were other concerns raised. Mind,
Dinsmore and I have concern for Aithinne, being
she is a neighbor and lacking protection—"

"Lacking protection? I fear you are mistaken in
this. Glen Eallach was given to me to hold by
Edward. Since Dunbar, I think he demonstrates he
now rules this land, not your king, John Balliol. It
is but a matter of time until Balliol surrenders. Already Challon holds Glen Shane, has married the
Lady Tamlyn. I give fealty to him as overlord of
Glen Eallach. All's well and happy, eh?"

"Except for tales where Dinsmore says that
Aithinne married Gilchrist—" Phelan was like a
dog with a bone and not about to let go easily.

"The Lady Aithinne," Damian corrected.

Phelan looked confused. "Beg pardon?"

"As you should. I amended your reference to my lady. She is *Lady* Aithinne. You referred to her in the familiar. I have not granted leave for this." Damian reached over and picked up her hand, toying with her fingers in a clear move of possession.

Phelan began again, "As you wish. Dinsmore sent word that the Lady Aithinne had married Lyonglen—"

"I am Lyonglen." Damian looked up at the servant setting down the goblet and pouring wine. "Shall you join us? 'Tis good French wine and not the dregs from last summer."

Aithinne stormed back and forth across the solar, so upset she could barely think. She felt she might start rattling and never stop. Stopping before fireside, she contemplated how she could have muddled up her life any worse. St. Giles was Gilchrist's grandson, she carried his babe, and if he found out about her tricks and deceits then he would loathe her as he did Moffet's mother. Now, the arrogant man almost taunted Phelan to go to Edward with his suspicions.

"'*I am Lyonglen,*'" she said in a high voice mocking Damian. Tossing another brick of peat into the hearth, added, "Aye, *he* is Lyonglen. Stupid, stupid, stupid man."

"All men are that way."

Aithinne jumped, clutching the amulet hanging before her breast, trying to still her heart. "Oona, one day you will appear out of thin air like that and scare me to death. I sent for you ages ago."

Oona smiled knowingly, coming to place her

hand on Aithinne's chest just to feel the thudding of her heart. You are in a bother."

"A *bother*? You do like to state the obvious in mild tones." Aithinne flung her hands in the air, helpless to see a way out of her situation. "That man is Gilchrist's grandson. He's in love with Tamlyn—"

"He was not in *her* bed last night, now was he, lass?" Oona pointed out shrewdly.

Aithinne closed her eyes, fighting against the tears. "Oh aye, he will take me. In the shadows he can pretend it's Tamlyn. He shan't see seven bloody freckles on my nose to remind him."

Oona reached up and pushed the hair away from the side of her face. "Only you worry about those bloody dots. They have faded—"

"Faded? He tapped each and every one today. He sees them. Bloody things may as well be warts." Despair was near overwhelming. "I am taller, not as curvy and I have this horrid shade of red to my hair."

"Och, lass, your emotions run high because of the babe. The first weeks always are full of tears. Everything seems so out of control. Ride this out, sweet child. All this will smooth out in the coming weeks. Then you will wonder why you were so distressed about freckles."

Aithinne stared at her teacher, her friend, a woman who was like a mother to her, and burst into tears.

"Oh, dear child." Oona wrapped her arms around her and rocked her, clucking her tongue. "Cry—it helps relieve the inner turmoils. Then dry your eyes and face life. Things are never as bad as we think."

"No, they are worse. Oona . . . I fear the spells and the potions are not holding his memories at bay."

She felt the fraile woman suck in a breath. "As to that . . ."

Aithinne's head snapped up. "What?"

"My craft was strong, lass, the drugs worked . . ."

"But what? Do not toy with me. I need to ken."

"The spells and drugs will only work to a point. There was no worry as long as he did not return to Lyonglen, did not see you again. He would mayhap recall shards of a dream, not knowing precisely what was real and what was just conjured within a drunken mind." Oona pulled her kerchief from her sleeve and dabbed at Aithinne's eyes.

"Only he has returned." Aithinne exhaled her fear. "How much will he remember in time?"

"'Tis hard to say."

"Do not yank my tether, old woman."

"I am not being evasive. I simply do not ken how much. He will have strong images of you, your scent, your taste. His body will ken yours. Pieces will come back to him, confuse him. He was only in the tower room so the rest of the fortress will not be in his memory to bubble up. But being in your bed, you, mayhap the time he wrestled with the lads and Einar . . ." She shrugged. "Some of it may return. It will be like a man taken by the drink. Some things might return. Others never will come to mind other than as a sense of something being familiar."

"Oona, that young man, the squire to the Dragon, he is Ravenhawke's son. The mother played him false, got with child hoping to barter the child for a better way of life. He stings with her betrayal. Do you not see, my deceit is not much different—"

"Which deceit is that, Princess? You have too many of them, I fear."

Aithinne whipped around to see St. Giles standing in the doorway, his expression aloof, accusing.

Chapter Fourteen

On the following morning, the sun rose over the hills that ringed Glen Shane, painting the sky with a hundred shades of pinks and purples. Aithinne was tired. She had been in the saddle for what seemed half her lifetime; she was stiff, hungry, and feared her stomach would roll in the next breath. It took all her will power to fight the urge. So while the dawnspring was breathtakingly beautiful, she really could not appreciate the majestic beauty.

She glared at the back of Damian St. Giles, riding beside his cousin at the head of the small column of cavalry and, in her current perverse mood, she wished for a stone. Not a big one, mind, just one of size to clot him between the shoulders to get his attention. Resentment still clouded her mind. Having summarily ordered her to ready herself to journey to Glenrogha, the arrogant man had assumed she would rush to do his bidding without one word of protest.

Oh, she understood the urgency for Julian's desire to speed home to his waiting lady wife. He missed Tamlyn. What Aithinne failed to see was the need for her to accompany these men of Challon. Worse, they were none too free with explanations.

When she protested the command, Challon said he was returning to Glenrogha and wanted Damian and her to come with him. He was not leaving them at Lyonglen. End of discussion. He would grant leave for their return once Damian's forces from Parvon were fetched. He did not like that Lyonglen was the center of a hot power struggle amongst Clan Bruce and two of the most powerful Highland clans—Comyn and Campbell. Something about Phelan's visit had set Challon on edge. As a result, he insisted that Damian and she would be better protected at Glen Shane. Her wishes or thoughts on the problem were given little consideration, and that left her furious. Accustoming herself to the highhanded command of Ravenhawke was hard enough to do. Now she had Challon giving orders as overlord.

She was also upset at facing her cousin Tamlyn again. She had always loved Tamlyn. As children they had been as close as sisters, often pretending to be twins as Rowenna and Raven were. Now that closeness would be tested, as she would be forced to observe Damian watching Tamlyn, know his true feelings for her.

Of course, she had not put up too much of a fuss about packing for Glenrogha. Coward that she was, she had jumped at the excuse to leave Damian's presence to do so. He was in a determined mood, wanting to know to what deceit she spoke of to Oona. Hence, when Lord Challon entered and announced he was returning to Glen Shane come first light and wouldst see Ravenhawke and Ai-thinne return with him, she almost felt like kissing her cousin-by-marriage for the timely rescue.

Other than helping her to her seat upon the mouse-colored palfrey, Damian had not uttered one word to her since they set out—which was both vexing and a relief, if she were to admit the truth. Her stomach fluttered again, warning of the morning sickness. At this point she wasn't too concerned about hiding it. Oona assured her men were never bright in seeing signs that a woman was with child. Pleading the long ride would be excuse enough.

As they rode across the deadzone, Aithinne spotted evidence of construction for a new curtain wall and a dry ditch moat. As they approached, the portcullis rose and a drawbridge was lowered. The first stamp of Challon's possession, Aithinne noted. Before, the gate had been simple. Already Glenrogha was bearing the mark of its Norman lord.

As the riders poured into the bailey proper, Tamlyn came flying out of the lord's tower, her skirts held high so she could run. As she pulled up, her eyes took in Aithinne, but then quickly shifted to the handsome man dismounting his black destrier. There was wariness in her expression, as if she were excited to see Challon, but unsure if she should openly demonstrate this before all the men.

Challon dismounted and passed the reins off to Moffet, then turned to see Tamlyn awaiting his notice. He showed little change, so it was odd to judge what reaction he had toward his new wife.

With a flash of frustration, Tamlyn composed her beautiful face into one of a lady proper and greeted him. "Well-come, Lord Challon. I hope your business was settled to your liking and the ride was not too tiring."

For several breaths the arrogant man just stared at Tamlyn, then he burst out laughing. "The mantle of proper lady does not rest well on my *faidhaich*."

"Oh, Challon, hush." Tamlyn practically jumped into the arms of her husband.

Aithinne's heart warmed as her cousin chided this fierce warlord, at Challon calling Tamlyn his wildcat. As she watched the two, she remembered what Moffet said about how Tamlyn handled Challon. It was very clear to all that Challon and Tamlyn were deeply in love.

Aithinne was nearly overcome by conflicting emotions. Her heart squeezed at the beauty of their feelings, felt envy that Tamlyn should be blessed by the pure love of her Dragon, and ached with resentment that Tamlyn not only had Challon's love, but had captured Damian's heart as well. It was not fair. Most women would kill to have what Tamlyn now shared with Challon. Were the Auld Ones not content enough with their magical union that they had to fix Damian's feelings on her cousin as well? It hurt. Pain lanced through her, but she did her best to mask the reaction under the pretense of being exhausted.

Challon hugged Tamlyn tightly. "I take it my wife missed me."

Aithinne was surprised when Tamlyn bit his neck lightly. "Had you taken me with you, then you would not have missed *me.*"

"Tamlyn, I explained why I did not want you to accompany me."

Putting her arms around his neck, she pulled up to his mouth. "Challon, hush and kiss me."

His fingers rubbed the growth of beard. "Mayhap I should bathe and shave first."

"Challon . . ." she growled a warning.

He leaned back so he could study her face, the laughter in his eyes turning serious. "I missed you, wife."

Then he kissed her. Oh did he kiss her! Aithinne so enjoyed their love. What she would not give to have Damian look at her in the same fashion.

Pagan, Challon's horse, nickered as if laughing at them and pushed Challon's shoulder. Julian

broke the embrace and looked around at the midnight steed. "I think he wants his feed and is tired
of waiting."

Aithinne's attention was pulled away from the
loving couple when her arm was touched. She
glanced down to see Damian coming around to
help her dismount. But, his eyes strayed to Tamlyn,
still in Julian's embrace. His pale gray-green eyes
watched them with a hunger that made her want to
kick him. Instead of holding back, she did just
that—nudged him with the toe of her boot, a light
jab in the ribs to draw his attention back to her.

Blushing at her behavior, Tamlyn came over as
Damian lifted Aithinne from the saddle. "Aithinne,
well-come. How fare you? We missed you at Beltane."

As Damian set Aithinne on her feet, she jerked
her elbow from his grasp. Angry with him, she
flashed him a look that would wither even the
strongest of men. Ignoring the vexing man, she embraced her cousin.

"Well wishes on your marriage, Tamlyn. I apologize for not being there." She smiled at Challon,
then lifted her brow. "So he went through the rites
of the Sword and The Ring? Mayhap *this* Norman
has value. Am I to stay in the same room? I am tired
from the ride and need to lie down." What she
needed was to get away from Lord Arrogant before
she broke down and cried or vomited. Or both.

"St. Giles is staying in that room. You may use
my old room," Tamlyn answered with a warm
smile, glancing uneasily from her to her husband's kinsman.

Aithinne glared daggers at St. Giles. "Why does
that not surprise me? He is so adept at usurping
what is not his." Tilting her nose in the air, she
passed him and strode into the lord's tower with all
the poise she could muster.

If she hoped to escape him, her wish went begging. He came up the steps two at a time and hurried to catch up with her halfway down the hall. She tried to pretend she did not hear him coming up fast behind her, but as she neared the stairs, he caught her arm.

"Aithinne, you appear pale. Fare you well?"

Aithinne frowned, then rolled her eyes. "Lord Arrogant the Observant. Please let me go. I am weary from the long ride and my stomach complains. I must have eaten something that did not agree with me."

His hand raised to stroke his thumb along her jaw. "Are you upset about something? You seem angry, distressed."

"Oh, and why is that? I am commanded to leave my home, ride when I am unwell, and then—" She caught herself before the words tumbled out, railing at him for wasting his love on a woman he could never have when another stood before him who loved him with her whole heart. She nearly choked on the tears welling within her throat. "Please release me lest you want me to blaw all over your boot."

"You are unwell?"

She exhaled impatience. "Save me from men who finally see what is about to bite them." Jerking away from him she fled up the stairs and into the room, slamming the door in his face.

Aithinne stood at the arrow loop watching the men below in the lists fighting with swords. Challon practiced using the claymore against one of his squires—Gervase, she believed the man was called. Tamlyn bustled about the room settling

Aithinne's belongings about the room. She smiled at her cousin.

"Tamlyn, you need not do all that. That is what servants are for." She knew it was a waste of breath, for her cousin rarely asked others to do chores for her.

"I do not mind. I have a restlessness in me these days, a lot of extra energy." Tamlyn smiled, but then it faded as the amber eyes ran over Aithinne, taking stock. "You concern me, dear cousin. Are you not well?"

"Oh, Tamlyn, I am sinking in a quagmire." Aithinne sniffed, then nibbled on a slice of dried apple, finding it settled her queasy stomach. "It might be worry . . . but I fear I am with child. All the signs are there. Oona says I am."

"With child?" Tamlyn echoed her shock. Then she grinned and put a hand to her belly. "I might be as well."

This night is our Beltane. Great magic rises. It touches your cousin Tamlyn at Glenrogha, and like the reflection of a mirror, it affects your life as well.

"Beltane?" Aithinne asked, hearing Oona's words in her head.

Tamlyn nodded and hugged herself. "I took Challon to the orchard."

Aithinne's eyes went wide. "Beneath your tree?"

"Aye. The blossoms were so thick they blanketed the ground. On his black mantle on the white blooms—it was like a dream."

"No wonder you glow with happiness." Envy filled Aithinne.

"How far along do you think you are, cousin?"

Aithinne bit the apple piece. "The apples ease queasiness. It comes in the afternoon, too. I always heard it was morning sickness that was the sign.

Only, Oonanne says sometimes it hits a woman in the afternoon as well. Are you experiencing it yet?"

"Not yet, but Bessa said it could come soon. So who is the father and how long?"

"Beltane," she admitted in a sigh. Pushing the wooden shutter wider, she stared out at the men below.

Damian had been practicing with Moffet, showing his son the way of the sword. Done, he pulled his sark over his head and went to the well. Drawing a bucket of water, he poured the whole thing over his head and then shook like a dog. When Moffet laughed, Damian pulled up another pail and then dumped it over the lad's black head.

Their laughter brought a sad smile to Aithinne's lips. Would Damian ever share such moments with the child they created? She tried to cast her mind with the kenning, to envision the future, only she could not tell where she would be a year from now.

"But you were not at the May Day ceremony—"

Aithinne laughed sardonically. "You might say I held my own ceremony."

"I do not understand." Tamlyn went back to unpacking Aithinne's kirtles and hanging them in the wardrobe.

Abruptly, Aithinne broke down crying. Tamlyn rushed to her and held her, rocking her. "Oh, Tamlyn, I have made a muddle of everything and I do not know how to put things right."

"Hush, sweet cousin, you shall sicken. Surely it is not as bad as you fear."

"Och, 'tis likely worse."

Challon opened the door, knocking as he pushed it wide. "Tamlyn, sorry, I fear you need come tend your silly husband."

Tamlyn gasped as she saw blood dripped down his hand. "Challon, what have you done?"

"Hush, wife, it is only a small cut. I was not paying attention to what I did in the lists and Gervase sliced my wrist. 'Tis minor, just it bleeds like a stuck pig. I need you to wrap it for me."

Tamlyn half nodded to Aithinne. "We shall talk more later. Sorry."

"Go care for your husband, Tamlyn. My troubles will still be here." Aithinne watched them walk away. "Still here and mounting, I fear."

Nervous at facing St. Giles, she had put off joining them belowstairs by fussing with her hair and gown. Truth be told, she was trying to look her best so she did not compare so unfavorably with her lovely cousin. Unable to put it off any longer, she arranged the long sleeves on her pale blue kirtle and then opened the door to go down to supper.

She jumped, startled when she found the doorframe blocked by the body of a tall man. Instant alarm spread through her. Who was he? What was he doing standing there, filling the doorway and preventing her leaving?

"Good eve, kind sir. If you shall move so I may pass?" She tried to sound calm, but something about this man, the utter stillness in which he held himself made her back up. A mistake. She saw the glint in his black eyes. This man fed upon fear. When she took the step back, he moved forward into the room and into the candlelight. The half shadows made his appearance fearsome, but seeing him in full light did little to dispel her deep unease. Madness touched his brain. In her whole life, Aithinne had never feared any man. She did this one.

"Tamlyn . . ." he finally spoke, saying the name in a breath. A drunken breath. She realized though she saw him full-faced, the light was to her back, hiding her countenance in the shadows. Many would mistake her for Tamlyn.

She tried to skirt to his side, hoping he would take the hint, but he moved to counter her leaving. Panic rising in her, she pulled up. Clutching her amulet, she tried to still the fear surging in her and drew on her tone of nobility. "I fear you have mistook me. I am not Tamlyn. I am Lady Aithinne Ogilvie, Baroness of Coinnleir Wood. Lady Tamlyn and I are cousins."

The white teeth flashed in something that resembled a grin, but there was no mirth in it. The expression lent on oily bile taste to the pit of her stomach.

"What stupid jest is this . . ." he growled.

Slowly she lowered her hand to the *sgain dubh* sheathed at her belt. Getting her hand around the hilt made her breathe a little easier. "'Tis no jest, sir. Lord Ravenhawke and Lord Challon returned this morn with me. All in the bailey saw Tamlyn greet me. I favor her, 'tis said. Though I am taller and have a red cast to my hair."

She had to steel herself not to flinch as those cold, empty eyes roamed over her face, her hair, her body. The show of teeth reminded her of what you would see on a hungry wolf in deepest winter.

"So you do." He lifted a lock off her shoulder, rubbing it between his fingers, studying it. "Your tits are not as big either, but are still more than a mouthful, more than a handful."

"Never speak such to me again or I shall see you flogged." She drew herself up to look down her nose at him.

Evidently it was the wrong thing to say. "You Scottish bitches. I have been flogged once because of your cousin. She owes me. I shall collect. Soon.

Mayhap you are smarter than the Glenrogha bitch—in heat for her lord and master every time he snaps his fingers. I watched them under the apple tree, rutting in the dirt—"

"Dirk!" Damian's voice was the most welcome sound Aithinne had ever heard. "What are you doing here?"

His hooded eyes lowered as he nodded toward Aithinne. "I was merely saying well-come to Lady Tamlyn's cousin that looks so like her. Rather puzzling the way God works, eh? You favor Challon and he has Tamlyn."

"By the grace of Edward," Damian corrected.

"I supposed our good king has given you Glen Eallach along with this bi . . . *lady*." The way he stressed the word said he did not mean it in a flattering fashion, but equated it on the level of a whore.

Aithinne stepped toward Damian and almost sighed relief when he pushed her behind him as he stayed facing the taller man. "You would do well to remember your place, Pendegast, or the whip shall taste your flesh once again. Mayhap it shall be my blade driving home the point."

"At your convenience, Lord Ravenhawke." Dirk Pendegast sketched a mock bow and then departed the room.

Aithinne was nearly sick from the evil coiling within that man, the foulness polluting the room even after he had taken leave. She was so upset she wanted to do something silly—like throw herself into the strong arms of this troublesome man. "I thank you for arriving when you did. Who is he?"

Damian whipped around and glared at her. "Sir Dirk Pendegast, a knight in Julian's cadre. I mislike the man. He tried to rape Tamlyn, Challon said, the day he took possession of Glen Shane. Pendegast and four others caught her out picking flowers.

Only by the grace of God did Challon arrive in time to stop them. What was he doing in your room?"

Aithinne stiffened at his tone, which bordered on an accusation. "Do not speak that question as if I invited him here, Damian St. Giles. I opened the door and he was there blocking the doorway. He thought I was Tamlyn. I tried to move past him, only to have him cut me off."

Damian gave a short nod. "Pardon me, the man troubles me. If he lays a hand on you, I shall kill him without second thought." His eyes skimmed over her as if assuring himself of her being unharmed. "You are very beautiful in blue, Aithinne."

Aithinne sucked in a breath, wanting to believe him, yet knowing that he looked at her and found her lacking next to Tamlyn. "I am taller than Tamlyn—"

For the first time his countenance eased. "And I am taller than Challon. And prettier."

She nibbled on the inside of her lip for an instant, her eyes drinking in his male perfection. "Aye, you are. Though he is nicer."

"Challon? They call him the Black Dragon. A man once the king's champion. He is the most feared warrior of these isles. Even Edward treads carefully around Julian Challon. I do not think anyone has called Challon *nice*. Ever. Not even Tamlyn."

"She loves him." The words popped out. The instant they did, she wished she could recall them, knowing they had the power to hurt the man.

He nodded sadly. "Aye, she does. And he loves her. Julian is a very troubled man. He needs peace, happiness. Your cousin has the power to heal him, make him whole again, give him the son he so desperately wants."

"She is very fortunate. They share something very rare and special." Unable to look at Damian any longer, she turned and hurried from the room before she could see just how unhappy that knowledge made the man she loved.

Oh aye. She was in love with Damian St. Giles. Fool that she was.

Chapter Fifteen

With mixed emotions flooding through him, Damian studied Challon as the man's eyes hungrily followed his lady wife's departure from the Great Hall. Tamlyn had come to report she had settled Aithinne for the night and was now going to seek her bed as well. Damian thought it endearing how she had asked Challon's permission.

Never could he envision the fiery Aithinne coming to ask his leave to retire. He almost snorted thinking of her, how she chafed at the orders he had given over the past couple of days. She would sooner take a knife to him than bend her will to his. Firebrand—what her name meant in the Gaelic. It was perfect for her, he thought. His Firebrand.

It brought him joy to seeing how Julian and Tamlyn were already bonding so strongly. Truly, he was happy for them. Yet, in the same breath, it also made him feel empty inside. He craved this same contentment, the closeness of their affection. "She is good for you, Julian. I have not seen you this happy in years."

"Aye, Edward has no idea what a prize he has given me. I am damn lucky, indeed." Julian concurred with a half-smile. "I have a feeling we both are."

"You are. For me . . . mayhap." Damian shrugged.

"Have you twigged if she lies about this so-called marriage to Lyonglen?" Challon asked, settling back in his chair to finish his drink.

Damian lifted the goblet to his mouth, paused and flashed his teeth in a grin. "Oh, she lies. I spoke with the gatekeeper of Lyonglen and casually inquired how often Malcolm the *Culdee* comes to Lyonglen. He said the priest comes only when called. So I asked when was the last time the man had been summoned to Lyonglen."

"And?" When Damian just smiled smugly, Julian nudged his foot with the tip of his boot. "Spill it. Do not keep me wondering."

"The guard said the priest was summoned one stormy night—first time since last Yuletide—a little over three moons passing. He came as quickly as a fast horse would carry him. Then departed with the dawn."

Julian yawned. "Interesting, but not quite to the point."

Damian nodded, then took a swallow of the wine. "The point being, the brothers started putting about the rumor that Lyonglen had married several sennights before that. Which means—"

"I raise a cup to the Dragon of Challon . . . brought low by love madness!" The slurred words rang out through the great hall.

All eyes turned in the direction Dirk Pendegast, who had stood and now lifted his cup to Julian. The man's eyes glazed from drink, it was clear that demons ate at his insides.

Damian gritted his teeth as he recalled earlier when he had found the man in Aithinne's room. She had been scared by Pendegast, but then, to Damian's disgust, he had long ago surmised the warrior liked females to cringe before him. One of

the best knights Julian had ever trained, his cousin
was disgusted by the man's sadistic bent toward females. Under a less careful liege, the tall knight with
black hair and eyes would likely prey on maidservants or rape women in warfare, proof of this was his
near taking of Tamlyn before Julian stopped him.

"Love madness?" A small twitch in Julian's jaw,
barely perceptible, bespoke of his controlled anger.
Only a fool provoked Julian Challon.

"Aye, 'tis a disease and you are infected, my lord."
The fool gave a mock, sweeping bow. "Mayhap
beyond cure. It can make a lapdog out of the strongest. Rot one's brain."

"Disease?" Julian probed, clearly wondering what
maggot had gotten into Dirk's foul mind.

Challon had stated a fortnight ago he had sent
word to Baron Pendegast, Dirk's eldest brother,
that he wanted Dirk recalled to the family holding,
that his services would no longer be needed. Unfortunately, thus far there had been no reply. The
Baron had hoped Julian would settle a fief on Dirk.
Damian knew that would never happen. Challon
wanted the man gone from Glen Shane.

Damian noticed Challon's right hand had decep-
tively slipped down to the hilt of Tamlyn's *sgain
dubh*, which he kept tucked at his belt. After Pendegast scaring Aithinne earlier, he would like naught
more than to see the repugnant pup taught a
lesson, but he had a feeling Dirk was not as drunk
as he pretended and deliberately provoked Julian
for just this sort of response. Mayhap he assumed
Julian's wound to the wrist to be worse than it was.
Tamlyn had pampered him all evening. Possibly,
Dirk assumed she did so out of necessity instead of
love. Dirk would never mistake to challenge Julian
in a fair fight otherwise.

To head off the coming confrontation, Damian

slammed his golden cup down hard on the table to draw Julian's focus from the knight. "Sir Dirk dips into the wine overly this night. Pendegast, close thy mouth, before you ruin our digestion with bilious nonsense."

"Any healer will attest to the truth. It is disease, say I. As with any disease, there is a cure. Does not our Church say women corrupt us, weaken us? No man should suffer such indignities to his honor and pride. Women should know their place. Obey their lords. A man never permits one to lead him around by his tarse."

Julian jumped to his feet.

Damian loosely restrained his arm and cautioned lowly, "Ignore him. His words spew forth from a green fount of jealousy."

"Healers bleed a man . . . draw out the foul poison crippling spirit and body. To sear wounds and prevent infection, you slap hot iron. For a man to cure this insidious sickness that saps his soul, he must have intercourse with another woman. Then and only then shall he rid his soul, mind, and body of this malady. If that does not work, he needs to discover they all are alike. Willing to lay with any man when his back is turned. A man is a fool if he thinks any one of them is special above others. A lady screams her pleasure same as the lowest swine girl. Sad when our mightiest warrior is brought low by cock fever."

Before Damian could blink, Julian tossed his dagger and with a thunk it landed tip first between Dirk's first and second fingers. Casually, yet with regal bearing, Challon strode to the table. He stared at the knight, not blinking, waited, allowing the man's fear to rise. Julian wielded silence as a weapon, one of his tools that always gave him the advantage. Finally when Dirk blinked, Challon reached out and snatched the knife back and then used the tip of the blade to pare his fingernails. "You were saying?"

Dirk reached for his cup, his expression surly though his tone was obeisant. "Nothing, my lord."

"What I thought," Julian responded with haughty disdain. With the clear dismissal, he turned on his heels and marched from the Great Hall.

Damian followed him. "You would do well to send that pup back to his brothers."

"I plan on it. I sent word to his brother to recall him."

"Good, because if you do not send him from here I shall end up slicing his throat. I found him trying to corner Aithinne in her room just before supper. She said, at first he thought her to be Tamlyn. I trust him not. Tamlyn or Aithinne—I do not want him near either woman."

"Do not worry. He is gone or I fear I shall have to kill him."

Pausing to glance back to the arrogant soldier, Damian asserted, "You might have to stand in line, Julian."

Damian watched Challon go on up to the next landing to the lord's chamber. He smiled as he saw Julian taking the steps two at a time, eager to be with his lady.

The emptiness that gnawed at his innards at supper now arose again as he wondered at the feeling of knowing someone awaited his return. With a sigh, he turned and stared at the long hallway, dark except for the torch burning in the sconces, about halfway down. No one waited for him. There was no body warming his bed—or his life.

His whole life he had carried the sense of feeling apart. Not a Challon son, just a cousin. Unwanted by his grandfather. He was half Scot and yet this land was strange to him. He wanted to vanquish this restless, hungry spirit within him—to belong somewhere. He wanted what Julian had—love, a home, a future. Someone waiting for him to come to bed.

He wanted Aithinne.

She alone could give him for what his soul thirsted for far too long.

His eyes were drawn to the door where she rested. Was she asleep or was the redheaded harridan waiting to hear his steps pass by? Mayhap someone waited for him after all.

With a smile, he started to take a step toward her room, only to have raised voices at the bottom of the stairs distract his attention. The small hairs prickled at the back of his neck, and his warrior's skills took over. Stepping so he was cloaked by the deep shadows, he looked down the stairwell to the floors below. Several of Julian's men were passing, coming from the Great Hall and heading out of the lord's tower. Talking, chuckling, loud enough to be heard, yet just at a level where most of the words were indistinguishable. They laughed at some jest and then moved on past.

One lingered. Dirk. He paused at the bottom of the steps, his hand on the newel, looking up, as if trying to decide something.

Damian's hand went to the hilt of his sword. If Dirk so much as put a foot on the first step he would be dead before he reached the third one. The torches on either side of the stairs illuminated the hard planes of Pendegast's face. A face a woman might mistakenly find comely—until it was too late.

After Julian had taken the three holdings, he'd ordered Dirk and the other men who attacked Tamlyn tied to the post in the bailey and given one hundred lashes. Pendegast was lucky Julian had not killed him, so great was his offense. As Damian stared down at the cold, empty eyes, he feared Dirk had not learnt his lesson. An oily taste filled his stomach as he realized he held his breath, ready to strike.

Finally, with one last chilly look, the man moved on. Something in his manner spoke to Damian that whatever poison that fouled Pedegast's mind would only grow worse. He bore the taint of madness. Uneasy, he glanced to the stairs. Both Moffet and Gervase slept in the hallway leading to the lord's chamber. They would protect Challon and Tamlyn.

He turned, his eyes going to the door where Aithinne slumbered. No one slept as sentry before her chamber. She had not even brought a lady's maid with her, so none else would be resting in the room. Even if there had been one, he would not trust her to be capable of defending Aithinne. If he admitted it, he would not depend on anyone but himself to see to the Lady of Coinnleir Wood.

He smiled. "Ah, the sacrifice. The code of chivalry says a knight must protect his lady. If she shan't have me in her bed, then I shall have to make a pallet on the floor." With a last look down the stairwell, he went to play guard.

Aithinne jerked up in the bed when he pushed the door open. She wore only a thin chemise, so sheer it was nearly his undoing. The dark circles of her breasts were clearly outlined against the pale material, bringing a wolfish grin to his face as he noticed how those crests became more defined the nearer he came to the bed. Even in the candlelight he saw her blush as she tugged the wolf pelt cover to her chest. Her long hair had been plaited; the braid hung over her right shoulder and down to the bed.

Her wide-eyed expression lent her an air of innocence. He knew that was a lie. Aithinne, his mistress of deceits. Only, as he looked at her he could not breathe, let alone care what she was hiding from him. He just needed her.

"What are you doing here, Lord Ravenhawke?" She tried to sound chiding, aloof.

"Take off your chemise, Aithinne." He began unbuckling his baldric.

"Go kiss the backside of your destrier, my lord," she snapped, her nostrils flaring slightly.

Whether it was with rising desire or anger he was not sure. Mayhap a mix of both.

"The command worked last time," he pointed out, grinning. "Ah, my lady plays hard to get this night. Fair enough. That being the nature of things, I thought you might be in need of a bed warmer."

"The night is not cold, my lord. So you may hie yourself on down the hall—or to the stable," she fussed.

"True, it is not cold." He leaned the sheathed sword against the wall, within reach from the bed, then sat on the edge of it. "But sometimes there is another cold that touches people, Aithinne. It comes from being lonely. Are you ever lonely, lass?"

He saw such sadness, such longing in her eyes before she pulled her knees to her chest and looked away. His heartbeat dropped to a low thud, her pain becoming his.

"Please . . ." came her whispered reply.

"Please what, Firebrand? That is what your name means, is it not?" Lifting the long braid, he toyed with it. "I think the name fits you well. You have a rather fiery temper and—"

Her head jerked up, the sadness still there so

tangible it was nearly a living force between them. "If you say freckles . . . I will . . . will kick you."

Damian chuckled, though everything within him wanted to soothe her pain, to bring a smile to her beautiful face. "Freckles? Ah, my lady, you are sensitive about them? Even in the bright sunlight I hardly notice them. By candlelight I cannot see them at all."

"Do not laugh at me, Damian St. Giles or I will . . . will—"

He reached out and lifted her chin with his crocked finger. "I do not laugh at you. Freckles have divine possibilities, Firebrand. Such as, since you have freckles in one spot—your nose—then you might have at least one or two . . . or three . . . elsewhere. A man might spend half a night hunting for them." Might spend his lifetime, he wanted to say, but feared she was not of a mind to hear that yet. "Since I am suddenly quite captivated by freckles, it would be a quest worthy of a knight of Challon."

Aithinne crossed her arms and buried her head against her knees. "Oh, go away," came the muffled request.

Still playing with the braid, he chuckled. "Cry and you will have puffy eyes and a big red nose come morn. Likely make your freckles stand out more."

"I could grow to hate you, St. Giles." Her hazel eyes lashed daggers at him. The words might have had some force if her chin had not quivered.

He traced the faint cleft in her chin with the side of his thumb. Some might consider that slight dip a flaw in the perfection of her beauty. Not him. It made her more real. Emotions overwhelmed him as he knew without doubt he stared into the face which had haunted his dreams, that kept him clinging to life when he was ready to give up because his whole existence had been hollow. He needed more to his life, wanted roots, a home, more sons like Moffet. Maybe a daughter with those ensorcelling eyes.

"Hate me?" He shook his head no. "You resent I have come into a life where you had final say in all. Now I tell you how things will be. You do not like that. You have been used to doing as you please for too long. Give it time, Aithinne. We will learn to work together for the good of Glen Eallach. You will do what is right for your people. So will I. They are now my people. When you come to trust that—trust me—maybe you will also trust me with the secrets you guard so jealousy."

She looked away.

"Coward," he chuckled.

Her head snapped back. "I am not a coward."

She started to slap him, but his quick reflexes caught her wrist before it made contact with his face. Grinning, he let her struggle against his hold. Then forced her palm down inside his sark's opening to the center of his chest where his heart beat. "I warned you, Firebrand, about trying to hit me. What would happen."

Distracted by the pounding under her hand, she stared where her palm met his flesh, in thrall by the magic rising between them. Then her eyes batted as she recalled what he said would be the punishment if she ever tried to strike him again. Aithinne tried to pull back as if she had been scalded, but he refused to let her go.

"I am sorry," she whispered the apology.

He laughed out loud. "That I do not believe."

Her smile tried to slip out. "Very well, I am not sorry. But I do wish you would go away."

"I do not believe that either. Your body puts lie to those words." He brushed the back of his hand lightly against the dark circle of her breast where it pressed against the thin material with each shallow breath she drew. She shuddered. "As your body becomes aroused, it speaks to me with its changes. No words are needed between us, Aithinne. Words can lie. This does not."

He covered her mouth with his, giving her no chance of protesting. He was not being fair. Fairness be damned. This night, he wanted to be with her, to hold her through the long shadows of darkness, feel her heart beating next to his. Awaken in the warm glow of dawn with her in his arms. He was a warrior. Anytime he went into battle, he waged war to win. The war he played out on the plane of her bed was little different. He wanted to win Aithinne's heart, take her hostage and never let her go. Mayhap he would tie her up and tickle her with a peacock feather until she surrendered and yielded all her secrets as well as her body.

Something about peacocks trigged the drunken images to float through his mind. He recalled there were no peacocks at Glen Shane. There were some at Glen Eallach, though. What had led him to the tower room at Lyonglen. He had meant to examine why the remembrance bothered him, but Aithinne had entered the chamber and he had told her to take off her clothes. Then his mind suddenly forgot all about peacocks.

Breaking the kiss, Damian gasped for air. His eyes searched hers. Words floated in the air, so he made them his own. "Half-measures never see the deed done, Aithinne."

He heard the small hitch in her breath and knew he had struck a cord within her. Yet, once again, his mind little cared for riddles as he stared at this pagan enchantress. The candlelight made her eyes seem to glow. Intelligent, penetrating, they held a power, a pull. Their directness might unsettle some men. Men too weak to accept the challenge flashing in their hazel depths. His mother had whispered tales of the *Cait Sidhe,* a race of witch women of the Picts. Lore said they possessed the power to assume the form of a cat under the rays of the full moon. He recalled Challon saying the women of Tamlyn's clan were descended from such females. As he stared at Aithinne he found it easy to believe she was some magical creature touched by the blood of the Fey—a witch. A woman a man would kill to possess.

Only she provoked his warrior's blood. The need to conquer her flooded his mind until he could no longer think. Only beg. "Touch me, Aithinne."

For several heartbeats she didn't stir. Then the corner of her mouth twitched as she rose up on her knees and moved closer. "Touch you how, my lord?"

"Any manner you wish. Burn me with your fire, Aithinne."

She pushed at his shoulders. "Get off the bed, my lord, you have too many clothes on."

He watched her for a second, wondering if she was trying to trick him. But his inner voice told him to take the chance. Trusting it, he slid off the bed and stood.

Aithinne's legs slipped off the bed, coming to stand behind him, her soft hands snaking around his waist to reach for the hem of his sark to pull it over his head. So damn slow, he had to grit his teeth at the ghostly friction upon his skin. He barely breathed until she tugged it off and tossed it to the floor. Molding her body against his bare back, she ran her hands up his chest and then slowly down to unlace his chausses. As the deft fingers nearly drove him to madness, he took over undoing them.

With a throaty purr, she slapped his hands and then nipped his back. Damian smiled and let her continue her game. She pressed her soft breasts to the curve of his spine while, like an idiot, he

balanced on one foot to undo the cross-lacings on
each boot in turn, then kicked out of them. She was
already shoving down the leathern hose, allowing
him to step out of them. With another rumble in
her chest, she brought her hands up the outside
of his thighs, nails lightly scoring his flesh.

Her questing hands slid around his waist, one
going up so the first finger could encircle his flat
nipple, the other going down, to the soft sack between his legs. She squeezed gently, causing his
staff to buck painfully. Damian leaned his head
back, closing his eyes, to ride the edge of the pain
pleasure threshold she brought to him.

"Is this how you wished to be touched, my lord?"

He smiled in delicious agony as she wickedly
added a pinch to the nub on his chest. It sent lightning arcing through his body to explode in his
groin. Sensations he never before experienced.
Aithinne's magical touch made it all new to him.

Spinning around, he caught her waist. She didn't
resist him. Instead her mouth met his, opening to
taste him once more. Slanting his head for a better
angle, he pressed his advantage, hungry for all she
could give him. Control—if there had ever been
such a thing—shattered as the kiss went on. And on.
He heard a low moan—her moan—felt it through
his skin and every drop of blood. Took it within him
and made it his own. Deepening the contact, he
issued the primitive male demand for her submis-
sion. Now.

His hands roamed over the swollen breasts, toyed
with the nipples until her breathing was ragged,
wheezing. Damian smiled, arrogant, happy, determined, as he pushed her back on the bed, then covered her with his burning body. Never had the primal
urge to mate torn through him with such savage
force, proclaiming this woman was his, his mate.

Aithinne was more than he ever dared hope, even in his darkest dreams, a woman with the power to make those dreams a reality.

The magic was voracious, like a forest fire consuming all in its path.

What he felt for her terrified him. But, by damn, he would possess, own her. Kill anyone who tried to take her from him.

The passion burned so bright the explosion came quickly, then immediately seared them all over again, pushing him to take her again and again.

Aithinne . . . firebrand. Aye, she had branded him.

In her bed he was no longer alone, empty.

Chapter Sixteen

Aithinne spent the better part of the morning hovering in her room for two reasons. The most pressing one was her sour stomach. The smells of cooking from belowstairs had set to the scurrying for the chamber pot at first light. Fortunately, Damian had already gone to break his fast before the urgency hit her. The other reason she remained—she was not ready to face Damian again after last night.

The door opened and she jumped fearing it was Damian. Only Auld Bessa strolled in. "I fetched you a tansy, lass, and some dried apples. Will ease the morning sickness."

It did not surprise Aithinne the old woman knew about the babe without being told. A healer, a witch, she was one of the Three Wise Ones of the Woods, women who watched over and cared for the people of Glen Shane and Glen Eallach. Bessa, Oona, and Evelynour were her teachers, showing her how to use the kenning, instructing her in the ways of herbs and plants.

"Ravens carry messages from Annwn—the Otherworld—for those wise enough to hear. Your soul kens this dark warrior."

Aithinne frowned, trying to avoid the speaking of

him. "You speak riddles, Bessa. I do not ken who you mean."

Bessa clucked her tongue, sounding out her disbelief. "These Dragons of Challon are worthy of reflection, child."

"Bessa, he confuses my mind."

"But not your body?" Bessa chuckled, shaking her head. "Tamlyn spoke nearly the same words the first time I brought up the Black Earl to her. Through the long days of my life I have seen the faces of many a warrior, looked into their hearts. Some were good men. Some needed killing where they stood. These men of Challon possess courage and fire. They are a breed rare. Their coming is the will of the Auld Ones, a blessing from them. Seven seasons past, I will have you ken, the laird of Kinmarch sought auguries about a man—one he called the Dragon. He felt in his heart this man would make a braw husband for our Tamlyn."

"The Earl Hadrian thought Challon would make Tamlyn a good match?" The tides surprised Aithinne.

"Aye, Evelynour foretold with the first awakenings of springtide a dark warrior would come to Glen Shane. Challon. His life threads are woven with Tamlyn's—there is no turning back for either of them. Only the visions were confused at first, hard for our seer to interpret. Slowly they became clearer. There were two men, not one. One who wrapped himself in the shade of the ravens. Another who came with the color of fog."

This night is our Beltane. Great magic rises. It touches your cousin Tamlyn at Glenrogha, and like the reflection of a mirror, it affects your life as well.

"Oona said as much to me on May Day," she admitted.

"Aye, the men are similar, the women similar.

Each pair charged with protecting our glens, our way of life here. A time of trial is at hand. You lasses need strong helpmates to see to what has to be done, to fight for you, protect you."

"Mayhap. But the path for Tamlyn and the path I must tread are different." Aithinne's heart burned. Challon loved Tamlyn. Very different.

"Sometimes, lass, we make things more complicated by our fashing over what might be, rather than facing what is. Let life happen. Accept it."

"If only it were that easy, Bessa. If only . . ."

"Mayhap it is."

Aithinne watched the witch go, despair rising within her.

Last night hurt her in ways she could not begin to understand. She loved Damian. And because she loved him, she could see that she had little sense or willpower where he was concerned. Oh, she was full of righteous plans on how to handle him, how to keep her distance. Each time she was with him, the stronger the urges grew in her foolish heart to throw reason and caution to the wind. She wanted a life with this arrogant man, and it was becoming clear she little cared what the cost would be. That only made her deceit about the child growing within her womb all the more damning.

Last night, she held nothing back from him, gave him everything he asked, and more. Now in the cold light of day, she regretted her wanton ways. She made everything too easy for the vexing man. From the very start she had felt a bond to him, knew that she had given away of piece her soul to the stranger in her bed. Just last night she lay with him with love in her heart. Oh, how she loved this arrogant, beautiful, aggravating man!

No matter which way she turned, she could only see the devastating consequences to come, feared them. She felt the need to confess her lies, her tricks she used in stealing him from his life, using him to get her with his child. Just as she summoned courage enough to tell him, she recalled the look on his face when he spoke of Moffet's birth, how he had been deceived—betrayed. Then, the complete coward, she tried to imagine if she just never told him. He made it clear he did not believe her assertion about marrying Gilchrist for the sake of Lyonglen. What would he think about her turning up with a bairn, especially one bearing the clear stamp of Challon, as all these men seemed to do?

"He will never accept the possibility of a second immaculate conception," she muttered, then shivered.

Noises from the bailey drew her to the arrow loop. Confused, she saw people running toward the stables. Shortly afterward, Challon came out carrying a bundle wrapped in his mantle. From the long hair, Aithinne judged it to be Tamlyn he held.

Not pausing, she rushed out of the room and down the stairs only to meet Challon, carrying her cousin on the steps, Damian right behind him. Grim of face, he hesitated for a breath, stared at her with such pain, then pushed by her and up the stairs to the lord's tower without a word.

Pausing at the first landing, Damian barked at one of the maidservants to send for Auld Bessa, the healer.

"Damian, what happened?" She caught his arm as he nearly headed past as if he did not see her. "What happened? Is Tamlyn all right?"

He tried to say something, frowned, then set her from his path and rushed up to the lord's chamber.

"Men!" She stomped her foot and then headed to the next floor after him. The door at the end of the hall was half open so she entered on Damian's heel.

"I called for the healer." Damian informed Challon. "I saw her about this morn, so she should be easy to find."

Aithinne moved farther into the room. "I am a healer as well, Lord Challon. Let me see Tamlyn until Auld Bessa is fetched. Is she all right? What happened?"

Challon rounded on her, fury in his dark green eyes. "Where the hell were you?"

Aithinne backed up a step, hit by the full force of redoubtable power the Black Dragon and unsure why he was angry with her. "I . . . I . . . was in my room, my lord."

"Why were you not with her? You and your *damn* kenning. Why did you not foresee this . . . stop this? What good are these powers if you cannot prevent something like this?" His accusation lashed at her.

Without thought, her hand reached for her amulet to steady herself against the wave of black despair and fury breaking over her. "I am sorry—"

"Julian, there was a guard with Tamlyn. He could do nothing to prevent what happened. I do not know what you expect of a woman. So do not blame Aithinne. You are just looking for a target to vent your misplaced anger. Save it for the one who deserves it." Damian glared at his cousin. Instead of reaching the man's logic, it only seemed to make the man's anger harden.

"Enough, Challon," Tamlyn's weak voice called from the bed. Her chiding reached through the Dragon's rage when Damian's had not. "'Tis not Aithinne's fault, so stop trying to scare her, Challon."

He whipped around, his face just as fierce, but suddenly his countenance softened as he set down on the edge of the bed and took his wife's hand. His other one reached out and cupped her cheek with such tenderness, such utter love, that tears filled Aithinne's eyes.

Hungrily, Aithinne's gaze sought Damian, desperately hoping to see even a faint echo of those emotions as he looked at her. Damian stood, arms crossed over his chest, one hand lifted so his thumb rubbed his chin in thought.

The gray-green eyes saw only Tamlyn.

A phantom knife slashed through her heart, and finally lodged in her womb. She distantly pondered if the wee being that slumbered there felt her pain, understood her helpless misery. She bit down on the inside of her lip to stop herself from doing something rash—like slapping the man silly. This corked brain male did not have too far to go. How blind could he be? How many ways could she show him she loved him?

"Aithinne, could you see a bath is sent up—" Tamlyn started to ask only to have Challon cut her off.

He blinked, clearly trying to focus on her and not the emotions clouding his mind. "A bath? Why?"

Tamlyn sighed deeply and forced a faint smile, rolling her eyes. "I am muddy, my lord. I wish to get rid of the filth and don a clean kirtle." She glanced to Tamlyn. "Please have one sent up. And ignore my lord husband. Dragons roar and love to snort fire. He forgets gentle souls get singed when he huffs and puffs."

Aithinne nodded, unable to speak for the tears clogging her throat. She turned to go, only to have Tamlyn add, "And take Sir Nodcock with you. I might bathe before my husband, and sometimes I am now forced do so before his squires, but I draw the line at his brothers and cousin." When Damian just stood gazing at her, she snapped, "Out, Lord Ravenhawke. You trespass on my privacy."

Her words finally hit him. He nodded. "Beg pardon, my lady. I am at your service. Just call—"

Aithinne did not wait to see the idiot groveling adoringly at the hem of her cousin's gown. Her hurried steps carried her down the spiral staircase, straight to the ground floor and then into the busy kitchen. Once there, she instructed the cook to set water to being boiled for a bath for his lady, and instructed meals for Challon and Tamlyn to be fetched to their rooms this night.

Once the chores were done, she donned her mantle and went out for a walk by the kitchen door. In the gathering fog, she strolled toward the back of the ward, past the kitchen garden and the long, neat rows of herbs tied to stakes, all the way back to the midden. Her melancholy seemed drawn by the refuse dump, maybe a reflection of her troubles. So much was wrong in her life and she could see no hope of righting it.

Splashes of color drew her eye. As the very edge of the midden, toward the rear of the heap, grew a new sapling, nearly as tall as she was—a hawthorn tree. Already it showed a display of beautiful white blooms. The delicate flowers of five petals were so beautiful, in stark contrast with where its roots drew nourishment. One of the three sacred trees—the others being the oak and ash—people called it the May Tree or the White Thorn. Often they hung a rag or a cloth from someone's clothing on the limbs, and made a wish upon it, for lore spoke the trees were magical and would grant them wishes if the person had a pure heart.

On impulse, she undid the ribbon from around the end of the braid, and with trembling fingers carefully tied it in a bow on the thin branch of the sapling. "There, my lovely White Thorn, who grows strong from the refuse of Glenrogha. Beauty from ruins. I ask no wish, just hope you grant me your blessings. I certainly need them. Come autumn, when your leaves drop, I shall return and move you to a place of honor at Coinnleir Wood, give you the love and care so that you grow strong. I shall not pick your blooms, though I would dearly love to take one back with me, as I ken 'tis a sin to harm you in form."

Behind the hawthorn grew a fat bush of broom, the flowers not as prettily formed, but a brilliant yellow. Her people used broom for protection. Obviously, Cook, who tended the garden and came to dump the refuse in the midden, would pluck anything considered to be weeds before they had a chance to grow very tall and take over. He deliberately left these two, knowing they were special and granted protection to Glenrogha.

Aithinne plucked a sprig of the brilliant yellow blooms. "I ken 'tis considered wrong to use your blossoms in menial ways. Rest assured I very desperately need your protection. Mayhap to save me from myself."

She inhaled its wonderfully sweet fragrance, a nice mix to the tangy scent of the hawthorn flowers. So strange to find the beauty of these two plants growing out of trash. "I wonder if there will be something beautiful to come of the refuse of my life."

Her hand cradled her stomach, thinking of the child slumbering there. A secret smile crossed her lips. There was the indeed the seed of something very special, rooting to take life within. Despite the misery flowing through her, she wanted this child— his child—craved to hold it. The bairn would come as winter lost is grip on the land, as the earth warmed and awakened to spring.

Life beginning anew.

She had come out here in pain, seeking a spot no

one frequented so she could have privacy with her sorrow. Living in a large fortress one saw so few places where one could truly be alone. The midden seemed the site to come shed her tears. Instead of crying, the beauty of the hawthorn and broom gave her a wee shard of hope, the will to carry on.

"He must not fight tomorrow." The voice was barely more than a whisper from the shadows.

Aithinne's head turned, as she tried to adjust her eyes to see who spoke to her. The words had scarcely been more than spoken on the breeze, so faint she almost feared she had imagined them. Then the mist seemed to gather form and a women materialized from it. Evelynour of the Orchard. The rising fog almost haloed her long white hair, lending her the appearance of an angel descended to earth. Named after the goddess of the orchard, no elder could recall a time when she was not teaching and protecting Clan Ogilvie. Despite being one of the oldest members, she appeared ageless, her years scarcely marring her serene countenance. Pale lavender edging toward gray, her eyes were so translucent many oft thought her blind. Her milky skin burned easily under the sun, so few ever saw her except at dawn or in the gloaming. She seemed most at ease in the *haar*, as if her grayness made her a part of the fog. The strongest of the Three Wise Ones of the Woods, her second sight beheld far-reaching visions that none dared doubt. Chiefs of other clans traveled great distances to court her wisdom.

She had trained Aithinne in the lessons needed to face life, guiding her in the ways of the stones and ravens. Through her, the oral history of their ancestors lived on.

After the death of her lady mother, Auld Bessa, Oona, and Evelynour had each played an important role in molding Aithinne, as well as Tamlyn and her sisters. Yet, in some ways Aithinne always felt closer to Evelynour, more like mother-daughter than teacher-disciple.

"Evelynour—"

"I came with words of import for you to hear, Aithinne Ogilvie. Heed them well or sorrow will own you on the morrow. He must not fight on the field of honor when the sun rises. He dies if he picks up the weapon in the stead of another. Please, child, listen."

Aithinne started toward the elderly woman. "I always listen, great mother. Your words show us the way."

As she drew near, Evelynour switched the tall white hawthorn staff from her right hand to her left, so she could cup Aithinne's cheek. "My beautiful daughter, child of the stones, terrible danger rides this land in the form of a leopard. A man of great power, he destroys, maims, his ugliness leaves ravens feasting on the bodies of the dead in his wake, rivers run red where he has been. You and only you can stop him from sweeping through Glen Shane and Glen Eallach. Nothing will be left standing—*nothing*. Our castles will be raised, our women raped and murdered, our men butchered. Before he is through, these two valleys will bleed."

Tears poured down the smooth, unlined cheek, summoning echoed emotions within Aithinne. "Tell me what I must do . . . what is happening? I do not ken what this is about. Why would we be in danger?"

"Your man will fight on the morrow . . . unless you prevent him. If he fights, he dies. Before his final breath he will kill another—justly, but that shall not mean aught to the leopard. He will come, with fire and sword, and all of Clan Shan and Clan Ogilvie will perish."

"Evelynour, I believe you, but do not ken—this leopard—King Edward? Why wouldst he come to destroy our clans? He has sent his dragons to hold these valleys for him."

"True, but it was chastisement, not reward. He sent the Earl Challon here as punishment for daring to raise a hand to him. On the morrow, Challon will seek to take the field of honor to avenge his lady. This is the true path. The way it must be. The leopard will accept Challon as the messenger of their God's justice. Only Lord Ravenhawke will seek to take his place, to fight as his champion. He must not. The leopard will perceive umbrage. Let no hand turn you from this purpose—you have to stop him. Do what you must—whatever you must—he cannot not fight in Challon's stead. He will die. We all will die—"

"I ought to beat you senseless!" The voice rang out, shattered the moment. "But then that would mean you would had sense to start with, and I have serious doubt about that, lady."

Shaken to where she could barely breathe, she rotated to spot a furious Damian stalking down the rows of herbs toward her. "The last person I wish to see—Sir Nodcock," she said under her breath to Evelynour.

Only as she turned back to pale woman, she had gone, vanished as she had come—with the mists. Aithinne blinked, almost fearing she was losing her mind and had imagined the whole incident, so strange were Evelynour's words. Looking down at the flower in her hand, she stared at the yellow blossoms in her hands. She forced her fingers to relax, not to crush the tender flowers, as she struggled to absorb the warning from her guide. She knew better than to disregard any foretelling from Evelynour. But, the enormity of the stark warning was taking time to sink into Aithinne's understanding. She needed a moment alone to absorb it all, try to make sense of the confused words. Time she would not get.

"I should strip a branch off that sapling and thrash you for your stupidity."

Still trembling, Aithinne stepped between the angry man and the hawthorn tree. "You shan't touch my tree. Any lackwit with a thimbleful of wherewithal kens to maim a hawthorn tree is to invite a life of nothing but ill-luck."

"Then I shall use my hand. You will eat your supper standing up for a week, Aithinne Ogilvie. You will sleep on your belly." His words sounded more a promise than a threat.

Oh, why could the infuriating man not leave her alone, give her space so she could try to use the kenning to twig the meaning of Evelynour's dour prediction? No, he had to come rushing in, breaking her solitude and threatening her and her tree. Damian was beyond angry with her, though she had no idea why. The man was most fearsome. Instinct said to flee from him, but she was not leaving him to possibly hurt the hawthorn. She titled her chin up in defiance and stood her ground.

"I did not quail before the bloody Dragon when he breathed fire at me, blaming me for I know not what, so I shan't quiver before you, Lord Ravenhawke. Save your bluster and haranguing for someone who can be intimidated," she snapped. "I wish to go home to Coinnleir Wood. This day. I have had enough of you highhanded warlords who take sport in pushing women around. Enough!"

As soon as the words were out, Evelynour's voice reverberated through within her mind. *He cannot*

not fight in Challon's stead. He will die. We all will die.
If she returned to Coinnleir Wood then there
would be no one to prevent him from fighting in
Challon's place. Only what place? Why would he
take the field of honor? It was to do with Tamlyn,
but she had no idea what was going on, and it was
making her scared. Very scared.

He paused, closed his eyes, and then reigned in his
temper. "I am sorry. My annoyance stems from my
fear of finding you harmed. No one could tell me
where you went. After what happened to Tamlyn——"

"What? What precisely happened to Tamlyn? Neither you nor your ride-over-you-rough-shod cousin
have told me anything. You may be Lord Lyonglen
now, but I am still the baroness of Coinnleir Wood
and I will not stand for this shabby treatment. I——" So
frustrated, she gave up and started to push past him.

Damian caught her upper arm and swung her
back around to face him. "Forgive me, Aithinne.
Men are not the most reasonable creatures when
someone they love has been hurt. Tamlyn was attacked by Dirk Pendegast . . . behind the stables."

He looked down at the toe of his boot. So sad, his
pain was hers, made worse because it was a pain
due to him loving Tamlyn. *A man is not the most reasonable creatures when someone they love has been hurt.*

She finally choked out the words. "Och, Poor
Tamlyn. Did he——" Images of the man, with madness tainting his hard black eyes, cornering her in
the room yestereve flashed through her mind. He
had thought she was Tamlyn.

"Challon and I caught him. Hopefully we
reached her in time." He finally look up, the pale
eyes full of tears. "I could not find you . . . so naturally I jumped to fears."

She nodded, glancing down at the pretty flowers
in her hands, unable to think straight.

"We heard there were stragglers camping on the other side of Lochshane Mòhr. We rode out to make sure they were gone. When we returned, Challon seemed to sense Tamlyn was in peril. Then we heard her scream and followed it."

"What happened to Pendegast?"

"He and the men are held in the oubliette."

"Will Challon hang him?"

Damian's head gave a slight shake to the sides. "Nay. Challon wants Trial by Combat. God will mete out justice."

She gasped as she focused on what he was saying. *On the morrow, Challon will seek to take the field of honor to avenge his lady. This is the true path. The way it must be. The leopard will accept this as God's justice. Only Lord Ravenhawke will seek to take his place. He must not. He will die. We all will die.*

"Nay!" The word was torn from her.

"I agree. Challon should not fight. He cannot fight. Even since the sacking of Berwick, he has been sick of soul. His mind should not face this. Dirk is too good of a warrior, the best Julian has ever trained. Challon is slowing down. I fear even a second's hesitation from him would give Pendegast the advantage. He will die. Tamlyn needs him."

Horror washed over her has Evelynour's words burned in her brain, crashing in her mind like breakers upon the shore. Only now did she comprehend what her teacher had tried to warn her of. Challon sought justice, punishment of Pendegast on the field of honor in Trial by Combat. Their God's retribution. In the combat, the righteous warrior was guided by the hand of their God—mayhap.

As she stood staring at Damian, the words echoed over and over within her head. *He will die. He will die. He will die. He will die.*

The world suddenly spun and then went black.

Chapter Seventeen

Aithinne stirred. She felt warm, secure.

Until the dream came . . .

Aithinne raced through the foggy morn, bright rays of the rising sun punching through the *haar*, piercing it with blinding shafts of white light. It burned her eyes, nearly blinded her with the peculiar brilliance. She searched, desperately. She had to find him.

Mighty destriers barded for combat were being led to the field and throngs of people milled about, walking by her, around her, bumping into her, spinning her about, faceless in the dream, though their fear seemed to hang almost tangible in the air. She pushed, shoved against them, trying to reach Damian. She had to find Damian. Stop him from throwing his life away.

Then she spotted him at the far end of the field.

Several people again moved between them, paying little attention to how urgently she battled to reach him. Hindered by their shifting positions, Aithinne could only see glimpses of the tall knight. She struggled against the careless bodies, furious at the serfs for blocking her path to him. Finally, they parted and stepped to the sides and she stared at the beautiful warrior in the face. All she could see was Damian St. Giles.

There was a vital, elemental power that emanated from this special warrior—the fire of a Dragon of Challon. Hairs on the back of her neck prickled as she watched him. The armor, covering his upper arms and thighs, and the mail habergeon were dark steel, the shirt and surcoat gray. *Another who comes with the color of fog.* The breeze stirred the black, wavy locks touched with a hint of dark fire, a mark of one bearing ancient Celtic blood. Long, curling softly about his ears, it brushed the metal gorget that covered the back of his neck.

Aithinne's breath caught and held as she stared into the gray-green eyes, shade of the foggy passes of Glen Shane in early morn. He was handsome— no, beautiful. And she loved him so.

He stood calmly while a squire buckled the metal greave, which covered his knee and shin. Despite the heavy mail and plate weighing on his body, he stood with a regal bearing at the center of the men, readying him for combat. Infuriatingly, the stupid man appeared to all as if he did not have a care in the world.

He accepted the leathern gauntlets from another squire, but did not put them on. His attention remained fixed on Aithinne as she approached. Reaching out, his elegant fingers captured her trembling chin and lifted it, forcing her not to turn away from his probing stare. She gazed at the arresting eyes, ringed with long lashes, as they observed her with a willful, incisive intelligence that was beyond the bearing of mere mortal men. The *last* man she would want to face as an adversary. The *only* man she would ever love. When she stared into those haunting eyes, the world narrowed. Nothing else existed.

There was only this knight all in gray.

His jaw was strong, square. The small mouth, etched with sensual curves, was seductive; it could lure her to forget her best intentions and surrender to him, asking nothing in return. A black curl carelessly fell over the high forehead, drawing her to reach out and push it back.

Images possessed her, singed her with an ancient fire as she touched him . . . of her hands on the bare flesh of his muscular chest, of how it felt to be kissed by this powerful knight. In a blink they were replaced by a horrible vision, of a sword piercing his body, the plate not holding. Of his blood soaking the gray shirt. It trickling from his mouth as his life force faded in the pale eyes.

Terrified, she reeled backward, her scream tearing through her mind.

Jerking awake, she sat up in the darkened room, unable to recall how she got there. It took her a moment before remembering she passed out by the midden, not so much as fainted, as she had been sucked into the void of farseeing. She shivered as traces of the vision—the foretelling—were still so real. What would be if she did not stop Damian. The only thing keeping the velvet blackness at bay was the flickering light of the candle on the table at bedside.

Her eyes cast about in the darkness seeking him. He was not in the chamber. There was a chill to the room, an emptiness.

She sat, her heart thudding painfully. So in the clutches of the kenning, she almost jumped from the bed to run after him, then she realized it was still dark. Night. There was still time to stop him.

"Your man is gone. I sent him away. Like all

males, they are useless when a woman faints. Give them a fire-breathing beastie to slay and they are calm, level-headed, full of purpose. Present them with a lass who has swooned and they go to pieces and only get in the way." Auld Bessa stepped from the shadows, gripping a pitcher. She poured a liquid in to a small bowl and then soaked a cloth in it. "This will awaken you. Put the rag to your face whilst I mix you a tansy to strengthen your blood for the babe. You must eat better. The bairn grows. You must give him the nourishment he needs."

"I would eat more if he would not make me so bloody sick," she grumbled.

"That shall pass as you two come to agreement. Male babes always cause the strongest problems, like they battle their *maither* for dominance from the instant they come into being." Bessa hummed a singsong melody while stirring the herbs in the cup of water. "The more violent the morning sickness, the more braw a warrior he shall be. You breed with a son that will one day be a legend."

Provided she stopped his father from destroying them all. A chill ran down Aithinne's spine. "Bessa, can you craft the forgetting potion as Oona does?"

Bessa snorted a laugh. "So that is what you plied on that bonnie man? Oona thinks highly of her spells to reinforce the potion, mayhap too high. With repeated doses it works—for a time. Life has a way of outflanking such craftings, so they are risky at best. Odd things set loose fragments; the more pieces that haunt him, the more he will struggle to recall. One with Fey blood, such as this man carries, will see him remember, lass. Not everything, but one day it will come flooding back to him. Some of it won't seem real, merely shards of dreams. Others will suddenly become very sharp in his thoughts. You think he shan't remember when he stares down upon his babe?"

"But Oona said it would keep him from recalling." She clutched at straws, still hoping.

Bessa nodded with a smile. "As long as he was never around you again, aye, there was nothing to summon forth those splinters of remembrances. But now you are before him, with him. You show little resistance in keeping him out of your bed. You took him, did you not? Had those nodcocks of your brothers and their pet Einar steal him away from Glenrogha on May Day? You only returned him when Challon's men grew too close to finding him in your bed at Lyonglen. You took him, used that braw warrior's body to get you with child. Worse, you do not hold too much shame over that—only that you might now be found out. You are a bold, sinful lass, Aithinne Ogilvie. You played a game of chance with the Auld Ones. Now you get more than you bargained for."

"Oh, do hush. Oft Oona and you love to poke me with a stick for my rash actions. Oona assured me the plan would work. I trusted her."

"Well, she told you the truth, but you heard what you wanted. The plan did work. You got the child you sought. Oona followed the path of what was meant to be. Just sometimes the trail is not precisely as we would wish."

"Bah, more riddles. I deal with the brew working or not concerning my Beltane antics later. I thought the forgetting potion would be the quickest way to handle the problem of the coming morn. Evelynour said—"

"Evelynour? When? She came here?" Bessa frowned, deeply shaken. "Why was I unaware of this? I was—well, nevermind, I grow old. My powers are not as strong as they once were. It takes more strength to use the kenning. Things that came so easily once now require more concentration."

"Oh, Bessa," Aithinne felt so distressed, seeing how flustered Bessa was by not sensing Evelynour's coming.

"Forget my failings. Tell me about seeing Evelynour."

"Aye, she met me by the midden with a dark augury. Said Challon would take the field of honor this coming morn to avenge his lady. Only Ravenhawke would seek to be her champion in his stead. She spoke he would . . . die if he did this, though he would kill Pendegast before he drew his last breath." A sob welled up in Aithinne's chest. "She warned if that comes to pass King Edward would take grievous offense. With fire and sword, he would come and destroy both glens."

Bessa backed up in shock, her hand flying to the side and knocking the picture over. "Och, what an old clumsy fool I am."

She sat on the bed's side and with an aging hand cupped Aithinne's cheek. It hurt Aithinne to recognize how ancient Bessa was. All three of the healers' days on this earth were numbered in few. She was not sure what the Shanes and the Ogilvies would do with their passing. They were the heart of both clans, the life force of their glens.

"Can you recall Evelynour's words?"

"She said Ravenhawke must not fight in Challon's stead. That if Challon fights for Tamlyn, King Edward will accept the judgment as their God's will. I surmise Challon has the right to take Pendegast's life in Trial by Combat. Damian does not, though the lackwit thinks he does. He wants to save Challon the pain in his mind at fighting again. Wants to give Tamlyn the man she loves if Pendegast wins."

"You could tell him about the child," she suggested.

Aithinne's body jerked from the suppressed sob. "Nay. He believes I lie about marrying Gilchrist—"

"Smart man, eh? You did lie."

"The lads said he was asking questions of people, getting different tales about what happened. He might not believe me about the child either. And even if he does, he will hate me. He was played false before—"

"Moffet? The pretty lad, squire to Challon?" Bessa asked, though her tone said she already knew the answer.

She nodded. "He is very bitter. What if he refuses to listen to me and fights anyway? Might not the warring questions I gift him with be the cause of him failing to focus upon the fight? What I tell him could slow his hand. I could be killing him . . ." She buried her face in her hands, against her bent knees, and cried. Finally, she looked up through tearful eyes. "What am I to do, Bessa?"

"The strongest magic any woman wields over a man is her body. You have the power to reach your braw warrior, bend him to your will—all without the need of any dark brew."

Aithinne took the cup Bessa handed her. "Mayhap, if he cared. But he loves Tamlyn, not me."

"Och child, you do seem to find trouble at every turn. You have lived in Tamlyn's shadow for too long, compared yourself to her, and in your mind see yourself as lacking. No man could love you when he has seen her, eh? Well, that is true in Challon's case. It does not mean 'tis the same with his cousin. St. Giles is much in the image of Challon. Did you ever stop to think, in his mind he has compared himself to the mighty Dragon, all these many years, and deemed himself not as good, too? Gives you a common ground to find pax, lass. You are Tamlyn's equal, in all ways. Stop letting yourself feel you are less. You want this man—fight for him. Brand him with your special fire."

Brand him with your special fire.

The words echoed within her as she watched Damian slashing away at the practice dummy. She had found him on the lists working in the torchlight. *Slash-slash-slash.* Spin, the sword singing through the air as he brought it down in an arc. Again and again. Killing Pendegast a dozen times over. A hundred.

Watching him scared her. He wore no sark, no vest. His muscular chest glistened with the sheen of sweat. She swallowed hard at the sheer perfection of his body. A warrior readying for battle. He saw nothing, felt nothing, but his single-minded focus of preparing for Trial by Combat.

Damian did not sense her presence. He blocked her out of his mind, his heart. She was nothing to him but a body in the dark, one that was formed in the image of the woman he loved. A pale substitute. On the morrow he would fight for Tamlyn. He would die. Even if he knew that his life would be forfeit, he would still fight.

The enormity overwhelmed her. How could she contest this?

She stood in the deep shadows, watching, crying silent tears. He was beautiful. Torches were set in a circle in the list proper, permitting him to continue practicing against the quintain. Everyone else had already had supper and gone to see their rest. Not St. Giles. The night was chilly, her breath vaporizing as she waited. Shivering, she had stayed here as along as she could. Much longer and she would risk getting chilblains.

"Damian," she called to him, but was not surprised

when he continued with the hacking and slashing at the wooden dummy. "Damian! Och, bloody man."

Risking that he would not strike her down before he reined in his killer's focus, she approached him, reaching out and putting a hand on his bare arm. He reared back, the sword raised. He stared at her so coldly, devoid of any caring. The long lashes blinked as he realized only she stood there. An odd flicker of emotion flashed in the pale eyes, but he quickly hid it behind a shutter of iron within his mind. What he had thought, she was not sure. She feared for an instant he believed her to be Tamlyn. With the hood of the mantle pulled up around her face and in the shadows, it would be easy to assume such.

Until he looked her in the face and saw the freckles, stared into her hazel eyes instead of Tamlyn's amber ones. Trying to be brave, she pretended that he did not have the power to crush her tender soul. Pretended. Failed. She almost closed her eyes against the tears that tried to come. Instead, she recalled her purpose this night was to save him, save both glens from a horror unimaginable. Her feelings mattered little when so much was at stake.

"The hour grows late. You should come in. It is chilly, my lord," she said softly.

His jaw flexed in stubbornness before he lowered the sword. "I am not ready to seek my rest." As he finally pushed back his killer instinct, his face gentled. "How do you feel? You worried me passing out as you did. Auld Bessa shooed me from the room. Said I was as useful as a boil on her behind."

"I am fine. Just too many upsets of late." She gave him a half smile. "Bessa tends to be rather colorful at times."

He returned a fleeting grin. "Aye, 'tis putting it mildly. She threatened to sprinkle some powder in my ale that wouldst make my manhood shrivel if I did not get from underfoot."

"You should come inside." She held out his gray woolen mantle to him. "The night is very cool. The fog blankets the land. You can sicken."

He shook his head, then restlessly changed the grip on the sword's pommel, half ignoring her. "I would rather continue to work off my poison. You should go inside. I wouldst not see you become unwell."

Her stubbornness surfaced. "I stand here as long as you stay."

"Tam—" he flinched as he caught the slip.

A knife to her heart. "No, I am Aithinne, not Tamlyn, though I am sure you would wish I were my cousin."

"I just have Tamlyn on my mind at the moment, Aithinne. I would never mistake you for each other. I see only the differences, not the likeness," he assured.

She managed a tight laugh. "Oh, of that I have little doubt. You plan to fight as Tamlyn's champion on the morrow. Do you not?"

He nodded, then looked away from her, unable to maintain her probing stare.

"Fool," she growled.

His head snapped up, glaring at her. "I am no fool. It is what must be. Julian has been sickened in spirit since the death of his brother Maxum. It was . . . not an easy death and it haunts him. Since wedding Tamlyn he is coming alive again. Even so, I am not sure he is truly prepared to take up the sword to kill once more. Berwick was . . . ."

She nodded when he could not go on. "Word of the sacking came, spread through the Highlands like wildfire. 'Tis spoke Edward went through the town with fire and sword."

He nodded. "Sounds so simple—with fire and sword. You have no idea. Three days, Aithinne, three days and nights. It *never* stopped. The killing. The fires. The screams. The smells. A town dying in this manner is a very ugly thing." He stared at the sword's blade as if seeing blood upon the surface. "Edward's crushing of Wales had been bad enough. Only Berwick was nothing but a demonstration of the Plantagenet's might. Madness. We were encamped at Hutton. At dawn of the first morn, Edward himself rode to the gates of the town. He called for their immediate surrender. The foolish . . . arrogant . . . stupid Scots called out, dared him to do his worst. He did. His very worst, Aithinne. You cannot imagine the . . . horror. Men, women . . . children . . . died—a thousand score. So many they needed burying in mass pits. Most still rot, now several sennights past—Edward's decree. He commanded the putrid corpses should remain where they fell, a warning to the Scots."

Bile rose in her stomach. 'Tis what would happen to Glen Shane and Glen Eallach if she failed to stop him. "Tamlyn does not need a champion, my lord. She has a husband. Through Trial by Ordeal he is made invincible because he is the instrument of your God's justice. You shall not have that shield."

"Enough, Aithinne. I shall discuss this no more."

"Damn you, all of life must be decided by you, no matter who else is affected. You fight because you love Tamlyn. You break your Commandments. Thou shall not covet another's wife—is that not one of your ten laws? You fight because you hold another man's lady in your heart, then your God will turn his back on you. You will die. Because you fight with stained honor, this valley and the valley beyond shall bear your punishment, the wrath of your king for your affront."

He shook his head. "You are not well, Aithinne. Please return to your bed, rest. Shortly the dawn will come, then this matter will be settled, finished. Then we can talk of the future—"

"There will be *no* future. Your arrogance shall summon vengeance from Longshanks. With fire and sword, my lord, fire and sword. What happened at Berwick will be visited upon Glen Shane and Glen Eallach. Your precious Tamlyn will die, Raven and Rowena . . . even I shall die, though that shall matter little to you." Tears streamed down her face to where she could barely think, let alone speak. "You condemn us all because of your love. A love that is wrong."

"You speak nonsense, Aithinne." He tried to put an arm around her. "Come, I shall see you to your room. You are not well."

She ducked away from his grasp and rounded on him. "Of course I am not well, you lackwit! You are not listening. You will not listen. You will die—"

He grabbed her, pulling her body against his chest, holding her while the sobs racked her. The strong, unyielding arms held her firm, despite her struggling against him. Then she didn't want to struggle. She wanted him to hold her through this night.

Stay with her when the dawn came.

Chapter Eighteen

"Sleep well?" Aithinne echoed sourly.

That was it? He was just going to walk away from her. Damn his blind eyes! This was not going at all as she hoped. Well, she had not really planned out what she was going to do to keep him from fighting come the morrow. She counted on him being his usual randy self to aid her scheming. Never before had he been reluctant to lie with her.

"I seek the solitude of my room this night. To prepare for the coming morn."

Over my dead body. She bit back the words before they escaped. "You do not wish to be with me?"

"If I stay with you, Aithinne, we will do little sleeping. I will need all my strength to face Pendegast. He is too good to gift with that sort of advantage." His hand reached out and cupped her face, his eyes looking at her full of emotion, almost awe.

If only it were with love.

Aithinne tried to smile, but her lips trembled. "What if I said, take off your clothes, Damian?"

"Ah, lass, you do not play fair." He kissed her forehead. "Rest well, Firebrand. Feel better."

He turned on his heels to leave, but she caught

his arm. *Think, silly woman,* her mind screamed. "Ah . . . eh . . . 'tis chilly in here. Could you please build up the fire before you go?"

Damian hesitated. She was never a convincing liar, too lacking in genuine guile. Laying the back of her hand against his cheek, she let him feel how cold she was. That much was no lie. She was cold, cold to the marrow, afraid she was not woman enough to stop him by fair means or foul.

He finally nodded and stepped to the fireplace, methodically laying several peat bricks in an alternating stack and then striking flint until the spark caught. The heady scent filled the air and the tendrils of warmth soon snaked through the damp room. She took off her mantle and laid it over the end of the bed, as he stood and dusted his hands off on his thighs.

"There, Aithinne. That should hold you through the night. Just add a brick now and again and you should stay comfortable. 'Tis a cool start to summer. I can see getting used to these Highlands will take a bit of doing."

Spinning, so her back was to him, she lifted her long hair over one shoulder. "Could you? I cannot reach the lacings on my kirtle. I did not bring a lady's maidservant and I would hate to awaken Tamlyn's to aid me." When he didn't move, she glanced over her shoulder. "Please, Damian. I should not wish to sleep laced into my gown."

After a long hesitation, he stepped forward and rather roughly tugged the leather lacings through the grommets. He separated the back of the gown, then his movements slowed, his large hands sliding inside the gown about her waist. His touch caused her heart to jump. The callused hands, toughened from years of using a sword, squeezed her soft flesh.

She closed her eyes and leaned her head backward

against his chest, rubbing it back and forth. All the
passion, all the love for this man rose within her,
words she craved to say, words to tell him of her love.
Words he had not given her the right to speak. Instead, she expressed what stormed through her by
reaching behind, her hands grabbing the back of his
thighs. She flexed her fingernails, digging into
his strong muscles. As if she could take and hold him
forever.

"Aithinne . . ." He breathed against her head,
both a warning and a near plea for her to let
him go.

She smiled when his groin bucked against her
derrière, felt confidence rise in her power to en-
thrall him. Greedily, he pulled her against him, increasing the contact. Savoring it. Then he went and
ruined it by very firmly setting her away from him.
"No, Aithinne."

She swung around, backing up in rapid steps so
she stayed between him and the door. "I curse your
'no.' You plan to fight for another woman on the
morrow, die for her. Damn your eyes. And you dare
say no to me? Think again, bloody Lord Arrogant.
You fight for Tamlyn come morn. Fine. Go ahead
and throw your life away for another woman. This
night you are mine."

The muscles in his jaw flexed in fury, though it
was nearly her undoing to see the glimmer of a tear
in his eye.

She was so scared, terrified of losing him, that
she did not care if he saved his love for Tamlyn.
Foolish now, what had seemed so important to her
before now mattered little. She tossed all her pride
to the wind, cared nothing for her pain. "Love
me . . . if only for this night."

Grabbing her by the waist he tried to lift her away
from the door. She wrapped her arms around his

neck and brushed her mouth against his hard lips. She savored his taste, making her dizzy. He fought it, his lips remaining firm, but not for long. Instead of trying to put her aside, he yanked her to him, his mouth devouring hers. His kiss was savage, taking all and giving no quarter, but then her surrender was his, always his.

He broke the kiss, gasping for air. "You bedevil my mind. I cannot think when I am around you. You are like mead hitting my blood. What am I to do with you, Aithinne?"

The woman in her rose to the pure male power surging through him. She reached up and stroked his cheek with her thumb. "Love me, Damian, just love me."

He turned to kiss the inside of her right hand. Closing his eyes, he rubbed his face against her palm. The kenning let her feel his inner conflict, but she'd be damned if she'd make it easy for him to leave her this night.

Then he was kissing her again. Not a gentle kiss, but one speaking his violent need for her. Damian kept his face clear of whiskers, in the Norman way, but it had been a while since he last removed them, so they were rough. That didn't stop her from responding in full measure. She held nothing back, pouring her love into her passion, letting her kisses speak so eloquently the words he would not grant her the right to say.

His hands gathered the kirtle up her thighs, then were on her flesh, as he walked her backward to the bed. Bending her back to the feather mattress, he unlaced his chausses and entered her in one hard plunge as though seeking to bring this to a brutal physical level rather than one spun from the magic of her love. She little cared. She would take Damian

St. Giles anyway she could get him, teach him the
power of her love for him.

He stretched her arms over her head, then tightly
laced his fingers with hers. He drove into her again
and again, slamming against her. Deep down, she
thought he was trying to shock her, punish her from
deterring him from his set path. Determined not to
let him have control, she arched, meeting each
fierce thrust.

Her release came, splintering her into a thousand red-hot shards. Instead of relaxing and enjoying the ecstasy, he increased his pace, driving her
even harder, not giving any retreat. She did not
want it.

"Again, Aithinne. I want to watch your eyes as you
come apart for me, around me," he growled, raising up on his elbows.

She purred, "Oh aye, Damian . . . again . . . and
again . . . and again." Wrapping her legs about his
waist, she increased the angle for his invasion of her
body, letting the emotional storm sweep through
them.

His mouth closed on her neck, scoring it with his
sharp teeth, then sucking hard. He would mark her
skin. She would wear the bruise proudly. Then his
mouth closed over hers and he kissed her until the
last shards of reason fled and only the consuming
flames of passion remained. Damian took her, devoured her with the hunger of a man seeking dominance or salvation.

Or one saying goodbye.

Fighting that horror, she loosened her fingers,
then fisted them in the thick black curls at the back
of his head. She tightened the grip, holding onto
the locks as though she would never let him go.
This was not a gentle coming together. They waged
war. She dreaded she fought a losing battle. Time

was running out. Damian was so wrapped up in his love for Tamlyn, his belief that she had saved him when he was dying, that he could not see past those visions he held dear in his heart.

This was their last battlefield. She *had* to reach him, cradle his defiant soul with her love and pray it was enough. If not, he would destroy them both. Destroy both Glens. She poured every ounce of her heart into the physical expression of her love, trying to show him there was something just before his eyes. Someone who loved him more than life. She held back nothing, giving everything he demanded, more than he asked. Pushing him as hard as he pushed her.

Aithinne was betting everything. Their future.

The sound of the door closing broke Aithinne's deep slumber. She fought the need to give into the sleep, sucking her back into the blackness, panic pushing her heart to slam repeatedly against her ribs. Instead of slowing, the pace only increased as she realized Damian was not in the room.

He was gone. Gone to his death.

"Och, fool. I might just take a knife to him. 'Twould solve all our problems." Her bare feet touched the cold stone floor as she slipped from the bed. Tossing open the wardrobe, she snatched up a plain sark and plaid kirtle and quickly slid them on. There was no one about as she made her way down the hall to the room where Damian was staying. The door was open partway so she entered without knocking.

In black leathern hose, gray shirt and studded black arming jack, he stood patiently while his squire, Dyel, fastened the buckle points on his long mail hauberk. Damian was aware of her presence.

She saw his jaw flex, but he continued speaking instructions lowly to Dyel. Kneeling, the lad strapped on the greaves and then pulled Damian's gray surcoat over his head.

Damian's pale eyes met hers as he hung the baldric around his hips and buckled it. With a faint gesture of dismissal with his hand to the door, he signaled the squire to leave them alone. "Wait just outside, Dyel."

"Aye, my lord." The young man gave a small nodding bow to Aithinne as he passed.

She waited until he stepped out in the passage. "You cannot fight this day, Damian. If you fight, you will die."

He tucked his dagger in his belt, determination showing in the set of the curves surrounding his mouth. "All women entreat their men not to fight, fear they are going to die. I regret you are upset, Aithinne. But this is how it must be. Please accept that. I need the focus of my mind. I cannot spare you a thought now."

"Nay, 'tis not just my fear. You will destroy us all. All of Glen Shane and Glen Eallach. 'Tis not my dread of losing you speaking. Last night Evelynour came to me beside the midden, carrying a dark augury. She warned me that if you fight you will die. Before you die you will kill Pendegast. When you do, both glens will be made to suffer Edward's wrath. He will accept Dirk's death in Trial by Combat as Challon's right. The same dispensation will not extend to you or our lands."

"Aithinne, there was no one but you by the midden. When you passed out mayhap you dreamed this—"

"Oh aye, I did dream it. After. I walked the path between Annwyn—the Otherworld— so I may see what will be if you do not listen to me. Damn you, Lord Arrogant, your way you die. We all die. Are you willing to take that risk, just to fight for Tamlyn? You of all people should believe in the power of the kenning. You have these things in you, do you not? 'Tis the blood of your *maithar* speaking to you. You know I utter truths."

"Aye, I know the ways of the kenning. 'Tis not so simple. I fight for Julian, as well, he is my brother—"

"Julian fights for himself this day." Challon's voice caused them both to turn. All in black, barded for battle, the man struck an imposing figure as he strode into the room. The Black Dragon. "Yea, we are brothers in the truest sense. Howbeit, this is *my* challenge. The combat will be fought before my people. I fight for my wife's honor. The people of Glen Shane judge me this day, as much as God, and ultimately the king shall. I rule here by right, but also by respect. Respect comes from my unassailable power. My people would lose respect if I let you fight in my stead. I would lose respect for myself." Challon turned his back to Aithinne as he lowered his voice. "Tamlyn is my wife, Damian. *I* fight for her. I have warned you about interfering in my marriage."

Aithinne closed her eyes against the wave of pain lancing through her. Even Challon was aware of Damian's feelings for Tamlyn.

"Dirk comes from a wealthy and powerful family, much favored by Edward," Challon continued. "I cannot hang him. Punishment *must* come from me, and in a fashion that leaves Edward no recourse. The First Knight of Christendom will understand and abide by God's law. You fighting in my stead will not have the blessing of the Church or king. Only I can face Dirk in Trial by Combat."

Damian pursed his mouth as he listened to Challon. His eyes moved toward the arrow loop, casting his sight far, deep in thought. Aithinne tasted regret as the stubborn man listened to neither of their arguments, blocking their words out.

Challon saw it as well, for her turned to face her. "He is not hearing me, is he?"

She shook her head sadly. "I know you do not place much faith in the kenning, Lord Challon, and sometimes it fails me when it should serve me best. Know that Evelynour is a true seer. She knew you would come to this land, to claim Tamlyn, several seasons past. Last night she warned me Damian must not fight. He would die. Then Edward will come with fire and sword."

Challon smiled, lightly resting his hand on the pommel of his sword. "Then there is only one thing to do. Damian?"

"Aye, Julian?"

When Damian swung back around, Julian moved so fast he did not have time to block as Challon yanked the sword's hilt straight out of the sheath and used it to ram hard against Damian's jaw.

Damian stood for an instant, surprise flooding his handsome face. Then his knees buckled and he collapsed to the floor.

Challon gave a small nod. "Sometimes, in dealing with Damian, the fewer words used, the quicker the resolution."

Aithinne sat with Damian's head in her lap. She lovingly ran her fingers through the black curls at his forehead, then traced his thick black brows. Placing a hand over his heart, she felt it thudding strongly, though in a normal rhythm. He was all right. "If only you would open that heart, my brave warrior."

She was not happy when he stirred just a short time later. She had hoped he would remain unaware until after the combat was done. His right arm moved to his chest and then back out as he struggled to pull from the darkness claiming him. Hoping to slow him, she pushed against his shoulder, but he only struggled harder.

He sat up, blinking. "How . . . long?"

"Too long, my lord. 'Tis done. You should rest a bit more." Aithinne lied without hesitation, hoping to prevent him from going after Challon.

Rubbing his bruised jaw, he glared at her. "For a woman who continually lies, you would think she might develop the skill better. Some day I shall beat you for it."

He pushed up to stand, without her help. As she tried to block him from leaving the room, he set her from him. "Do not interfere, Aithinne."

"You cannot leave. Damian, wait! Please, by all that is sacred to you, hold!"

Not heeding her call, his steps hurried down the hall and took the stairs, two at a time. The steps were too wide; Aithinne could not follow at that pace. She picked up her skirts, going down as fast as she could. By the time she reached the courtyard, the irritating man had already mounted his destrier left waiting by Dyel and spurred him from the bailey. Not even looking back.

"Curse your black head, Damian St. Giles." Not bothering to saddle a horse, Aithinne ran toward the gate, only to have Challon's Norman gatekeeper call after her as she ran through the open portcullis.

She did not even slow.

Ravens fussed in the distance over the passes of Glen Shane as she approached the field. Aithinne saw this as an ill omen. Her lungs burned, but she pushed on, fearful she would be too late. Aithinne raced through the foggy morn, bright rays of the rising sun punching through the *haar*, piercing it with blinding shafts of white light. It burned her eyes, nearly blinded her with the peculiar brilliance.

She panicked as she realized her dream had been made reality!

She searched, desperately. She had to find him. She had to stop him even if she had to lie down before the hooves of his charger.

Mighty destriers barded for combat were being led to the field and throngs of people milled about, walking by her, around her, bumping into her, spinning her about, faceless in the panic, though their fear seemed to hang almost tangible in the air. She pushed, shoved against them, trying to reach Damian. She had to find Damian. Stop him from throwing his life away. Somehow she had to stop this vision from unfolding.

Then she spotted him at the far end of the open field.

Several people moved between them, paying little attention to how urgently she battled to reach him. Hindered by their shifting positions, Aithinne could only see glimpses of the tall knight. She struggled against the careless bodies, furious at the serfs for blocking her path to him. Finally, they parted and stepped to the sides and she stared the beautiful warrior in the face.

All she could see was Damian St. Giles.

There was a vital, elemental power that emanated from this special warrior—the fire of a Dragon of Challon. Hairs on the back of her neck prickled as she watched him. The armor, covering his upper arms and thighs, and the mail habergeon were dark steel, the shirt and surcoat gray. *Another who comes with the color of fog.* The breeze stirred the black, wavy locks touched with a hint of dark fire, a mark of one bearing ancient Celtic blood. Long, curling softly about his ears, it brushed the metal gorget that covered the back of his neck.

Aithinne's breath caught and held as she stared into the gray-green eyes, shade of the foggy passes of Glen Shane in early morn. He was handsome—nay, beautiful. And she loved him so.

Then he turned to Challon, who was being made ready for battle by his squires, Gervase, Michael, and Vincent.

Aithinne finally breathed, nearly swooning, as she comprehended Damian was not going to fight. The tears she had been holding broke free on a sob, torn from her. He caught her in his arms and pulled her to his chest.

"Shhh . . . my lady. You do not want me to fight. So I do not fight. And yet you cry anyway. Is there no pleasing you?"

Suddenly, the people lining the edge of the field stirred again as Tamlyn came running toward them, Moffet on her heels. She pulled up when she saw the wooden rack holding five lances. The color drained from her face. Shoving to break free of the people blocking her path, Tamlyn headed straight for Julian, clearly determined to stop this at all costs.

Aithinne felt dreadful. She knew what the woman, who was like a sister to her, was facing.

Ignoring his furious wife bearing down on him, Julian examined one of the lances, running his hand over it. "Gervase, change this one out."

"Aye, my lord." Gervase immediately set to doing Challon's bidding.

"Challon, I want this stopped. Now!"

"Tamlyn. I see you found a way out." His lashes

made a small sweep as he swung around to stare at Moffet. "I cannot imagine how."

Damian's son blushed and lowered his green eyes, knowing he had failed his lord.

Patting the lad on the arm to assure him, Damian handed Challon the Glenrogha claymore. "I honed the edge myself last night, Julian."

"Damian, take Tamlyn away—" Julian requested.

Nodding, Damian reached out to take Tamlyn's arm. "He is right, Tamlyn, let me take you back to Glenrogha."

She backed up. "Why? So my idiot husband can get himself killed and I do not have to watch? You think that, you are as big an idiot as he." He put a hand on her upper arm to lead her from the field. "Take your hand off me, Damian St. Giles, or I shall claw your eyes out."

"Tamlyn, calm yourself—" Julian began, only to have her cut him off.

"I shall be delighted to calm myself—when you come back to Glenrogha with me and forget this nonsense."

Julian exhaled and glanced skyward as if seeking patience. "I already explained why these steps are necessary. That swine dared to touch you. No one touches my lady and lives. This is the only way."

Tamlyn shivered as she saw there was no changing his mind. "Fool! Stupid, arrogant fool!" She choked on the words. "You risk all, Challon. What is honor without your life?"

His arms encircled her, pulling her to his chest, and letting her cry. "You have so little faith in me, Tamlyn? I was the king's champion, the best in all the Isles. I wish you would return to Glenrogha. If you are here you might divert me and I need no distractions."

"If you insist on getting yourself killed, then I am

going to be here to go to you and kick you for it."
She tried to laugh, but a sob of pain escaped her.

"If you will not return to Glenrogha, stay to the
sidelines and permit me to prepare myself. I would
prefer not to give you a reason to kick me." He
lifted her chin and lightly brushed a kiss to her lips.
"Please, go with Damian."

Tamlyn hugged him tightly, crushing him to her
as if to hold him and protect him. She stepped back
and then glanced around her. Looking at Gervase,
she barked, "Give me your knife."

He blinked, startled by her command. "My lady?"

"Don't act the lackwit." She held out her hand
and snapped her fingers. "Your knife. Give it."

"But, my lady . . ." He glanced to Challon, in
search of guidance.

"I swear, Challon, you must deliberately seek
dullards for squires." Tamlyn turned and spoke to
Aithinne, then reached over and snatched the
knife from Damian's belt. She noticed all the men
except Challon backed up a step. She chuckled de-
risively. "Dolts."

Tamlyn ignored them and leaned down and
sliced away at the hem of her woolen kirtle. When
she had cut a thin band, she straightened up,
handed the knife back to Damian. Stepping to
Julian, she tied the tartan sash of black and green
around the middle of his left, upper arm. "If you
are determined to go through with this, then you
must have a lady's colors."

Aithinne sobbed as Julian caressed the back of her
cousin's head in such love. Challon loved Tamlyn so,
and no one doubted how the lady of Glenrogha felt
about the dark warrior who was now her husband.
Their love was so beautiful. She felt envy and knew
they were the luckiest people on this green earth.

Oh, why could they not live in peace without the ugliness of the world intruding on their lives?

"Moffet." Julian called the one word command.

The young lad took hold of Tamlyn's arm. "Come, my lady, you must follow me."

Tears filled Tamlyn's eyes as she nodded, though she continued to stare at him. "Julian, I . . ."

"Go with Moffet, my lady," Julian urged gently. His eyes looked to Aithinne, beseeching her to help Tamlyn face this. "Care for my lady?" His plea was almost whispered.

Aithinne nodded, turned, and followed Tamlyn.

At the side of the field, Aithinne stood next to the trembling Tamlyn. Soon, Damian joined them to watch the two men ride to the center of the field. Challon, all in black and on the black horse, was a striking contrast to Pendegast, who wore a brilliant scarlet and yellow surcoat over silver mail and plate, and sat on a snow-white charger.

Aithinne put her arm about Tamlyn, and felt the quiver ripple through her cousin's body when Malcolm spoke, asking if Challon and Pendegast accepted one man lives, one man dies in Trial by Combat, believing this to be God's will. After affirming this, each turned his mighty horse and retired to his end of the field. The squires stepped up on the mounting blocks and placed the battle helms on the warriors.

Malcolm dropped a white cloth, it fluttering to the ground. Then two warriors spurred their steeds, lowering their lances into place.

Aithinne closed her eyes as the lances crashed into each knight, unable to watch. She heard the crowd groan, and several called, "He held! Challon held!"

It was a living nightmare. The sounds of the

horses, the lances breaking and splitting. Knowing they splintered against armor that protected flesh and bone.

"Two passes. Three more to go," Damian said.

The horse screamed as they started the next run. Damian's body jerked as the crowd exclaimed in horror. Unable to bear it, Aithinne opened her eyes, to see the last charge had flipped Challon over the back of his mighty destrier, Pagan, and slammed him to the ground.

Tamlyn moaned, her grip on Aithinne's arm so hard she would leave bruises. Aithinne, like everyone else, held their breaths to see if Challon rose.

Dirk dropped the broken lance, then pulled his mace and chain from the side of the saddle. Slowly, Challon staggered to his feet, only to have Dirk's chain and ball catch him across the back. There was no plate there. Only the heavy hauberk stopped the ugly weapon from mauling flesh and bone. Pivoting his horse on its hind legs, Dirk came at Challon again, the heavy spiked ball slamming repeatedly into Challon's back and helm.

Tamlyn screamed. Grabbing Damian's arm, she begged, "Stop this! For God's sake, stop this madness! He is *killing* Challon!" She started to push past Damian, but he caught and held her arm.

"Stay back, you'll get Challon killed, if not yourself."

Dirk came at Julian again. As he swung the mace, Pagan flew at the other steed. Head lowered, the midnight charger crashed into Dirk's mount. Using teeth and hooves, the screaming animals reared, fighting with the same hatred as the men. Nearly berserk, Pagan tore into the other horse's flesh, blood gushing down the animal's white neck. The dueling stallions unseated Pendegast, the magnificent destrier likely saving Challon's life.

Aithinne swallowed back bile, watching as Challon yanked off his badly dented helm and tossed it to the ground. She reeled, faint. Not seeing Challon's face, but Damian's. The kenning told her she now faced the point where Damian would have met his death. Would Challon die in his place?

At each end of the field, the great swords had been stuck in the ground, left for the warriors to claim if they could reach them. Challon now headed for the Sword of Glenrogha. Dirk watched for several breaths as Challon's staggering steps carried him to the mighty weapon. With one more glance, he turned and ran toward his.

Again, the furious black horse came to take a role, blocking Dirk's path, preventing him from reaching his sword. Giving Challon time.

Challon reached the sword. Instead of pulling it from the ground, he collapsed to his knees before it.

"What is he doing?" Tamlyn's voice broke as she strained against Damian's grip. "Julian, get up!"

Aithinne buried her face against the back of Damian's shoulder, unable to watch. She feared while changing the path of their lives, she saved Damian, but had condemned Challon to death. She could only sob her sorrow.

Challon looked up at the sword as though it were a cross and he offered prayer. His face of such angelic beauty stared transfixed at the golden stone in the hilt. Aithinne kept experiencing that slippage. One instant it was Challon, then next she blinked and it was Damian. The gray clouds broke and a shaft of brilliant morning sun shone down upon Julian and refracted through the amber in the hilt of the great sword, as if he received a blessing from On High.

Finally rising, Julian yanked the weapon from the ground and turned to face Pendegast. The blades

clanged and rang out, again and again. Dirk
backed Challon up with the force of his blows. Finally, Challon's blade deflected the downward arc
of Dirk's. Using the momentum, Julian spun his
whole body completely around, and then delivered
a kick to the center of Dirk's plated chest. Pendegast appeared exhausted, while amazingly, Challon
gained a second wind.

Never had she seen a man so controlled, so powerful with his every movement. Small wonder the men
called this warrior the Black Dragon of Challon.

Julian spun once more. The force of the turn saw
his sword carry Dirk's right out of his hands, flying
through the air. It landed, embedding in the earth
and wobbling with the force.

Shoving her hand into her mouth, Tamlyn bit
down on her knuckle as Dirk picked up one of the
half-broken lances and wielded it. Since it was
longer than the sword, he was able to keep out of
harm's path while swinging it as a club. Meeting
each thrust, Challon used the claymore to whack
off chunks of wood from the lance. Dirk quickly
backed up until he finally neared his broadsword.
He tossed the now considerably shorter lance at
Challon's head and lunged for the weapon.

Throngs of people cheered, called warnings, and
moaned with each turn of events, clearly rooting
for Challon.

Dirk came up in a round swing, intending to slice
Challon through the midst, but Julian jumped
back, arching like a cat. Even so, the tip of Dirk's
sword ripped through the surcoat and hammered
the plate underneath.

Aithinne felt as if she absorbed the blow to Challon. She worried about Tamlyn and the child she
carried, fearing how this all affected her.

Just then, Pagan charged across the field. He'd

set Dirk's stallion to running. The poor animal, weakened by the blood loss, collapsed at the side of the field. Now Pagan came back, to again fight at his master's side. Dirk panicked and gave an overhead blow to Challon, driving him down on one knee. Using the claymore as a shield, Challon swung the sword behind him to protect his shoulder and back. Dirk moved in and slammed his knee to Julian's chin. It sent him sprawling backward, open to a final blow before he'd be able to recover.

Aithinne screamed, "No!" in the same breath as she heard it from Tamlyn.

The monstrous black destrier flew at Dirk, rearing high, hooves slashing. He caught Pendegast hard on the head with a hoof and continued to pound at him even after the man was down.

Sickening, Aithinne turned, seeking Damian, wanting him to hold her, warming her.

Only he held Tamlyn.

Michael rushed to help Julian to his feet, while Gervase and Vincent took charge of Pagan. Finally standing on his own, Julian went to the still excited horse, patted his forehead and whispered to him.

He ordered, "Get that . . . carrion off the field." Several men obeyed him, dragging Dirk's body away.

Tears streaming down her face, Tamlyn jerked away from Damian and ran to Challon.

As he finally looked at her, Damian's face was haunted. He almost seemed to reel from her silent accusation. They stared at each other, the wind ruffling his black hair. He was so handsome, everything she could want in a man.

And he did not love her.

He said nothing. There was nothing he could say. Turning, he rushed to Challon, leaving her alone. So very alone.

Chapter Nineteen

Aithinne looked at the endless flow of people and animals up ahead, winding at a snail's pace along the road to Berwick, and as far as the eye could see. Turning in her saddle, she noticed it was the same behind her. She sighed. Exhausted. Frustrated. Sweat dripped to her brow; she swiped it away with the back of her hand before it hit her eyes. A small stream trickled down her spine, itching unbearably, only it was impossible to do anything whilst on the back of a horse. She suffered in silence. Complaining would not change a thing. Gritting her teeth, she rode on along with the Challon cadre.

Now that she was over three months along, the babe had made peace with her body. The sickness did not come as often, nor was it as severe. She welcomed the respite. Presently, the heat was making her ill, enough so she was not sure if she could hold it in. August was always the hottest time of year for the land, but this season it seemed worse than usual. The whole of Scotland labored under a long drought.

Somehow it seemed to mirror her soul. Her life.

The high heat mattered little. Edward Planta-

genet, King of England, Lord Paramount of Scotland, had commanded a Parliament called for late
August, and anyone of note was to appear before
him and take oaths before the new ruler of the
Scots, now that all of Scotland had been brought to
heel. Every noble, freeholder, clergy, burgess, and
vassal—over some hundred score—would bend
knee to the new monarch of the land, give extorted
oaths of fealty and homage, and be made to sign an
instrument of their acceptance.

Lord and Lady Challon, Lord Ravenhawke and
Lady Coinnleir had been requested to show. Both
Julian and Damian knew there was no ignoring the
royal summons.

Aithinne sat upon her mouse-color mare,
Gràdh—Darling—riding beside Tamlyn. Her cousin
guided Goblin—her wedding gift from Challon—
with less than her usual adroit skill. Aithinne was
concerned. Tamlyn was a superior rider, but she
seemed to be distressed beyond the uncomfortable
circumstances and transferring that unease to the
nervous horse. The black mare kept breaking ranks,
dancing sideways, sweating in fear. The horse again
swung wildly, sidestepping, then backing up to
where its flanks crashed into the side of *Gràdh*.

"Tamlyn, have care!" Aithinne frowned, trying to
steer her horse out of the path of Goblin, but
Tamlyn kept looking about her, as if she really did
not see what was happening. It was clear she was
panicked, though the reason why was not.

"Sorry." Tamlyn looked at her with worried eyes,
looking so unlike herself.

Aithinne frowned, but at the situation more than
Tamlyn. "What troubles?"

Tamlyn smiled, but there was no humor to it.
"Nightmares. The likes I hope you never have.

Nightmares of what I fear we are heading into and there is no escape."

Just then the wind shifted, carrying upon it a sweet, sickening odor, warning of what lay ahead. Aithinne reeled from the foul stench, reining hard on *Gràdh* to keep her from bolting. Unable to abide the fetor, she reached out and snatched up the hem of her kirtle, pulling it over her mouth and nose—the only way she could breathe.

Grim of face, Challon barked, "We are downwind of Berwick." The Dragon's horse pranced sideways, as he turned it back so he could speak to them. "Tamlyn, Lady Aithinne, there is no way to prepare you for what lies ahead."

"By the Holy Virgin, what sort of brainsickness is this?" Damian gasped. "There are no words to describe this foulness."

"It is no more than I feared." Challon moved his steed back in position next to Damian, then he glanced over his shoulder with worry at Tamlyn. Julian replied lowly, so Aithinne could overhear only part of his words. ". . . remember to thank Edward for the coming experience . . . commanded the bodies should be left until Scotland was brought to heel. I fear it is precisely what has happened."

Damian stared at Julian in horror. "Not even Edward would subject us to this. Think of the ill airs. He cannot . . . no man would—"

Challon warned, "Tell Edward whatever he wishes to hear . . . mayhap we might escape Berwick with our heads."

Despite the heat of the hot August day, Aithinne shivered.

Trying to control her revulsion, Aithinne fixed her eyes on Damian's back, where he rode next to

Challon. Hot resentment bubbled in her blood. Resentment was good. Anger was good. It kept her mind focused on wanting to kick him, instead of opening her mouth and screaming at the horrors about them as they rode through what was left of the town of Berwick. She did not want the images of dead bodies, over four months decomposed, to be burned into her memory. Thus she targeted Damian.

"*Ceann-clò*," she muttered, calling him a blockhead in the Gaelic.

Tamlyn had proved too excitable, unable to handle her mount. Fearing she would unseat herself, and possibly be trampled under the hooves of the spooked horses, Challon had lifted his wife from the back of Goblin and now carried her before him on his mighty destrier.

"Sir Nodcock troubles naught what happens to me," she groused under her breath.

Moffet riding to her left said, "Beg pardon, Lady Aithinne. Were you addressing me?"

"Nay, I merely made comment that your lord father could not care less if I fell off my horse and were stamped to death," she said sourly. This whole ugly situation was wearing her down. She was ready to cry. Instead, she vented her pain and aggravation upon Damian, hoping to get through this foul miasma.

"That is not so, my lady. My father asked that I ride next to you, assure you were protected."

Finding distraction in the high dudgeon, her mouth compressed into a grimace, determined to continue on with her peeve. "Oh aye, I oft settle for crumbs from the table."

The handsome lad on the verge of manhood offered her a smile. "Methinks, Lady Aithinne, you speak in riddles."

"Gervase!" Challon called.

"Yea, my lord." The squire spurred his steed past Moffet and Athinne to catch up to his liege.

Challon, still cradling Tamlyn in front of him, spoke over her head. He tossed the man the reins to Tamlyn's riderless mount. "Take the reins on Goblin and lead her. Ride in front of us with Vincent and Michael. Carry the standard high. Let everyone know the Dragon of Challon comes."

Hard-bitten and dour-faced, Julian and Damian rode behind the phalanx formed by the squires, forcing their way into the fallen town. Aithinne's heart broke as they spurred past women on foot, tearfully hiding behind their kerchiefs. Women with haunted eyes that bespoke their loved ones had died in this wasted town. Aithinne went back to holding the hem of her gown to her face, so desperate not to gag at the overwhelming pall, floating in the air like a black fog. Her tears stained the rust colored material.

The horses' hooves clattered over the wooden bridge, spanning the wide, dry ditch meant for defense, and then into the arched stone entrance of Castle Berwick's bailey, finally their journey's end reached. Off to the right, Aithinne spotted the Douglas standard draped, half dragging in the mud. Blue stars on a silver field—the flag that had flown over the castle's ramparts before Berwick was invaded by the English in spring. Now, the proud Douglas standard was splattered with horseshite, object of English spite and ridicule.

Aithinne fought dizziness as they finally came to a halt and the squires took control of their mounts. Damian came and helped her from *Gràdh*. His eyes stared into hers for a long instant, so many thoughts swirling in the pale depths—sorrow, fury, regret—

but he said naught. Too near fainting, Aithinne let the moment pass and turned away.

So shook by Damian, she immediately slammed hard into the chest of another. Phelan Comyn. His hands caught her by the elbows to steady her. Unsettled for some reason, she jerked back, but his grip held her firm. She glowered at him, unblinking. Something in his manner made her feel as if she looked into the face of a stranger.

"Aithinne, how have you been? You are as lovely as ever." The handsome man smiled, but it had as much warmth as a hungry wolf salivating over a newborn lambkin.

"So sorry to learn you are going blind as well as lackwit, Phelan." Once more, she tried to yank away from his hold.

The smile remained in place, though there was a hard edge to his eyes. "And as sweet of nature, I see."

Damian moved in to the edge of her vision. "Let go of my—"

"Lady wife, Lord Ravenhawke? I think not. There was no marriage performed at Lyonglen—not for your grandsire, not for you. The priest was called, but for last rites, methinks." His expression glowed triumphant.

"By my English laws, mayhap 'my betrothed' would suit better. Howbeit, I avowed I was wed to the Lady Aithinne before Challon, her brothers, and Dinsmore. Then repeated the claim before you, with Challon as a witness." He lifted his black brows in triumph. "You forget I am half Scot. I respect the way of my lady *maither*. Old Pictish law says if a man declares he claims a woman as his wife before witnesses and she gives her aye, then they are wed. Edward commanded me to take the Lady Aithinne to wife when he granted the charter to

Glen Eallach, same as he ordered Challon to wed one of the Earl Kinmarch's lady daughters. Edward was too busy putting the boot to Scotland's spine when Challon married with the Lady Tamlyn. I hope to gift him with the satisfaction of a Christian ceremony whilst we are at Berwick. I think he will be most pleased."

Phelan's eyes shifted between Aithinne and the black-haired man who just stole Phelan's joy at causing a bit of mischief. "Some say you are naught but a bastard, another dragon from the litter of Michael Challon."

"I loved my sire, but also looked upon Michael Challon as a second father, since he fostered me. If I were his likelylad, I wouldst find naught but honor in the hand of fate. Howbeit, think twice if you plan to drag that worn-out tale to Edward to tattle. I can tell you 'tis one he's heard a score times over. He knows from whose loins I sprang. Even if it were true, it would make no difference. I am Lyonglen now. Edward raised me to such. He is the law of this land. What he says is what will be. If you do not know this, you shall learn in the next few days." Damian smiled as he took Aithinne's arm. "Now, excuse us. You need to get in line with the rest of the Scots, whilst I escort my lady out of this killing heat."

Halberd-bearing minions in dented jacks stood at the entrance to Castle Berwick's courtyard, asking of the arriving people, "English or Scots?"

Aithinne noticed the English were steered to the right and quickly led into the cool stone castle, out of the scorching noon sun. Scots were not so lucky. They were herded into a queue to the left that slowly snaked outside the bailey through a side postern door and then into the inner ward. From there, they were forced across the cobbled courtyard and were actually hustled toward the kitchen. She frowned at the deliberate humiliation. The Scots were shepherded into the castle proper through the servants' entrance. An insult. More cruelly, they were not permitted to break from the long line to get a drink of water or even to relieve themselves. Double ranks of armed guards, nearly shoulder-to-shoulder, held their halberd points like a schiltron, turning the Scots back to the queue should they attempt to leave it.

The dark stones of the castle sweated in the summer humidity. The whole area reeked of pine-pitch from the torches lining the walls, trying to mask the repellent haze hovering over the streets.

The walk from the gatehouse to the Great Hall seemed to take forever. By the time they entered, Tamlyn looked barely able to stand. Aithinne needed to lie down, but she judged her cousin looked even worse. Even so, Tamlyn nervously took Aithinne's arm, lending her support. "I am not sure which of us is in worse shape."

"The air is suffocating. I cannot breathe." Aithinne felt her knees weakening and was glad when Damian suddenly wrapped an arm around her, adding his strength. She smiled up at him weakly.

Challon came rushing up. "I've secured a room. The four of us shall have to share the bed. I told the squires to bed down on the floor for added safety. There is just no space in this madness. Come."

Aithinne dabbed the wet cloth to the back of her neck, fighting lightheadedness. She had stripped down to her chemise and cared not that squires for Challon and Damian were carrying in their baggage. She had to cool down or she was going to be ill.

"We have to share the bed, but 'tis large enough." Tamlyn sat on the end, leaning against the bedpost. "The mattress is not too lumpy. I brought some ground walnut leaves. I shall sprinkle them on the bloody thing before we go down to supper. It will chase away the fleas, if there are any. I suppose we are honored in getting a room so spacious in this crush. All of Scotland is here it seems. I must admit, I am a bit overwhelmed. Unlike Raven and Rowena I have never been to court. I am not used to all these . . . people."

Damian entered wearing a grin. "'Tis not much, but it might make you ladies more comfortable." It was a small wooden footbath. Moffet and Vincent carried in buckets of cool water."

"Not much . . ." Aithinne laughed. "I would pay its weight in gold. Thank you."

"I wish I could do more for you. If there had been any way around it, I would have left you behind. I would do all to prevent your mind from being burdened with this . . . horror." Damian took the damp rag and pressed it to her forehead. "You look unwell, my lady."

She watched his pale eyes, wondering if she should ask the question gnawing on her mind, or just let it be and try to get through this ordeal, once they were back home, then face the situation. Instead she asked, "How long must we remain in this cesspit?"

"As long as Edward wishes. We have to think of Glen Eallach and Glen Shane. Let us get through this torment, then we shall make haste to return home, and merciful heaven, never step foot within a hundred leagues of here."

Aithinne nodded, but knew neither distance nor

time would ever erase the image of dead bodies
being picked over by ravens. It was bad enough
such things happened in this world. Worse to know
a man used it as a means to control a conquered
country.

"I suggest, Aithinne, you rest after you unpack.
This eve promises to be a long one."

Aithinne trembled as she sat on a bench outside
of the chamber, awaiting an audience before the
king, despite the lateness of the hour.

No sooner had the Challon party retired to their
chamber after the long supper and were trying to
settle in bed for the night, than a servant came
knocking with word the king wanted to see Lord
Ravenhawke and Lady Coinnleir and summoned
them forthwith. Challon seemed less disturbed by
the command, saying Edward slept little and often
carried out court business late into the night. Even
so, Aithinne feared Phelan had somehow gotten
Edward's ear and spread his poison. Damian never
said anything, just dressed as quickly as possible. He
remained silent as he took her arm and led her
through the castle to where Edward stayed.

Upset by the pending audience, she jumped up
and started pacing again, only to have Damian
glare at her. Nothing new in that. He had been glaring at her all evening, ever since the bloody know-
all king had taken great pleasure in announcing in
the Great Hall—before the English nobility present
and a large portion of Scotland—that she was with
child.

Aithinne shut her eyes against the image of the
whole horrid affair in her mind, but could never
forget it. Damian had escorted her into the Great
Hall, behind Tamlyn and Challon. Tamlyn and she

had just made their curtsey to the king, and what did the arrogant man do?—he told Tamlyn and her to arise that he understood heat was stressful on ladies carrying babes in their bellies! Then he went on to talk about his beloved late queen, Elinor, and how she had fatigued in the early stages of breeding. By all, she wished the bloody Englishman to perdition. He even slapped Challon and Damian on their backs and congratulated them!

"Could not even wait for a bloody how-do-you-do?" she muttered under her breath, putting her thumbnail to her mouth, and was tempted to chew on it.

"What do you say, Aithinne?" Damian asked drolly, knowing she was talking to herself and not him.

"*Amadan.*" Calling him a fool was not the smartest tact to take with the angry man, so she removed her thumb and forced a smile. "Why, nothing, my lord. I just wondered how much longer we must wait, that is all."

He folded his arms over his chest, crossed one leg over the other, and leaned his shoulder against the wall. "We wait until we are called. All night if need be. I am sure Edward will be mindful a woman *breeding* fatigues easily and shan't keep us dawdling too long."

She paced the length of the small hall, and tried to think of something to do with her hands—other than strangle Damian St. Giles. Several people— Richard de Burgh, Elizabeth, his daughter, and a stranger went by and were given admittance.

"Gilbert de Clare, Earl Glouster, and son-in-law to Edward," Damian informed her who the man with the de Burghs was. "You might as well stop pacing and sit, Aithinne."

Figuring she did not need to annoy him any more than he already was, she sat. Getting restless again, she huffed. "'My Seeding of Scotland Campaign. I see the lords of Challon wield their mighty *swords* for the good of England.'" She mimicked the king's words in a high tone, unable to just sit still.

Damian had closed his eyes and pretended to sleep. At least, she thought he pretended. She leaned close and peeked up at him, trying to discern if he really slumbered in that position. "'Tis not a good policy to mock the king in funny voices," came his advice.

"What about unfunny voices, my lord?"

"Use any voice you wish—once we are back to Glen Eallach. Here you do so at peril of losing your life," he cautioned.

She wiggled her feet back and forth. "How can you sleep standing up like a horse?"

"A horse does. I, howbeit, am not sleeping." He yawned, stretched one arm out, then refolded it. "You best use this time to compose yourself before we meet with Edward. All this jittery flitting around might convince him you have something to hide. Of course, you lie to him like you do me and you could find yourself in very hot water."

Figuring it best to skirt that particular path, she asked, "Do you?"

"Do I what? Sleep standing up? A warrior learns to sleep at any chance he can, any position."

"Nay, do you wield your mighty *sword* for the good of England?" Aithinne tried to make it sound playful, but it hurt to think that was a possibility. It was bad enough she feared he came to her bed because she was an echo of Tamlyn. To think it might also be commanded by the English king, merely to see Scottish ladies breed with English babes, saddened her.

"Every chance I get. I have not heard you complain about my thrusts and parries." He opened an eye. "And do not think to try to slap me because this time I *will* turn you over my knee."

"Slapping you never crossed my mind." She straightened her spine and scooted back in the chair.

He gave her a nod. "Then we progress in our relations. Heartening."

"Actually, I was thinking of strangling you. And another time I thought of chucking a rock at you."

"Anything to keep life from being boring. What games do you play next? Poison the mead—" He stopped in mid-thought and stared at her intently.

A blush spread up her neck and face, making her feel faint.

"Oh, Challon, hush." Tamlyn's voice shattered the tense silence. Thankfully.

Challon sounded implacable. "I do not care, Tamlyn. I told you, you go nowhere without me or an escort."

"I am not taking an escort to the garderobe, Challon. That is asking a bit much." Tamlyn glared at her husband, who glared back. She then came to sit by Aithinne. "Is *he* making you take an escort?"

Damian opened his eyes. "*He* is not."

Tamlyn stuck her tongue out at Challon.

"*He* escorts her same as Challon does you. Stop grousing at Julian. There are just too many people about, too much rage looking for a spot to vent. They have to swallow the dictates of Edward. They might see you—two Scottish females as coming through all this with none of the heavy hand offence Edward has applied to them—and view you as a surrogate for their anger. Especially now that Edward gloated before all that you both breed with child."

Aithinne glanced down at her fingernail, suddenly

intent on pushing the skin back so she didn't get the sore split at the side. Very important chore.

She knew Damian was right. There were people about—both Scot and English—who did not wish them well. The confrontation that had occurred earlier, just after they had left Great Hall, came to mind. Sir John Pendegast, the elder brother of Dirk had blocked the hallway, along with another brother. They were not happy over Dirk's death in Trial by Combat, nor that Edward accepted it as God's will. She feared they would have provoked a fight with Challon, had not the Bruces—Robert, Edward, and Nigel—come along and stood at Challon's shoulder.

There was a family resemblance between Dirk and his brothers, though John's eyes lacked the taint of madness Dirk's empty black eyes had held. Howbeit, there was a strong hint of greed and need for power that flickered within them that made her fear this man. The Bruces might have caused him to back down for now, but she was sure he had not dropped the matter.

The door opened and people came out, their conversation heated. They spared no heed to the other people in the hall, but moved off in rapid strides. The elderly man, holding the door, glanced at Challon and then Damian. "The king wishes to see the Lord Ravenhawke and the Lady Coinnleir—alone."

In silence communication, Damian looked to Challon, who merely arched an eyebrow. Taking Aithinne's elbow, he whispered lowly, "Do us all a boon and save your lying ways to use on me. I consider it a result of high spirit, one I can curb in time. Edward shan't view it in that light. So keep your tongue behind your teeth. Am I understood, Aithinne?"

Chapter Twenty

Damian gave Aithinne's elbow a small squeeze for support as they were ushered in. He should have used the time while they were waiting to prepare her for this ordeal. But he was still too furious to use common sense after learning Aithinne was with child. Now he regretted letting his temper get the better of him.

Being a warrior, he had long ago learnt to put away emotional problems until he calmed down and could analyze them with a level head. Others oft wondered why he tended to appear to ignore dilemmas, only to act much later. He never liked to rush into situations, rather held back and analyzed them, then acted accordingly. It saved fraying on his emotions.

He was still trying very hard to avoid facing Edward's revelation, so instead of preparing Aithinne, he traded jibes with her, tweaking her nose. The corner of his mouth twitched with a suppressed smile—the nose with seven freckles. Now he would have to hope she was smart enough to see through his lies, and if they were fortunate, wise enough to keep her mouth shut.

"Come. Have a seat, Lady Aithinne," King Edward

of England entreated. As he looked up from the
document he was studying, his drooping eyelids—
so like his sire's—lifted over those vivid blue eyes,
shrewd eyes that missed little. Naturally, he noted
Aithinne looked to Damian for cue. "Ah, already
the female looks to you for guidance. As it should
be. A good beginning, Lord Ravenhawke."

"Thank you, Sire. She has quickly learnt who her
master is," Damian replied with a careless negligence.

"Gilchrist let her run wild, We fear. So the chore
of taming this hellion must not be an easy one. We
do not envy you. These females of Clan Ogilvie are
too headstrong, too spirited."

Damian shared a smile with the king he did not
feel. "I have little taste of a coward dog or horse. I
find I warm to spirit. Yea, more trouble with which
to deal, but I tell myself that she will breed that
spirit in my sons. I believe your beautiful Queen
Elinor was a woman of spirit. Did she not follow you
to Acre on the Crusade and save your life?"

Edward's face softened as memories of his queen
filled his mind. "That she did. A Muslim fell on me
with a dagger and stabbed me. I managed to fight
him off, kill him, but the dagger was dipped in
poison. They said I would not survive the toxin
pumping through my blood. Our queen would
have none of it. She said I would recover and she
would have any man saying otherwise put to death.
I dared not contradict her, so had to get well. Now
balladeers sing how she saved my life by sucking out
the poison. Our queen was a warrior." He paused,
a sadness filling him. "I miss her so."

Damian noticed how he had dropped the royal
'we' with that statement. Few ever doubted Edward
loved Elinor. Most wish she were still around to
curb his Angevin rages. His eyes swung to the

rough-cut slab of red sandstone. At supper, Edward had it directly behind him using it as a makeshift table, and a golden pitcher and two goblets sat on the uneven surface. It seemed out of place, odd, when Edward was trying to impress the Scots with the English riches that he'd be compelled to use such a poorly chiseled stone as a tabletop.

Edward followed Damian's eyes. "Ah, you admire the Stone of Scone."

"Not sure admire is the correct word. I guess I assumed the Scots would crown their monarch on something a bit more ornate." Damian recalled his mother describing the Stone of Destiny, upon which Scottish kings were crowned, as being smooth as glass, black and with Pictish symbols all around it— and much bigger, almost like a footstool. The slab of stone before him looked hurriedly dressed and not something that would be the cornerstone of Scottish regalia.

Damian leaned his elbow on the arm of the chair and stretched out his long legs.

"We understand from Anthony Bek you wish a formal betrothal—banns called as proper at Kinmarch by the *Culdee* there. We shall be sending a priest of papacy to these remaining Celtic Churches. These *Culdees* are rebel makers. They give the sermons in their tongue, not Latin. We are told they even marry, father sons. The office of priest passes from father to son."

"So it seems," Damian agreed. "Still, I would like this done as quickly as possible, but in the proper fashion. Set the way I shall go at Lyonglen. Think it would fix it in the Scots' minds the way of things."

Edward was glancing through the parchment documents, instruments of Scottish nobility's oaths to him as the ruler of Scotland. He waved his hand absently. "Actually, when We granted you the charter to Glen Eallach, We made the lady and her brothers your wards. The males need to be fostered, finish their training for knighthood. The lady We advised you to breed into a loyal subject." He smiled in a gloat. "'Tis good to see you followed Our will. So what is the concern?"

"As your man, I wish your blessing upon the union." Damian sighed. "Of course, she is hardly what I anticipated for a wife. Challon got the pick of the litter with Lady Tamlyn. Lady Aithinne is a bit taller, but that works since I am taller than Challon. She is not as *full* of figure. And then she had those marring freckles on her nose. Still, she is healthy, strong . . . fertile. While I could take her to wife and be done with it, I prefer to have it done the English way. As to the brothers, they have received no training as pages, so are not ready even to be a squire. I have already started to correct Gilchrist's oversight."

"Admirable. You have made good use of your time away from Us."

"So you give leave for the marriage?"

"Troubling tales reached our ears . . . that the lady married Gilchrist before he passed on, in order to keep control of Lyonglen."

"Dinsmore. Consider the source. The fool carried jests of Aithinne's brothers. Seems the lads love to torment Campbell as a pastime. Sad the man believes everything you tell him." Damian stifled a yawn. "Beg pardon, Sire, but wielding my sword for England's glory does keep me up nights."

"Does it?" Edward's cold Devil's-breed eyes watched Damian. Then he burst out laughing. "We are sure England appreciates your diligent efforts. If the Dragon's two bastard brothers are working as hard to beget babes on Lady Tamlyn's elder sisters,

come spring all these Pictish heiresses will be bred
into loyal English subjects. We agree on the assessment of Dinsmore Campbell, so it would be easy to
dismiss his ramblings. But Phelan Comyn carried
similar tales."

"Comyn? Cousin to Earl Buchan and Lord Bade-
nock? The commanders of the Scottish forces de-
feated at the Battle of Dunbar?"

Edward nodded, and then sat. "But he did not
support them."

"Nor did he support the English side. Methinks
Phelan Comyn looks to his own interests. 'Tis my
understanding he was once a suitor for the lady.
Gilchrist rejected him. He has only come circling
like some carrion bird to feast upon the carcass of
my grandsire. He greeted us when we arrived,
dragged up that I was Michael Challon's bastard."

"Much the same thoughts We hold on the man."
Edward nodded. "Well, what say you, Lady Aithinne? Do you want this dragon for your mate? Or
shall you have Phelan Comyn?"

Damian's fist closed at the side of his leg, reign-
ing in ire against Edward's probing. The king was
testing, prodding, to see what sort of reaction he
could provoke from Damian. Instead he offered a
countenance that said he was full of ennui. He kept
his smile hidden as Aithinne looked to him before
replying to the king. He waited until he offered her
a faint nod.

"Ah! We like this female." Edward slapped his
knee. "We spot intelligence flashing in those odd
eyes, but she is smart enough to take her lead from
you, Lord Ravenhawke. A wise woman."

"Whilst I have problems accepting my fate decided without my say—"

"Ah, she goes and spoils it. We are giving you say.
We just asked." He wagged a finger at her. "So tell

us, do you want Ravenhawke or Comyn for you lord and husband?"

"Since I would rather kiss an adder than Phelan Comyn, I am left with one option."

Edward rang a bell, and Anthony Bek came in with a servant. "Bishop, come join us in a toast and then you can affix a seal to the betrothal agreement between Lord Lyonglen and Lady Coinnleir. We are becoming quite the matchmaker in our graying years. The marriages between my English lords to Scottish ladies shall see Scotland secure in our control. A great day, is it not?"

He lifted the golden goblet to them. "May you both be as happy as I was with my queen. Give me strong sons to foster. Our lands will grow strong through these unions."

Pouring water into the pot to heat over the campfire, Tamlyn looked to Aithinne. "Soon we shall reach Glen Shane, tomorrow, I think. I am so weary of travel, but will feel relieved when we get home. I am glad Challon received permission for us to leave Berwick so early. I do not think I could have stood it there one more day. Lucky for us, Edward agreed the foul air was no good for women carrying babes."

Aithinne only spared her cousin a half interest as she watched the men riding out to patrol, unease fermenting within her. Challon and Damian had left half their men to guard them and ridden out without bothering to say why. She did not like the furtive looks passing between the two men.

"You are not speaking to St. Giles?" Tamlyn asked.

Aithinne tossed away the small pebble she had

been holding. "Nay. I wish never to speak to Sir Oaf again."

"Is it because Edward and he decided your fate, betrothed you to him without a by-your-leave?" Tamlyn sighed. "I would think you more abhorrent of the fate, dear cousin, if the man was not in your bed so much—if you did not carry his child. You will want the babe to be born in wedlock, eh?"

Aithinne stared off into the woods, listening to the babbling of the burn. It sounded so cool, so inviting, the first creek they had passed in their travels that was more than a trickle because of the drought. "Please, do not remind me of my past foolishness. Since that man came into my life it has been one big muddle, a coil that just seems to tighten about me like a rope."

"Lass, you cannot tell me you hate the idea of being his lady. I have known you too long. You see nothing but him. Your heart is in your eyes each time you see him. And I do not use the kenning to see this truth."

"I will not lie to you. That is my deepest wish. Only it was . . ." She swallowed the sob welling up in her.

"Was what, Aithinne?"

"You were not there . . . heard the things he said to King Edward. He did not just hurt my pride, Tamlyn, he laid it in the dirt. Humiliated me before his monarch. Mocked me—and my freckles."

Her cousin exhaled deeply, dusting her hands on the side of her kirtle. "I fear neither you nor I were cut out for the world of male intrigue. I do not understand it all, but our men tell Edward what he wants to hear. That does not meant the thoughts are theirs, but cut to placate this king. I am sure Damian did what he had to to see you safe, see Glen Eallach secure."

"Do you not chafe that Challon was commanded to take you to wife, seed you for the greater glory of England?"

"Oh aye, I worry over that every time I lie with the vexing man . . . at least once or twice a day." Tamlyn's laughter was musical. "Talk to Damian, Aithinne. Discuss the bairn—"

"Oh, like you discuss your babe with Challon?" Aithinne regretted the words as soon as she spoke them. "Sorry. I grow older with each day, but no wiser."

"I ken the feeling. Aye, I had not told Challon, now I shall pay for that. Curse the bloody king. I kept hoping for the right time. Our marriage is still young. Pendegast cast a pall over the news of the child. Seems we were both undone by Edward Longshanks."

As the darkest part of the gloaming fell on the land, Moffet sat down on the far side of the large flat rock log, following Aithinne's instruction to turn his back to her as she undressed.

"When my lord father bade me to watch you, Lady Aithinne, I am not sure this is what he meant. Watching you entails that I see you."

"Hearing serves just as well. With your back to me you can view all threats coming, eh?" She smiled at the back of the lad's head. "I appreciate this boon. I must get the smell of Berwick from me or I may be sick."

"Does the babe make you sick?" He paused. "Beg forgiveness, Lady Aithinne. 'Tis not my place, but I heard King Edward say you and Lady Tamlyn carry babes. Is it true? Do you carry my father's child?"

"Aye, I carry your half-brother. He made me ill in

the beginning, but he seems to have made peace with my body."

"You know it is a boy? Are you touched with the kenning, as my lord father calls it?"

"Aye, I see things sometimes. I am not able to control it. Just odd bits and pieces come to me."

"In your dreams sometimes?" His question sounded pointed.

As Damian's child, he might carry the power within him. "Do you feel it?"

"I am not sure. I never did before. Only . . ."

"Only what, young Moffet?" she asked, slipping out of her chemise.

"Since my body began to change, my voice change, I have been having dreams. Sometimes these dreams happen. I often wonder if I am imaginings these things," he confessed.

"The kenning is generally in females of Ogilvie blood," she explained. "I surmised your grandmother has Ogilvie blood in her from some line and she passed this on to your father. Speak with him. Mayhap it comes with manhood in males."

"Will you wed with him?"

"Your king ordered it."

"Good. My father is happy with you."

Aithinne bit the corner of her lips. "Mayhap."

She laid her folded clothes on the flat rock and then stepped into the pool. The soothing waters were not very cool, due to the summer heat, but it was enough. Surely, heaven could not feel this blissful. Holding the bar of soap in one hand, she floated toward the middle where it was barely chest high. She ducked her head under and then surfaced to scrub her hair. She loved a good bath, but this time it was more. This was healing. The thick miasma of Berwick clung to her, permeated her hair, so this washing was both for cleansing her body, but more so her soul.

"If it was only so easy to be rid of troublesome men," she muttered before ducking under to rinse the soap's foam from her hair. It would take more than one lathering to be rid on the foul stench, at least to her mind.

She broke the water, swiping it from her eyes, only to spot Damian sitting on the flat rock instead of his son. Arms crossed and legs stretched out before him, the white sark almost shimmered in the deep gloaming. He was so handsome—and more than a little perturbed.

"What part of 'you do not go anywhere without me' do you not understand?"

She crossed her arms over her chest. "I told Tamlyn I went to scrub Berwick's foulness from my skin, my hair."

"You should have asked me to accompany you, Aithinne."

"You were busy talking with Challon. Then you rode out with him. I asked Moffet to stand watch."

"Aye, I sent him to bed. Where you should be," he carped.

More than fed up to her ears with males bossing her around, she ducked down and scooped up a handful of the soft silt from the bottom of the pool. As he opened his mouth to continue his diatribe, she tossed the loose muck into his face.

He stood and wiped it off, spluttering where a bit had hit his mouth. She should feel bad for being so wicked, instead she chuckled. He flung the silt away, glancing down at his shirt.

"You witch. I should beat you." He sat and unlaced the cross ties on his boots and kicked out of them.

"He who raises his voice or fists is a dullard and

cannot win the dispute otherwise." She smiled her triumph.

He undid his leathern hose, placed them on the rock next to her kirtle and then waded into the water. "Quite true. But then, it shan't stop your bare bottom from stinging after I put my hand to it."

She let go with another fist full of mud, hitting him square on his warrior-honed chest. Such action was not nice, but she certainly enjoyed it. She could not stop the laughter from bubbling up. It felt good after so much tension of the last few days.

"Wench. Enjoy yourself. I am in arms' reach now." To prove it, he reached out. She held her breath until his hand took her shoulder, the beauty of his bare chest making her want to touch him back. "The water must be a sacred spring of Annis. It feels divine. You also sound of better spirits than you have of late. Enjoy the respite. We travel at first light. We will be riding fast and hard, Aithinne. Challon wants to reach Glenrogha as soon as possible. I do not blame him. I fear we are being followed."

"Followed? Who follows us? Why?"

"I am not sure who—yet. It is more of a feeling. I get this sense . . . I just know."

"The kenning. 'Tis your mother's blood. You are gifted with the ways of our people. It mostly shows in females with blood from Clan Ogilvie. I have it, but cannot control it. I try, but when I get upset or worried ofttimes it is blocked at a time I need it the most. You might speak with Moffet about it."

"Moffet?"

"Aye, he speaks of dreams. Did it come as you changed from boy to man?"

He nodded. "As a matter of fact, it did."

"'Tis not many males carry the ability to farsee."

His pale eyes seemed to almost glow in the gloaming. "Am I special, Aithinne?"

Unable to meet the haunting stare, she looked down, and then gave a faint nod.

"Suddenly gone shy? Why?"

She shrugged, having trouble putting in to words all the things that bothered her.

"You owe me."

Startled, her head snapped up. "I do not ken what you mean."

"Edward."

Her spine stiffed at the mention of the English King. "I owe you naught for Longshanks. He is your ruler, not mine."

"You may not like it, but he rules Scotland now. And if not for me, you could have found yourself betrothed to Phelan Comyn or Dunny Dinsmore." His grin was wolfish, taunting.

"Instead I find myself betrothed without my leave to a man who thinks I am not too bright, who lies at the drop of a pin, is not as pretty as my cousin Tamlyn, my tits are not big as hers—and have dots on my nose."

He laughed. It was the last straw. She had been so brave. She put up with the long journey, being uncomfortable every step of the way, hot, worried sick, and tired. Then she was dragged through a town where the idiot fool of a king had left bodies killed in a slaughter over four months gone, just so he could parade half of Scotland before them. She had been scared, leered at, laughed at, had to stare into the faces of women not too different from her, and know her life had changed, but not in the manners as theirs.

"I would take a swing at you, Damian St. Giles, but you would use that as a reason to beat me." So instead she tossed the chunk of soap at him, the playful mood spoiled.

He caught it, then pulled her to his chest. "Shhhhh, lass. I promise not to beat you . . . ever. Oversetting yourself cannot be good for the babe." His heart beat strong and steady, increasing speed the longer he held her. "The babe is mine, is it not?"

"Why you lackwit—" Aithinne bit his chest.

He jumped, startled. "Owwwww. Why do you bite me?"

"You told me I should not hit you. You said nothing about biting," she pointed out, trying to push away from him. "Of course, the bairn is yours. He is—"

"He?" Damian asked awed. "A son?"

She nodded, "'Tis what I see with the kenning. What Oona and Bessa see also."

"Of course, those with Challon blood tend to sire only sons with black hair and green eyes. My blood is through one of the few female Challon lines, but I was true with the black hair and green eyes. So you have an idea of the looks of the child I bred upon you." He lifted her chin. "Aithinne, all the things about you I said to Edward—"

She looked away. "Do not remind me, my lord."

"I was forced to let him think I did not see the value in you. Edward is crafty, and any weakness in his eyes is a tool in his hands. Tamlyn would be the means by which Edward could compel many things from Challon, the same as he could seek to use you to see my will complies."

"He would be sorely mistaken, eh?"

He shook his head. "Blessed with the kenning and yet she is blind. Sometimes, Aithinne your thoughts are very muddled." She opened her mouth to argue, but he spun her around. "Enough blethering. Close you eyes and let me tend you, my lady."

Lifting her hair over one shoulder, he soaped her back. Scrubbing hard, as though he understood her need to be rid of the foul miasma of Berwick. Her head lolled, loving his strong warrior's hands stroking her tense muscles. "Duck to rinse off."

"I was enjoying it," she almost whined.

"Do as I say, wench."

"These Dragons of Challon love to bark orders," Aithinne fussed, but did as he said.

And, oh, was she glad she did! He ran those clever hands over her shoulders, upper chest, trailing the thick foam from the soap up her neck. He allowed it to slither downward, the lather creeping across the tops of her breasts. She dipped down to stop it from moving over her nipples. A chuckle rumbled in him, aware of what he was doing to her.

She leaned her head back against his rippled chest, feeling the muscles flex at the contact. "*Amadan.*"

"Oh aye, I am a fool for you Aithinne." His hands followed the path of the soapy foam over her breasts and then down upon her belly. "Our babe grows here. Do you know how humbling that is? Your breasts are fuller. Here, I just assumed you were getting fat."

He laughed as she spun around and started to shove him. He caught her and pulled her with him, floating and treading water, so she was almost lying upon him. "I like teasing you. 'Tis so easy to get a rise from you."

"Oh, is it, my lord?" Her hand pressed along his chest, moving between their bodies until she curled her hand around his rigid shaft. "I seem to have a rise from you, Ravenhawke. Doing your duty for king and country, wielding you mighty sword for Edward?"

His white teeth flashed in the night. "Oh, that

rankles you, does it not? You would have me say I lied to Edward, that I take you for my pleasure, not for duty. Do you really need those words, Aithinne? For one blessed with the kenning, you cannot see the truth in me?"

"I told you, my emotions mess it up. I have never been able to control it, sometimes do not even understand it. Auld Bessa thought I would one day be as powerful as Evelynour. It will not happen. I cannot find that inner place inside me where I can reach within to hear," she confessed sadly. She wanted to tell him how she looked into his heart, saw very clearly when her brothers brought him to Lyonglen. Since then, she tried very hard not to walk in his thoughts, too fearful to see how deeply he loved her cousin. From that point on, she had trouble reading his emotions because she blocked the kenning as much as possible, unable to bear the pain of seeing Tamlyn in his thoughts.

But she was not sure he was ready to hear that truth yet. She knew he still hurt from the betrayal by Moffet's mother. Mayhap in time, she would be able to speak of it. Of course, the day would come soon, as the arrival of the babe would tell him the date they had made him.

Instead she distracted him through pleasuring his body, moved her hand down the long, swollen length of his erection, then back. Hearing his hiss as she repeated the action.

"Wrap your legs around me, lass," he gasped between pants. "Let your body speak truths to me."

Chapter Twenty-One

Damian jerked awake before dawnbreak. Not sure what woke him, he reached for his sword to assure himself it was within easy reach and out of the scabbard. That feeling of being watched was increasing instead of lessening. A queer itch between his shoulder blades, one he could not reach. He was not able to dismiss it or shake the sensation; the presentiment only grew.

He feared the kenning was speaking to him. It generally happened that way. The unease mounted for about three days, flashes coming, generally stronger at night while he slept. Without fail, on the third day the visions would be strongest and his dreams would become reality.

As yet, he could not tell from where the ill wind would blow. Was it from stragglers lurking in the hills? Even since Dunbar, many of the Scots had taken to hiding from the English, serfs seizing the opportunity to escape their servitude to some lord and turning to the ways of brigands to survive. Others, he worried, were Scottish rebels still lingering, hoping to attract followers to the cause. Rumors of a commoner, a William Wallace, were spreading across the land. The man's father, Alan Wallace, had

signed the roll at Berwick, but no one saw anything
of the son. They feared he and some of his cousins
planned to cause problems, harass the new English
rulers. If Edward thought Scotland was subdued, he
was in for a big surprise.

Damian was also concerned about John Pendegast's reaction to Dirk's death. He made it clear he
was unhappy Edward accepted it as legal Trial by
Combat. The confrontation at Berwick warned the
Pendegast's would not allow the matter to drop despite Edward declaring it as God's judgment. They
would come at Challon when the advantage was in
their favor.

Of course, Damian was not too happy with
Phelan Comyn, either. The morning after he had
taken Aithinne before the king in answer to his
summons, Julian and Damian had had a second audience with Edward. It had been Julian's intent to
get the king to grant permission to leave parliament early, that the heat and the dismal condition
of Berwick left it an unfit place for a lady breeding
with child.

Damian had been displeased to find Comyn already there, wearing the smile of a cat with pigeon
feathers about its mouth. It quickly became evident
why, as he pressed claims about being betrothed to
Aithinne. Damian had refuted them at all points
and, backed by Challon—a man just proven pure of
heart through Trial by Combat—the king had accepted Damian's assurance the child Aithinne carried was his. Comyn had not been happy. Was the
man muttonheaded enough to try to attack them
on the road to Glen Shane?

He did not like Dinsmore either. There was
something wormy about the man. Oh aye, he was
a total lackwit. Just for amusement, Damian had
dropped the lads' sobriquet in a few ears—known

gossips—Edward's included. The king howled with laughter over Dunny Dinsmore. In short order, all through the land would be calling Campbell by the new name of Dunny.

"Too many enemies," he muttered under his breath.

Rolling to his side, he fitted his body against Aithinne's, holding her back against his chest. He placed his hand on the rounded tummy where his babe rested. He jerked it back when he felt a small quiver. The child? In awe, he waited for another sign of movement, but there was nothing.

He ran his palm over her hip, smiled pleasure to have her sleeping against him. Being his usual randy self around her, he would love nothing better than to take her. But he had been foolish enough once tonight at the pool. He would not take that risk again, not until they were safely behind the walls of Glenrogha.

"A miserable night ahead." He permitted himself the luxury of nuzzling her hair before closing his eyes. "Ah, my little liar . . . my precious little liar . . . how I love you."

The *haar* swirled about him so heavy he could barely see a horse's length ahead of him. The damn fog seemed to swallow the landscape, blanketing everything. Damian spurred his steel gray steed, Galleon, back to the column. Urgency breathing down his neck. He rode on recklessly, virtually blinded by the thick mist.

He had to reach Aithinne. Save her.

He reined the horse, pausing but for a moment as he heard the ravens high in the hills of the Passes of Glen Shane. Ravens that were both a welcoming— they were nearly home—and yet, a dark augury in the same breath. The shrill cries broke the stillness of the isolated Highland glen, telling him something was not right. Startled, scores of ravens took to the sky. Their discordant cacophony set his teeth on edge. For a peculiar instant the world held its breath as the heavens were turned black. The fog swirled about him, the loch breeze ruffling his hair, as his eyes followed the spiraling path of the noisy blackbirds.

An ill omen, whispered the kenning to his mind. He had to get back to Aithinne. Save her. He must save her and his child she carried.

Galleon reared slightly on his hooves as Damian spun him about-face, then spurred him, driving the great stallion as if demons chased them, rushing to get back to Aithinne before it was too late.

As he rode over the crest of the knoll, the kenning slammed into him. He could see it all unfold before him. Men lurking on the far side of the hill, lying in wait with crossbows. Drawing his sword, he rode in a race with Death to save her. If he did not reach Aithinne in time she would die. Nothing—nothing mattered more than saving her. He wanted to live with Aithinne, with their child, to see his son grow strong and healthy, become a man. Still, he would give his life without hesitation to protect her.

Riding hard, he galloped past the assassins. They were too startled to do more than let loose several poorly aimed bolts from their crossbows as Galleon galloped past. He thought he was free—until the last one caught him in the side of his thigh.

Challon, already alert to the pending attack, saw Damian riding flat out to reach them. He pulled the squires into a phalanx, long shields unslung, before Tamlyn and Aithinne. Gervase and Vincent were helping them down from the horses, trying to position them between the animals to use them as a protective barrier. Arrows plowed into the side of Gervase's steed, the mighty horse going down in a stream of blood and agony. He saw the young man's agonized expression, but Gervase did not hesitate before moving in front of Tamlyn, covering her with his shield.

Damian's eyes searched for Aithinne. Vincent was guarding her. But then riders came from behind them. Now they were trapped between those using the hillside as cover to let lose their hail of arrows and the riders coming from both sides of their flanks. Challon, Michael, Deyl, and several other men-at-arms, turned their mounts, spurring them to charge the riders, meeting with swords clashing. Damian spared them but a glance as he leaned forward, driving Galleon toward the riders closing in on the far side.

Aithinne swung around as she spotted the horsemen arriving to their rear. Galleon intercepted them, swords drawn, Damian clashed with one, dispatching him quickly. As he turned to get back to Aithinne, another bolt slammed into his right shoulder, at the edge of his breastplate. The pain was a fire, nearly causing him to drop his sword. Gritting his teeth, he spun Galleon as a third bolt hit his thigh again, not far from the first one, the agony causing him to reel in the saddle. Aithinne screamed and started toward him. Gervase made a grab for her, but it was too late.

The arrow slammed into her chest . . . blood spreading over the front of her sark.

"NO!!!!" Damian howled his madness.

He jerked up, his hand already about the pommel of his sword, ready to fight to save Aithinne. His heart pounded as he realized he was still in the tent and it was near dawning. Sweat poured down his chest as he adjusted to it only being a dream.

His stomach rolled. Nay, not a dream. The kenning . . . showing him what would be. Desperately, he cast his mind inwardly, trying to recall all parts of the dream, but already some of it was slipping away, fading into mist. But not the sense of fear.

He blinked as he saw Julian on one knee before him. "Sorry to disturb you, Damian. We need to move out. I want to be well down the road to Kinmarch before sunspring."

"Julian . . ." he started, then hesitated.

But then, Julian did not need to be told. "It grows worse?"

He nodded. "The images are strong. We shall be attacked. It is a sickness at the pit of my stomach. Julian . . . this is bad. I am scared . . . scared I will lose her."

Julian's eyes shifted to the sleeping Aithinne, his face ashen. "This kenning has saved us before. Recall the time you warned of the ambush. I know I railed at it after Tamlyn was attacked. I am a warrior. I trust what I see. I do not understand this . . . this . . . gift . . . this curse. But surely, 'tis not just to torture you. Bad enough we have to live through some of the terrible tragedies of life, without some higher power taunting you, saying see what will be, and you can do naught to stop it. Trust this is a warning so we can save those we love."

Damian sucked in a ragged breath and nodded. "We can ride hungry. Better that than die on a full belly."

Damian leaned over Aithinne, his eyes hungrily drinking in her serene beauty. He noted the shadows that touched the skin under her eyes. She was tired, needed more rest. The journey had been grueling on both Tamlyn and her. The long days in the saddle were hard enough on men. A woman with child needed plenty of rest to see the babe root strong.

The fear of losing her once more rose, nearly pushing him to panic. Drawing on his warrior's mien, he swallowed back the emotion. He could not afford to let his emotions rule or he would be of no use to her. He had to trust that Julian was right. These visions were given to him for a reason.

With trembling fingers he lifted her hand and brought her delicate fingers to his mouth and kissed each finger in turn. "Awaken, my lady."

She shivered and then yawned. "Hmmm . . . 'tis morn already?" Then she yawned even bigger.

"That is the most unladylike yawn I have ever seen," he teased.

"Go kiss your horse's arse, my lord." She gave him another yawn and stretched. "Can we not rest a bit more? Please? I am so weary. I am sure Tamlyn is tired as well, though my perfect cousin never shows it."

"Aye, Tamlyn is always flawless, while you, my gentle betrothed, are naught but a swort hag . . ." he leaned over and kissed her freckled nose, "with dots on your face."

"My lord, you *are* a horse's arse."

He shook a finger at her and she playfully snapped at him. "I am adding biting to the list of activities you are to refrain from indulging."

The wench gave him a half smile. "*All* biting? I seem to recall you rather warmed to me *biting* you."

"Take your freckles and get dressed. We move out as soon as all are dressed." He gave a light slap on the tempting rump.

She tugged her sark on over her head. "I want to bathe in a steaming tub when we reach Glenrogha, then sleep for a week."

"Sounds reasonable. I may join you."

The leathern hose on, he used the crossties to

secure his boots. The dream brushed against his mind, stirring that unease within his chest. His logical warrior's mind wanted to dismiss it as naught more than a nightmare, stemming from his fear of losing her. Only the kenning had been right too many times for him to pay no heed to it.

"Aithinne," he came up behind her, sliding his arms around her and pulling her back against his chest, holding her gently, "have you felt anything with the kenning the past three days?"

She shook her head no. "I fight the images of Berwick in my mind. I cannot open myself to it or those eyeless bodies are there waiting. I have to block against those horrible things rooting in my thoughts. To wield the kenning with intent, you have to be at peace with yourself and all around you, that is why the Three Wise Ones of the Woods keep a solitary life. Everyone's thoughts, their feelings crushing in on you, could be brutal. I guess that's why I never sought to strengthen this within me. Sometimes . . . 'tis better not to know things . . . not to see into another's heart. It saves you pain, my lord."

The last sentiments seemed directed toward him. He opened his mouth to ask what she meant, but was prevented when Julian pushed open the flaps.

"Ready?"

"Almost." He hesitated, wanting to tell Aithinne so many things, but the squires stood behind Julian waiting to take down the small tent.

There would be another time. There *had* to be another time.

Damian had ridden ahead, scouting to see if he could spot anything untoward. Nothing. As far as the eye could see. Finally giving up, he rode back to the column and straight to Julian. Reining Galleon to ride beside his cousin, he spared a glance over his shoulder at Aithinne and Tamlyn. He was worried about the women, especially Aithinne. She seemed wan. Frowning, he wished he could take her before him, ease the burden of the ride for her.

"Our ladies are not used to being in the saddle as we are, Julian. Aithinne shows strain," Damian said, knowing there was little he could do to alleviate her suffering until they reached the safety of Glen Shane.

Julian turned back, his eyes falling on Tamlyn. "The journey has been rough for them, in more ways than one. I wished I could have spared them the horrors of Berwick."

"Wished we all could have been spared the horrors of Berwick."

"No one should suffer through that hell. Tamlyn did, long before we got there. She seems to walk in my memories . . . see things I would sooner forget. 'Tis not easy being married to a witch. Tamlyn says Aithinne's abilities are even stronger. Methinks lying to a woman of Clan Ogilvie must be damned hard." Julian's dark green eyes skimmed over Damian. "Or lying to you, for that matter. Not that I have ever tried. Has anything else come to you?"

Shortness of temper rising, he snapped, "Merde, the kenning is not blowing your bloody nose." He gritted his teeth. "Beg pardon. My spirit is ragged."

"You are a warrior. Put it aside, Damian. We need our focus and our wits. Worry clouds that."

"Tell me you are not worried about Tamlyn." He laughed in challenge.

Julian's right hand caressed the pommel of his sword. "Damn straight I am, but I will only be able to protect her if I am at my best. I am a warrior. That is my value to her."

"Your value to her is she loves you. I do not think she cares that you are a warrior." Damian frowned as they crested another rise and started down into the thickly shrouded glen. "Damn, I hoped the fog would lift by now. Maybe we should consider going to Lyonglen instead of Glenrogha."

"That would keep us on the road nearly twice as long. If someone is planning an ambush, then we would be vulnerable to attack longer. I will send riders up ahead to Lochshane and Glenrogha both, marshal forces to come meet us."

Julian turned in the deep seat of the war saddle and called, "Michael, Moffet—"

Damian's hand shot out catching his cousin's arm. "Not Moffet. I would keep him close to reassure me. If you send him ahead, my mind will be worrying about Aithinne and him both. This way they are in one spot. My attention will not be as divided."

"Vincent." The squires spurred their mounts to catch up.

"Moffet. Stay with the ladies. Keep close watch on them. Michael, Vincent, each of your take two men-at-arms with you. Michael, go to Lochshane and charge my brother to ride out and meet us with a column. Vincent, ride to Glenrogha and pass the orders for riders to come. Be alert."

They watched the riders go off, and in a short space disappear in the thick fogbank. Damian feared they might have sent the men off to their doom, yet knew there was no other choice. "God speed."

The muscles around Challon's mouth tightened. "Now we wait."

"Challon, we must stop." Tamlyn clucked her tongue, signal to Goblin to up the gait so she could ride aside her husband.

Challon glanced to Damian, seeking his silent guidance. Both knew Aithinne and Tamlyn needed to stop. The horses needed to stop, but that sense of urgency was heavy on his mind.

"I regret the pace is taxing, my lady, but we hope to reach Glenrogha around nooning. We can rest then—safely."

She glanced at Damian as if it were his fault, then fixed her gaze on Challon. "Men. I am sorry if women carrying bairns are bloody inconvenient, but Aithinne needs to rest. Her back is killing her, sharp pains. I fear if you maintain this punishing pace, it will put the babe at risk. So put that in your mouth, my lord husband, and suck on it."

Damian turned in the saddle and noticed Aithinne's countenance was ashen. "Damn." He spun Galleon on his back hooves and set the horse back to the middle of the column until he reached her. Pulling beside her, he noticed she was struggling to sit upright in the saddle. "Tamlyn said your back distresses you?"

She nodded, her lower lip quivering. "Beg pardon, my lord, I cannot ride much farther . . . it hurts. I need to rest, drink some water."

Challon was watching, so Damian gave him a slight shake of his head to the negative, to let him know they could not ride on. "You should have said something, Aithinne."

"I knew you wanted to reach Glenrogha." She tried to give him a fleeting smile, but it seemed beyond her.

The column turned off to an incline of a small knoll. It had a good view of the surrounding areas, yet was secluded by a small stand of trees, thus not leaving them in the open. Damian lifted Aithinne from the saddle and led her about half way up. He unfolded his mantle and placed it on the ground for her.

Sitting slightly behind her, his fingers kneaded the small of her back. "That help?"

Accepting water Moffet fetched for her, she gave him a smile and then drank. "I do not mean to be a burden, Damian."

"Hush, Aithinne. Just feel better."

"The rubbing helps. Thank you."

His eyes inspected the terrain, searching for anything out of the ordinary. A breeze swirled around them, welcome for it was cool and had the promise of rain with it. The first rain in weeks.

He tried to focus on the dream. He recalled fog, not rain. If it rained, then the path to Glenrogha should be safe.

"You still fear someone follows us?" she asked looking over her shoulder at him.

He exhaled and then nodded. "I cannot shake the sensation. I had a dream last night."

"A troubling one, from your expression." She reached up and ran her thumb over his brow. "You worry."

"Pieces of it faded, as dreams are apt to do. Other fragments linger." He caught an apple that Challon tossed to him. Taking his knife he cored it and sliced it for Aithinne. "Tell me about Phelan Comyn and Dinsmore Campbell. Especially Comyn."

Aithinne made a sour face and chewed the apple chunk before answering him. "Not my favorite things to talk about. What do you want to ken? You think one of them is following us? Why?"

"I barely know either of them, hence my asking. Just considering possibilities."

She shrugged. "Dinsmore is a pain, but not likely to cause trouble for anyone outside of himself, my assessment. Not too bright. However, often those most lacking in wherewithal can be quite cunning. They catch you off guard. Phelan . . . I am not sure.

When I saw him at Berwick, I had the sense of never really knowing him. He paid me court several seasons past. I thought mayhap Gilchrist would arrange a marriage. Then I caught him coming out of the stables—and he had not been seeing to his horse. I deemed it the height of foolishness, and lacking in respect for me, for him to swive a serving wench when trying to win my hand in the same breath."

"On the morning after you and I met with Edward, Challon and I went to visit the king alone. Phelan was there. Edward's bit of mischief."

"Mischief. How?"

"He said Phelan came to him with a claim that you were betrothed to him—"

"Why, that swine." Her revulsion was clear. So was her fury.

He picked up her hand. "Hear me out, Aithinne, before you lose your temper."

Her amber eyes with the green streaks narrowed on him. "Speak."

"He said the child you carry is his."

For a moment, she looked like she would hit him. Instead she glowered at him, before getting to her feet and started down the hillock to the horses. She was livid. He expected it. She saw his question as one of doubt. Well, it had caused him an instant of feeling like someone had punched him in the gut. Most males would react the same way. Then reason kicked in.

Jumping up, he grabbed his mantle and followed her. "Aithinne—"

"Do not *Aithinne* me!"

When he tried to take her elbow she ducked away from him, so he blocked her path to *Gràdh*. "I did not believe him, Aithinne. But . . ."

She looked at him as if he crawled out from a rock. "He lied. That is all I shall say on the matter."

"I believe you."

"Oh, go away, Sir Nodcock."

She started toward the horses again, but he caught her arm and would not let go when she tried to pull away. "I did not believe him about the child, but I did wonder . . ."

"Ooooo . . . I promised not to hit you, but you really should stop opening your mouth and letting all that stupid fall out, or I shall be obliged to close it for you—with my fist." Her eyes flashed daggers at him. "Let go . . . now . . . Lord Ravenhawke."

Demons nibbling at him, he held fast. "When you came to my bed . . . that first night at Lyonglen—"

"Damn your eyes. I will tell you this once—since you seem determined to step squarely in the cow pie of your stupidity—I came to you a virgin."

The words sprang forth, along with the regret, but too late. "You came to my bed experienced in the ways of the flesh, not a trembling virgin. I did not take your maidenhead that night. There was no blood."

"If you do not leave me alone, I will show you blood."

Challon came slowly up the hill, frowning at Damian as though he could not believe his cousin acted as such a knave. "Come, Lady Aithinne. Let me aid you to your mount. Sir Nodcock is too busy getting his booted foot out of his mouth."

Chapter Twenty-Two

The attack came. Just as he expected.

The rain clouds had sounded high in the passes all morn, but thus far had not broke to pour their life-giving blessings upon the parched land. He had so hoped for rain. There was no rain in his dream. Since they were near the two cold-water lochs, enough moisture hung in the air to see the haar stayed heavy and low to the ground. The damn stuff swirled about him as he rode ahead to scout the landside.

They were on the vast holding of Kinmarch, thus they should be nearing Glen Shane anytime.

He patted the horse's neck, soothing the sweating animal. His own nervousness was infecting the horse. Trying to reassure the beast, he spoke to him. "Galleon, 'tis impossible to see very far down the trail—or any direction for that matter. I will be glad when we are within the curtain of Glenrogha. You earn extra rations of oats for all your hard work."

The horse nickered softly and tossed his head up and down, bringing a chuckle to Damian.

Tamlyn had told Julian the mists, which perpetually hovered before the passes of Glen Shane, were part of an ancient warding placed upon the valley by the first lady of the glen. Supposedly, they screened the passes, hiding them so none could find the entrance. For centuries, no invader had put foot on their soil in this pristine pocket in the Highlands. Not until Challon had come. Her people saw that as an omen and accepted Julian's arrival as blessed by the Auld Ones.

"I wonder . . . might this damnable *haar* be a blessing instead of a hindrance this day?" Damian asked.

In his dream he saw the fog as having left them vulnerable to attack. What if the mists were the key to saving them? If their party could reach the passes, could the sacred mists enfold them within the protection, close behind them, and block out the ones with evil in the heart from finding a way to follow them through? Mayhap the shrouded landscape was their salvation to surviving.

Excited by this possibility, he lifted his reins to turn Galleon.

Then he heard them. The ravens high in the hills of the Passes of Glen Shane.

The black birds let him know he was close. And yet, in the same breath they were the harbingers of his nightmare. The shrill cries disrupted the muffled stillness of the mist-shrouded Highland glen. Warning him it had begun.

Startled, scores of ravens took to the sky. For a peculiar instant the world held its breath as the heavens turned black. Upset by the discordant cacophony, Galleon reared slightly on his rear hooves as Damian spun him about-face. He did not blame the animal. The screeching set Damian's teeth on edge. The fog swirled thicker about him, the loch breeze ruffling his hair, as his eyes followed the spiraling path of the noisy black birds.

Time had run out.

* * *

He had to reach Aithinne. Save her.

As he rode over the crest of the knoll, the kenning slammed into him. Men. On the far side of the hill, they were lying flattened to the ground, waiting to ambush the column. Some were clearly archers with longbows. A few had the more costly crossbows—an assassin's weapon.

Drawing his sword, he raced with Death to save Aithinne. Nothing—nothing mattered more than saving her. Without hesitation, he would give his life to protect her. He knew he likely rode to his death.

As he galloped past the assassins, a few let loose with hastily aimed bolts from crossbows. One slammed into the side of his thigh. Just like the dream. His warrior's mind tried to block the pain but, white hot, it spread out in both directions within his leg muscles. Fortunately, it had struck the side or he might bleed to death before he reached Aithinne.

Fully anticipating danger, Challon reacted to Damian galloping to the column. He quickly pulled the squires into a phalanx before Tamlyn and Aithinne. Arrows slammed into the shields as tall as a man, while behind them, Gervase and Vincent aided the women to dismount. They circled the animals until the women were between the horses, trying to use the animals' massive bodies as a protective barrier. Three arrows plowed into the side of Gervase's steed. With a groan, the horse went down on his front knees in a stream of blood and agony. Damian saw the young man's agonized expression, but he never hesitated to move before Tamlyn, covering her with his shield.

Damian's eyes searched for Aithinne. Vincent

guarded her on one side, with Moffet moved in to cover the other. "Oh, God, protect them. Please."

Swinging Galleon around, he prepared to meet the riders as they attacked from both flanks. And they came. Like Hell unleashed, Challon spurred forward to charge the ones arriving from the left. Damian faced a half a score appearing to the right. They were trapped, surrounded. There would be no aid from the garrisons at Lochshane or Glenrogha. The riders—if they'd gotten through—had not had time enough to reach the fortresses and return with the much-needed reinforcements. They were on their own, battling for their lives.

Using his knees to control Galleon, leaving his hands for his sword, he intercepted the attackers. With slashing precision, he dispatched one and then turned to block a blow from a second. Galleon reacted as he'd been trained, tearing into the horse of a third rider, unseating him. Then the expected bolt sliced into the flesh of Damian's right shoulder, a freak shot hitting at the narrow point where the breastplate ended and the shoulder spaulders covered the upper arm. The pain was so bad he could hardly grip his sword, so he shifted it to his left hand, thankful warriors learned to fight with both.

Reeling from the raw throbbing, he gritted his teeth and reined the destrier to look for Aithinne. Make sure she was all right.

Time stilled as his eyes met hers. About them the battle raged, swords clashing, orders being barked, horses screaming. Suddenly, the noise faded, leaving only the discordant screeching of the massive flock of ravens circling overhead.

He could only see Aithinne. Saw her scream as another bolt slammed into his thigh, not far from the first one. Saw her shoving to get away from Gervase.

Damn woman. She was so beautiful with the long hair with the cast of faery fire flying about her. The face that had haunted his dreams for years. After all these years of wondering if she was real, he had found her. Only to lose her. Regret surged up in him that he had not spoken the words of love to tell her of his deepest feelings, let her know it was never Tamlyn—she was always the one who owned his heart.

She broke free of the squire, nearly shoving him back against the horse. Her running steps coming straight for him.

The kenning flooded through Damian's heart, molten certainty boiling his blood. If he did not reach her, they both would die.

"NO!" he screamed.

Forcing himself to lean forward in the saddle, he spurred Galleon to Aithinne. "Get down!" He yelled, hoping she would obey him. "Too much to ask," he muttered.

Driving the spurs deep into Galleon's sides, he caused the animal to leap through the air before her, just as the hail of arrows came. Two hit Galleon's flank, one in the withers, but the valiant destrier held firm, a true warrior. Damian took one to the chest, an arrow from a longbow—the one meant to kill Aithinne. He felt the barbed tip punch through the chest plate, the force driving him off the horse.

Aithinne rushed to him, but he was grabbing her by the shoulders pushing her down to the ground, struggling to use his body to cover her and at the same time trying to reach his dropped sword with his left hand.

Just as his fingers closed around the pommel, a new horror filled him. A whole column of riders came at a gallop over the hillside, riding under the standard of a goshawk on a field of half-red, half-gold.

"Just who the bloody hell is trying to kill us?" he wondered aloud, as he saw Challon dismounting before them.

Tamlyn came at her husband in a run, grabbing his sword arm. Challon, sparing her a heartbeat's notice, spun her around behind him. The mighty Dragon of Challon stood ready to kill all to protect his wife, his downed cousin, and Aithinne.

"No, Challon, no! The goshawk is the pennon of Grant Drummond. That is Duncan MacThomas with him. They ride to our aid. That's Aithinne's brothers and Einar with them."

Aithinne pulled Damian's head into her lap, her tears falling on him as she stared at the arrows protruding from him.

In short order the combined force of Lyonglen, Drummond, and MacThomas killed most of the attackers; the few remaining took to the hills, fleeing for their lives. Damian finally leaned back and enjoyed his head resting in Aithinne's lap, gazed up at her beautiful face. Sucking in a deep breath, he realized that two English knights had just been saved by two Scotsmen.

"What do you think about Goshawk for the name of our son?" he asked Aithinne. A laugh bubbled up in him, but he choked and flinched in pain instead.

"Oh, do hush. I am going to name him Nodcock after his father." Then she burst into tears.

"I command you to hush, wench. Surprise me for once and obey me." His hand reached for hers, their fingers locking.

Riders cantered back, the handsome Scotsmen returning. Challon dropped his sword tip, reached out with his left arm and encircled Tamlyn. "I never thought I would want to kiss a Scotsman before, let alone two."

One carried a man, gagged and with his hands tied, slung crossways over the shoulders of his horse. As they stopped their mounts, the Scot in the Mac-Thomas blue plaide dumped the man before Challon. "Figure you might want this, Dragon." Dismounting, he flashed a wolfish smile, the brilliant blue eyes made all the more intense by the hue of the woolen tartan.

The man had landed face down in the dirt, so Duncan MacThomas kicked him in the ribs and then used the toe of his boot to roll him over. Aithinne and Tamlyn gasped when they stared at Phelan Comyn.

Challon frowned. "I was betting the Baron Pendegast was behind the attack."

Cursing in Gaelic, Tamlyn marched over and kicked the man in the side. When he rolled away, she kicked him in the groin. He jerked, trying to retch.

Duncan looked up at Grant Drummond. "Mayhap I should cut the gag off him. If he blaws with it on, he will drown in it." He did not sound too concerned.

Drummond leaned forward, elbow resting on the high cantle to the saddle. A brow arched over his dark gray eyes. "Now that would be a crying shame, eh?" With a sigh, he dismounted and came to extend his hand. "Grant Drummond at your service, Englishman."

"Strange times, eh? Saving Englishmen and killing Scots." MacThomas shook his head. "*The enemy of my enemy is my friend*—a Scots saying. Of course, had these two lovely ladies not been with you, Grant and I might have sat back and watched the happenings."

Tamlyn kicked Phelan again, this time in the arse.

"Kick him again, Tamlyn," Aithinne called. "Kick him for me."

When Challon held out his hand to MacThomas, the man glared at him, then looked to Grant. "I saved his English hide. Does not mean I have to shake hands with him."

"What do you want to do with this offal? I would kick him, but seems your lady wife is doing a proper job of it." Grant smiled, watching Tamlyn.

Damian pushed to a sitting position. "Take the gag off him and cut the bonds."

"What?" Aithinne and Tamlyn said in the same voice.

"Help me up." Damian looked to Challon.

His cousin grimaced at the arrows protruding from his body. "You stay down. I shall handle this. I shan't take long."

MacThomas stepped to Damian, gave him a hand over Aithinne's protest. Of course it was not a gentle hand. The man grinned at Damian's groan as he set him on his feet. "Since you are talking, this did not do much damage." He examined the chest-plate with the arrow sticking out of it. "Penetrated the plate, but the jack over the mail stopped it. Must hurt like hellfire. You will have a nasty bruise."

"Help me out of it." Damian knew there was no way he could reach the buckles to remove it.

MacThomas snorted. "Bloody Englishman suffers blood loss. Thinks I am his ghillie."

Moffet stepped to Damian and began undoing the arming points at the shoulders and the band looping across his back at the waist. Once undone, Damian dropped the chest plate. "I need to be able to move without encumbrance. The arming jack and mail will be enough."

Aithinne stepped in front of him. "Sir Nodcock, just what the hell do you think you are doing?"

Damian leaned forward and kissed the tip of her nose. "I would kiss you once for every freckle, but I am tired."

"We need to get you to the Glenrogha so I can tend the wounds," she insisted. She turned to Einar. "Lord Ravenhawke needs help to get to Glenrogha."

"Einar, ignore your princess." Damian forced a grin for Aithinne. "As soon as I dispatch this vermin, then we go to the fortress."

Tears flooding her eyes, she shook her head to the sides. "No! You are too weak."

Challon took hold of Tamlyn, who was going to kick Comyn again, and pulled her back. "I am just evening the odds, my lord." She batted her eyes at him.

"You cannot fight," Aithinne choked out as Moffet handed Damian his sword. She rounded on him. "Stop aiding him, you lackwit. You want to get your father killed?"

"He shan't be fighting, Aithinne," Challon assured her. "I will deal with the man who dared threaten my lady."

Damian shoved Aithinne into Moffet's arms. "Hold her. I have never raised my hand to you lad, but you let her loose and I shall turn you over my knee."

"Yes, Father." He nodded.

"Argh! Sir Nodcock the Second!" Aithinne screamed her rage. "Are all the men in this family created with sheep dung for brains? It does not make me view the coming of my child with hope."

Challon blocked Damian's path to the man on the ground. "I am unharmed. I will—"

"Tamlyn and you were put in harms way because of me, Julian. Comyn was coming after me.

Aithinne is to be my lady wife—this day *I* fight for her."

Damian's words echoed the ones Challon had spoken on the morning he faced Pendegast. The two men watched at each other, each feeling a brother's love, each understanding the warrior in the other. Challon finally nodded and stepped back.

Aithinne marched over and kicked Comyn. "You did not kick him hard enough, Tamlyn."

Her cousin smiled. "Och, I apologize." She delivered another blow to the man's lower back. "Ouch . . . that hurt my toes!"

Grant laughed. "Hey, Englishmen, why don't you just rest on your laurels? I think your ladies have this problem in hand."

"You mean in foot." MacThomas laughed loudly.

Grant pulled his knife from his belt. "You are sure you want me to set him lose?"

"Set him free and give him a sword." Damian lifted his sword, ready to avenge his lady.

Grant cut the bonds on Comyn's hands and the man immediately untied the gag about his mouth.

MacThomas spat at the man. "Bah. Just kill him and have done with it. Englishmen and their code of honor. Bloody boring."

Damian looked at Phelan. "What did you hope to accomplish? Kill me and then run to Edward and hope he would give you Aithinne and Lyonglen? Are you that stupid?"

"He tried to attack Lyonglen," Hugh offered. "That's why we rode out to meet you. He was going to seize it while you were gone. Guess he figured we could not hold it. Grant and Duncan came along and counter-attacked from the rear. Set them to running."

Comyn wiped the blood from his mouth, looking

at Aithinne with hatred. "I hope to kill you both, and that English bastard she carries. Why would I want her after she has lain with an English cur?"

"You are losing blood, Damian. Get it done," Challon prodded. "You do not hurry, you will pass out, then I will have to kill him."

A cornered animal look came into Phelan's eyes, knowing the instant he took the sword Duncan held out to him he was a dead man. He glanced around, clearly trying to see if there were any of his soldiers lingering with the hope to help him. None remained.

As Duncan pushed the sword to him, pommel first, Phelan jumped, knocking Moffet into Damian, and snatching Aithinne by her long hair. Pulling her back against him, he wrapped his arm around her neck and tilted it at an odd angle.

"Stay back. Stay back or I will snap her neck like a twig." Just to prove he would, he jerked her neck sideways, causing Aithinne to cry out.

Suddenly Einar moved. Before Phelan was aware of the big man behind him, he threw his knife, the long blade striking Phelan in the middle of his back. Damian and Challon jumped Phelan, pulling Aithinne away from him.

Damian hugged her tightly, letting her cry on his good shoulder, feeling the peace of knowing it was over.

Einar walked over and bent to remove his knife from the dying man. Before extracting it, he gave it a twist to make sure the deed was done. Pulling it out, he wiped the blade clear of blood on the man's arm. "No one harms my princess and lives."

Damian sighed and looked to Challon. "Pendegast . . ."

He nodded. "I know. Later—"

One minute he was standing. The next he was

looking up at people hovering above him. Aithinne knelt to place his head in her lap.

Deward knelt before him, holding the cup. "Einar, help him sit, we need to get this draught into him, help fortify his blood, until we can get him to Glenrogha and remove the arrows. Oona mixed it. Said we would need it for the wounded."

Damian stared up at the three faces that looked the same. For a moment, as another wave of pain rolled through him, he pondered if he was not seeing everything in threes. Then he recalled— Hugh, Deward, and Lewis—Aithinne's brothers. Deward—at least he thought it was, pressed the cup to his mouth. "Come, new brother, drink your fill. Forget what pains you."

Forget what pains you. Why did the words seem as though he had heard them before?

He struggled to turn his head, to see Aithinne.

Beautiful Aithinne . . .

The days and nights were the same. A living hell. Damian gasped through the heated haze, the words nearly panted out as the fever burned bright through his body, his mind. "Send for the priest."

"Nay!" Aithinne pressed the cool cloth to his forehead, it growing hot almost immediately. He saw her struggling to be strong, hold back the tears that struggled. If by will alone, Aithinne would not let him die. His Firebrand would hold tight to him. "Malcolm can stay at Kinmarch. You do not need him."

Damian managed a feeble smile, hearing her determination, her love in the refusal. "Aye 'tis time, Aithinne. Fetch the *Culdee*. He is needed."

She did not say anything, just shook her head. Hands trembling, she clutched his between hers, squeezing it tightly. Huge tears shown in her eyes, but he saw her refusing to let them fall. His poor Aithinne. His valiant warrior.

As he gazed at that worried face, he relived all his dreams again. Over and over. Of the time when he had been wounded and nearly died. Her face had come to him in the hazy dreams of fever, demanding he not die, she would not let him die. Same words she had chanted these past days. The other dreams visited him. Odd dreams mixed with memories of her. One very peculiar one of him drinking from a cup her brothers offered, then followed by him chained to a bed and him yanking on the chain trying to get free. Of him taking her in the big bed in the tower of Lyonglen.

You must speak your deepest wish.

Look at me. You are my wish. I want to see your eyes when I take you . . . when I make you mine.

He looked to Einar standing in the corner, keeping watch over his princess. "Fetch the priest, Viking."

Einar's pale blue eyes shifted to Aithinne, watching her with love and worry. Damian could read his thoughts. He feared what Aithinne would do if Damian died. Then the man turned his stare back to Damian.

"Do it, Einar. And be quick about it," he ordered.

Aithinne's head snapped around to glare at her personal guard, daring him to obey. The poor man seemed to shrink in size under her withering attention, but then nodded to Damian that he would comply. Opening the door, he frowned at Aithinne once more and then left.

"You will not die, Damian St. Giles. Your body rages with a fever because it fights the poison, the festering. If you were dying that battle would cease and you would become cool. Your body struggles because it wars to live. And so you shall." She took the cloth off his forehead, wetted it, and then swabbed his face and chest.

Oona came in carrying her herb box, and behind her was Moffet with a bucket of steaming hot water. "I ground up enough herbs for more poultices, to hold us through the night. I told Einar to go to Malcolm by way of Kinloch and seek more herbs from Lady Raven. My supplies wane." She poured a mound of dark green leaves and powder into the center of the large cloth, folded it and then dipped it into the hot water.

When she placed it on his wound, Damian jerked up in the bed, hissing in agony. The wound was hot and festered; applying the heat only made the pain throb a hundred-fold. "God's teeth, old woman, I think you seek to hurry my demise along." He growled. "Do not dare cackle at me, you crone."

"You have the will to fuss, Lord Ravenhawke, then you have the will to live," Oona pointed out, as she pressed the hot pad harder against his wound. "Here, lass. Keep the pressure on, whilst I make another. Let us keep switching them, keep the poultices as hot as he can stand to draw the poison from his flesh."

Aithinne pressed the hot cloth and herbs to the wound, nibbling on the corner of her lower lip. Sweat broke out on his forehead. "Deward, heat some bed bricks and place them all around him."

"God's breath, woman, I am half cooked as it is."

"Half-measures never see the deed done." As soon as she uttered the words, her eyes flew wide and he saw she wished she could call them back.

Damian watched the woman he loved so much. Though he had never spoken the words to her.

"I sent for Sir Priest—"

"If you want extreme unction, then you shall go

to your Devil. I shall not permit Malcolm to speak them over you. So there, Sir Nodcock."

He laughed, but that made his shoulder hurt worse, so his smile faded. "Aye, I think it best he speaks the words over me. I may have the pagan raisings of my *maither* woven into my beliefs, but I am a Christian knight as well. But there is another purpose in calling for Malcolm. The child."

He saw the light of understanding flicker in her hazel depths. In all her worry, she had forgotten about the child she carried. Her free hand slipped to her belly, her eyes finally shedding the tears she had been so valiantly holding back.

"Aye, the babe. We need to speak words of marriage, so our son will have my name." He wanted to laugh, but held back thinking he could not stand the pain. "Anyone ever warn you about being careful for what you wish?"

Aithinne cautiously studied his face. Holding her breath.

Oona chuckled and she lifted Aithinne's hand and switched the poultice. "Constantly."

"You once thought to marry my grandfather to save Lyonglen, protect its people. Well, the gods are laughing this night. You hurriedly sent for the priest, to speak words of marriage for you to wed Lord Lyonglen. Malcolm failed to come in time. Let us hope I have more staying strength than my grandsire."

"Oh, do hush your gub. Who says I would wish to wed such an arrogant man? I am thinking of marrying Dinsmore as soon as we plant you in the ground. He shall make a grand father for my son."

Damian knew what she was doing, but he could not stop the reaction. His hands grabbed her upper arms and desperately tried to raise up. Molten agony poured through his body to do so, but he wanted to look her in the eyes, nose-to-nose. "Witch," he said through gritted teeth.

"Aye, 'tis what I am."

"One with freckles," he added the jibe, knowing it would get her anger on the rise.

"Oooooo . . . Sir Nodcock!" She glared at him, then burst out crying.

He smiled. "Silly . . . freckled . . . female . . . I . . ."

Everything swam around him and he closed his eyes, unable to draw on his strength to fight any longer, so he fell back on the pillows panting for breaths.

"Aithinne . . ."

"Yes." She sobbed, burying her face against his chest.

"I remember."

She slowly sat up, the hazel eyes warily watching his. "Remember what, my lord?"

"Everything."

The long lashes batted innocently. "Everything what, my lord?"

"Do not play coy, lass. I recall it all. You had those three mooncalf brothers feed me something this crone conjured up—" He grimaced as Oona slapped a new poultice to his shoulder. "Then you shackled me to your bed."

"I know not what you mean," came the little liar's reply.

The brothers against the wall shifted uncomfortably, Deward and Lewis looking to Hugh for their sign. "Sister," he said, "we go to the Great Hall. Surely, 'tis time for supper."

"Run, you cowards." He laughed to their departing backs.

"That is why you insisted I took your virginity when I questioned you—"

"Poor man, the fever consumes his mind," she said to Oona.

"Ever my little liar. Aithinne, you really should cease telling falsehoods. You are no good at it." He reached up and caught her chin between his curled finger and thumb, forcing her to look him in the eyes. "No more lies betwixt us. You took me, used me to get with child, did you not, hoping to convince Edward you carried the heir to Lyonglen?"

She closed her eyes and swallowed hard. Finally, she nodded. "I know you shall hate me for it. But if you will just live you can hate me all you want."

"Why would I hate you for it?"

"Because of . . ." Aithinne caught herself before she spoke about Anya. Her eyes shifted to Moffet, poking the fire, recalling he did not wish his son to know the circumstances of his birth.

"Not the same, lass. She thought to gain coin. You were doing it to protect the people you love. Besides, it was meant to be, eh? I was coming to Lyonglen. I would have claimed you. Edward already told me to take you to lady wife or stick you in a nunnery. I do not think you would have permitted me to stick you in a nunnery. I think you would have drugged me, chained me to your bed, and gotten with child."

She shrugged. "Sounds a reasonable conclusion."

"I love you, lass."

Her face turned to stone. "You tell me, do not lie, Damian St. Giles. I tell you, do not lie to me either. I looked into your heart the first . . . night. I saw the truths within you."

"Ah, that is why you believe—"

"I ken—"

"You saw what I *thought* was the truth. I saw the face of my dreams when I came to Glenrogha. Challon told me I was mistaken. Said I needed to seek the answers elsewhere, that it was not Tamlyn's face that had come to me in dreams. When I came to Lyonglen and saw you I understood it had been you. All along."

Her chin quivered. "How can you be sure?"

He reached up and tapped her nose seven times. "Because the woman in my dreams has seven bloody dots on her nose."

"My freckles?" She beamed. "Well, that being the case, Sir Nodcock, stop this nonsense about dying. I refuse to have a corpse for a husband."

"Yes, Aithinne."

Epilogue

"My lord, my Princess." Einar burst into the bedroom, out of breath and excited. "Word just came from Glenrogha. Lady Tamlyn has given birth to two babes—a girl they named Paganne and a son called Christian."

"Thank you, Einar," Damian said, crossing the room to sit on the bed by Aithinne, as the door closed again.

She clutched the black-headed babe to her breast, his wee fist waving defiantly in the air. "Well, fie on her. Once again, the perfect Tamlyn has to prove she can do everything better than I can."

Laughing out loud, Damian smiled at his wife and babe. He leaned to the woman who was his reason for living and brushed a kiss to her cheek. "If you want twins, my lady, I shall have to work harder wielding my sword for England the next time."

"Next time? If you think I am going through this rigmarole again you *are* corked-brained, Sir Nodcock. If just one man ever gave birth and understood the pain, you would all be more careful about wielding your mighty swords." Pulling up her knees, she rolled the precious little boy so he was inclined back against her thighs, letting her stare at the angelic face crowned with thick black waves. "Well, Challon may have a son and a daughter, but neither can be as perfect as my Darian."

There was a knock on the door and when it opened, Moffet peaked in. "Father?" The young lad looked hesitant to enter.

"Come, greet your new brother," Damian smiled, proud of both his sons.

Moffet edged toward the bed. "He is so small."

"Small? You give birth to this braw babe and then see if you want to call him *small.*" She smiled smugly. "Bet neither of Tamlyn's babes is as big as Darian."

Damian chuckled. "Aye, he is taller and he is prettier."

"Just like his father."

Moffet grinned. "I hate to tell you this, Father, but I do not think you are prettier than Lord Challon. My lord is the most handsome of all knights in Christendom."

Aithinne chuckled when the baby grasped her finger with amazing strength. "And I bet you think the Lady Tamlyn the most beautiful of all ladies in Christendom."

"Aye, she is beautiful, but not as beautiful as you, Lady Aithinne. My father married the fairest lady I have ever laid eyes upon. I can only hope that someday I wed one half as beautiful as you."

"Without the seven bloody freckles on her nose," she added.

Moffet looked puzzled. "You have freckles, Lady Aithinne?"

"Oh, I do love your firstborn son, Damian."

"I love both my sons—and my wife." He kissed her on the forehead and then hugged his eldest son. "Moffet, if ever on a Beltane night someone offers you a potion that grants all your deepest desires, do not hesitate to believe."